REQVIEM FOR ATHENS

A historical novel of ancient Greece

DAVID S. ALKEK

Copyright © 2012 David S. Alkek
All rights reserved.

ISBN-10: 1480119350
EAN-13: 9781480119352
Library of Congress Control Number: 2012919544
CreateSpace, North Charleston, SC

Dedication page

To all who realize that we can learn from the lessons of history for today.

Chronology of Events

All dates are BCE

386 Foundation of Plato's Academy
382 Birth of Phidias
371 Battle of Leuctra
378 – 354 Second Athenian Empire
356 Birth of Alexander
356 – 346 Second Sacred War
351 Demosthenes' philippics
347 Plato dies
342-338 Aristotle tutors Alexander
338 Battle of Chaeronea
336 Assassination of Philip
335 Alexander destroys Thebes
334 Foundation of Aristotle's Lyceum
334 Battle of Granicus
333 Battle of Issus
332 Alexander founds Alexandria in Egypt
331 Battle of Gaugamela
323 Alexander dies
322 Aristotle and Demosthenes die
313 Ptolemy moves capital to Alexandria
309 Phidias returns to Athens
307 Phidias dies

One talent equals 6000 drachmas, approximately $60,000 in 2012
One drachma or ½ drachma equals one day's wage.

List of Historical Characters in Alphabetical Order

All other Characters are Fictional

Aeschines – Athenian orator and ally of Phocion
Alexander the Great – Son of Philip of Macedon
Antigonus – general and successor of Alexander
Antipater - Philip's general and ruler of Macedon in Alexander's absence
Aristocus – an ally of Demosthenes
Aristotle – philosopher
Attalus –general of Philip
Bessus – general of Darius
Callisthenes – historian, nephew of Aristotle
Cassander – son of Antipater and later King of Macedon
Cleander – general of Alexander
Cleitus – friend of Alexander
Cleopatra – daughter of Attalus, wife of Philip
Craterus – a senior general of Alexander
Darius – The Great King of the Persian Empire
Demetrius Phalerum – ruler of Athens under Cassander
Demetrius Poliocretes – son of Antigonus
Demosthenes – Athenian orator
Dinocrates – architect of Alexandria
Epaminondas – Theban general and leader
Hephaestion – Alexander's closest friend and companion
Hermeias – Aristotle's father-in-law
Hyperiedes – ally of Demosthenes
Isocrates – philosopher, teacher of rhetoric
Lysimachus – boyhood friend, general and successor of Alexander
Olympias – wife of Philip of Macedon, mother of Alexander
Parmenion – Philip and Alexander's general
Pausanias – assassin of Philip
Perdiccas – successor of Alexander
Philip – Alexander's physician

Philip – King of Macedon
Philotas – son of Parmenion and commander of the Companions
Phocion – Athenian political leader and retired general
Plato – philosopher
Ptolemy – general of Alexander and King of Egypt
Pyrrho – cynic philosopher
Roxana – princess and wife of Alexander
Seleucus – general and successor of Alexander
Speusippus – philosopher, successor of Plato
Theophrastus – Aristotle's successor at the Lyceum
Xenocrates – Plato's successor at the Academy

Ancient Greece

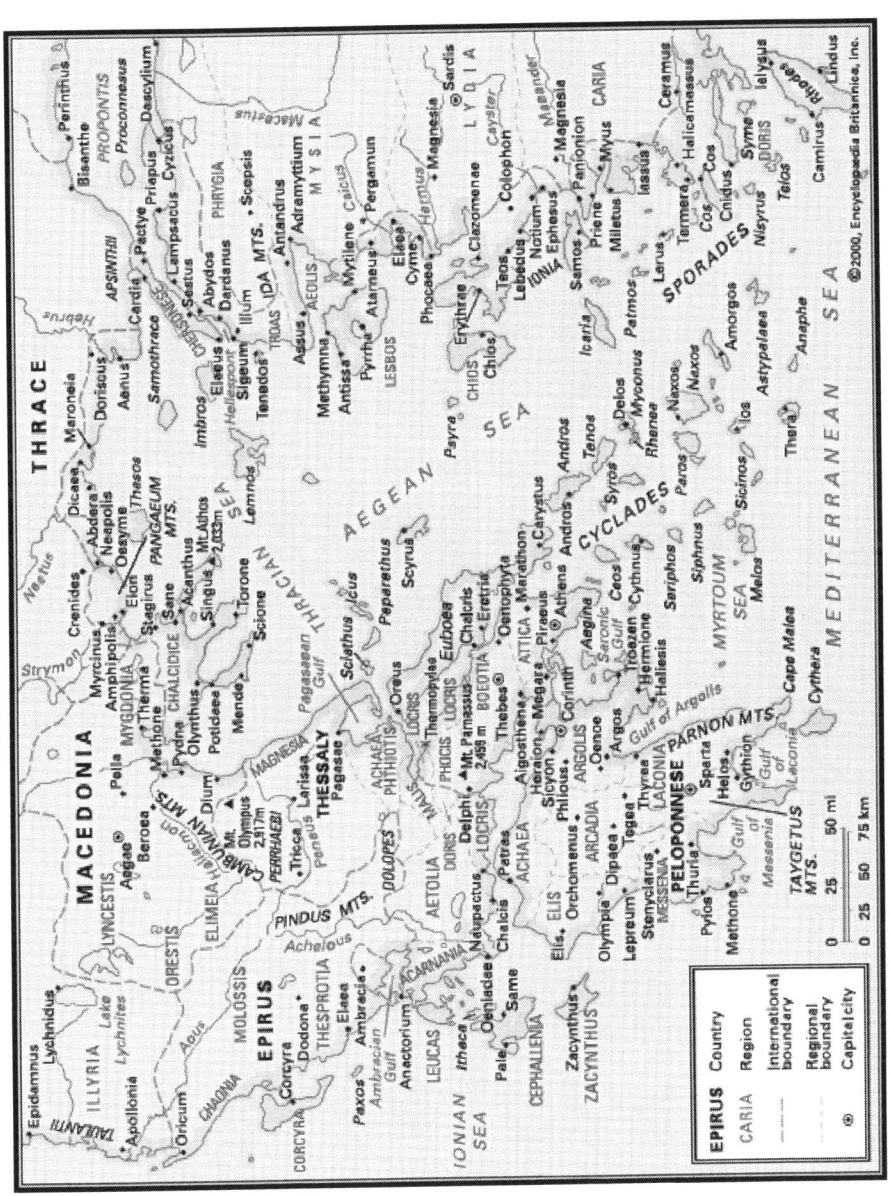

Alexander's Campaigns

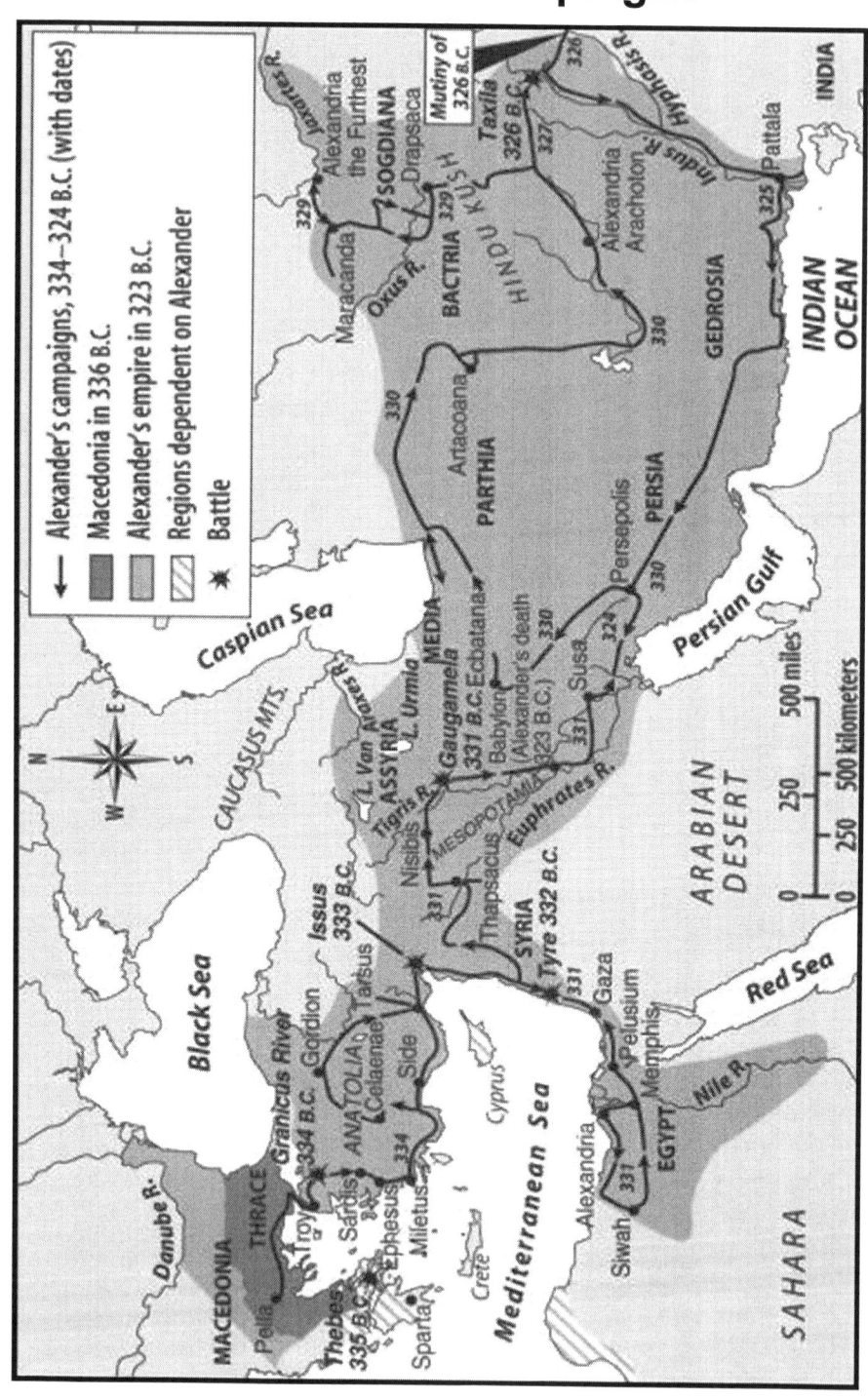

I THE WORLD OF GREECE

CHAPTER 1

Piercing screams, like those of a person being tortured, shot through the open doorway and across the courtyard, where the men had gathered in anticipation. The screaming stopped, and a woman appeared in the doorway clutching a red, wet, wailing mass. She held the infant up, displaying it to the men. Their voices rose, as in a chorus as they said, "A boy." They congratulated Aristippus, slapping him on the back, while the women helped the mother and cleaned the newborn.

Aristippus was exhilarated, accepting congratulations from his family and friends. "It's your second son," said a friend, Sosus. "You named your first son Meletus after your father, as is our custom. What will you name this one?"

"I will name him Phidias after my father's oldest brother."

"Yes, I remember your uncle," said Sosus. "He was a brave soldier. Didn't he die in the wars with Sparta?"

"It was a sad thing to our family, especially to my father. I hope this younger Phidias will be like him."

Ten days after his birth, Phidias formally received his name and was welcomed into the family in a religious ceremony that invoked the gods' blessings on the new infant. Extended family of aunts, uncles, and cousins, as well as close friends, gathered around the hearth in the largest room of the family's home. The hearth, a sacred place, held small statues of the family gods, candles, and an incense burner, which today was filled with the precious substance. The slaves passed around wine and food while the men danced in a circle, singing and waving their hands. The women passed the infant around, each acknowledging that he looked like his father and would be strong and smart.

Aristippus, the prosperous but not wealthy owner of a small estate, raised olives, grapes, and sheep. Working his farm had weathered his skin beyond his thirty-odd years, and his body bore scars from past wars he had fought for Athens. A fair and honest man, he did not beat his slaves and sold his grapes and olive oil at fair prices.

* * *

A year or so after the naming, Aristippus stepped from his house and walked past the gate. The large orange disk had just cleared the distant hills and shone warm on his face, outlining his medium frame. Mist still crouched in the low areas but would dissipate with the warmth of the day. From his vantage point on the hill his walled house stood upon, his dark brown eyes surveyed his fields. The solidly built stone compound had been in his family for generations. The building lounged like an old man on the stony hill, surrounded by smaller hills like adoring children.

He also owned a smaller house inside the walls of Athens, three miles away. He used it to entertain guests, and his sons would live there once they started attending school.

Aristippus was proud of his second son, and Phidias thrived on the spoiling affection given to Greek boys. Aristippus noted that at five, he was developing the skills that a Greek child should have. He could run fast and throw a ball. He also showed a quick intelligence and wanted to read his father's scrolls and letters. He already knew the alphabet.

After the births of Meletus and Phidias, two years apart, another boy joined the family, then a girl, and finally, another boy. Until the age of six, children stayed at home and lived with the women of the extended family in their quarters, the *gynaceum*. There were no slave children to play with, for slaves were not allowed to have children. If a slave gave birth, the baby was taken away and abandoned in the hills.

One morning, after his breakfast of cheese, bread, and fruit, Aristippus wiped his face and arms with a cloth from a basin of water a slave had brought to his room. He wrapped his linen tunic around him and threw it casually over his shoulder. Men did not wear undergarments, and sometimes they wore a single, one-piece chiton with holes for the head and arms. In winter they wore woolen cloaks over their tunics. It was summer, so Aristippus wore only his white tunic. His slave put oil into his hair and tamed his dark curls with a comb.

"Not too much oil today, Strabo. I will put on more after my exercise and bath at the gymnasium."

The slave nodded and knelt down to tie the straps of his master's sandals. "Will you be coming home for dinner, Master, or staying in the city?"

"Tell the mistress that I will return before dinner." With that, Aristippus stepped out into the portico, where he noticed the children playing around the fountain, splashing water at one another. Phidias was chasing his younger brother, and Aristippus saw Meletus stick out his foot and trip him. Phidias fell spread eagle across the tiles, scraping his knees and hands, bellowing as giant tears flowed down his cheeks.

Aristippus quickly walked over. "Wait here," he said to Meletus as he picked up Phidias. He carried him to the fountain and washed off the blood and dirt. "You will be all right," he soothed his son. "Your feelings are more hurt than your knees. Go to your mother so she can put some unguent on them."

After Phidias ran to his mother, Aristippus turned to Meletus. "I know that boys play rough and it hardens their bodies. You are his older brother, and you should not take advantage of him. When he goes to school, I expect you to protect him. I am afraid that he may not be the strong soldier his namesake uncle was. But, he may one day be smarter than you, and then he will repay you for all your bullying. If I were you, I would go and tell him you are sorry."

"Yes, Papa," the youth said meekly.

Aristippus did not have to box his ears; the stern reprimand was enough. He very seldom had to lay a hand or a stick upon his children. Their mother could discipline them by scolding and her wooden spoon, and only had to threaten them with telling their father. Aristippus was firm but loving, and his children, as well as all his acquaintances, knew him to be a person of good values and a man who kept his word.

In the city, Aristippus made his way to the open area surrounded by markets. He'd lived all his life in Athens and knew most of the men of his class by name. Many acknowledged his greeting as he passed knots of men in active conversations or single strollers going to and fro. The monotonous white color of the Athenian tunics intermingled with colored robes, and with the head coverings of men from Asia, Africa, and the Mediterranean. The occasional brightly colored robe of the *hetairai*, the Greek courtesans, made a statement—a walking advertisement.

The pleasant scents of ripened fruits and vegetables flirted with Aristippus' nose and palate. Maybe he would pick up some on his way home, but now he was on his way to conduct business. He entered the large square surrounded by a shaded portico, under which merchants manned stalls filled with goods from all parts of the world. All around, men congregated in couples or small groups engaged in often animated discussions.

Aristippus threaded through the crowded square looking for the merchant, Plotinas, who might purchase his grapes, aware of the energy filling the Athenian atmosphere. The mélange of colors, people, smells, and sounds stimulated the senses and heightened emotions.

It was in the streets and open meeting places of Athens that the politics of the polis and the competition of business spiced the life of the citizen. A vigorous intellect, competitive enterprising, and an easily excitable temper were hallmarks of the Athenian personality. The citizen of Athens kept his body healthy by exercise in the gymnasia and palaestra, living in the open, and eating and drinking moderately. He kept his mind healthy by hard bargaining in business, arguing in the Assembly and the courts, and partaking in heated discussions in the streets.

Was it the nearness of the sea, the competition among the traders, or the personal freedoms that made Athenian life so vibrant, so excitable? Aristippus realized it was all of these things that gave him and his fellow citizens a resilience of temper, a sharpness of wit, and the courage to defend their economic and political freedoms.

"Hail, Plotinas," he called, waving at his merchant friend a few steps away.

They greeted each other as the old friends they were, each asking about the other's family.

After a decent time, Aristippus turned to business. "I want to talk to you about my grapes. I think I will have a good harvest."

They haggled over an hour.

"The grapes will be large and sweet."

"But there will be too many on the market."

"But trade has expanded, and there is more demand."

"But labor costs have increased."

"But slaves do most of the work."

"The political climate is unsettled."

"But it always is."

And on and on. The Greeks always conducted business in this manner; it was expected.

Finally they agreed. Aristippus would deliver so many wagonloads of grapes, and Plotinas would pay him an agreed-upon sum. They embraced, laughing.

"That's enough business for today. Let's go to the gymnasium," Aristippus said. "I need to exercise off that fine dinner from last night, and it looks like you can afford to exercise off several dinners."

Plotinas guffawed and slapped Aristippus on the back, agreeing with him as they walked to the open palaestra next to the gymnasium.

They entered the gymnasium and took off their tunics. All men and boys exercised or played sports naked. They folded them and placed them with their sandals on benches lining the walls. After working up a good sweat, the men went outside and splashed their bodies from the fountain, washing off the dust from the city and the sweat from the gymnasium. They sat in the sun and dried off, while slaves applied oil to their hair and bodies, before they returned and dressed.

Exiting into the portico outside the gymnasium, Aristippus approached a loud discussion. One of the men punctuated his argument with flailing arms and stuck an index finger into the face of the man opposite him to make his point. Aristippus recognized him as the owner of a fleet of trading ships. The man lowered his hand and, turning, saw Aristippus. Recognition lit his eyes.

"And what do you think, Aristippus? Should we go to war with Thebes against Sparta? What will you do, if we have war?"

"I will do what my city asks of me. I do not favor war, because it brings hardships and dead fathers and sons. But I have no love for Sparta, which has slaughtered our citizens and strangled our city since the great Peloponnesian war. If Athens calls, I will fight."

"Brave words," another man said. "For you may be called upon to act on them as well."

Athenians were nothing if not proud of their cultural and intellectual prowess, jealous of their political freedom, and willing to prove their patriotic duty to Athens by fighting for her. Aristippus would have to stand by his statement soon enough.

During these prosperous years of Athens' second empire, men made and unmade their fortunes at unprecedented speed. The new rich, whom the Greeks called *neoplutoi*, spent their wealth ostentatiously, erecting lavish houses, dressing their women in costly raiment, and putting on outrageous banquets with the most expensive food and drink their money could buy.

Inevitably, as in all societies, the clever and aggressive became wealthy while the simple people became poorer. The freemen of the cities had less than when they'd been tied to the land. In the countryside as in the cities, the slaves did most of the work and kept low the wages of free men.

Aristippus was of a shrinking middle class. He despised the newly rich, who flaunted their wealth, but also distrusted the lower classes, who found more and more ways to use their political power to despoil the propertied classes. Thus the foundation of social upheaval and class struggle was laid.

One evening, after spending a few days doing business and attending the Assembly, Aristippus invited a few of his old friends to dinner at his house in the city. These were men who either still had lands that they patiently cultivated, or had given up farming and become businessmen. The host served roasted lamb and his best wine from his own estate. Fresh fish from the port and seasonal fruits and vegetables from the market filled the tables.

Aristippus was not sparing in the food and entertainment for his guests, but neither was he lavishly ostentatious as the tasteless rich were wont to be. The pretty young flute players, the *auletrides*, sang and played. Dressed in short linen skirts, the girls danced around the guests, playfully flirting by tugging at their beards or sharing a sip of their wine. After the sweets were served, the auletrides retired. Servers refilled the wine cups, and the conversation turned to more serious matters.

Plotinas raised his cup in a toast. "Here's to our host. If the grapes he sold to me make as fine a wine as this, we will both be rich."

The other guests laughed and nodded agreement as the six men raised their cups to their host.

"But will we be able to continue such fine dinners if the Assembly raises our taxes again?" asked Glaucas. "They are always adding to the theoric fund, because more and more of the unpropertied classes want it."

The Assembly provided the theoric or divine fund to the populace for the price of admission to attend the games or plays that made up the sacred festivals. Because the masses of laboring people complained that they could not afford to miss work to attend the Assembly, they were also paid for that. Many hundreds were given free bread at the temples, also at public expense.

Stilbo slammed his fist on his couch. "The politicians elected by the Assembly are buying the votes that keep them in power. The one who promises the most increase in taxes for the rich, and to give more to the masses, is the one who will be elected."

Another raised his voice, "I heard that the last count of the voting citizens showed that over half own no property. We who have property are taxed so that they may go to the Assembly, where they vote to tax us even more. Something must be done."

"You're right," said Plotinas. "Men of the middle class, small landowners, and businessmen such as ourselves used to make up a sizable number. We could balance the power between the rich aristocracy and the common people. Many of our class have lost their wealth or land and can no longer mediate between the rich and poor. I'm afraid we may see even more violence between the two."

Mylias spoke up. "The politicians are straining to discover ingenious new sources of revenue. They require so-called 'voluntary contributions' from the rich to pay for public enterprises. I hear of increasing numbers of outright confiscation of property for the smallest pretext. Men are beginning to hide their wealth to evade the aggressive squads of tax collectors. I understand that they can even enter your home and seize goods for back taxes."

"It's outrageous what the democratic masses are doing," said Stilbo. "If money is taken from the rich to give to the poor, then we shall all be poor."

Aristippus raised his hands. "My friends, I am no advocate of what the unpropertied populace is doing to our city, but I am no lover of the rich merchants and bankers either. The intellectuals at Plato's Academy and Isocrates' school disdain those whose wealth seems to be inversely related to their culture and taste. I hear Plato said that Athens is in reality two cities: one city of the rich, the other of the poor, and each at war with the other."

The men exhausted themselves with frustration over the increasingly violent conflict between the classes.

Their anger at the democratic-dominated Assembly finally spent, Cleamas spoke up. "We have enjoyed your hospitality, Aristippus, but we had better all go home before the streets are deserted except for the thieves."

Ruffians had organized themselves into thieving bands that preyed on men who walked the darkened streets. The wealthy had responded by hiring their own gangs of thugs to protect themselves.

"I will send my slaves to accompany you to your homes," Aristippus assured them. "They will carry torches and are armed with knives and clubs. You will be safe."

They all thanked their host again and bid him goodnight, still harboring thoughts about the political future of their beautiful city.

The next day Aristippus returned to his estate. On the way there, his mind churned over the discussions of politics, class conflicts, and, of course, war. These issues had always been part of Greece, and Athenians had dealt with them since Aristippus could remember. He had lost his uncle in the war with Sparta, where he had been wounded himself. Would his sons have to fight? What of this war between the rich and poor? Would it become bloody?

His mind was picturing a troubled future when he spied his children playing inside the gate. Their laughter and young innocence dispelled his gloomy thoughts, and he smiled.

He saw Phidias look up first and call, "Look! It's Papa!"

They all yelled and ran to him, and he squatted and hugged them all, kissing each in turn. Meletus was at school in the city, so Phidias was the oldest at home. He would turn six in a few months and join his older brother.

Aristippus held his hand as they walked to the house. "You will be going to school soon. Are you ready?"

"Oh yes, Papa," Phidias said as he looked up into his father's eyes. "I'll be staying with you and Meletus in our city house."

"That's right, and I will be there frequently. The slaves will take care of you and Meletus. Are you a little afraid?"

"Oh, Papa, I'm not afraid. You and Meletus will protect me from mean men. He's told me about school. He says that he has fun with the other boys, but sometimes they get into fights."

"Are you scared that you might have to fight another boy?"

"I don't think so. I've fought with my brothers many times."

Aristippus laughed. "Yes, you have. Your mother has washed dirt and blood from your young bodies many a time."

They entered the door, and Phidias ran shouting to his mother, "Mama, Papa's home!"

Aristippus watched him go, proud that he was becoming older and would be going to school, proud he was a healthy, smart, happy child, but troubled with the feeling that the future he was growing into was uncertain.

CHAPTER 2

Soon after Phidias' sixth birthday, Aristippus took him into the city, where he would live while he attended school. His father could afford to send him to one of the best schoolmasters in Athens. Since the teachers were paid, they had to prove their ability to teach their charges the basics of reading, arithmetic, music, and gymnastics. They also had the responsibility of developing the moral character and discipline of these boys. Girls did not attend school but were instructed at home by their mothers.

Schoolmasters had wide latitude in their teaching methods and had absolute authority. They maintained a strict discipline, sometimes with the aid of a sandal or a birch rod.

Aristippus sat down with Phidias on a bench and spoke with him as Meletus and a slave waited to accompany him to school on his first day. "Listen to the schoolmaster, my son. Do as he says and pay attention. If you do, you won't get into trouble and he won't whip you. Do you understand?"

"Yes, Papa." Phidias had heard from Meletus how strict some of the teachers were. Some were known to whip boys until their backs bled. "I'll do everything he says, Papa. I'll be good. I don't want a whipping." His eyes revealed a fear of the unknown.

"Then off you go, Phidias. Learn well, and make me proud of you."

"I will, Papa." He left, as every other boy in every other time, with mixed feelings of joy and fear as he skipped off to his first day of school.

* * *

When Phidias was about eight, the teacher caught one of the boys cheating. "Oneiros, son of Medias, stand up," the teacher commanded. "I observed you cheating. Come up to the front of the class and take off your chiton."

The boy did as he was told and stood naked in front of the class with his head bowed in shame. "Phidias and Glaucon, come up and help me," the teacher said. "Glaucon, turn your back to Oneiros. Oneiros, you hold on to Glaucon's shoulders. Phidias, take hold of Oneiros' ankles." They obeyed and the teacher flogged the boy across his back with a birch stick until it drew blood. The disciplined boy whimpered as tears ran down his face. He did not cry out, however, for he knew that the other boys would tease him later as a coward if he did so.

Oneiros got no sympathy from the other boys, who all knew he was receiving the expected punishment for cheating. Athenians were taught to be good bargainers and astute politicians, but dishonesty was not tolerated. The lesson was not lost on Phidias and the others, and no more cheating took place under that master.

Like all the boys, Phidias played with hoops, marbles, and stuffed balls. At about the age of ten, he began to play a game called *astrali*, which consisted of cubic knuckle bones with numbers on them. The object was to toss a pair of these dice and add up the numbers on top. The boys wagered their marbles or other toys against one another, just as their elders did for money.

One summer day, Phidias joined a group of boys playing astrali outside the school. The sun turned the bare backs of the players a richer tan as they watched the dice being tossed on the hard ground. Phidias noticed that one of the boys, a loudmouthed bully named Leontas, was winning more than any other. He was about a year older than most of the others, and a lot of marbles and balls lay on the ground in front of him. Phidias watched Leontas carefully, and observed that he handled and threw the astrali in such a way as to influence their fall.

As Leontas was about to toss the dice, Phidias grabbed his hand. "You're cheating!" he yelled.

Leontas jerked his hand out of Phidias' grasp and hit him in the mouth, splitting his lip. "You dare call me a cheat!" he screamed into his face. "Shut your mouth or I'll shut it for you. If you don't like the way I play, then go find another game. You call me a cheat again, I'll beat you up."

Phidias left, holding his hand to his bleeding lip. He washed his face at a fountain and walked home in silence, resentment simmering inside him at the injustice and humiliation he had suffered.

At dinner that night, Phidias poked absently at his food, while his father and older brother talked of the day's happenings.

At one point, Aristippus turned to his son and said, "Phidias, you have been very quiet and that's not like the bright boy I know, who is always asking questions. What is bothering you?"

"Nothing, Papa."

"I notice that you have a split and swollen lip. What happened? Did you get in a fight?"

"He probably got hit and ran away like a coward," said his brother.

"Quiet, Meletus," his father commanded. "Phidias, tell me exactly what happened."

Phidias told him the whole story with the cheating bully. His father listened without comment, slowly nodding his head as his younger son described his embarrassment.

After Phidias finished, his father stroked his beard and said, "You will be faced with people like that your whole life, and you will have to learn to deal with them. If you give into their bullying or flee like a coward, that will only encourage them to do it again and again. You must stand up to them. If you are weaker than they are, then you must gain allies. That is what Athens does if she must fight Sparta or Thebes."

"What should I do, Papa?" Phidias asked.

"You have to recover the honor you lost when Leontas hit you, and you did not defend yourself in front of the other boys. You're a smart fellow, so I'm sure you will find a way. I have confidence that you can do it."

The next day at gymnastics class, Phidias gathered together three of his friends. They had all suffered from the bullying of Leontas. Phidias told them of the incident and showed them his split lip.

"I know. I was there and saw it," said one boy. "Why didn't you hit him back, Phidias?"

"Because he is bigger and would have beaten me up. He would bully everyone even more and get away with it. We have to stop him."

"But how?" asked another friend. "He's bigger than we are."

"We have to work together. We have to become allies, like the other cities do when they have to fight Sparta. I have a plan."

After the teacher dismissed them for the day, the four boys waited until Leontas came down the street. Phidias confronted him, while the others surrounded the boy.

"What do you want, another bloody lip?" Leontas asked, showing Phidias his fist.

"No, I want to give you one, you bully," Phidias said. With that signal, the four pounced on Leontas. Phidias punched him in the eye, knocking him to the ground.

With his hands over his face, Leontas began whimpering, "Don't hit me anymore." All bullies are cowards at heart. Other students had gathered around and were laughing at him.

Phidias stood over him. "Now you know how it feels to be on the receiving end. You better not bully me or any of my friends again or we'll give it to you worse than this." After that they heard no more of Leontas, for he had begged his father to send him to another school.

* * *

By the age of sixteen, Athenian boys were expected to pay more attention to physical development. Preparing their youth for the rigors of war—their ever-present reality—had been a constant theme throughout Greek history. Their sports in particular were militarily related. They had to run, often long distances, carrying a spear and shield. They had to jump, wrestle, hurl the javelin, and, of course, ride a horse and hunt.

Phidias worked hard at developing his strength and endurance. He was not as heavy and athletic as his older brother, who often teased him about being smaller. He developed his strength by lifting and carrying large stones and ran long distances in winter, often carrying a shield on his back. In the summer months, he swam in the ocean. He gained a reputation as a strong swimmer and often taught other youths how to swim. Twice he saved the lives of drowning men.

During an exercise one day in the palaestra next to the gymnasium, Phidias fought with a wooden sword and shield against another youth his age. He could see that the other boy, Hippias, had sharpened the end of his sword, instead of fighting with the usual rounded edge everyone was supposed to use.

"Ho, Phidias, I hear that you are proud of your skill with a sword. Let's see what you can do against me."

"I'll take that challenge," said Phidias. "I can see that point on your sword, but I'm not afraid of it. In fact, I intend to crack your skull under that leather cap."

The boys thrust and parried until the dust they kicked up coated their sweaty bodies. Both displayed their skill and stamina, while Phidias carefully avoided the sharpened sword. The sound of wooden swords smacking against shields or one another resounded over the exercise yard. Other youths stopped their practice and stood around the pair in the bright sunshine, watching the skillful duel, encouraging one or the other. Suddenly Hippias pushed his shield against Phidias', and then raised his sword as if to hit him on the head. Instead, Hippias thrust his shield under Phidias' shield, lifting it up. He then thrust his sword under his shield, aiming his point at Phidias' exposed genitals.

Anticipating the maneuver, Phidias came down hard with his sword, inside his own shield, on Hippias' extended forearm. They both heard a crack as Hippias howled and dropped his sword. He threw off his shield and knelt down, grabbing his broken arm. Tears streamed down his youthful face.

One of the instructors who had been watching the duel came over to the stricken Hippias. "I saw your fight," he said, "and I congratulate you, Phidias, for your courage and skill against his sharpened sword. Let's take Hippias over to the gymnasium where I can treat his arm."

After splinting and bandaging Hippias' arm, the instructor said, "It will heal fine. You'll be able to use it again, but not for the next two months. You may not wrestle, fight with the sword, or throw the javelin, but you must still run, jump, and ride."

Hippias later told Phidias that he was sorry he had tried to injure him.

"I accept your apology," said Phidias, "and I'm sorry I broke your arm."

"I guess I deserved it," Hippias said. "Will you be my friend? I promise to be yours, if you agree."

They clasped hands and embraced, sealing a friendship that would last. They fought side by side in exercises and confrontations from then on.

One day when he was seventeen and in his last year at the school, Phidias had just finished an afternoon of wrestling, javelin throwing, and mock combat. He and some of his classmates walked over to where they had left their clothes on benches under the portico outside the gymnasium. They continued laughing and ribbing one another as they scraped the sweat and oil from their bodies with stirgils. After they had finished cleaning and cooling off, they put on their short tunics.

"Let's go down to the port, Phidias," Hippias said to his friend. "There's always something happening down at Piraeus. Maybe a ship has brought in some pretty new slave girls for sale. Of course, we can always visit the *pornai*."

"You're always thinking about girls and sex," replied Phidias. "I know you're seventeen, but why do you want to visit the cheapest brothels in Athens? Don't you have slave girls at home?"

"My father won't let me touch them," Hippias said. "He keeps them for himself and my older brothers. Anyway, what will it hurt? If we can't afford to pay pornai, we can always examine the goods. You know, they hardly wear any clothes. That's why they're called *gymnai*—naked."

Phidias turned to some other older youths. "Come on, fellows. Let's go with Hippias down to Piraeus and try to keep him from making a fool of himself."

The other boys laughed and one said, "Yeah, we may have to protect him in case we run into some wharf rats or students from other schools."

The busy road to the port less than five miles away was busy with merchants, farmers, and tradesmen. The boys filled the time with good-natured joking and jabbing one another. As they entered the precincts of the port, the crowds grew thicker, the sounds louder, and the smells more offensive. They wandered around the market marveling at the variety. Open stalls displayed a colored cornucopia of fruits and vegetables; freshly caught fish swam in barrels of sea water; terracotta jars filled with wine and oils sat in rows; and rolls of multihued red, gold, green, and blue cloth spilled out over tables. Men hawked gold and silver jewelry, precious stones, amulets for good luck or successful lovemaking, and foods of all sorts.

Fascinated by the riot of color and objects, the students continuously joked and pointed out things to one another. Words painted on the houses indicated the services provided inside. On the walkway in front of them was painted an arrow pointing ahead with the statement "beautiful pornai." Eventually they found themselves in a small open area with a raised platform at one end. "It's the slave market. Let's see if they have anything interesting," said Hippias.

"You mean young girls, don't you?" Phidias laughed. They pushed their way closer as a large black male was led off the platform. All slaves were exhibited nude, so any serious buyer could examine the goods as they would animals for sale. "He's probably from Nubia. The men from there are known to have large phalluses. Look at his. Wouldn't you like to have one like that instead of your little thing, Hippias?"

Hippias hit Phidias on his arm. "At least I use mine, instead of making love to myself, like you do."

"Shut up, fellows. Look what they're bringing up to sell," exclaimed one of the others.

Indeed, a group of five females, aged about twelve to nineteen, were being led onto the platform. The girls were of olive skin, flawless in youth, with dark eyes and long black hair falling across their shoulders and backs. Their firm bodies shone in the sun, pert breasts pointing their nipples as if advertising their fertile youth.

"I wish I could get my hands on those," rasped Hippias. "Too bad they won't let us touch them."

"Those dark beauties must be from Syria or Egypt," said Phidias.

"As a matter of fact, they are from Rhodes," said the slave auctioneer. "They were sold by their parents to pay off debts. What am I bid for these beauties?"

"I would give you ten drachmas for them," said Hippias, "but first I want to feel their flesh."

"Shut up, Hippias. You don't have any money," said one of the other boys.

"Maybe not, but I would bet they would enjoy my hands running over their bodies, someone as handsome and virile as me."

"You're full of offal, Athenian pig," yelled a young man from a group to their right.

"What do you know, son of an ass?" Hippias yelled back.

"I'm from Rhodes, and we attend the school of Isocrates. I say, you smell like the fish from Piraeus. You probably act like one in bed too." The group of students next to him guffawed and made rude gestures at Hippias.

Phidias came to Hippias' defense. "Are we going to take that from a bunch of foreign students? Let's show them how Athenians defend themselves."

With a yell, Phidias and his friends fell on the group from Isocrates' school. Fists and stones flew, and a stick or two beat heads.

"Look out, Phidias!" Hippias yelled, as he blocked a stick from a youth about to hit his friend.

"Thanks," said Phidias. He and his friend ran together at two of the other students, knocking them over. The two helped each other up and fought back to back, defending one another.

After a time, the general melee and individual fights tapered off as the bruised and dirty boys gathered around two older boys who had squared off.

Herodus, the largest and most athletic Athenian, and a large youth from the other group had thrown off their tunics so as not to tear or dirty them and faced off, circling for an opening. They grappled with each other, wrestling, hitting, and kicking one another until blood ran down their faces. It was generally accepted in fights such as this that all was fair except biting or hitting the genitals.

The youths from each side yelled their support to their champion as a group of bystanders gathered to watch the fight with them. At last Herodus took the other youth down, mounting his back and beating his head into the ground. The youth lay motionless as blood oozed from his nose. Herodus rose and said, "He lives, but with a few scars to show for his battle with Athenians. Anyone else care to challenge me?"

The young men from Isocrates' school did not answer him but helped their bruised and battered comrade back to Athens.

Phidias and his companions dusted themselves, washed off the blood and dirt at a fountain, and started back toward the city. They'd had enough of a good time in Piraeus, and none of them were thinking of girls or sex anymore.

Phidias looked at Hippias and put his arm around his shoulder. "Looks like your lip is busted and swollen, but I don't see any cuts on your face. You'll still have your good looks for the girls." He smiled at his friend.

"Thanks, one of my teeth is loose, but I gave it back to the guy who hit me. He had a bloody nose. I hope we see them again. I'll give him more than a bloody nose next time."

"Boy, Herodus really took care of the big guy," said Euthyphro, the youngest of the group.

"Are you all right, Euthyphro?" asked one of the others.

"Yeah, I picked up a stick to protect myself, but not before one of them tore my tunic. It was my best one. My mother will kill me."

"Better your tunic than your head."

They all laughed and joked their way back home, recounting blow by blow their recent battle. The retelling would get more embellishment each time it was repeated, at home and at the school.

CHAPTER 3

At eighteen, Phidias was admitted into the second of the four stages of Athenian life, which consisted of child, youth, man, and elder. For the next four years, he would be a member of the *epheboi*—the soldier youth. He would belong to a regiment that lived together in barracks. Organized as a community with its own government, the epheboi would be trained in their duties as soldiers and as citizens.

During his first year, he was allowed a visit to his family. Phidias showed off his distinctive uniform with pride. He had been issued a leather breastplate, which he wore over his short chiton, that reached only to his mid-thigh. He carried his brass helmet but left his shin-protecting greaves at the barracks.

His father embraced him. "I am proud of you, my son; you will make a fine soldier." Aristippus knew that Phidias had good stamina and athletic skills, but he was still too thin. He had to gain more muscle if he was to be successful on the battlefield.

"I love you, Phidias," his mother said. She hugged him and wiped a tear that had fallen onto her cheek. "You are becoming a man before my eyes."

His sister also kissed him. "I love you too, big brother." He squeezed her back with a big grin.

Phidias' two younger brothers gushed with admiration and touched parts of his uniform. "Tell us everything, Phidias," Cimeas, the older one said. "I can't wait to be an ephebos."

The whole family, except for his older brother, Meletus, an elder ephebos who was not at home, ate together that night, and Phidias' father allowed everyone to drink some of his best wine—watered down for the women and younger boys. They drank to Phidias' health, glad to have him home for a while.

The next day, Phidias walked with his younger brothers over their fields and told them of his life as an ephebos. "We are drilled strenuously, from dawn until we fall exhausted into our bunks at dark. We also must attend lectures on geometry and how to reason and argue, which they call rhetoric. Also, we study Greek literature and music. We govern ourselves. We meet in our own assembly and elect our own leaders, generals, and judges. Of course, these are usually older epheboi."

"You ever have time when you can rest or enjoy yourselves?" asked Diocles, the younger.

"We sometimes meet and sing in groups, and our regiment practices and gives a performance to the whole group. But our first year is mostly physical training, and it's really demanding. Athens believes in producing well-rounded citizens, strong in body as well as mind. Next year I will be assigned garrison duty on the frontier."

For two years, the young men were entrusted with the early defense of Athens against attack from without or from disorder within.

"Will you be afraid?" asked Diocles.

"I don't think so. I'll be ready by then. We can defend ourselves if we have to."

Phidias could see the pride in the way his brothers looked at him. He threw back his shoulders, tossed his long curls across his back, and smiled broadly. He clapped his hand on the older brother's back and said, "You'll be an ephebos one day, and you'll be trained to fight too."

* * *

While on garrison duty, Phidias had to take his turn standing watch at night. Falling asleep on watch was considered a serious dereliction of duty. A soldier during war could be put to death for such an offense. An ephebos would be whipped and expelled from the regiment. During his duty as watchman one night, Phidias noticed his fellow guard, an older youth, starting to nod.

Phidias walked over and stood beside him. "That was quite a dinner we had tonight," he said, starting a polite conversation as if he hadn't noticed his fellow nodding.

Instantly alert, the youth replied, "Yeah, I guess I had one cup of wine too many. I'm glad to have your company tonight, Phidias." He knew Phidias would not use this episode against him.

Known to be a fair-minded young man, Phidias didn't abuse his authority over younger boys or try to undermine or talk against his older colleagues. His many friends knew of his keen intellect and sense of humor. When a youth stepped out of bounds, Phidias was known to take him aside and remind him of the virtues that make an Athenian citizen, but he did so in a sincere way, without a condescending lecture. The other youth always took his advice, for Phidias lived according to what he said.

At the assembly near the end of Phidias' twentieth year, when they were electing their officers for the next term, one of the older youths rose to speak. "I nominate Phidias, son of Aristippus, to be a judge."

Phidias stood and was recognized. "I thank my brother ephebos, but I am only twenty and not as experienced as older epheboi."

The youth who had nominated him told the assembly of Phidias' intelligence and judgment in several circumstances.

Another added, "Phidias shows much control over his emotions and is not easily angered. He balances intelligence with good judgment and a sense of humor."

Another added, "He has been a good example to us all, because he is virtuous in his actions and loyal to his friends."

The first youth added, "I nominate him because he will be a fair and discerning judge."

The chief judge, who was one of the eldest of the epheboi, said, "Indeed, Phidias shows more maturity at his age than many men twice his age. He will make a very fine judge indeed."

The assembly elected him judge. During the next two years, the other judges looked up to him for guidance, and the epheboi elected him chief judge his last year.

* * *

At the end of their time as epheboi, the youth, at the age of twenty-one, participated in a deeply meaningful ceremony. All of Athens turned out for the sacred and colorful event. The participating youth were spaced along the route from the port of Piraeus to Athens' gate. They all wore short, belted chitons that bared their arms, and carried unlit torches.

In the marketplace of Piraeus, the main priest of Athena and the chief of the Assembly both lit the torch of the *strategos,* the elected general of the epheboi. The chief of the epheboi then ran to the next youth about fifty yards away. After lighting his torch, they both ran to the next, and so on until the whole class of torch-bearing epheboi joined the last youth at the gate of the city.

Another priest of Athena led them through the city to the Temple of Agraulos, where they placed their torches in holders around the inside of the edifice. They had been instructed to encircle the altar and stretch out their arms over it. The flickering light of the torches revealed the solemn emotions enveloping these handsome young men. After four years as comrades who shared meals, discipline, fun, and maturing hardships, they considered one another as brothers. They would defend each other in peace and war.

They then recited the oath required of all men who would become citizens of Athens: "I will not disgrace the sacred arms, nor will I abandon the man next to me, whoever he may be. I will transmit my native city not lessened, but larger and better than I received it. I will obey those who are judges, and the established laws, and whatever regulations the people may enact. If anyone shall attempt to destroy the statutes, I will not permit it, but will repel him both alone and with all. I will honor the ancestral faith."

Their training as epheboi completed, they were officially free from parental authority and admitted as full citizens of Athens.

Phidias and the other youth entered into the active political and social life of Athens, and they continued to exercise their bodies as well as their minds. After exercising at the gymnasium one day, Phidias and some other young men stood around talking and joking while they were drying off before putting their clothes back on.

Hippias took his friend Phidias aside and said, "Lysias, Agelaus, and I have been invited to attend a dinner at the house of Myrtilas tonight. I was told to bring a friend. Myrtilas, as you know, is extremely wealthy. The food ought to be very good. You can also expect that there will be auletrides for our entertainment. Will you come?"

"I have no other plans tonight. I think I'll join you," Phidias said. "Some good food and wine will be a good reward for our hard exercise."

"And don't forget the pretty auletrides," said Hippias.

"Oh, of course," said Phidias. "Maybe we can ask our host for a private room, so we can mingle with the girls after the dinner." He grinned and winked.

Hippias laughed and slapped him on the back. "You're always thinking, Phidias, but thinking of what?" They laughed together.

The four young men met and walked out to Myrtilas' villa, perched on one of the hills outside the walls. "I understand that our host is very rich," said Lysias.

"He owns a fleet of merchant ships that trade all over the Mediterranean. He has houses on Lesbos and in Syracuse, as well as this huge estate in Athens," said Agelaus. "It is said that he has over a hundred slaves and supports two well-known hetairai, who are very cultured courtesans. He's unmarried, although his children from his dead wife are grown and live in Asia."

"I can't wait to see his house," said Phidias.

"And the auletrides," said Hippias.

They laughed and joked their way to the villa. From the main road, they followed a torch-lit path to the gate in the wall surrounding the estate and rang the bell. A tall, muscular black slave, stripped to the waist, admitted them and escorted them into the house, where a handsome, young white, male slave, also bare-chested, greeted them. He sported a gold hoop in one ear, and his body shone with scented oil.

The young visitors whispered to one another pointing out the expensive mosaics, art, and furnishings. The slave escorted them into a large room with couches for the guests against the walls. Two men would share each couch, where they would eat while reclining. In the center of the room stood eight beautiful young women. They wore their hair braided and tied up by ribbons of many colors, and gold earrings dangled from their ears. Their thin cotton skirts barely covered their thighs. Pinned at the shoulders, the short dresses were gathered at the waist by gold braided ropes. The opening left in the middle of the chest came to the waist and allowed their youthful breasts to peak out and sometimes become completely exposed. The girls seemed to encourage this titillating show.

The young men's eyes filled with excitement, and they could hardly concentrate as they met their host, who introduced them to the other men. Half-naked slaves brought around trays of wine and appetizers. After some pleasant conversation, their host asked his guests to take the places he had appointed them. Myrtilas had taken a liking to Phidias during his conversation with him. "Phidias, you come share my couch."

During the dinner the auletrides played light flute music while the men ate and discussed politics, literature, and philosophy. As the dinner wore on, the slaves diluted the wine less and less until they served it full strength.

When the *epikomen*, the sweet dessert, was served, the girls began to dance. Toward the end they pranced around the room, flitting from couch to couch, caressing faces, giggling, and allowing a kiss on a hand or shoulder. The sensual show aroused all the young men. They had heard of such dinners but had never participated in such a lavish one.

After the girls finished their dance, Myrtilas said, "It looks like we could all enjoy a warm bath, and perhaps a cold splash for the young men." Everyone laughed. He assured them, "The girls will still be here afterward and for the rest of the night."

The men carried their newly-filled wine cups and followed Myrtilas to the large enclosed bath—really a small pool. Benches and hooks for clothes lined the room. Slaves brought fresh towels while the men stripped and stepped into the hot bath, still joking or talking.

The younger men horsed around, playing, splashing, throwing cold water from standing vases at one another, and imbibing several more glasses of wine. After a time, Hippias said, "I'm not feeling too well. My stomach is cramping."

Myrtilas motioned to a slave who quickly took Hippias into the courtyard, where he could vomit. "He'll be all right," said the host. "A little too much wine and excitement for one who is not used to it. I guess he won't be able to enjoy the rest of the evening. Too bad."

The young men calmed down and started conversations with the older men. Phidias sat on the side of the pool talking with Myrtilas about his fleets and the ports they visited, water from his dark curls dripping down his broad, tanned shoulders. His fit, youthful body contrasted with the older man's pale skin and portly belly covered with dark hair. Phidias, anxious to experience the world outside of Athens, devoured all talk of foreign places, like a hungry dog presented with raw meat.

"You have undoubtedly been exercising your athletic and military skills," said Myrtilas as he felt Phidias's chest. "You have a good, solid physique."

"Thank you, sir. I am proud of my physical strength but also wish to improve my mental skills."

"Are you also proud of these?" asked Myrtilas as he reached between Phidias' thighs.

Phidias caught his wrist and gently pushed it aside. He smiled and said, "I use them for women only."

"Why only women? You can enjoy the company of men like me in more than just eating and conversing."

Phidias looked around and noticed that all the other guests had melted away. He didn't know whether his young friends were with the auletrides or with the older men. "Pardon me, sir, but I am not inclined to have that kind of relationship."

"And why not? It is common practice for a rich, older man to take a youth into his home. Come live with me, and I will give you many nice things. And you can call me Myrtilas."

"Thank you, Myrtilas, but my father is getting old. If my father's health fails, I must help my older brother and take care of my mother and younger brothers and sister."

"That can be arranged."

"Pardon me, sir—I mean, Myrtilas—but isn't it in the statutes that a person who has a relationship of this kind with his own sex is banned from serving in public office?"

"How foolish you are." Myrtilas chuckled. "You may be too young to realize that the public is cynical and turns a blind eye as men get around that law. Look at the notorious Alcibiades. He lived during the great Peloponnesian war between Athens and Sparta and was a leader and general after Pericles died. He was openly homosexual, if I may use the term.

"As a matter of fact, I can help your political career. I have need of a handsome, intelligent man in the service of Athens. You could help me in my business affairs."

"I appreciate that," Phidias said, "but I have no desire at this time to enter public service and have no interest in business. I am still young and, as you say, inexperienced. I must learn more about the political side of life. After all, I've been separated from it while an ephebos. Maybe after I've learned more about Athenian government, I will become active in it. Now it's getting late and I must go back alone into the city." He was anxious to leave a conversation that had become embarrassing to him. "I appreciate your offer of friendship and would like to always consider you a friend, if I may."

"I admire your strength of character," Myrtilas said. "Not every young man in your position would refuse my offer. Yes, I will remain your friend. Call on me if you need anything. The slave will show you out. He will carry a torch and walk home with you if you like."

"Thank you, Myrtilas, for all your hospitality." Phidias rose, dressed, and left.

Homosexuality was commonly accepted in ancient Greece, attributed by some contemporaries to a fear of overpopulation. More than likely, it had to do with the exclusivity of male social life. Young men knew only other men and prostitutes and no women other than their mother and sisters, until they were married. After marriage, all political and intellectual contact was with other men, and occasionally professional courtesans, the hetairi.

By the time Phidias had reached young adulthood, religious cynicism and moral decay in Athens was growing along with the increase in luxury and the political turmoil. The rich and intelligent classes lost their faith in the traditional gods while the masses still clung to their myths. However, new faiths imported from Egypt and Asia competed with the old Olympian gods. As the traditional religion fell out of favor, individuals felt freed from its moral restraints. Strong moral scruples and civic devotion no longer ruled people. The rich had become obsessed with protecting their wealth, while the lower classes had become equally obsessed with finding ways to take it from them.

Phidias was already aware of the social and political conflicts unraveling the fabric of Athens society, and the dinner at Myrtilas' villa had opened his eyes wider to his city's seedy underside. For many days after his experience there, he wondered about it. His thoughts brought many questions to his troubled mind.

What did he really think about sexual relationships, the morals of the wealthy, and the gritty reality of Athenian politics? It was all so confusing. What were his own values? What did he really want to do with his life? He knew he didn't want to join the young men who had no direction in their lives. He would find his way, discover what he wanted, and fulfill his promise.

CHAPTER 4

Some months after Phidias had dinner with Myrtilas, he met him on the streets of the city. Phidias was pleasant to the man, without encouraging anything further. He immersed himself into public life, discussing politics, and attending dinners and symposia. Realizing he didn't know as much about literature, philosophy, or foreign lands as many of the older men, Phidias absorbed as much as he could from them, but he wanted more.

He was enjoying dinner one evening with his family when, after the meal, Aristippus excused his wife and daughter so he and his four sons, for Meletus was also present, could continue their discussion.

"Athens is going to have a war with Thebes," said Aristippus. "Epaminondas' strategy completely defeated the Spartans. That had never been done. Now Thebes has become too powerful."

"What will Athens do, Papa?" Cimeas asked.

"Athens will form an alliance with Sparta," explained his father. "It's always the two weaker cities against the stronger."

"Will you fight again, Papa?" Diocles asked.

"No. I am too old, but Meletus and Phidias will fight."

"No, I won't," said Meletus, raising his voice. "Let Athens hire more mercenaries. Why should I spill my blood? What has Athens done for me except tax my father into poverty?" He pounded his fist on the table and reached for his wine cup.

"What do you mean, what has Athens done for you?" Aristippus exploded. "You are a spoiled son who has taken the prosperity, education, and culture of the greatest city in the world for granted. You live well because of your trade in goods. You have not even married."

"Yes, Meletus, when will you marry and move your family out to the estate?" Phidias asked. "Father will need you more since he is getting older."

"I don't care to yet," Meletus replied.

"You are living with a woman, aren't you?" his father asked between clenched teeth.

"So what if I am." Meletus was defiant. "Many men of my age and older have taken women. Why do I have to marry? To have children? For what? So they can be marched off to fight? Many Athenian women try to avoid pregnancy and, if they do carry a baby, will abandon it. I am happy with my life, and I don't care what you or Athens says about it."

"How dare you talk that way!" Phidias raised his voice in anger. "You took an oath as an ephebos, or don't you remember? You promised to protect your city and to improve it by your citizenship."

"I help Athens by my trade, but I will not sacrifice my life for her. What will you do, Phidias," his voice dripped with sarcasm, "if Athens and Thebes go to war, sacrifice yourself on the altar of patriotism?"

"I will fight for my city." Phidias stuck his chest out with pride. "I am twenty-two and a citizen of Athens. It is my duty, and I will uphold my honor by defending her."

"Well spoken, my son," said Aristippus. "I would go with you if I could."

"So would I," said Cimeas.

"And me too," added Diocles..

Phidias smiled at them. "I know you would. You'll be epheboi soon enough and will become good soldiers." He turned to Meletus. "I'm sorry you think that way. I have always looked up to you as my older brother, but I strongly disagree with you. Perhaps you will see how this hurts our father and you will change your mind."

"Perhaps I will...someday, but not now." With that, Meletus stood and stomped out of the room. He left early without saying good-bye to anyone and returned to the city.

Weeks later, Phidias bade farewell to his family and marched with some of his friends to fight Thebes. After camping for the night, Phidias strode to where his friend, Hippias, had prepared a site for them to sleep.

"We will meet the Thebans near the town of Mantinea," Phidias said. "I heard the officers discussing the coming battle."

"I know we will win," said Hippias, "because we have the help of the Spartans, who are fearless fighters.""Don't be over-confident, my friend. Remember, Epaminondas destroyed them at Leuctra. The Spartans had never been defeated on the open battlefield. He had developed new tactics. Greeks had not fought that way before."

"Will our generals know how to counter his strategy?"

"I hope so," said Phidias. "We'll follow their lead and show the Thebans how hard we can fight."

"We'll fight side by side and protect one another," Hippias said, feeling confidant. "I know I can rely on you, because we're brothers."

"Hippias, I feel closer to you than I do to my brothers. I pledge my blood and my honor to you. But this is our first battle. We've never faced an enemy or killed a man. I'm a little worried."

"You'll be fine, my friend. You have great skill with a spear and sword; I've seen it." Hippias smiled knowingly. "I know you'll have the courage Athens demands of you. Remember, I'll be there to help you."

"And I'll be there for you." With that they embraced with a firm commitment. Phidias didn't want to show the fear that all young soldiers felt before their first battle.

Two days later, Phidias stood on the left side of Hippias facing the Thebans across the open field. He beat his spear on his friend's shield and smiled at him. A line of sweat marked his upper lip, and his face was pale. Hippias returned his salute by touching his spear to Phidias' shield. The command was given, and they ran yelling at the opposing force, which seem to be at an angle instead of parallel to the Athenian and Spartan lines.

Halfway across the area dividing the two armies, an arrow found its way and pierced the outer part of Phidias' right thigh. He screamed in agony and fell to the ground, dropping his spear and shield. He was aware of his companions rushing past him as he grabbed at his leg. Trained for such circumstances, Phidias pushed the arrow through until he could grasp the pointed end. Tearing off some of his chiton, he tied it above the wound. Then, while holding on to the pointed end with his right hand, he broke off the feathered part with his left and pulled the shaft out. Blood followed the arrow, dripping onto his right hand. He quickly retied the bandage over the wound to staunch the flow. Then he lay back and helplessly watched the chaos of battle.

Hippias fell with his companions upon the Theban line with a loud yell, their flank was firmly fixed against the enemy. Spears and shields clashed and blood ran, soaking the ground. Hippias missed his friend guarding his left but felt secure that on their left flank were the Spartans. He knew they would hold their line and push back the Thebans. Thrusting with his spear, he killed two Thebans, but it broke in the body of a third. He drew his sword and defended himself against his foe.

In hand-to-hand battles in which a soldier looked his enemy in the eye and knew he must kill him or be killed by him, time seemed to stretch in odd ways. The battle had raged for an hour that seemed like half a day when Hippias became aware that the Athenian line to his right was giving ground. He heard shouting and, peering over down the broken ranks, he saw that the Thebans had turned the Athenian right flank and were enveloping them. As his head was turned, a Theban thrust his spear through Hippias' throat. It was only in that instant, before he fell dead, that Hippias remembered that Phidias was not there to protect his left side.

The Athenian flank was completely turned and they were routed, while the Spartans stood their ground and were surrounded and slaughtered. Two of Phidias' companions helped him flee from the carnage. The Thebans won the battle, although their great commander, Epaminondas, was killed. The brief hegemony of Thebes was finished.

Phidias returned home, and his mother and sisters nursed him. The wound healed, but he would walk with a limp for several months. His father and his younger brothers congratulated him and said how brave he was and how well he had fought for Athens, even though they hadn't won the battle. Phidias thanked them but didn't have the courage to tell them that he'd never crossed sword or spear with the enemy.

All winter he lay on his bed and felt sorry for himself, wondering whether he was a coward, a failure, a traitor to his city. He thought of his best friend, Hippias, and how brave he was in his first battle. He asked himself, if he had been by his friend's side, would he have saved his life? He felt guilty that he had not been there.

He began to walk with the aid of a stick. By spring he could walk down to the vineyard and ride a horse across the fields. To while away the hours and days, he read all the books his father had in his house. Books, of course, were papyrus scrolls covered with a leather sleeve. His father had copies of Homer's classics, the histories of Herodotus and Thucydides, some plays, and the writings of some philosophers.

On a day in early summer, Phidias sat in the sun outside the gate, gazing over the green vineyards with their ripening fruit. He had taken off his chiton and wrapped it around his waist so he could feel the sun's heat on his chest. He felt aimless, like a boat without sail or oars, with no goal. He could no longer be a soldier or work in his father's fields, and he didn't want to go into trade like his brother. He liked to hear about places outside of

Greece. He was curious about the world, the stars, and what caused things to be the way they were. He found his mind questioning the old myths and beliefs as he read all of his father's books. He would ask his father to borrow more books, or better yet, he would study with some masters.

One summer night as Phidias sat reading, his father entered his room. "What are you reading?" he asked.

"Herodotus' history, Father. It's fascinating. I have learned so much about the Persians and Egyptians that it makes me want to visit those places."

"How would you get there, my son? You have no money. You have no skill, trade, or education. You can barely walk."

"I've got to do something, Father. I can't just live at your house forever."

"Yes, you could. You can help me run the estate. Meletus does not seem to want to."

"My younger brothers will be able to help you soon, and perhaps I can talk sense to Meletus. I want to study. I want to go to Plato's Academy."

"What will you study? Mathematics? Philosophy? What can you do with those, except to be a teacher to others and argue about what is real."

"I don't know, but I admire Plato. He was a student of Socrates. I hear Socrates was the best philosopher Athens had, until he was killed."

"Yes, he probably was. I remember being a young man when the Assembly voted to give that harmless old man the death penalty. It was a tragedy. But you won't be a philosopher. Why don't you go to Isocrates' school and learn rhetoric and how to argue in the courts. You can become a rhetor. You can make money defending people and go into politics. Politicians always know how to get rich. After all, they make the laws."

"You sound bitter, Father."

"It's true," Aristippus said. "This city is coming more and more under the power of the masses, who are controlled by the politicians. They control the Assembly and elect the generals. They don't know how to run a city or prosecute a war. If a general or admiral loses a battle, they fine him or exile him. Is that any way to reward service to Athens?"

Aristippus sighed. "Well, anyway, I'm getting cynical. It seems that politics is the only way to get ahead these days. Why don't you go to Isocrates' school?"

"I don't want to be a politician. The rhetors are hypocrites. They will argue for or against any side in the courts or the Assembly. I believe in what is true and will defend it. I want to find out how things really are. I want to talk to other men from all parts of the world. I want to read all kinds of books. I want to learn more."

"What will you do my son?"

"Father, I have made a decision. I will go tomorrow and ask Plato, if I can join his Academy. Will you help me?"

"I know that the families of students are expected to donate to the Academy. After all, they don't charge their students, and the teachers have to eat." Aristippus paused a moment. "All right, I will give the rent from one of my houses in Athens to the Academy if you attend."

Phidias grinned, "Thank you, Father. You won't be sorry. I will study hard. You will be proud of me."

CHAPTER 5

One day when Phidias was still an ephebos, he noticed a group of young men in distinctive caps strolling through the marketplace. They all carried canes and wore the same short cloak over their clothes. "Who are those men?" he asked an older ephebos.

"They're students in Plato's Academy. I think they put on too many airs."

"Why do they dress alike?"

"They wear those caps and gowns to show they belong to the Academy and to set themselves apart."

"I overheard some of their conversation," said Phidias. "They seem to be very smart."

"They flaunt their self-importance and supposedly superior intelligence. I went to a play, a comedy by Aristophanes, that poked fun at their affected manners and dress."

Impressed with the bright students, Phidias ignored his comrade's criticism. He decided to learn more about this school.

Plato had built his school on land that was a recreation grove outside the gates of Athens, named for the local god, Academus, and thus the school became known as the Academy. The first university of its kind, it officially was dedicated to the worship of the muses and was therefore technically a religious fraternity. It was called a *museion*, or museum, but, rather than a collection of objects, it was a place dedicated to pursuits of the muses, such as poetry, music, mathematics, and philosophy.

Plato believed in the education of women as well as men and allowed them to attend his school. Students were not charged fees, but, because most of them were from the upper classes, their families were expected to give generously toward its support.

Phidias applied to the school, and Plato, impressed with his intelligence and eagerness to learn, admitted the young man to his Academy.

Phidias found that Plato and the other instructors taught by a combination of lecturing and dialogue with the students. They often posed problems, especially in mathematics or astronomy, for them to solve. Sometimes questions of philosophy or political science would be posed, and then the students were encouraged to argue points. The heady atmosphere of intellectual discussion stimulated Phidias' mind.

Students often continued their arguments about political or philosophical points outside the school on the streets and marketplaces of Athens. One day, Phidias and some of his friends were discussing forms of government. They had strolled into the open area below the steps leading up to the Acropolis and the beautiful Parthenon that graced its peak.

One of the students was saying, "And Master Plato distrusts democracies. He says that it tends to become rule by the masses. They are largely uneducated and can easily be influenced by clever speakers."

"The government of the city is too important to be in the power of the uneducated," said another.

"But Master Plato doesn't favor a king or aristocracy either," said the first student. "The government should be in the hands of intelligent men, like philosophers."

"Yes," said Phidias, "men who have no desire for power or wealth but only for the welfare of the city-state"

"I think democracy has many weaknesses," said one of the students. "Master Plato told us how the jury that was dominated by the people condemned Socrates to death."

"It's true," said Phidias. "That was because it was swayed by the arguments of a man who disliked Socrates' teachings."

"You see," said another student, "in a democracy, a skillful orator can sway the Assembly."

"That can be good or bad," said one. "Pericles was a good orator and a good leader."

"The Master said that a person who wants to be elected by the people promises to give them more. Maybe grain, or payments from the Theoric fund," said another.

Phidias' friend Hesiod added, "That's the way in a democracy. When a person is elected, he gets the Assembly to tax the people with property to pay for the things he has promised the masses to get their vote."

"It's a dangerous game," said Phidias. "The person who promises the most to the masses is the one who gets the most votes."

While they were discussing the pros and cons of various forms of government, they began to collect knots of bystanders, who joined in the arguments. Politics was the lifeblood of Athens. It fed on the energy of the Greek soul and fertilized its temperament. Inevitably, whenever such a controversial subject was the topic, emotions soon overcame reason and talking transformed into shouting and shoving.

A man who thought Athens' democracy was the best possible government violently opposed Phidias, who defended Plato. The man threw a fist at Phidias. He blocked it with his cane, but it knocked off his cap. Phidias pushed away his attacker and picked it up, yelling at his comrades, "Let's get out of here."

They backed out of the crowd of arguing and shouting men, and made their way toward the Academy. "Why can't men just argue reasonably, like we do at school?" asked a younger student. "These men on the street get violent." He shook his head in disgust.

"They aren't trained like we are," said Phidias. "Master Plato has taught us to leave our feelings aside and use only our reasoning."

"That's easy to say," said Hesiod, "but when politics is the issue, emotions take over. It seems with that, and with religion, there is no good intellectual discussion."

"You're right there, my friend," said Phidias. "We just saw that in action."

They all laughed in agreement.

Not long after the political brawl in the marketplace, Phidias and a few of his friends were in a spirited discussion on the use of taxation of the wealthy to feed and house the poor. They had just heard a lecture on the topic and were anxious to debate it. "Let's ask the instructor," said Phidias. "Sir, may we go to the school of Isocrates and debate the students there on this subject?"

"It's possible," said Lycon, the teacher of politics. "You know that Isocrates's school specializes in teaching rhetoric and the art of debate. They are trained to argue cases in court and must take either side to defend."

"But we study law and politics also, and in this case moral philosophy as well. We can hold our own."

"I will see about arranging a debate," Lycon agreed. "I know one of the teachers there very well. See if you can gather four of your friends together to go."

Phidias talked to some of his friends. "I'm trying to organize a debate with students from Isocrates' school. We have a lot of experience and training in class. I think we can probably win a debate."

Iophon, the oldest of the group, said, "Isocrates' students are trained in rhetoric. They're known for their skilled argument. We may be humiliated."

Phidias replied, "We can tell them that we want to debate the topic of taxes for the poor. We can use our knowledge of moral philosophy as well as politics."

Hesiod agreed, "We are smarter and more well-rounded in our studies. We can beat them. I'll go with you."

"Iophon," Phidias said, "you of all of us have the widest knowledge of government and politics. You've been at the Academy for over three years. You could be our leader."

"Okay," said Iophon. "You've convinced me. I'll gather two other men who can argue well. I think we can more than hold our own against Isocrates' school."

Instructors from the two schools arranged the debate, and, a few days later, the group from the Academy entered the grounds of Isocrates' school, a collection of low buildings with Ionic columns, a long stoa or covered walkway, and a small temple. Trees and open fields surrounded it, but it was not nearly as large as the Academy.

They were welcomed and led to a portico raised four steps from an open area in which sat the faculty and students, eager to hear the debate. The Academy instructor was also there. The Isocrates' headmaster asked their names and introduced them to the assembly. He also introduced the five students who would debate them.

The rules were that each side would take turns of a measured time in which to speak. The members of each team would alternate until all ten had spoken. Since they were guests, the students of the Academy were invited to speak first. Phidias agreed to start, followed by three other members and ending with Iophon, considered to be the strongest speaker.

The headmaster announced the topic for debate: "Is it morally right to tax the rich to feed the poor? You will have a short period in which to gather your thoughts and begin."

The students from the Academy put their heads together. Iophon said, "This should be straightforward. We should argue for the affirmative, that it is morally right. To bolster our argument, we have the moral laws, the laws of the gods, and the fact that Athens has already passed such statutes."

Phidias said, "In addition, if we force our opponents to take the negative stance, then they are arguing against those laws and statutes. This should be an easy debate."

"Our teachers in politics and philosophy have prepared us for this," said another.

"Go to it, Phidias. Give them such a strong argument that they are defeated before they even start," replied a fourth.

Phidias, eloquently and with unassailable logic, laid down his arguments: "It is the moral law given to us by the gods and put into practice by the state to take care of those who, by no fault of their own, are sick, destitute, or maimed. The state has no wealth of its own but must obtain it through taxes. Those who have more property and wealth should pay more taxes because they have been blessed by the gods. The taxes obtained by the state from the wealthy can then be used to support the less fortunate."

After he finished, Phidias sat down, satisfied that he had built an impregnable argument. His fellows smiled and patted him on the back.

A student from Isocrates' school arose and began to speak. "What is morally right? Where do morals come from? Who says what is morally right or wrong?" He began with the morals of the gods, explaining that their actions, as depicted in the myths, revealed that they engaged in acts of rape, incest, torture, murder, lying, deception, and other acts the Athenians considered immoral. "If the gods do these things, then are they moral?" he asked.

He next pointed out that what Athenians consider moral acts are considered immoral or vice versa in other countries. He told of how the Egyptian pharaohs married their own sisters and the kings of some Asian countries murdered all their brothers on gaining the throne, so that none would be left to contest their reign. He then illustrated the immoral behavior of the poorer class, who engage in stealing, murder, drunkenness, and rape. "Is it therefore moral to support people who act immorally?" he asked.

The students then debated back and forth about morality: Was there an absolute standard of morals? And if so, where does it come from? Are morals relative to a time and place, that is, do they change according to circumstances? Do extenuating circumstances, such as war, plague, or famine, justify the suspension of morals or the institution of new ones?

Whatever the students of the Academy argued, the Isocrates students seemed to counter brilliantly. They turned the Academy's arguments on their heads and made them appear absurd. Iophon tried to bring the argument back to the original thesis that it is right to take care of the poor, but the last and most talented debater of the other school closed by destroying all his points. As he finished, the audience clapped and cheered.

The Academy students were embarrassed and demoralized. The headmaster thanked them for coming and escorted them from the school. He thanked their instructor for the opportunity to debate the learned students of the Academy. "And feel free to return again for a debate. Our students need the practice," he said with a smile. They each went to their homes with heads down, like beaten dogs with tails between their legs.

The next day they returned to the Academy. Plato had heard about the debate from Lycon. He asked that all the debaters come and relate to him the course of the debate.

Iophon laid it all out. "Whatever arguments we had, they seemed to turn inside out. They made us look absurd. We thought our reasoning was sound and logically presented. We don't know what went wrong."

Plato said, "You were foolish to try to debate the students of Isocrates. They are trained to argue any point and make excellent lawyers, if you ever have need for one. They reduced your arguments and thesis to the definition of the words themselves. Words have different meanings, depending on their use and contexts. Thus the words 'right,' 'moral,' and 'good' mean different things, depending on how we are using them."

* * *

In his third year at the Academy, Phidias was invited with his friend, Stilpo, to attend a dinner at the home of Eucleides, a well-to-do and learned man. Eight men were attending the dinner, and Phidias shared his couch with Stilpo. During the dinner of fish, roast duck, vegetables, and fresh-baked bread, auletrides played musical instruments and danced around the room.

One in particular kept exchanging glances with Phidias. He was mesmerized by her eyes that twinkled like stars surrounded by a dark halo. Her blond hair, braided and interwoven with bright blue ribbon, hung down to her lower back. Long lashes fluttered as she smiled when she looked at Phidias. He could barely concentrate on his food and conversation.

After the dinner, attendants swept the floor and passed around perfumes. They took the dishes away and poured fresh wine for all the guests. In the typical *symposion*, or drinking together, attendants kept the wine cups full while the guests engaged in games; watched professional entertainers; matched poems, riddles or witticisms; or, as in Plato's famous dialogues, discussed politics and philosophy.

Eucleides spoke, "I propose that each of you in turn submit a riddle for all to solve, or recite a poem that you have created. It may be serious, comical, or lascivious. Being the host, I will begin, then pass to the person on my right." He gave them a riddle, which they all began to ponder. The guests gave many solutions. Some were extremely funny, so all laughed. Some wits were sharpened while the flowing wine loosened tongues.

As the guests took their turns, Phidias had time to compose his poem. The loveliness of the auletrid moved his sensual feelings. When his time came, he said, "I have a poem that I have composed tonight, inspired by the beautiful auletrides provided by our guest. I dedicate it to him." He glanced purposefully at the auletrid who had held his attention all evening and then recited:

> "Good food and wine to sate our taste
> Nor we to drink or eat in haste.
> We fill our cups and toast with wine
> The friends herein with whom we dine.
> Fluted notes, dance, and poet's rhyme
> Cool hot emotions for a time.
> Bright talk fills our symposion,
> The mind's hearty companion.
> Auletrides light heart's desire
> And energize our loins with fire.
> Beautiful hair and eyes alight
> May warm our beds and souls this night."

As he finished, he raised his wine. All the men clapped and lifted their cups. The auletrides, returning the favor, smiled, bowed, and began to mingle with the guests. The beauty, whom Phidias had lost his heart to, danced to his couch, her face alight with smiling eyes. Erect nipples tented the light fabric flitting open between her full breasts as she approached, and he held out his arms to envelope her warm, perfumed body. She raised her pale arms around his curl-draped neck and placed her full, moist lips on his.

After the arousing kiss, she grasped his hand and pulled him toward the door. Phidias noticed that all the auletrides were engaging the guests in flirting conversation or caresses. She led him to a small bedroom lit with fragrant candles. Again he pulled her into his arms and kissed her mouth, then her cheeks and neck. She pushed his robe off his shoulder until it hung around his waist and gently ran her hands over his chest, massaging his firm pectorals and tweaking his nipples. His manhood stood fully erected and pressed against her abdomen as he lifted her shoulder drapes and let them fall away from her firm breasts. She pressed them against his warm chest.

Disengaging herself, she led him to the bed, removed his robe, and pushed him gently onto the cover. Looking sensually into his eyes, she loosened the cord around her waist, letting the light skirt fall to the floor. His eyes drank in the soft, flawless skin covering her young curves and secret parts. He reached for her hand and pulled her to his chest. She nestled onto his body, his legs open and enveloping hers.

The time passed in ecstatic delight, each sensually stimulating the other into explosive orgasms. Phidias had never had an experience such as this. His other sexual escapades had been with the pornai. He paid them to do whatever he wanted, but this auletrid seemed to know how to arouse him to dizzying heights and stimulate him in ways he had never known. After hours of sexual play, they lay exhausted, her perspiring body across his broad chest.

"My name is Phidias. What is yours, my lovely?"

"Danae," she said, smiling.

"You have brought out sensual feelings I never knew existed. You are not only the most beautiful auletrid I have ever seen but the most talented."

"Thank you, sir. I appreciate your flattery for a simple orphan girl. Pleasing the guests of my master is what I am trained to do. I am in turn pleased that you like me."

"I not only like you, I love you," Phidias murmured.

"It is not agape love, but erotic love," she advised. "Enjoy it for the moment, for it will pass until reignited by another. Now rest and sleep. The slave will bring you water in the morning and escort you home." She rose, ran her hand once more from his lips to his chest, and left the room, trailing her clothes behind her.

II THE MENTOR AND THE LOVER

CHAPTER 6

While Phidias studied at the Academy, the lectures of a particularly bright and energetic teacher impressed him. His name was Aristotle. He was not very much older than Phidias but had been at the Academy for several years. He had dark brown hair and a beard. Full of intelligent energy, his mind inquired into many aspects of knowledge. His genius shone through eyes that pierced to the heart of the matter he was dissecting, or the mind of the person he was conversing with.

His father had been the court physician to the king of Macedon and had taught his son some anatomy, endowing him with a lifelong interest in the subject. Deciding that Aristotle needed to broaden and polish his Macedonian heritage with Greek culture, he sent him at the age of seventeen to Athens to study with Plato at his Academy.

The young man immediately caught his master's eye. Intelligent and hungry for knowledge, he seemed to soak up everything he could from anyone he met. But whereas Plato was more interested in philosophy, Aristotle's mind was more taken with the practical aspects of this world. He was not averse to arguing with his master about points he disagreed with.

Aristotle's incisive mind and broad interests captured Phidias. There seemed to be nothing that he had not inquired into, and he was willing to expound upon it all. Phidias eagerly attended Aristotle's lectures on biology, physics, logic, politics, and ethics.

Once, after a particularly interesting demonstration on biology, Phidias approached Aristotle. "I ask you, Aristotle, do you believe that all animals are related in some way?"

For his part, Aristotle had taken a liking to this eager student, who was curious about so many things. He enjoyed discussing his stimulating questions. "I not only believe that they're all related, I will show you. Come with me to my work room."

He displayed to Phidias the carcasses of a dog, a lamb, a chicken, and a fish. "Let me show you something." He pointed out that all of the animals had the same organs: heart, liver, stomach, and intestines. "The fish do not have lungs like the others because they breathe underwater and have these openings I call gills that the water flows through."

Aristotle showed Phidias his collections of insects, plants, and animals. "We all know about the sexual union of animals such as sheep, dogs, and oxen. However, I believe that other animals, such as beetles and also plants, have sexual union." He explained his thoughts to the eager student.

"I will eventually collect all my notes on anatomy and will write a book on the subject. Come with me tomorrow to the butcher's. I can probably find a pregnant dog or cat to take with us. I would like to show you the similarities in the development before birth of animals such as sheep, dogs, cats, and rabbits."

Phidias was excited. He was eager to know about anything Aristotle could teach him, and that was a lot.

One day while sitting with Phidias in the shade of a large oak tree, Aristotle said, "What interests you, my young friend?"

Phidias replied, "I want to know everything, yet I don't know how to begin, how to organize my inquiries."

"Let's put them into categories, Phidias. First, are you interested in the heavens, that is, the sun, moon, planets, and fixed stars?"

"Yes," Phidias replied. "How and why do they move? What keeps them up? What are they made of?"

"Next, are you interested in the manner of inanimate things, how objects move, why some fall and others rise, and what is their most basic substance that comprises them?"

"Yes, yes, all those things."

"Then are you interested in why men act the way they do?" Aristotle continued. "What makes a person happy? What is the basis of friendship?"

"Yes, Aristotle, and tell me also why the different classes fight with one another for power in the *polis*, the city-state? In your opinion, what form of government is best, a king or monarchy, an aristocracy of the nobles, or a democracy of the people ?"

"I agree with the master Plato that democracy has some good points, but also some deep faults. I have read his idea of a government by philosophers, who own nothing and live in a common community. I disagree with it. I think it is too idealistic and won't work."

"What do you think is the best form of government?" Phidias asked.

"I think a combination of a type of aristocracy and democracy is probably the best. I would like to do a study of all the forms of governments in the Greek city-states and write a book about it. Would you help me?"

"I would very much like to help in the study," Phidias said, excited by the prospect. "I've wondered about the different ways that cities such as Sparta, Thebes, and Corinth govern themselves. They have different laws than Athens, yet seem to thrive in what they do. So what makes a good government?

"I also would like to make a study of other non-Greek countries—Thrace and Macedonia, the cities of Asia, Egypt, and Persia. Some of those lands have ancient histories. They fascinate me."

"I will help you channel your investigations," Aristotle replied. "Tomorrow, at a midmorning lecture, I will discuss astronomy and why the planets move the way they do. Now let's go to our homes, for I am invited to a symposium tonight to discuss some of the political questions you have posed."

* * *

When Phidias returned to his father's house not long after that discussion, his mother told him that his father was not feeling well and would not be joining him and his younger brothers for dinner. Phidias went to his father's room and found him propped up in his bed on several cushions, pale and breathing laboriously.

"Mother said you are not feeling well, Father. What ails you?"

"Phidias, I'm glad you're here. I have difficulty of late climbing the steps in the city. I have to stop every little way and catch my breath. Sometimes I cough up pink, foamy phlegm. Also I have tightness in my chest if I exert myself. I am getting old and feel I do not have many years, possibly even months, remaining to me."

"Father, please don't speak that way," said Phidias as he took the old man's hand and choked down tears.

"One must be realistic, my son, and face the fact that life will end. We are not gods."

"Oh, Father. I never think about death. I merely assumed you'd be with us for many more years. You're not as old as some men I know. Perhaps you can visit the physicians at the Temple of Aesculapius."

"I don't think they can help me. Some men age and become weaker sooner than others. I've had a hard life. I have fought many wars for Athens and have been wounded. Yes, I feel the life left to me is short and I must do some things before the end comes. And you should think about the end of your life, my son. It makes you want to put more meaning into your life each day. For all the days that the gods give us are precious. We should not waste them.

"Now I want you to do something for me. I want you to write down the will I wish to dictate. Your bother Meletus, as eldest son, will inherit the house, the fields, and the slaves. He must take care of your mother and younger brothers and provide for your sister's dowry. Now that he has married, he seems to have a better head on his shoulders. I think he will do a good job with the estate."

"I think so too, Father. I only ask one favor before we write your will. I want to remain at the Academy and teach there if possible. I will gladly give any lands you may leave for me to Meletus. He is good with numbers and knows how to manage slaves and make decisions. I only ask for the house in Athens for myself, so that I may be close to the Academy."

"I have heard from Plato that you are a good student. He is impressed with your accomplishments and eagerness. You have learned much, my son, but there is still much more about life that you must know, life outside of the Academy."

"I feel you're right, Father. I want to explore the world beyond Athens beyond Greece." ,

"I don't mean only in that way," his father said, smiling. "You must learn about how and why men act the way they do, about the dirty world of politics, and, of course, about women."

"I have had sexual relationships with women, Father."

"I don't mean just sexual relations. You will be married someday and have a family. You must educate your children. They are all great responsibilities."

"Yes," said Phidias, "but you have taught me. I will marry and have a family someday, but now I want to remain at the Academy and be a teacher."

"I knew you would probably say that. You're a scholar and I'm sure you'll be a good teacher and perhaps even write a book. Now get paper and stylus and let's get to work."

Phidias dutifully wrote down the wishes of a dying man. Sorrow filled his heart as the finitude of life struck him in the face. He heard the words of the man who had sired him, raised him with a loving discipline, and given him the opportunity for his education. This courageous man was facing death, yet was calmly dictating his will. Phidias hoped that he could face death with the same equanimity.

Six months later, his father was dead. The family had a modest ceremony, attended by over a hundred, who spoke of the honest and virtuous man that had been Phidias' father. He listened to the warm compliments men gave to Aristippus, for he had many friends. Phidias vowed that he would live a life that had as much meaning. He felt that he had a long journey in which to do it. He was only twenty-seven.

* * *

A year or so later, after attending a lecture on ethics by Plato, Phidias followed the master, who was walking along a path away from the stoa. He quickly caught up with him and politely said, "Master Plato, are you engaged in important thought or may I speak with you?"

"Phidias, I am always engaged in thought and expect to be so until I am dead. For isn't it true that whoever does not think is as good as dead?"

"Indeed it is, Master. I believe that is what distinguishes us from the other animals. Aristotle said that since we have the distinctive power to think, we are obliged to use it to improve ourselves and our world."

"How wise Aristotle is," Plato said. "He has been my best student and will most likely succeed me as master of the Academy. What is it that you wish to discuss?"

"I've been at the Academy for seven years and have helped tutor the younger students. Now I wish to be a full-fledged teacher, like Aristotle and the others."

"What is it that you would teach, Phidias?"

"I am interested in the interactions of men and of cities and countries. I've studied the societies and governments of Greece, Egypt, and Persia, as well as Syracuse and other Greek cities outside of Greece. I have read the histories of Herodotus and Thucydides. I can teach the history of the Persian Wars and the Peloponnesian War, of the struggles between the Greek classes, and, of course, the history of our city since the time of Solon, the great lawgiver."

Plato nodded and placed his hand on Phidias' shoulder. "I have watched you teach the younger students, and I heard some of your lectures on history and governments. Aristotle has told me how you helped him. I'm glad you want to continue to investigate these matters. The study of men and how they act and think is, in my mind, one of the most important of all things. Of course, the history of Greece and other countries enlightens us about the character and motives of men. The Academy has need of a person who is interested in such a subject. We could use a teacher for it. Do you think you could do it?"

"Yes, Master Plato, I know that I can."

"I believe that you can, also. I would be glad to have you as a teacher at my Academy. I welcome you as a colleague." With that, the old man reached out and embraced the younger one and kissed him on the cheek.

CHAPTER 7

Not long after Phidias assumed his teaching duties, Plato invited him to accompany him to a symposium hosted by Mynilas, a rich merchant known to have read the classics and attended some lectures at the Academy. During the dinner, the usual auletrid flute-players were present, but there was also a hetaira, who ate with Mynilas on his couch.

Phidias noticed Plato adding extra water to his wine, which he sipped sparingly during dinner, and that he declined the undiluted wine served afterward during the symposium. Phidias imitated his master, guessing correctly that he wanted to keep his mind clear for the discussion.

After the dishes were cleared and the floor swept, Mynilas told the auletrides to leave the room. He raised his cup. "Here is to our beloved Athens. May the democrats who rule the Assembly become aware of their weaknesses and elect a strong Archon. Then, perhaps prosperity will return and there will be an end to this accursed class warfare." All the guests agreed, lifted their cups in the air, and drank.

"All of you are familiar with Aspasia," Mynilas said, motioning to the woman on his couch. "I have invited her to our symposium to enliven the conversation with our illustrious philosopher, Plato, the pupil of Socrates and founder of the Academy. Here's a salute to Plato." Again they raised their cups and drank.

"My dear, Aspasia," Mynilas said, "would you like to ask Plato a question?"

"Thank you, my lord," she said. "I would like to ask the master, why have men not created a perfect society? What is the best form of government?"

"Those are good questions, Aspasia," Plato replied. "Let us look at the first. Men have not developed a simple paradise on earth because of greed and luxury. They are not content with a simple life but are ambitious, competitive, jealous of others, and greedy for more. The results are one man competing and vying with another, one society encroaching on another, one city-state struggling for more land or wealth, and then war. There are inevitably rich and poor classes in every society, and the interests and needs of these classes will always bring them into conflict with one another. Any ordinary city is in fact two cities: one the city of the poor, the other of the rich, each at war with the other. We see this in Athens today."

"I understand what you mean, Master," said Phidias. "But can a perfect society, or one that is governed perfectly, not educate and train its citizens to live in harmony without class conflicts?"

"Behind these political problems lies the nature of man," Plato explained. "States and their governments are as varied as the characters of the men who make them up. Therefore, we shouldn't expect to have better states unless we have better men."

"But who should rule the state, Plato?" asked Aspasia.

"Now there are classes or types of men," said Plato. "Those who like to trade and produce and are absorbed in accumulating wealth; those who do not care about material goods but whose pride is in power, conquest, and the joy of the battlefield; and those whose delight is in learning and meditation. These last yearn not for goods, nor for victory, but for knowledge.

"Therefore, in the perfect state, the commercial classes would produce but not rule; the military classes would protect but not rule; but the classes of scientists and philosophers would be nourished and protected, and they would rule."

"But how will these philosophers become rulers?" Phidias asked.

"Statesmanship is a science and an art. Those who are to govern should spend years in perfecting their craft in special schools designed to train the philosopher-kings. Until philosophers are kings—or the rulers of this world, having the spirit and knowledge of philosophy, and therefore wisdom and political leadership, are joined in one person—then and only then will strife ease between cities and states."

A general discussion followed, with several questions aimed at Plato. Phidias also fed leading questions to him.

After the discussion, attendants passed wine around for a final toast. This time Plato and Phidias filled their cups, feeling relieved and assured that their discussion had gone well. Plato raised his. "I would like to toast to our generous host, Mynilas, for his delicious food and wine, and to his most beautiful guest, Aspasia, whose wit and intelligence match her beauty."

All raised their cups and said, "To Mynilas and Aspasia."

The guests rose and began milling around, engaging one another in conversation. Aspasia eased her way to Phidias, acknowledging compliments on her way.

"Hello, young master Phidias. I was impressed with your comments during our discussion. Plato must be proud of his young teacher."

"Thank you, Lady Aspasia. I was indeed flattered that Master Plato asked me to accompany him. It has been an honor to listen to your disputation with him. Thank you for your compliment, but I still have much to learn from Master Plato and Aristotle."

"I would like to inquire of you a personal matter," she said, smiling. "Do not think it forward of me or be embarrassed, for it is my calling as hetaira to seek after men's needs. Do you have a regular partner, Phidias, one for sexual and emotional intercourse as well as the intellectual kind? I have heard that you do not lean toward relations with your own sex."

"That is true, Aspasia. I have had much experience with pornai and auletrides, as is expected of one of my age, but I have no steady partner, if that is what you are asking."

"Then I would like to invite you to a dinner at my house one week from today and introduce you to a hetaira friend of mine. She is a lovely woman a few years younger than you, well-read in Greek literature and philosophy. She also plays the harp and sings. Will you come?"

"I would be honored to come to your house and meet your friend. It will be a delight to meet a woman as cultured and educated as you.

"Then I'll see you a week from tonight. Be happy and healthy, young Phidias. You have much to look forward to." With a flick of her robe and a wink, she turned and joined the other guests.

Phidias was not sure exactly how to take her last remark. Had she meant it in reference to his career as teacher and philosopher, or did she imply an enlightening sexual experience? He would have to see.

* * *

The hetairai, literally "companions," were at the top of the class of courtesans in ancient Greece. Unlike the pornai, who were mostly of Asian birth, the hetairai were usually from the citizen class. They had either fallen from respectability or fled from the stifling seclusion of Athenian women. They lived independently and entertained in their own homes, luring lovers who supported them there. They dyed their hair blond, because Athenians seemed to prefer it, and wore flowery robes required by law. Some of them were well-read or attended lectures and entertained their guests with educated discussion. No man was ashamed to be seen in their company; even philosophers contended for their favor.

When the day of the dinner at Aspasia's house arrived, agitated anticipation filled Phidias, his active imagination creating scenes of sensual pleasure with a heavenly body and the face of a goddess. His lectures to the students that day tended toward the sexual mores and practices among the various cities of Greece and the world around them.

That night Phidias wore his best robe and put scented oil in his hair. A slave with a torch came to escort Phidias to Aspasia's house. A large wooden door in a thick wall with family gods on each side invited the visitor to knock with a bronze ring in a lion's mouth. The slave did so, and another large male slave opened the door. The spacious house was furnished with obvious wealth and good taste. The slave motioned for Phidias to go through the courtyard to the dining room at the rear. Bronze and stone statues of gods and heroes adorned the entry and courtyard. Plants surrounded the courtyard, where water splashed musically from a central fountain. Torches placed tastefully around it lit the way to the dining room.

Phidias entered with self-conscious anticipation and was immediately recognized by Aspasia, who came over to greet him. "Welcome, Phidias. I hope your week went well. Come in and meet my guests."

"Thank you, Lady Aspasia," said Phidias as he took a cup of wine from a slave serving it on a brass tray.

Aspasia introduced Phidias to the most famous sculptor and architect in Athens, a foremost orator and politician, and a philosopher from Miletus. At last she came to the person that Phidias admitted to be the most beautiful woman he had ever seen. "And this is Thais."

Phidias barely heard her as he drank in the vision before him. Blond hair with a reddish hint crowned a cream-colored face and fell in tight ringlets down her shoulders and across the mounds her full breasts made in her robe. Her light blue, almost transparent, robe was crisscrossed over her chest by a gold cord that wrapped around her waist and then hung down from her flat belly. Phidias stood transfixed by the beauty standing before him. Her long lashes flirted over dark eyes that spoke of intelligence and seemed to search his very soul.

An embarrassing moment passed before Aspasia woke him from his trance. "Phidias, are you all right?"

"Yes, Lady Aspasia. I'm sorry. I was so taken by the beautiful apparition before of me. I thought it might be a goddess who would soon vanish. I am pleased to make your acquaintance, Thais."

"Likewise, Phidias," she replied. A sound like music emanated through full, scarlet-painted lips that pouted in a face that could be a model for a sculptor. "I have heard great things about you from Lady Aspasia. She says you are one of Master Plato's most brilliant students and a teacher. What do you teach?"

"Lady Aspasia flatters me, I'm afraid. There are teachers and students far more talented and learned than I. Aristotle is by far the most brilliant and may one day equal the Master himself. I teach a subject that is rather new at the Academy. It is the comparison of politics and government in the various cities and countries of the world and at various times."

"How interesting. And do you think Athens' government is the best?"

"It has been superior at times and at others has been deplorable, depending on who or what group was in power. This seems to be true in all countries."

The polite discussion continued until Aspasia announced that they should all take their places for dinner. Thais, of course, was placed with Phidias, as he expected. The dinner was an orchestrated masterpiece, with one course after another of rare and delectable foods served by beautiful slave girls all dressed in matching costumes. Auletrides danced elaborate choreography accompanied by flute, harp, and tambourine.

After dinner, Aspasia effortlessly led the discussion and made sure to bring everyone into it, including Thais, who proved to have a mind as beautiful as her face. Phidias was enchanted. He had never been with a woman who had possessed both attributes. After all, in Athens, women were not formally educated like men.

During the discussion, Phidias heard himself offering intelligent discourse, as if he were in a different world. He didn't know whether the pink haze that enveloped him was from the wine or emanated from the enchantress next to him. He didn't care which, but found intoxicated pleasure in it. He was dimly aware that the more formal discussion was over and guests were rising to relieve themselves or engage in smaller conversations. Thais excused herself and Phidias talked with another guest.

Aspasia intercepted Thais outside the dining room. "Well, how do you like our young philosopher?"

"He not only has a handsome face and body but possesses brilliant conversation. He really interests me. I thank you, Aspasia, for introducing him to me."

"What are your intentions with him?" Aspasia asked.

"I plan to ask him if he wants to spend the rest of the night at my house. If he does, and the evening passes in mutual enjoyment, I may ask him if he wishes a more permanent relationship."

"He is not rich like some of the merchants, Thais, but only a poor teacher."

"Wealth isn't everything, Aspasia. I have enough invested from my last lover to live comfortably. It might be fun to have a young and virile man as a partner."

Aspasia laughed, "I know what you mean. Well, good fortune to you and young Phidias."

Later that night at Thais' very comfortable house, she led Phidias to the bedroom and, after undressing him, told him to lie down on her bed. In stimulated anticipation, Phidias watched her light several candles around the room. Stepping out of her dress, she brought a bottle of scented oil to the bed and began to massage Phidias with it.

Beginning with his toes and feet, she expertly massaged and stroked his legs and thighs before moving upward. She then advanced to his abdomen and chest, kneading the firm muscles he'd developed in the gymnasium. He sucked in a deep breath and raised his buttocks as she tickled and twisted his nipples. Then she progressed to his arms, hands and fingers, alternating with firm pressure and gentle stroking on his sensitive palms.

Proceeding to his neck and face, she lightly massaged and kneaded his strong features and ended by combing her fingers through his dark curls. Although his eyes were closed, his body tingled with sensual excitement. His hot skin twitched around his erect nipples as Thais' fingers made every nerve of his skin stand at attention.

Then Thais gently stroked his private parts, expertly kneading them. He groaned and thrust his pelvis upward. Just as Phidias thought he could not withhold his climax any longer, she stopped, mounted him, and began her rhythmic motion. He sighed and reached up, cupping her firm breasts and rigid nipples. Her experienced orchestrations produced mutual climax for both. She reached down and squeezed his pectoral muscles until they hurt, accentuating his orgasm.

In echoing shudders, she collapsed on his chest, burrowing her face into his neck, her hair splayed across his chest. Phidias, panting and exhausted, put his arms gently around her and stroked her long tresses.

After recovering, and gently kissing his face, Thais rose and cleaned them both from a water basin. Then, after pouring each of them a cup of wine, they exchanged small talk until, spent by emotion, sex, and wine, they fell asleep in one another's arms.

The next day, and for several days thereafter, Phidias sent notes of affection to Thais. She responded by inviting him to her house, where they enjoyed light dinners followed by fervent lovemaking. Phidias was intoxicated, a slave to a feeling he had never known before. He felt that he couldn't get enough of her. He felt that he could not be without her touch, her smell, the sound of her voice.

After several weeks and one particularly pleasing evening of a fine meal and wine followed by tender sex, Thais asked Phidias, "Would you like to live with me in my house? You spend most of your time here anyway, when you are not at the Academy or attending lectures and symposia."

"I would very much like to live with you, Thais," admitted Phidias. "But I have nothing to pay you for my upkeep. My only income is from what my students' families pay."

"You don't have to worry about money, Phidias. I have income from investments from past lovers. We have a wonderful relationship and make a beautiful couple. As you have seen, we have many invitations to dinners. I have plenty of room in this house. You can have your own bedroom and a room for your scrolls and desk, where you can study and write."

"It would be like living with the gods to live with you, for I love you."

"Let's not speak of love or the gods; let's just enjoy the time we have together. Then it is settled. I will send slaves to your house tomorrow to move your belongings."

Phidias could hardly sleep that night. He was captured with emotion as his mind swept through the implications of Thais' invitation to move into her house. He knew that her hetaira tradition forbade her from emotional entanglements that might harm her.

Although she had never said the words, Phidias felt in his heart that Thais shared his feelings. He was sure that what he felt was love. It was obvious to him that Thais enjoyed the relationship as well, for why else would she invite him to live with her? He knew she wasn't doing it for his money, for he had none. Call it love or infatuation; he felt that they were immersed in each other, body and soul. Was he sure of this? It didn't matter.

Phidias' relationship with Thais was becoming the subject of comments among his acquaintances, and the two of them were invited to dinners and symposia. Although some of Phidias' closest friends chided him for not getting married, underneath, they were jealous that he was living in the house of a beautiful hetaira that he didn't even have to support.

It had long been the tradition of Greek men to marry in their late twenties or early thirties to teenage females. Marriage was for having families and maintaining society. But this tradition, as well as sexual morality in general, had been declining for many years.

More and more men imitated the actions of Meletus and Phidias, living unmarried with women. Some merely lived together without the rituals of marriage; others, like Phidias, kept a hetaira; while some married men had concubines.

This behavior was even the subject of a popular play by Aristophanes. He had one of his characters say, "Is not a concubine more desirable than a wife? The one has on her side the law that compels you to retain her, no matter how displeasing she may be; the other knows that she must hold a man by behaving well, or else look for another."

So Phidias had no moral qualms about living with Thais. It was not only accepted but fashionable among the upper classes. Besides, he enjoyed the relationship. She satisfied him emotionally, sexually, and intellectually. Completely immersed, he didn't care that it may not be morally correct; he was enjoying it.

CHAPTER 8

One day Phidias participated in a discussion Plato was having with Aristotle and some students. "Knowledge is possible only through *Ideas*," said Plato.

"What do you mean by ideas?" asked Phidias, although he was familiar with Plato's thoughts.

"I speak of *Ideas* with a capital because they do not rely on the senses but are real. They remain unchanged, even though the senses may be deceived or even die."

"How are they unchanging, Master?" a student asked.

"In mathematics, every triangle you draw is imperfect and can be erased, but the idea of triangle and the form and laws of all triangles are perfect and everlasting. This is true of all geometry.

"Likewise, the classes of things are more real than the individuals that comprise them. *Man* enables us to think of all men, *table* of all tables, *light* of every light that may ever shine. Individual men and tables may be destroyed, but the ideas *man* and *table* survive."

"What about abstract ideas, such as virtue or beauty?" asked Aristotle.

"Abstractions are also real in this sense," said Plato. "Individual acts of virtue are forgotten, but virtue itself has a permanent reality. The same is true for qualities such as beauty, largeness, the color red, and so forth."

"I don't see how this can pertain to science," argued Aristotle. "After all, what we observe in nature has its own reality."

Plato replied, "The world of science is not composed of individual things but of *Ideas*. History is the story of *man*, not of men. Biology is not the science of individual organisms but of *life*. Philosophy itself is the science of *ideas*."

Aristotle was not convinced by Plato's reasoning. After the discussion, the participants dispersed and Aristotle sought out Phidias. "I really don't agree with Plato," he said of his master. "I don't think ideas or abstractions have a reality of their own. I think they're just handy names that we can use. History is made by men, for who else acts it out? The science of biology is developed by studying individual organisms. There is no such thing as 'man' in a large sense. It is only a category we use to group all men together. The only thing that exists is real men—men who are born, age, and die."

"I see what you mean, my friend, but I also understand Plato's arguments," said Phidias.

"I truly admire Plato and his philosophy," Aristotle returned. "I do like to argue with him and may do so tomorrow, but it's meant to be as philosopher to philosopher. I love him as a father."

"I also love him," said Phidias, "but I admire you, too."

Phidias held Plato on his highest pedestal. He admired this brilliant philosopher who had sat at the feet of Socrates. He had read everything the master had written and absorbed all his teachings. However, he listened with growing appreciation of Aristotle's arguments against some of Plato's thoughts.

* * *

The political situation in Athens had been in turmoil for some years, with the upper, middle, and lower classes almost coming to open battle. Arguments and sometimes brawls warmed the streets, but the real fire was fanned in the Assembly. By this time, the poorer classes had maintained a majority in the Assembly, and the educated and well-to-do, despairing of winning a vote, stayed away.

As the weaknesses of democracy became overwhelming, Plato could not help criticizing it. "The average intelligence of the Assembly is fallen so, that it is easily swayed by demagogues," he said to one of his friends with obvious disgust. Phidias, also present, was sympathetic to Plato's feelings.

His friend replied, "I recently went to one of Aristophanes' plays. He really poked fun at them, showing that the unethical politicians who rule the Assembly are leaders of bumbling idiots. Phocion, who opposes Demosthenes, despises the Assembly. I was present when he gave a speech there. He is known for his honesty, you know. Afterward, they applauded him. He turned to me and said, 'Have I unconsciously said something bad?' I laughed."

Plato also laughed, "That's like Phocion, all right. Even our colleague, Isocrates, criticizes the Assembly. He said that it makes so many bad decisions, that it just as well should be paid by Athens' enemies."

The next day, Plato lectured his students about government. Phidias wanted to hear what he had to say. "The democrats turn out to be as bad as the plutocrats," he said. "They use the power of their numbers to tax the middle and upper classes and to vote doles to the masses and offices and salaries to their leaders. They pander to the multitudes until liberty becomes anarchy. Our moral standards are debased to vulgarity, and there is no respect for age, position, or wealth. As the rampant pursuit of wealth will destroy an oligarchy, so the excess of libertarianism will destroy a democracy."

"But, Master," a student said, "isn't it better for the common people to have a say in government, and that they not be dominated by the wealthy few?"

"Yes, to an extent, Phaedrus. However, when liberty becomes license, then dictatorship is near. The rich, afraid that the masses that control the government will bleed them dry, will conspire to overthrow it. If successful, they will set up a strongman and strangle the masses, or, as is more likely, some ambitious demagogue promises everything to the masses, surrounds himself with a personal coterie and armed men, kills his enemies then and his friends, and establishes a dictatorship."

"What kind of government would you have, Master?" Phaedrus replied.

"You know my thoughts about a best possible state in which philosophers rule. I know this may never be, although we can hope that at least intelligent and philosophical leaders will arise. In a conflict of extremes, of plutocrats against the masses, the philosopher who preaches moderation is shouted down. He is like a man fallen among wild beasts. If he is wise, he will retire and wait until the storm passes."

His students continued the discussion in class, and later in the streets.

As if by prediction, the next day, armed thugs hired by the wealthiest families roamed through Athens, beating and killing the poor and unlettered. Finally, their blood lust satiated, they melted into the hills.

Two days later the Assembly met and posted armed guards around itself.

The leader of the Assembly, Antiphanes, spoke. "My fellow citizens, you have seen the treachery of the rich, who want to despoil you of your liberty by force. We will not be intimidated." He continued by naming the atrocities and victims of the slaughter.

Working the crowd up to hysteria, he made a proposal. "Because the wealthy are a threat to our liberty, I propose the following laws: First, that all of them will be taxed at fifty percent of their wealth. Any who cannot or will not pay will have their property confiscated by the state."

The men cheered wildly in agreement.

"Please quiet down, my fellow citizens. I have a more important proposal. We need a permanent committee, a body of *nomothetai,* lawmakers, who have emergency powers to deal with lawbreakers and punish them. This is so that we do not have to call the entire Assembly to do so, which involves taking you from your jobs."

The men again met his remarks with enthusiastic applause.

One of Antiphanes friends, as planned, stood up and raised his voice. "I say we vote on the proposals put forth by our speaker, Antiphanes. In addition, I propose that he be the chairman of the committee of nomothetai."

Overwhelming cheering filled the gathering, and, as in one voice, the Assembly voted to give its power to a small committee, headed by a convincing and skillful speaker.

Pouring out of the meeting, gangs of men broke into several houses of the rich. Fortunately most were at their country estates. The mobs stole what they could and ruined what they couldn't. They smeared feces over murals, threw garbage into fountains, and overturned and mutilated statues. The hapless slaves were beaten or killed. One owner's daughter was in the house watching over the slaves and was brutally raped and murdered.

Carrying torches, the mob was preparing to march out and set fire to the estates, when Antiphanes stopped and addressed them. "Do not kill the rich or destroy their property, citizens. We need them to pay the taxes. Do not fear; we will make them pay for their treachery—and pay, and pay."

The leaders of the rabble nodded in agreement, threw down their torches and bade everyone to return to their homes.

Disturbed by the excesses of the mob and the influence of demagogues, Plato began to write a book in which he revised his ideas of the best state. He titled it *Laws* and described a city placed inland away from foreign trade and influence. It was to be administered by a council, which would enforce the laws of how much property a man could possess—not too much and not too little. He wrote that a man must marry between the ages of thirty and thirty-five, and drinking in public amusements was to be regulated. Women would have equal educational and political opportunity with men, and all education was to be regulated by a minister of education, the state's highest official.

The state would decide which gods were to be worshiped and in what manner. Any citizen who questioned the state religion would be imprisoned, and, if he persisted, was to be executed. This was more like Sparta than Athens and was a far cry from Plato's youth, when his hero Socrates doubted the existence of the Olympian gods and was tried for it.

Despairing of the tendency of politics to degrade into anarchy and despotism, Plato withdrew further from Athenian public life. He showed his distaste for the chaos of democracy. "I favor an aristocracy," he said. "The government should be in the hands of competent rulers, not demagogues or the masses."

"But it is Athens' freedoms that have created its culture, Plato," his friend rejoined.

"Yes, but it is the degradation of politics and morals that are its downfall. I think that the disciplined and strict morals of Sparta would be better. Look how stable their city is."

"It is stifling," Phidias argued. "All Sparta trains for is war. They don't produce philosophy or literature."

"That may be true," said Plato. "What I yearn for is peace in my old age. I would abolish war, and, yes, poverty too. Perhaps I love justice more than truth itself." Plato sighed, and his friends saw the sadness and resignation in his eyes.

If Athens' most revered philosopher could not find much to say in praise of Greek freedom, then Greece was ripe for a king.

CHAPTER 9

Phidias stirred with the gray light of dawn spreading through the high-set window, having fallen asleep with Thais in his arms. He looked over to where she lay, her blond hair forming a halo around her peaceful face, and becoming excited with the memory of the night's lovemaking he reached for her. As he enveloped his arms around her breasts and moved his pelvis against her backside, she hummed an awakening tone. "Go to sleep," she said." Don't you ever tire?"

"I never tire from making love to you," he whispered as he tweaked her nipples and rubbed his enlarging member between her buttocks. He could feel her stir in response, pushing her pelvis backward and putting her hands over his. He pulled her around to face him and kissed her, at first teasingly, then as she reciprocated, passionately and more deeply. After playful intercourse, Phidias collapsed on her in quivering exhaustion. He murmured, "I thank the gods for sending you to me. Are you a goddess?" He smiled and kissed her gently.

Thais stroked his back and laughed lightly. "No, but you're my Adonis." They shared a laugh and kissed again.

This morning exercise had caught Thais not yet fully awake and ended before she could reach her own climax. She had pretended it, as she had been taught by experienced hetairai. She had enjoyed the lovemaking because it made Phidias feel good, but it left her unsatisfied.

Phidias rolled onto his back, still regaining his strength. After a few moments, he kissed her and rose. "I would rather stay in bed with you all day, but I have to get ready for the Academy." He stepped to the water pitcher, poured some into the basin, and splashed the cold water onto his face and chest and cleaned his still half-erected organ. After he grabbed his cloak and threw it around him, he reached over and kissed Thais, who had closed her eyes and turned onto her side. "Good-bye, my love," he said.

"May the gods bless you with a good day, Phidias," she smiled. She knew the slaves would take care of his breakfast and lunch. She had instructed them to do so, for he should not have to concern himself with those things of her house. She slumbered for a while but then awoke and, lying abed, reflected on why she had chosen the life she had.

* * *

Thais remembered when she was thirteen, just after her initiation into the periodic menstruations of womanhood. Her much older brother, Marthonis, had just taken a wife, who was only a few years older than Thais. As was the custom, the couple had moved into Thais' father's house. Thais made friends with Elysia, her new sister-in-law.

After a few months of wedded bliss, the fragrance of new romance faded from the bloom. Elysia was relegated to the menial chores of the other women of the household, while her husband went out to be with other men. One day Thais found Elysia crying in her bedroom.

"What's wrong, my sister?" she asked.

"Oh, Thais, I miss my family so much. When Marthonis brought me from my town, I was so happy to be with him that I forgot my fear about a new home in a great city. Now he only talks with me when he wants something, especially sex. We hardly see each other. He is gone all day with your father, attending business or carousing with other men his age. I do what your mother tells me—helping with the cooking, weaving, mending, and other chores. I feel like one of the slaves."

"I hear my father talk with Marthonis about politics or the latest play. Does he ever take you to the plays or talk to you about them?" asked Thais.

"In my town we had no theater, and I had no schooling, as you know. Whatever I learned of the gods or our Greek heritage, my mother taught me. No, Marthonis never talks to me of anything except the food or his clothes. When his friends come to the house, I am not allowed to see them but must remain in my room. I feel that I am only a useful tool or a plaything for him. I feel so alone." She started to cry.

"Oh, Elysia," Thais soothed as she hugged her. "Don't cry. You have me and my mother. We are your friends."

"I remember my grandmother told me that it was not always this way," Elysia said. "She told me that her grandmother was very active in social life. She argued politics with the men in the market, attended lectures and symposia, and even wrote poetry. She was respected by other women, and even men. It was not unheard of at that time for women to walk freely about the town without a veil. But my grandmother said times gradually changed, as the customs of the Persians and other barbarians seeped into our Greek culture, and women were gradually secluded, veiled, relegated to menial service, and shackled to the home."

Thais had not realized that it had not always been as she knew it now. She suddenly felt choked with empathy, for Elysia's plight grabbed at her soul. In a couple of years at most, her father would arrange a marriage with some older man whom she wouldn't know. How would she know if he would love her or treat her well? How would she know what his family would be like? Would his mother despise and abuse her? What of his father and brothers?

Thais refused to be subjected to that. A strong-willed girl, she vowed to become independent. She knew other women had left their homes and families. She knew of auletrides and hetairai.

About a month after her fourteenth birthday, her father announced at dinner with the whole family present, that he was promising Thais to a wealthy merchant from Thebes. Everyone applauded and congratulated Thais. She thanked her father, but in her heart she hid her fear and loathing of a life like Elysia's.

Afterward, Elysia came to Thais' room where she found her quietly crying. "Don't waste all your tears now, Thais. You may have to save some for later. I know what you must feel. I was in your place only a few years ago. It is fearful."

"Elysia, I will not be married to some old man and waste my life in the back rooms of his house. I want to be an educated, independent woman. I want to be free to walk the streets and be friends with whomever I choose, even politicians and philosophers. I will not be someone's sex slave," she fumed as she beat her fist into the bed.

"What will you do, Thais?"

"I have seen hetairai in their beautifully colored clothes walking proudly through the markets, men greeting them with respect. I will meet one. I will ask her to help me leave home and become one like her."

Elysia was incredulous. "Thais, you will not marry nor have children?"

"What use have I for children? Only the pain of childbirth and the drudgery of raising brats, just to have them leave my home. No, I will be my own person, a woman of independence respected for my mind as well as my body."

Soon afterward, while Thais was accompanying a slave to the market to buy food, she saw a hetaira. Her bearing impressed Thais, head held high, telling her slave what to buy, arguing with the sellers. Her beautiful gown was obviously very expensive. Telling her slave she was going to another stall to pick out some fruit, Thais walked over to the hetaira and spoke.

"Beautiful lady, I would like to talk with you."

"What do you want, my child?"

"Can we step over here under this portico so we will not be overheard by anyone?"

Humoring the girl, the woman ushered her behind a column. "What do you want to talk about?"

Thais exposed her feelings about the stifling life of women and the fate that awaited her if she became married. She told how afraid she was of a life like that. She told her of Elysia and what her grandmother had said. "So I want to be like that. I want to be like you, free to walk the streets of Athens, to choose my friends, to attend lectures and dinners. I want to talk of literature and history, of philosophy and poetry. I want to be free and independent."

"I will help you, my girl. I will help educate you and help you become a woman. Not just a woman, but a woman of the city and the world. I will introduce you to businessmen, politicians, and philosophers. You can feel free because you will be free. What is your name?"

"My name is Thais."

"I am Aspasia. I will meet you here tomorrow. Bring what personal items you want from home and hide them in your cloak. Don't worry about clothes. I will take care of that. As to your family, I will inform them through a public official that you have left the care of your father and are now a member of my household. Don't worry; everything will be fine. I will be your new mother, and you can look forward to a new life."

She did as Aspasia told her, and, in the cold grey hour before dawn, she packed her personal belongings, kissed her mother good-bye, and closed the door on her previous life. Her mother cried but told her that she understood her daughter's emotional turmoil, for she had felt it also at her age.

Aspasia taught Thais the graces of being a lady, a woman unattached to men. She read poetry, especially that of Sappho, the most famous female poet of ancient Greece. She learned of erotic love, the love of poets and playwrights.

"But what of making love itself?" she asked one day. "I'm afraid that I won't know what to do. Will it hurt? Will I like it?"

Aspasia replied, "Don't be afraid. I will teach you. I won't let you make love until you are ready. You must believe me that you'll know yourself. When that time comes, when you meet the right man, when the circumstances are right, you will know."

Aspasia took Thais to dinners and symposia and taught her how to have polite conversation with men, how to flatter them, and how to appeal to their emotions. Aspasia showed her how to dress, apply makeup, dye her hair, eat properly, and, of course, how to exercise her mind.

When Aspasia thought the time was ripe, she introduced Thais to the mysteries and ecstasies of sex. Men, whom Aspasia knew and respected for their tender and experienced lovemaking, initiated Thais to that magic realm.

She showed Thais how to avoid pregnancy, for there were many methods available. She taught her how to excite men emotionally, how to tease them, how to sexually arouse them, and how to maximize their pleasure, as well as her own—both physically and mentally.

Over time Aspasia introduced Thais to young men of wealthy families, businessmen, and aristocrats, all of whom paid well for her company. She also enjoyed the association of learned men and philosophers, who rewarded her with knowledge and fine conversation.

With Aspasia's careful tutelage, Thais developed the air of a cultured courtesan. She dressed in the finest clothes died in patterns of flowers and foliage. Hairdressers coiffed her tresses, and her makeup was perfection itself. She walked the streets of Athens with an erect bearing, drawing the admiring glances of everyone she passed. All of this would have been for naught had she not the beauty of face and body to go with these appurtenances.

At the dinners Aspasia took her to, Thais was the center attraction, the woman all men wanted to be with. She did not disappoint. Her conversation sparkled with knowledge and wit; her flattery titillated; and finally, her sexual prowess brought men to their knees.

When Thais had passed her twentieth birthday, Aspasia introduced her to a widowed wealthy banker. Clineas was in his early forties and lived the good life. He entertained lavishly, but with taste, in his magnificent home. Not of the obnoxious neoplutoi, he didn't flaunt his wealth, but used it to support artists, poets, and philosophers. He attended lectures at Plato's Academy and could converse easily on philosophy, literature, and, of course, politics.

Thais was impressed with the gentleman, and they developed a deep mutual relationship. She provided youth and beauty, while Clineas gave her expensive presents and intellectual stimulation. Sex was the icing, the spice that completed the gourmet affair.

She became his exclusive hetaira and moved into his house. Two years later, he bought her a very comfortable house of her own and put it in her name. He also provided her with the rent from another of his houses for her slaves and expenses. Thais truly felt love for this man, although she had never said so.

After an especially delectable dinner and night of sex, Clineas confessed to her. "Thais, I know that it's not proper for a gentleman to say I love you to a hetaira, but that is what I feel. You know that in the time we've been together, you've meant more to me than anything. You bring out the best in me. I feel the energy of youth, not only sexually but in my mind. I believe that you could keep me young forever."

" I doubt that I could keep you young, although you certainly act it." She laughed. "Only the gods can make us immortal, but they have given us happiness." She cupped his face in her hands and kissed him deeply, trying to express her feelings without actually saying that she loved him. Aspasia had impressed upon her that hetairai should never give themselves completely to any man.

During their third year together, Clineas was tragically drowned when his ship was lost in a storm. Thais fell into mourning, refusing to see anyone and wearing rough clothes and no makeup. Clineas' will left her with enough wealth and yearly income to live independently for the rest of her life, but even this did not ease the ache or fill the space in her heart, vacated by her warm and giving lover. But time heals all wounds, as the poet says, and Thais, with Aspasia's motherly assistance, reached out again for companionship.

She developed mutual friendships with other hetairai—intelligent, refined, and worldly women. Not all love is sexual or erotic love, and she enjoyed the freedom to be a woman and talk with others of her kind. Only women can share the feelings, fears, and joys that are peculiar to their sex. After a time, when Aspasia apparently thought she was ready for male companionship again, she introduced her to Phidias.

Phidias was a young man who had no wealth or refined culture, but had a mind as beautiful as his body. She found that her soul, as well as her flesh, found companionship with his. No, it was more than that. Could she call it love? She never thought she would feel that way about a man after Clineas' death, but this was different, deeper. She knew in her mind that it was dangerous, but her heart denied it. It told her to fling caution and reason to the wind and enjoy this life while she had it.

* * *

One day as Thais was tending to her housekeeping, telling the slaves what to do and what to buy in the markets, Aspasia came to visit. They hugged warmly and exchanged kisses on the cheek. Thais had fruits and wine served in the portico by the fountain.

"I haven't seen you in a while and decided you needed a visit. How have you been?" Aspasia asked.

"Very well; my life is very contented, very happy."

"That's good, my daughter, but be careful that you protect your happy heart, for it can be broken."

"I know that, Mother Aspasia, but it is hard to tell my heart that. Phidias loves me, too."

"All men confuse erotic and agape love. He must realize in the back of his mind that you are hetaira, and your profession does not allow for a permanent relationship like marriage."

"He may know that," said Thais, "but his heart beats with mine. I will not push him away or abandon him."

"That is well for now. Let's allow time to do what it will. Our fate is in the hands of the gods." Aspasia took a sip of her wine before changing the subject. "I would like to invite you tomorrow night to a small dinner I'm having."

Thais smiled. "Phidias and I would be delighted to come to your house. You always serve fine dishes."

"I am not inviting Phidias. There will only be hetairai. You know all of them, old friends of mine and yours. Your time has been monopolized by Phidias for too long. You need a break, some female conversation."

"I could do that during the day, like I am with you right now. Why do I have to come without Phidias?"

"Because I think it best." Aspasia reached for Thais' hand. "Because I want you to keep your mind open, even if your heart is closed. Besides, a gentleman friend of mine is also having a symposium tomorrow night, and I suggested that he ask Phidias. Don't worry, he won't be crying in his soup alone that evening."

"All right," said Thais. "It might be fun to get together with the girls over some wine again. I'll come."

"Good. That's settled." Aspasia rose and kissed Thais on her cheek. "Tomorrow night, then," she said.

After Aspasia left, Thais sat down on a low couch and watched the water play over the stone statue in the courtyard as she sipped thoughtfully at her wine. Was she really in love with Phidias? What did that mean anyway? Would she marry him if he asked her? Probably not. She couldn't; she wouldn't—ever. She wouldn't give up the independence she had worked so hard for, then throw it away, only to live like her mother and her brother's wife.

What of Phidias? What were his feelings, his plans? He was a philosopher, a student, a teacher. She could see that learning and teaching were his true loves. Did his fellow philosopher, Aristotle, say that the highest virtue of a man was to use his mind, his reasoning? When he was with her, she tried to satisfy his mind and his soul as well as body. He seemed to forget the world outside their bedroom. But, she knew that with the morning's light his mind passed to other matters—history, science, and philosophy.

Thais enjoyed their relationship and knew that Phidias reciprocated her feelings. But deep in her soul, a tiny voice whispered that it could not last forever. Nothing lasts forever, does it?

CHAPTER 10

At this time, the political turmoil in Athens was coming to a boiling point, the fire being stoked by the orations of Demosthenes. He had developed into a talented orator who spoke eloquently and fervently against the growing power of Philip of Macedon.

As a young man, Demosthenes had been cheated out of most of his inheritance when his father died. He had talent for writing arguments, but his slight build and lack of ability to argue in public hampered him. He studied rhetoric for a while at Plato's Academy, where he trained his body as well as his mind. His trainer had him run uphill carrying a shield and spear. His teacher told him to memorize and recite a speech while doing it, so he could learn to control his breathing. He exercised his voice by speaking above the roar of the waves at the beach. To aid his diction, he placed pebbles in his mouth and forced himself to articulate well in spite of them.

After spending a few years at the Academy mastering the art and science of oratory, he left and developed his own career as a rhetor. Hired orators who acted as professional lawyers and politicians, rhetors argued cases in court or before the Assembly. Some, like Demosthenes, were honest and noble, while others were simply hired mouthpieces without strong ethics. As Athenian politics grew more intense, rhetors on both sides of issues rent the atmosphere with their campaigns.

Demosthenes became one of the wealthiest of these lawyers and was well-known for his technical ability and sometimes flexible morals, for he could be hired to defend either side. Citizens paid him large fees for introducing and arguing in favor of laws before the Assembly.

In spite of his wealth and reputation, he earned the integrity of defending Athens against its own degenerate politics. He raised his powers of oratory to their supreme effort and urged Athens and all Greece to resist the threat of tyranny from Philip of Macedon.

* * *

Phidias grew up during the period of Athens' second empire, in which she was again powerful and her citizens accumulated great wealth. He remembered, when he was about twenty-four, going with his father, who was to speak at the Assembly. He knew his father was concerned about the decay in morals and the lack of good sense in Athens.

Aristippus rose to speak at the Assembly. "My fellow citizens, when we formed our new Confederation after beating the Thebans, we promised our allies that we would not conquer or colonize any lands outside of our surrounding Attica. Instead, you have sent armies to conquer Samos and islands off the coasts of Thrace and Macedon. Athenians are now colonizing those islands. This is an arrogant and unwise policy that will only gain the enmity of our allies. Some have already protested, and I promise you that the others will withdraw from the Confederation and may even go to war against us."

A man in the front row stood up and yelled, "Let them! We have wealth and power and will crush any opposition."

Many in the Assembly cheered and raised their fists.

Aristippus held up his hands for quiet. "I see that my warnings have fallen on deaf ears. I am too old and have suffered too many wounds in Athens' wars to defend her again. I am trying to do it now with my words. Don't throw away our hard-earned prosperity and political power by using policies that failed with our first empire a hundred years ago." He sat down amid cheers and boos from the Assembly.

Not long afterward, Aristippus' warnings came true.

Athens ignored the advice of level heads like Aristippus and used force to coerce or punish any of its wayward allies. That year, several cities and islands declared a Social War of rebellion. All of Athens' allies left her and, after two years of war, she was forced to sign a peace treaty, acknowledging their independence. Athens, indeed, lost not only its second empire, but was left without allies, without effective leaders, without wealth, and without friends. Fortunately, Aristippus died two years before this and didn't have to witness the humiliation of Athens that he had warned against.

Meanwhile, the kingdom of Macedon in the north was growing in power. While Athens was engaged in the Social War that ended her second empire, Philip seized territory all along the European coast of the north Aegean, including the lucrative gold mines of Thrace. His thoughts then turned to the south.

At a celebration of his recent acquisitions, Philip raised his third cup of wine. "To the Athenians."

The officers and members of Philip's council, sitting at tables, littered with scraps of the feast, looked at each other with raised eyebrows.

"They have given us literature, art, and philosophy," Philip continued.

The guests nodded; they knew their king admired Athenian culture.

"They are also politically stupid," he roared.

The men laughed.

"A few years ago they lost the rest of their empire. And now they're engaged in a war supporting Phocia against the Amphictyonic League. Weakened Sparta is their ally."

More laughter rolled like thunder through the men.

The city of Phocia stole the treasury at Delphi, the home of the sacred oracle. This was a sacrilege, and the Amphictyonic League, composed of the cities of Boeotia, Locris, Doris, and Thessaly, declared war against Phocia. Athens and Sparta fought for Phocia in what was referred to as the Second Sacred War.

"Let the Greeks fight each other," said Antipater, Philip's senior general. "They will be easy pickings for us, when they come begging for our help."

Everyone raised their cups in agreement and drank deeply that night. They had reason to celebrate, for the Macedonian treasury was bursting with gold from the Thracian mines and the sale of Greeks from the captured lands in the north Aegean into slavery.

The war in the south lasted ten years, while Philip trained his army. As the war turned against the League, it turned to him for aid. He was waiting for the opportunity, and his expertly trained army was ready. He marched swiftly south through the open passes and overwhelmed the Phocians and their allies.

The spoils he took from Phocia he gave back to the Oracle at Delphi. Philip was invited to join and become leader of the League. Hailed as a protector of the shrine, he was invited to preside over all the Greeks at the Pythian Games. His star was rising.

* * *

During Athens' struggle with Phocia against the League, Demosthenes began his *phillipics*—famous orations against Philip and Macedon.

He was furious that Athens had not awakened to the threat and was using its depleted treasury to hire mercenaries to do its fighting.

Phidias and Aristotle were as concerned as many Athenians about Athens' losses and her resistance to the growing power of Philip. They attended a meeting of the Assembly to hear Demosthenes, whose campaign against Philip had become strident.

Demosthenes rose to address the Assembly. "My fellow Athenians, there you sit with your fat bellies, gold rings on your fingers, and slaves in your homes. You eat well and sleep soundly at night, while mercenaries defend our city.

"Have you no shame? Where is the patriotism that strengthened Athenian hearts and spears in the great wars against Persia? Where is the spirit of our Goddess, Athena? Have we given it away to mercenaries? You have allowed the wealth of our last empire to make you physically weak and morally decadent. Now you are using our depleted treasury to hire mercenaries to defend you.

"You are especially blind to the dagger at your throat held by Philip, the tyrant of the north. He says he will be the leader of all the Greeks and invade and conquer Asia. I say that it's only a ruse. His true ambition is to subjugate all Greeks to himself as king."

He looked with piercing eyes, his lips pressed with scorn, over his rapt audience. By this time, the theoric fund, which had been set up to pay the populace to attend games and festivals, had been so extended that it strapped the state. The Assembly had made it a crime to use this fund for any other purpose. Demosthenes recognized that the welfare state was bankrupting the city and hampering its defense. He was determined that the fund be used in a war against Philip.

"I propose—nay, I insist—that the money that is paid to citizens to attend the religious ceremonies and plays should be used instead to pay citizens to defend our state. Why waste more money on mercenaries who have no love for Athens, when we can use the same funds we are already paying to our citizens to defend our own city?

"You Athenians have become degenerate slackers who have forgotten the military virtues of our forefathers. Yes, war may bring death, injuries, and privation, but times bring circumstances when war is necessary. This is one of those times. We must regain the excitement of battle, the thrill of heroic deeds, and the glory of victory. Recall the Greek heroism that captured Troy and turned back the Persian hordes from our shores. A new power from the north again threatens our Greek liberty.

"Athenians, I warn you to arm yourselves and fight the Macedonians. Retain our allies and colonies in the north. Do not listen to the party of peace who accepts Philip's gold. They say that his leadership will bring peace and unity to Greece. But at what price? It will not be his leadership but his overlordship. Would you let those unlettered barbarians overrun our brilliant culture, trample our liberty under the hooves of their cavalry, and extinguish the light of civilization with their bloody hands?

"I will not! I will lay down my life to defend our glorious Athens, lamp of knowledge, teacher of the world. Citizens of Athens, join me. Arise in this time of crisis and resist the barbarian of the North!"

Most of the citizens in the Assembly rose and cheered wildly. "War !" some yelled. "Down with Macedon!" and "Death to Philip!" called others. A sizable minority, who favored a peaceful accommodation with Philip, remained silently seated.

Phidias and Aristotle quickly left the hysteria unleashed by Demosthenes. They not only did not share it, they feared it.

CHAPTER 11

After Aristotle gave a lecture on the four types of causes of things, Phidias approached him as he was answering some questions. When he finished, Phidias pulled him aside. "Take a walk with me around the arbor; I want to talk to you."

Phidias asked him some philosophic questions about the final cause of a man. "What is that cause for which we are made? Why are we here?"

Aristotle carefully explained that because it was obvious that our minds were unique and placed us above all living things, then it was our minds which gave us our cause. It was the use of them, then, that was our final purpose. "But you already heard me expound on those ideas. What is the real reason you wanted to talk to me?"

By this time their paths had wound into a shady grove. Phidias looked around to make sure they were alone. "My friend," he said, stopping and turning toward Aristotle, "the speeches of Demosthenes and his party opposing Philip are disturbing me. I'm afraid they may goad Athens and much of Greece into war with him. They can't win. His army is too powerful."

Aristotle nodded. "Yes, it saddens me to see Demosthenes dividing Greece. It would be best for all Greeks to unite under Philip and fight our real foe—Persia."

Phidias replied, "And Demosthenes' accusation that the peace party accepts Philip's money is hypocritical, for it's well known that his war party receives gold from Persia."

"I love Athens," Aristotle said. "Macedon gave me life; she is my home. But Athens taught me how to live. She opened my eyes and my mind. This is where I feel alive, where I work, teach, and learn. I am for peace and accommodation with Philip. Not because I have received any money, but because I think it is best for Greece."

"But Aristotle, the leaders of the war party think of you as a Macedonian and supporter of Philip. They don't know you aren't in his pay. You have a large following, and many men look up to you. I fear for your safety."

"I'm aware of my position," Aristotle replied. "I'll be careful to express my political opinions only around our friends. I don't want to give Demosthenes a pretext to exile me. However, I am keeping my bags packed."

"Then, are you thinking of leaving Athens?" Phidias asked.

"I don't have any plans right now, but I'm keeping all my options open. Who knows how the political winds will blow. If it becomes too dangerous for me, and I leave, will you come with me?"

Phidias was silent a moment. "I don't know. I've never lived outside of Athens."

"If we go elsewhere, it would be an opportunity for you to study other cultures. You may learn a lot."

Phidias looked down and shook his head. "I don't think so. How can I leave Thais? I love her so much, as I'm sure she loves me."

"She is a hetaira, Phidias. She has no ties to you, and you should have none to her, save the sexual ties of erotic love. She will find another lover, as you can find another woman."

"That's not true," Phidias insisted. "Thais and I feel the bonds of love as much as any married couple. Parting would break both our hearts. I would die without her."

"I doubt that. But I won't argue with you about your feelings. Perhaps another day, when your mind is not beclouded by your heart, you will reconsider what I've told you. For now, let's just clasp hands of friendship and return to our students."

* * *

Although Aristotle argued energetically with Plato's thoughts and conclusions, the scientific part of him fought the rest of his life with the philosophical side he had gained from Plato. Neither side actually won. Aristotle was at the Academy for almost twenty years and became its outstanding teacher before Plato's death.

Plato died near the end of the war with the Amphictyonic League at the age of eighty. All of Athens came to mourn him. Aristotle built an altar to him and gave his eulogy, giving him almost divine honors.

"My fellow Athenians, fellow Greeks, and fellow citizens of the world, be prepared to shed your tears with me for the passing of the most brilliant light of Athens, the philosopher Plato. Although not the lawgiver like Solon or the leader like Pericles, his thoughts and words were the guide of leaders and lawgivers. Although not a poet like Aeschylus, Sophocles, or Euripides, his philosophy sang like poetry. His intellect may not have been as high as some other philosophers, but he outshone them all because his intellect was so broad. He taught us of eternal values and morals. He wrote about forms of government we should adopt. He told us how we should educate our children, free our women, and regulate our personal lives. He wrote it down, so that posterity may study and learn and put his teachings into practice.

"Most importantly, he gave us an enduring record of our beloved philosopher, Socrates. It was Socrates, the self-proclaimed gad-fly, who pricked our consciences and poked holes in our comfortable ideas. He made us question old traditional thought and examine carefully our own lives. What are justice, truth, and virtue, and how do we attain them? He made us look critically at the old myths and the Olympian gods. Unfortunately, this led to his prosecution at the hands of political and religious traditionalists. They could not stand that he should question their beliefs, so they condemned him to death.

"Socrates never wrote anything. All that we have of him is through Plato. Socrates is immortal because of him. Now, Plato is immortal. He joins the other great men and gods of Athens and Greece who have brought light to a dark world. His perfect form has risen to join the realm of the perfect forms that he so cherished. We will miss his brilliant mind, his incisive tongue, and his literary wit. We shed tears and beat our breasts that we no longer share dialogue with our teacher, our philosopher, our friend. But we will always have his memory in our bosom, his image in our mind, and his writings on our shelves.

"I will miss you, my friend. The world will never be the same since you have lived in it." Aristotle began to choke as tears ran down his face. He excused himself and sat down as Isocrates, Demosthenes, and Phidias spoke. Many eyes were wet in Athens that day.

CHAPTER 12

Aristotle was reflecting on his old teacher as he walked through the marketplace on his way to the Academy. He already missed their discussions. Even though he disagreed with much of Plato's philosophy, he greatly admired and loved him.

His thoughts turned to the time he first came to Athens. A brash youth from Macedon, he thought he knew a lot of science. Plato took him under his wing, and, like a father, introduced him to new knowledge. His mind was opened and soon filled with new ideas. For almost twenty years, he listened, learned, and did his own research, formulating his own ideas. Suddenly men shaking their fists and yelling at him jerked him from his fond memories.

"Macedonian!"

"Philip lover!"

"You're no Athenian!"

"Traitor!"

Vegetables and fruits soon followed the epithets, and some found a target on Aristotle's tunic, staining it. He ran to the Academy, shocked and frightened. He knew that his support of Philip was unpopular, but now he realized that it was also dangerous. With Plato gone, he felt there was nothing holding him in Athens.

That evening, Aristotle told Phidias about his experience in the marketplace.

"I told you I feared for your safety," Phidias said. "What are you going to do?"

"I received a letter from someone I knew as a student at the Academy. His name is Hermeias, and he's king of a small country in upper Asia not far from the Hellespont. He heard of Plato's death and invited me to stay with him for a while."

"Will you go?"

"I'm considering it. With Plato dead, there's really nothing for me in Athens. Speusippus has succeeded him as master of the Academy. This episode today in the street will influence my decision to accept Hermeias' offer. Will you go with me if I go?"

"Why would I leave Athens," exclaimed Phidias, "especially for a barbarian country in Asia?"

Aristotle patiently replied, "Hermeias is not a barbarian; he is Greek and studied with me at the Academy. Come with me and see more of the world beyond Attica."

"I'm sorry, but I won't leave Thais. We love each other. I couldn't bear to leave her."

"I understand your feelings for Thais. I can't argue against passion. Continue your teaching at the Academy. I'll go, but we will see each other again. Greeks are making the world smaller."

* * *

Aristotle decided to go to the court of Hermeias, where he enjoyed the easy life and high, dry climate and married the daughter of the king. They were planning to move into a palace the king had built for them when tragedy struck. The Persians knew of Hermeias' support of Philip of Macedon and assassinated him. Soon afterward, Aristotle's wife died in childbirth.

Philip's messengers kept him informed of the events. "Hermeias was a friend and would've helped our forces after we crossed into Asia," he lamented to his general, Parmenion.

"Persians are trying to hamper us, as they interfere in Greek affairs elsewhere. Just give me the order, Sire, and I will cross the Hellespont," replied Parmenion.

Philip shook his head. "Not yet. We have to unify all the Greeks first. We can't leave enemies at our back. I also must train a successor, in case anything happens to me. Alexander is still young."

"His tutors are training him, Sire."

Philip looked away and stroked his beard. "I want to take him away from those tutors. They were selected by his mother. He should be removed from her influence. He is my son and heir."

"Who would you have tutor him?"

"I have my mind to bring someone from Athens to teach him Greek culture. I hear that Aristotle, the Athenian philosopher, is on Lesbos. He married Hermeias' daughter, who died in childbirth."

"That was tragic," Parmenion agreed.

"I knew Aristotle as a youth in my father's court. I wonder if he would come to Pella. Perhaps Aristotle can teach Alexander to be an educated Athenian."

"The young prince is very headstrong, Sire."

Philip laughed, "Like his father, I hope. But he's too much under the guidance of his mother, I fear. I'll write a letter to Aristotle on Lesbos, inviting him here to tutor Alexander."

After reading the letter inviting him to Macedon, Aristotle thought about the prospect—not an easy decision. Why should he go to Macedon? He considered it logically. On the positive side, he would be paid well and pampered at the court of a rich king, and he would have the freedom to study as he wanted. Philip was an intelligent and courageous king whose power would continue to grow. He would also have a hand in training the future king of Macedon. Besides, it was the country of his birth.

On the negative side, he hadn't been back to Macedon in over twenty years and knew few people there. It was semi-barbarian and a cultural and intellectual backwater. How would he be treated, perhaps as little more than a slave? Maybe Philip's son was a headstrong, spoiled brat, or, worse yet, stupid. Most of all he had come to love Athens as his mother. She had raised him, taught him, civilized him, and made him one of her own. Athens might go to war with Macedon. How could he forsake his adopted mother for her enemy?

Aristotle pondered a way to solve his dilemma. He would go to Athens, see what the political climate was, and discuss the move with some of his trusted friends.

* * *

After two years' absence, Aristotle found Athens' political atmosphere even tenser. For the most part, he stayed at the Academy. He didn't want to give the impression that he was involved in politics.

Phidias was glad to see his friend again. "I'm happy to have you back in Athens," he said," but I'm afraid parties on opposite sides of accommodation with Philip are going to spill blood in the streets. Demosthenes is fanning the flames of war."

Opposed to Demosthenes and his party supporting war against Philip was the party of peace, led by Aeschines and Phocion. Phocion, an elder statesman and talented general, was considered the most honest man of his time. He had been elected *strategos*, or commander of the army, forty-five times, surpassing even the great Pericles. He knew that Athens did not have the wealth or the forces necessary to go to war with Philip and tried to convince the Athenians of this.

Aeschines had served with Phocion in several wars and supported his advice of compromising with Philip. He also was a fine orator and had spoken publicly against Demosthenes.

"Demosthenes has brought an indictment against me," exclaimed Aeschines to Phocion, "charging that I've accepted Macedonian gold. That hypocrite! He accepts Persian gold to oppose Philip."

"He attacks me indirectly through you," Phocion said. "He knows what respect I have with the citizens of Athens."

"I can't wait to face Demosthenes in court," said Aeschines. "If he accuses me of accepting bribes, I will throw it back in his face. What if Philip pays us? It is still to the advantage of all the Greek, including Athens, to unite under him to fight the Persians."

"Old Isocrates will support you at court also," Phocion assured him. "He's written a letter to all the Greeks advising unity. He knows that even if Philip sends money to us, we are sincere in our desire for peace and compromise. The Greeks have fought each other for centuries. We need to quit shedding each other's blood and spill Persian blood instead."

"I know I can rely on you for your support, my old friend," Aeschines said. "I will see you in court tomorrow."

Phidias accompanied Aristotle to the trial. Aristotle covered his head with his cloak to disguise himself. All Athens turned out for what was expected to be a spectacle of oratorical display between the two best orators in Athens. Although Demosthenes, like most orators, wrote his speeches in advance, Aeschines could speak extemporaneously. His background as an actor enriched his skill as orator.

"Of course, this trial is all about politics," said Phidias.

Aristotle nodded. "Demosthenes will argue for Athenian liberty against the threat of Philip's tyranny. Aeschines will argue for Greek unity under Philip to fight Persia."

"And both will accuse the other of accepting bribes," Phidias chuckled.

"There are strong voices on both sides of the issues. It'll be interesting to see which way it goes," said Aristotle.

After the trial, in which Aeschines successfully defended himself against conviction, Aristotle confided to Phidias, "Even though the jury didn't convict Aeschines, I don't think Demosthenes and his party are finished. They will continue to press for war and may again charge Aeschines with accepting Philip's money."

"What are you thinking, my friend?" asked Phidias.

"I think that Philip will continue to put pressure on all the Greek states to accept his leadership. He makes no pretense about his desire to invade Asia. All of the Peloponnesus except Sparta is already behind him."

"But Athens is not," said Phidias.

"No, Athens is not—yet. The factions are still fighting between war and compromise. Demosthenes will continue to harangue the populace, appeal to their sense of freedom and independence. He will work up a frenzy of patriotism, defending against the threat from Philip. I'm afraid the anti-Macedonian fervor may make it too warm for a native Macedonian known to favor Philip, like me."

"What will you do?"

"Philip has asked me to come to Pella to tutor his son, Alexander. I think I will accept his offer. Why don't you come with me? You should broaden your horizons beyond Athens."

"I told you I wouldn't go with you when you went to the court of Hermeias. As it turns out, I was right. You have returned a widowed father. Why would I forsake Athens, and most of all Thais, and go to Pella?"

"I want you just to think about it. The passion for war with Philip will become an unreasoning hysteria. It will not be pleasant for you as a friend of mine. You can always return to Thais after things have calmed down."

"Right now my mind is not to leave Athens or Thais. However, for your sake, I will keep it open."

Aristotle felt that his life might be in danger if he stayed in Athens. He would leave, but he wanted to convince his friend and colleague to go with him. He decided he would find a way to pressure him.

CHAPTER 13

A warm fall day in Athens found Thais sitting on the side of the fountain in her courtyard, listening to the playful splashing and watching pigeons peck at the crumbs she threw on the stones. It had been several years since Phidias had moved into her bed and her heart. She had realized that their relationship would not last forever, yet it had grown stronger and stronger.

She gazed past the gurgling pool, picturing Phidias walking with his students in the orchards of the Academy. His reputation as a brilliant teacher made him popular with his students. She had heard that many praised him in the streets of Athens.

Phidias had told her about Aristotle's invitation to accompany him to Pella. He said that he would never leave without her, that he loved her so much that his heart would break if he left her. Thais knew about love, separation, and broken hearts. She didn't want to experience them again.

But what of Phidias? What was his destiny? Should he remain in the soul-calming life she had given him? Should she influence him to stay? She admitted her love for him tempted her to do that. But would her own self-interest prohibit him from fulfilling his life's goals? Perhaps he should follow Aristotle and experience the world outside of Greece.

She grabbed at her heart as the agony of her dilemma made it ache. "Oh, Athena," she prayed aloud, "patroness of our city, I beseech you to help me to do what is right. My heart will break if Phidias leaves me, but if I prevent him from his opportunity to grow with Aristotle, I will be racked with guilt. I am lost either way. What should I do?"

No decision was easy when hearts would be broken as a consequence. She thrust her face into her hands, the tears flowing between her fingers and spotting the sun-dappled stone at her feet. The pigeons moved around her, cooing and looking for further crumbs, oblivious to the shuddering sobs coming from the woman sitting on the fountain.

Between classes at the Academy, Phidias strolled through the groves deep in his own thoughts. He was completely in love with Thais, and, through the years they had been together, he knew she reciprocated. He found himself thinking of her even during classes and discussions he was leading.

He began to think practically about their relationship. Would Thais continue to love him if he could barely put food on the table from what the students and their parents paid him? She had been generous these many years, but would there be an end to it? He wanted to live with her forever, but would she keep him, a poor philosopher? He decided he would try to make more money. He would tell her that he was quitting the Academy. He would go into business, asking his brother to set him up in exporting olive oil or something. That might prove to her how much he loved her, how much he would sacrifice for her. "Oh ye gods," he prayed, "if you can hear, help me."

That evening at dinner, Phidias told Thais of his plans to quit teaching and to ask his brother to set him up in business.

"What? Are you crazy?" she screamed. "You know nothing of business. You don't even know how to bargain with the food vendors!"

"I'll learn. I'm smart. My brother will teach me. I want to make more money to support our household."

"What do you care of our household? All you ever see of it is the dining room and bedroom. I think all I am lately is a source of food and sex for you. I'm getting tired of all your insatiable need for lovemaking, of fulfilling your libidinous appetite. I'm going to bed. You can sleep in your own room. Goodnight."

Over the next days, Thais withdrew herself further from Phidias, picking arguments over insignificant things and refusing sex with one excuse or another. Phidias was distraught, at his wits end over what to make of Thais' moods and words. He lost his appetite and became careless with his habits.

One day he came upon a group of students talking under the portico. Hearing his name mentioned, he stopped behind a pillar to listen.

"What has become of Master Phidias of late? His mind wanders during a lecture. He stops, looks blank, and then asks us what he was saying. Is he getting senile?"

"He's only in his forties, but maybe he's sick. Have you noticed he's lost weight? His face looks thinner."

"And his robes. They're soiled and frayed on the edges. He really needs new ones."

"Some of my friends are wondering if we should stop going to his classes. What do you think?"

"I don't know. Let's go to the gymnasium and talk to some of the others."

Phidias was devastated. He had always enjoyed the adoration of his students, but this completely destroyed any satisfaction he felt. Could it be that bad? What was happening to him? He had to get a hold of himself.

He decided to seek counsel from his friend and found Aristotle in one of the halls speaking to a group of men and students. As he entered, he heard one of the men ask Aristotle, "What is the best life? What is the highest aim we should look for in a life?"

The lecture and discussion continued while Nichomachus, a nephew of Aristotle, took notes. Aristotle said that we seek happiness or flourishing in life as the highest goal. All other things, such as wealth, fame, power, and intelligence, we use as means to that end.

As the audience broke up into small groups, discussing what they had heard, Aristotle walked through the crowd, acknowledging colleagues and thanking them for their comments. As he started down the steps of the temple, Phidias reached his side.

"May I accompany you? I have something I must discuss with you."

"Certainly, my friend," Aristotle said as he patted Phidias on the back.

Phidias poured out his feelings to Aristotle, a picture of a heart bleeding with love but beaten back by indifference. "I don't even know if she loves me anymore. I don't know what to do."

"And I don't know that I can tell you what to do. All I can do is give you my opinion. Maybe Thais loves you, or maybe not. She is hetaira. You are not bound by ties of marriage, and she must feel that she is getting older and may need more financial security for later years. You have the rest of your life and work ahead of you. You have a brilliant mind and should not waste it."

"I know these things in my head, but my heart is so torn apart that I can't think clearly. What should I do?"

"I can venture some advice. Perhaps you should quietly reason out your options and talk to Thais again. Try to put your emotions aside and think logically. A way will open for you. Remember what I said in the lecture, that a man should use his mind and the talents he has to attain his greatest good or happiness."

Phidias looked at Aristotle with saddened eyes and admitted, "You're a very wise and true friend. I will do as you say. Thank you," he murmured as he clasped Aristotle's hand.

The next day Aristotle had no lectures, so he went to the home of Thais. Sitting in a small but comfortably furnished parlor off of the courtyard, Aristotle and Thais were served fruit and wine mixed with fruit juice.

"Thais, I believe you know why I have come to see you," started Aristotle.

"It is Phidias."

"Yes, it's Phidias. He's emotionally distraught. He sometimes skips his lectures, and his students talk about his absentmindedness. His classes have suffered and parents have stopped sending him money. He's at his wits end about his relationship with you."

"I'm aware of Phidias' emotional dilemma, Master Aristotle. We have had our talks. Frankly, I'm tired of his slobbering sex and fawning ways. He's smothering me. I need air. I can't breathe. I'm an intelligent woman and I miss my independence. He needs to be independent also, and perhaps will do well to leave me and even Athens for a while. After all, he is forty-five years old, and I am not getting any younger myself. I don't love Phidias anymore. I want you to take him with you, if and when you go to Macedon."

"I know you two have had a great love and I'm sorry to see it end thus. However, I do believe you're right. He needs to broaden his worldview, become more educated, more traveled, and go with me to Macedon. Phidias has great talent as a historian and must not waste it. In addition, Philip is the most powerful monarch in the Greek world and may someday be lord of all Greece. It would be a great opportunity to be at his court, which is where the history of Greece will be made in the coming years.

"I also will be entrusted to the teaching of his son and probable heir, Alexander. It's a wonderful opportunity to mold the mind of a future king of a powerful country. Phidias would share it with me."

"I will help Phidias make up his mind, Aristotle. I wish you well in Macedon."

"Thank you, Lady Thais. I have enjoyed the wine and our conversation. Good-bye."

After Aristotle left, Thais ran, threw herself onto her bed and cried deeply into her pillow. She loved Phidias but knew that she had to let him go. No one must know how her heart was breaking. No one must see behind her seamless facade.

That night she had her slaves prepare a sumptuous meal with oysters, fish, lamb, and fresh-cooked vegetables, served with their best wine. The most expensive dinnerware, candles, and flowers graced the table. Neutral conversation of the events around Athens filled the time while they ate.

After the slaves cleared the dishes, Phidias told Thais of his plight, of his love for her, and of his fear of losing her. He told her of Aristotle's offer of taking him to Pella and Philip's court, and of his conflicted feelings toward making any decision. "I don't know what I should do. If you tell me you love me and want me to stay, I will. Perhaps we can make tender love and rekindle that flame of our youth," he said softly, putting his hand on hers.

She pulled away her hand and threw wine in his face. "Don't you dare talk to me of love. Your groping sex disgusts me. Not only do I want you never to touch me again, but I don't want to see you anymore. I have only pretended to love you these last few months. I have bitten my tongue to keep from screaming in protest every time you place your grasping hands on me. I had this dinner prepared as my last good-bye. Now get out. Leave my house. You can sleep at your brother's tonight, and I will have your possessions sent there tomorrow. Yes, and all your precious books, too."

"Please, Thais. Don't do this. I will die. I love you. I know you still love me. You can't mean what you say!"

"I mean every word. Get out of my house and my life!" she screamed. "I never want to see you again." Phidias rose and, like a beaten dog, retreated through the door and the gate. With burdened shoulders and tear-blurred eyes, he dragged his feet through the streets to his brother's house

The next day it was a struggle for him to get out of bed and stumble through the day. He avoided his classes and sought out Aristotle. "Thais threw me out. She doesn't love me anymore. I know you told me to use my head, to reason out what I should do, but philosophy eludes me when my emotions are in such turmoil. There is nothing left for me to live for."

Aristotle grasped Phidias by his shoulders. "My friend, you have much to live for. You have much you can contribute, to fulfill the function for which you were made. You remember when I gave that discussion about happiness? I said friendship is the chief aide to it. Indeed happiness is multiplied if it is shared. A friend is one soul in two bodies, a single mind and a single purpose—each other's happiness. Therefore, I extend my hand of friendship. As my friend and equal companion, I want with all my heart for you to accompany me to Macedon, for it is there that your heart will heal and your mind will help the destiny of Greece."

Phidias let go of Aristotle's hand and embraced him. "I accept your friendship and will gladly go with you to Pella."

# III PELLA, CROSSING THE THRESHOLD

CHAPTER 14

The king sat on his white charger, as strong and athletic as its rider. His armor shone in the bright Macedonian sun as he watched the phalanx practice their maneuvers. They turned as one at the command of their officers, like the disciplined machine they were. He nodded his head in approval, his helmet covering the brown hair beginning to gray. Handsome and strong of body and will, Philip was a magnificent specimen, a rough barbarian king trying at times to be an Athenian gentleman.

At the end of the exercise, he turned his mount toward the palace. He had heard that Aristotle had arrived and wanted to meet the Athenian philosopher whose fame preceded him.

Having changed armor for a royal robe, he received Aristotle and his friend in his private chambers. He offered them cups of wine poured by a boy slave. "Welcome to Pella, Master Aristotle. I'm afraid it's not Athens, but I hope you will help me make it more so."

"Thank you, Sire," Aristotle said. He turned to Phidias. "I would like to introduce to you Master Phidias, who will assist me in tutoring your sons and those of your nobles."

"Welcome, Master Phidias. If Aristotle vouches for you, then you must have intelligence and a gift for teaching."

"Thank you, Sire," said Phidias. "I hope to merit your trust."

"Phidias will teach history and geography, his specialties," Aristotle explained, "whereas I will concentrate on philosophy, morals and ethics, and political science."

"Excellent," the king said, rubbing his hands. "I hope you will teach young Alexander how to be a king. I trust you will make an Athenian gentleman out of him, something I have tried to do but failed, sadly to say." He laughed heartily, drank down his wine, and poured another cup. "More wine?" he asked.

"Thank you, no, Sire," Aristotle declined. "I am tired from our long journey and would like to rest. Do you have any more questions for me or Phidias?"

"Only when you want to start your teaching?"

"We would like to meet your son tomorrow morning and the rest of the boys in the afternoon, if that's all right with you," Aristotle said.

"I will have the youths brought to the building you will use. My servant will show you the place. Now you may go, clean up, enjoy a pleasant dinner, and rest. Again I welcome you to Pella with open arms." The king lifted his cup in a salute, and the two men left.

After the two philosophers departed, Philip had a warm feeling of accomplishment. He had succeeded in bringing the famed Aristotle to be the tutor of his heir. Phidias was a bonus. He began to reflect on how fortunate his life had been.

* * *

The third son of the king of Macedon, it was by improbable chance that he was even king. As a teenager he had been sent by his father to Thebes as surety for a treaty—a sort of hostage. Fortunately he lived in those three years with Epaminondas, who developed the first principles of strategy for Greek warfare, which finally destroyed Spartan power. Philip no doubt absorbed some ideas from the great military strategist. It was also in Thebes that he was exposed to Greek culture, especially the art and literature of Athens.

When Philip was about twenty years of age, he accompanied his two older brothers to battle the Illyrians, who had invaded Macedon. In the ensuing battle, his oldest brother, King Perdiccas, and his other brother were killed. The shattered army retreated back to Pella.

The next day, the army encamped on safe ground and held an assembly. The Macedonian army was composed of the nobles and free men of the country and was, in effect, its governing body. The leaders of the army hailed Perdiccas' son as the new king. He was but a baby, and Philip was named as regent to rule for him.

Suddenly Philip found himself the acting King of Macedon and leader of the army that had been defeated by the neighboring Illyrians, who would certainly return after the winter to invade and possibly conquer Macedon.

Intelligent and strong-willed, Philip would show that he was worthy of the throne. During his years in Thebes, he became familiar with Greek methods, as well as their strengths and weaknesses. He had studied the organization of the Persians and the campaigns of the Greeks. Over the winter following the army's defeat, Philip trained the infantry and cavalry in new tactics. He was a strict disciplinarian yet inspired a loyalty from his troops. He would have to earn respect from the older officers.

In the summer, they met the Illyrians again in battle. This time, they completely destroyed them. They would not be a threat again.

Thebes' brief hegemony under Epaminondas had ended with his death, and Athens, Sparta, and Thebes had fought to a stalemate. Macedon's new king used this lull in Greek politics to forge the army he would use to further his ambitions. He had seen how weak and divided Greece was. He would unify it and invade Asia.

He developed a radically new army and strategy, forming his fighters into two ranks sixteen deep, as opposed to the normal Greek line of six to eight ranks. He called this a phalanx, and it presented an impenetrable wall of long spears up to twenty-three feet long to the enemy. Philip's second component was a large cavalry, known as The Companions. His strategy was for the phalanx to pin the enemy down while the cavalry attacked from the flanks, with the hapless enemy between the two. Whereas the object of Greek strategy was to break the enemy front and pursue it, Philip's object was to destroy the enemy on the battlefield.

He led his new army in several battles against Macedon's neighbors, extending and strengthening its borders. Each new battle further proved Philip's courage, cunning, and brilliance until the leaders of the country put aside his young nephew and crowned Philip King. He was twenty-three, and he decided he would put his strong ambition to practice.

Not a general to command from the rear, Philip fought with his men. "I lead by example," he told his officers. "How will my men fight with the courage and discipline that I demand of them if I don't share it?"

"True, Sire," said one of the older generals, "but you can eat better than they. You could have more meat and finer wine. After all, you are the king."

"I am the king, by virtue of my leadership and example. I have the love and loyalty of my men because I share their food and hardship during our campaigns. They also love me because of these." He pulled up his tunic, revealing the scars from battles on his torso and limbs. "Don't speak to me of good food and drink. We will have those, and more than enough, when we celebrate our victories." He laughed and took another gulp of wine.

After a battle in northern Thrace, an officer brought news to Philip. "The enemy has been crushed."

"It was a good day, thank the gods," Philip said. He took off his helmet as a young man helped him remove his breastplate, covered with splattered blood. The teenager was a son of one of the officers and served as a squire until he was old enough for battle. "We shall rest and tend our wounded, then in five days begin our march to Pella."

After they returned to Pella, the army celebrated its victory. Philip and his officers filled the great hall in the palace and ate, drank, and laughed until it seemed their bellies wouldn't take any more. The men shared the excitement of battle, reciting episodes of courage, sacrifice, and bloodshed. Some of the younger men started to throw food until a senior officer called them down.

Then the king stood up on his dais and spoke in his wine-hoarse voice above the din. "I propose a drinking contest for my generals, and I will join them. The man who can hold the most wine before vomiting or passing out will win this golden goblet that we took from our enemy." He held up the heavy, jewel-encrusted cup for all to see.

Cheers and laughter filled the room as the men drank one cup of wine after another. The officers laid bets on who would win. They staggered and spilled wine, and some passed out or left to vomit. Philip, enjoying the rowdiness and laughing, urged on the others.

After a time, five men remained, including the king. He stood up, weaving and holding onto the table. "I will add another prize to the contest," he announced over the commotion. He turned to a servant, "Bring in the girl."

Accompanied by bawdy comments of appreciation, a beautiful, white-skinned girl of about sixteen with long, braided hair was brought in and placed next to Philip. "Here is a Gallic beauty. Look at those green eyes and red hair. She was to warm my bed tonight, but I will award her to the man who is last standing."

Everyone cheered.

The men laughed and yelled louder, cheering on their favorites. Wine sloshed down their faces as they lifted unsteady hands to numb lips. One by one, with wine dripping from their chins, the generals fell down, sick or unconscious, until only Philip remained. The entire hall cheered their king as he grabbed his trophy and stumbled from the hall.

* * *

After Philip consolidated his power in the northern provinces, he turned his attention to politics in the south. Athens was absorbed in the Social War that ended her second empire. He took advantage of the situation and seized the cities of Amphipolis, Pydna, and Potidea—possessions of Athens on the northern Aegean. Athens sent a message to Philip. He read the letter, presented to him by a messenger, protesting his seizure of their cities and the selling of the captives into slavery.

He smiled and replied, "Once Athens was indeed powerful and could back up its protests with swords and spears. That day has passed, and now she is hard pressed by her former allies. Those allies she abused when she had the power. Now they will wear her down and impose an embarrassing peace.

"For my part, I admire the culture of Athens, home of Pericles, Euripides, and Plato. I do not want to destroy Athens, but I must have the cities to protect my frontier on the northern Aegean.

"Take this message back to Athens. 'City of Athena and birthplace of Greek art and literature, I hold your culture in the highest esteem. However, I will not return to Athens any of the cities I have obtained.'" He rose and stated forcefully, "That is all. You may return to your beloved Athens."

A few months later, he led a campaign to capture Methone. The city would not give open battle but defended itself stubbornly behind its walls. Philip had a meeting with his commanders after an unsuccessful day of attacking the city.

One of his generals spoke up. "Methone must have warehouses of food. They have withstood our siege for a month and laugh at us from their walls."

Philip replied as he raised a cup of wine, "They won't laugh for long. The new siege engines I had designed arrived today. We'll batter down their gates tomorrow."

The next day, the engines made slow progress against the determined defenders. Each time they advanced to the gates, volleys of arrows and stones forced them back. Philip's patience was as exhausted as his men. "Bring all the archers," he commanded. "We will place them to the sides of the engines to keep the defenders from the walls. I will lead them."

"But Sire, "one of his generals protested.

"I said, I will lead them. I am the king." He slammed his sword against a shield. No one gave further comment.

The attack was successful, but a stone hurled from the wall found its way to Philip's left eye, blinding it. He wrapped a rag around his bleeding wound and, with increased determination, led his army into the defeated town. The slaughter would have lasted all day if he had not stopped it.

Philip decided to make an example of Methone. He had the walls of the city torn down and sold all of its citizens into slavery. Other cities took note of his successful siege engines and of what happens to those who opposed him.

* * *

After the Sacred War in which Philip helped Phocia and the Amphictyonic League defeat Sparta and Athens, he was given the honor of presiding over the Greeks at the Pythian Games. At these games he used his considerable diplomatic personality to win many of the city-states into an alliance. His goal was to create a Greek Confederacy, under his leadership.

Not long after he returned to Pella and a period of peace, Philip began developing an interest in his son, Alexander, now a wild lad of thirteen. Alexander was an ideal youth—physically athletic, good in sports and hunting, and fair of complexion. A handsome, some would say even pretty, young man, his golden-brown hair hung in massive curls that picked up the sun's highlights like a halo. Bluish-green eyes burned with intensity in a clear face that Alexander would keep clean shaven. That would become the style of all Greeks later.

One day Philip watched, with Alexander at his side, as his men brought in horses from the Thracian plains to train for his cavalry. Philonicus, a Thessalian, brought in a huge, prideful black stallion Philip had paid a huge price for. The wild steed tossed his long mane over a strong neck and his muscles rippled as he reared high, forcing the men to back away from the flying hooves. One after another of Philip's best trainers tried to calm and mount the spirited stallion. All failed, some even suffering bites and kicks from the rebel horse.

Philip laughed, "He's a true warrior, a real match for his Macedonian captors. He will make someone a fitting companion in battle, if anyone can ever tame him."

"Let me try, Father."

Philip looked with amused surprise at his son, "What did you say, Alexander?" He was thirteen, not old enough to grow a beard or go to battle. What could this boy do that his best horse trainers could not?

"Let me try to tame the black stallion. I know I can. I have tamed other horses. I have a talent; they like me."

"I don't know, Alexander; you might get hurt. I don't want anything to happen to the future king of Macedon." Philip paused and reconsidered. This might be good experience for the young prince. "All right. Philonicus, hold the reins for Alexander. He will try to ride the stallion."

"Before I try, Father, would you give me a promise?"

"And what is it?"

"Will you give me this horse if I tame him?"

Philip smiled and clapped Alexander on the back. "Spoken like a prince, making a bargain with a king. And what will you give if you fail?"

"If I fail, I will pay the price of the horse."

His father laughed, "All right. You have a bargain."

Alexander was no fool. Even then, his keen observation served him well. He would not attempt a dangerous feat without assessing his chances for success. He had noticed that the spirited stallion reared and fought the handlers when his back was to the sun. The horse was afraid of its shadow that danced on the ground in front of him.

Alexander went into the corral and took the reins. The stallion started and shook his head, his eyes staring wildly at the beardless youth. He seemed to say, "How dare you test your puny body against me. I will show you!" He reared his forelegs and whinnied.

Alexander took the bridle and turned the horse around until it faced the sun; then, holding the reins tightly, he raised his hand to pat its huge neck. The horse settled down and allowed the boy to stroke him. Alexander advanced his hand to the long jaw and snout of the steed, all the while gently whispering to him. He walked him slowly forward, being careful to keep his face in the sun while continuing to murmur and stroke him. When he was sure he had calmed the mighty stallion, he stopped, said something to him, and reached into his short tunic. He pulled out an apple and gave it to the black giant, which took it greedily.

The horse stopped and pawed the ground, obviously nervous and eager to run. Alexander gently released his outer garment and let it slide to the ground. Then, in a sudden leap, he mounted the steed. The stallion snorted and looked back at this diminutive creature on his back. Alexander saw that he was allowed to settle himself and drew in the reins, all the while speaking quietly to his mount. When he realized the giant between his legs had accepted him and was anxious to go, Alexander gave him his rein. He allowed him to run at full gallop, urging him with a commanding voice and a firm kick in the side.

Alexander held this reins back, keeping the stallion's head up so he could not see his shadow, allowing the horse to run faster and faster around the corral. He laughed, his golden curls bouncing around his head.

The king and all the other men were laughing, clapping, and yelling the name of Alexander. It was a sight to behold, the giant black stallion accepting the calming and commanding hand of the handsome boy on his back.

When Alexander dismounted, he brought the horse to his father. "Is he mine then?"

"He is yours. You deserve him—a princely horse for a prince."

"I will name him Bucephalus. He will carry me to many battles and conquests."

"My son, Macedon is too small for you. Seek out a larger empire, worthier of you." Philip already saw a bright future for this boy.

* * *

Philip turned to Antipater, his most trusted adviser, and admitted, "Alexander is approaching manhood." He was proud of how his son had tamed Bucephalus.

"Indeed, Sire, he shows intelligence as well as physical bravery. He has a presence that men admire in a young man."

"That's why I have to start grooming him for the inheritance I plan for him, for he will be king one day."

"He is already going on hunts and training in the soldiers' exercise yard. He may be ready soon to be sent as a squire in battle," said Antipater.

"I don't mean only his military skills. I could do that and have already engaged an officer to oversee it. No, I have thoughts of his personal development. It's time that he be removed from his mother's hands and influence. I will replace the tutors that Olympias has arranged."

"The queen will not look kindly on your taking her son from her."

"I don't care what she thinks. She has too much control over him, and he needs to become a man. I have composed a letter, requesting a new tutor from Athens."

"From Athens, Sire?"

"Yes, I want him to be educated and accepted beyond Macedon as a cultured Greek. I want him to have every educational advantage I didn't have."

"Who are you engaging as his tutor?"

"I am asking Aristotle, the best student of famed Plato. He is a brilliant philosopher who has knowledge of many subjects. I want him to train Alexander's mind, as my officers will train his body. Most of all, I want him to help my son prepare for the legacy I am designing for him."

Later, Philip talked with Alexander and told him he had invited a new tutor for him.

"But why, Father? I like my tutors."

"The new tutor is Aristotle of Athens. He is renowned for his brilliant mind. He will help you learn many things. Things that will help you become a wise king someday."

"What will mother say? I don't want to leave her."

"Alexander, my son, you will be fourteen soon, and it is proper that you should leave the women's quarters and be trained with the other noble youths. Your half-brothers will also join you under Aristotle's tutelage.

"I'm not doing this for myself or to spite your mother. I want you to have the education that I did not. I want you to be taught by a philosopher, so that you may not do a great many things of the sort that I am sorry to have done."

"All right, Father. I will do as you say. I want to be a king like you." Alexander obeyed, but in his heart he told himself that he would be freed from his overbearing father someday and would be a strong king in his own right.

* * *

Yes, Philip was proud of his accomplishments. He had used diplomacy and negotiations as well as military action to increase his power and his influence with the rest of Greece. He knew that selling the captives from his campaigns into slavery did not endear him to other Greeks, but that was better than slaughter. Besides, the money from these slaves and from the gold mines of Thrace was more than ten times the value of the silver Athens drew from her mines at Laurium.

He was not ashamed to use whatever devices he could manage in his diplomacy to further his plans. He broke promises and treaties if it was to his advantage. In his reasoning, if cities, territory, or allies could be won with double dealing, then that was cheaper and better than shedding blood. For him there were no morals in government, and he considered lies and bribes a humane substitute for slaughter. He was generous in victory, however. Some said he was too generous, but he realized that with mercy he could turn a foe into a friend. He never slaughtered captives and gave better terms to Greeks he defeated than they gave to each other. He knew that with lenient terms he could turn an enemy into an ally. His goal was to unite Greeks behind him as their leader, not as an alliance opposing him.

Philip poured himself another cup of wine and congratulated himself again. Aristotle would help him train Alexander to be his heir, who would help him conquer Persia.

CHAPTER 15

When Philip was still a young king, he visited the island of Samothrace, where he sought an alliance with their king. After a banquet in his honor, he met a striking woman.

Her dark eyes flashed in a cream-colored face framed by auburn-red hair that hung in braids to her waist. Scarlet ribbons were woven into her tresses and wound around her black dress, outlining her full breasts. Around her narrow waist coiled a cleverly designed gold snake, the head serving as a clasp on its tail.

Philip couldn't take his eyes from her as she stood in animated conversation with two other men, occasionally throwing her head back in laughter at some clever remark. "Who is she?" Philip asked one of the nobles of the island.

"Her name is Olympias. She is from Molossia, where her brother is king of Epirus. He became king rather young, after their father and mother died."

"Is she married then?" Philip asked.

"No. She is here with some of her women friends. I am told she came to attend the Dionysian rites."

"Introduce me to her."

"Philip of Macedon," she said after their introduction. "I have heard what a brave warrior you are. Perhaps you will tell me of your conquests some time. Have you enjoyed your time on Samothrace?"

She beckoned a slave passing with a tray of wine-filled cups. Philip gave one to her and took a fresh cup for himself. She raised her brows and smiled as her hand grazed his. Philip felt a flush that prickled the roots of his hair and beard. He couldn't think clearly; his words stuck in his throat. "I...went hunting with the king. He showed me some of his warships."

"Interesting," she said, smiling. "I'm sure the ships made for brilliant conversation. Was the hunting at least exciting?"

"We hunted wild sheep. There are no lions or large animals on this island."

"Too bad. Would you like to experience something really exciting? I'm going to attend a religious ritual tomorrow night. Would you like to come with me?"

"What kind of ritual?"

"It is a celebration of Dionysus. It will be a rite of initiation into their worshipers."

"I don't know, Olympias. I am not a religious person. I am familiar with Dionysus, and I have heard of his mysterious cult. I enjoy drinking the wine that his divinity blesses."

"Oh come on, Philip. You will have the excitement of a new experience. I hear you enjoy the exhilaration of battle. There is nothing to be afraid of. Besides, I will be there to protect you." She laughed.

He laughed with her. "It will be my pleasure to go with you to the rites." He raised his goblet. "To Dionysus."

They both drained their cups.

The next night before the ceremony, the initiates were given lighted torches in the courtyard of the Temple of Dionysus. They then marched silently in single file, a flickering snake of flames, into the surrounding hills. They came to a clearing surrounded by trees and were led through about a hundred members of the cult, all scantily clad in short linen clothes that revealed the men's chests and part of the women's breasts. They wore grapevines twisted in their hair and around their bodies.

The newcomers took their places before a large fire, in front of which stood a stone altar, containing a bound lamb. The leader told them to toss their torches into the flames.

Standing behind the altar were three figures. A man in the center wore only a short skirt of animal fur, his hair tousled and entwined with vines and leaves. Around his neck hung a gold cup on a chain. The women, who flanked him, wore loose, white linen dresses that floated freely, allowing enticing peeks at curves and shadows through the sheer fabric. Their wild hair was also braided with vines.

Music from hidden flutes and drums filled the compound, and the two women began to dance away from the man. They pranced and twirled around the fire and the initiates, stepping and jumping, flailing arms and twisting their heads. They passed cups of wine spiced with herbs among the initiates, and continued to dance as the music became louder and faster.

The dancers came back from a basket at the edge of the clearing with snakes in their hands. They continued with the rhythm, now with the snakes coiling around their arms, necks, and bodies. They twirled and gyrated as if one with the snakes, their dresses clinging to their glistening skin that reflected the mesmerizing flames.

More cups were passed among the group, and Philip began to feel a lightheadedness that was unlike the wine intoxication he was familiar with. In the back of his mind he thought that there must be some drug in the wine. He didn't care; he was hypnotized, both by the rituals and the woman beside him. The female dancers stopped and took their places at the sides of the man.

At that point, the half-naked priest approached the altar and the lamb. He raised a sharp knife that seemed to be aflame from reflection. After chanting a prayer to the God Dionysus, he slit the animal's throat. Bright red blood splashed onto his arms and chest. He caught some of the blood in the cup he had removed from his neck, and turned to face the initiates. After another incantation, he went along their line, pouring the blood onto their heads. The priestesses followed him with the spiced wine and encouraged the group to drink deeply as blood trickled down their necks and bodies.

Olympias started to gyrate with the music, her head moving in a circle as her arms waved in the air. The two women yelled out the god's name , and the newcomers all echoed it. Olympias jumped toward the fire, whirling to the music. The rest of the group followed, dancing around the fire.

Philip saw Olympias go to the basket in the shadows and return with two snakes in her hands. She danced wildly, twisting and fondling the snakes in her flailing arms. Philip, intoxicated with the ritual wine, the wild rites, and the exotic woman with the snakes, was hopelessly entranced.

After that hypnotic night, Philip couldn't get Olympias out of his mind and returned to Pella determined that he would have that enchantress for his wife. He searched for an opportunity to visit Molossia in Epirus and sent a message to her brother proposing an alliance.

Molossia lay north of Greece and south of Macedon on the Ionian Sea. It would protect Philip's right flank if he were to face a combined Greek force. Its king would also welcome an alliance with his strong northern neighbor.

After the successful negotiations, the King of Epirus gave a banquet to celebrate in Philip's honor. Wine and fruit were passed around as the dancing girls entertained. The two kings toasted one another. Philip didn't ask why the other side of his couch was unoccupied. He soon discovered the reason.

The senior guard opened the door to the hall and bowed low to a woman who took two steps into the room and stopped, surveying it with piercing dark eyes. Of regal bearing, she wore a long black robe trimmed with gold ribbon. The same gold ribbon and white shells were braided into her red hair, leaving ringlets to dangle in front of her ears.

The boisterous hall hushed to a murmur as all eyes turned to this dark apparition. Philip was enthralled. Never had he seen a woman take control of so many men with only her presence. Her eyes found Philip's and remained there as she strode with easy grace to the raised platform and stood beside him.

The king didn't know that Philip had met Olympias on Samothrace or that she had introduced him to those mysterious Dionysian rites.

The king said, "This is my sister, Olympias. Olympias, may I present…"

"I have already met King Philip, the brave conqueror from Macedon." She held out her hand.

Philip took it, memories of wild rites and dancing with snakes flooding his mind. His mouth opened, and he heard himself say, "It's a pleasure to see you again." He helped her to his couch and joined her.

The Molossian king raised a toast to Philip. Before he could sip, Olympias said, "To you, Sire, may the gods bless all your triumphs until you lead all in an invasion of Asia." Philip raised his cup in acknowledgment and met her unflinching gaze. Fire shone in those eyes. She smiled and drained her cup, then turned and motioned a slave to refill it.

Enthralled, Philip struggled through a haze of emotions as he exchanged talk with the alluring, dark beauty. She fascinated him with talk of portents, the will and actions of the gods, and how she could read them. "I am a descendent of Achilles on my father's side," she said, as if all who knew her were aware of that fact. "The great hero of Troy was raised to Olympus as a god, but not before he left behind my ancestor."

"And what is that curious belt around your waist? It looks like a snake. Is it a symbol of Achilles?"

"Yes, it is a snake, but it has nothing to do with Achilles. It was my pet. Its name was Argos, like the ship of Jason, for I allowed it to wander through the palace."

"You allowed this snake to roam your brother's palace?" Philip could hardly believe it. He hated snakes. "It wasn't poisonous, of course."

"It was poisonous when I befriended it, although I had its poison sacs removed at my brother's insistence. I have others in a basket in my chambers. Would you like to see them?"

"Perhaps later." Philip was anxious to visit her chamber, but not to see her snakes.

She said in a low voice, "I'll send a message with my slave to you later when it's safe for you to come to my room."

He raised his cup and winked. "You must promise to keep your snakes in their basket."

She laughed and saluted with her cup. "I promise."

When the rest of the palace was asleep, Olympias' slave girl led Philip to her room. Candles flickered in the corners while fragrant smoke floated from a bronze brazier next to one wall. Olympias wore a loose-fitting white gown with her hair combed down around her shoulders. Philip could trace the nipples that tented the gown and could barely make out the shadow between her legs.

He was immediately aroused. She opened her arms and, without a sound, he stepped into them, enveloping her with his own muscular limbs. They fell across the bed and sank into the soft purple linen.

Olympias placed her hand across Philip's mouth and rose from the bed, strode to the center of the room, and threw off her robe. She wore only a thin gold chain, fashioned like a snake around her waist. Philip was completely captivated. He wanted to grab this apparition and ravage her.

She turned and walked to the censer. Grabbing a handful of herbs from an adjacent bowl, she threw them onto the burning coals. A plume of smoke filled the room with its intoxicating aroma. She danced through it, chanting in a tongue that Philip did not understand. He was mesmerized by this enchantress, who continued her incantations. She came to Philip and slowly undressed him as the smoke encircled her. She ran her hands over his broad, hairy chest and cupped them around his strong erection. He groaned.

She fell silent and slipped into the bed next to him, and he folded her body into his and devoured her like a famished beast.

She had done her magic. Philip was hers.

Philip's personal and sexual life was as wild and free as his political one. He liked boys, but he liked women more and planned to marry as many as he could. This was expected of Macedonian kings. When he met Olympias, however, he was completely captivated by her spirit. She enchanted him. He asked the king for her hand, knowing that it would be a good alliance. She would be his first wife.

"It will be a good union," the king told his sister. "Philip has an army that will soon dominate all Greece, and then he will invade Asia with its untold riches."

Olympias stuck out her chin, "I will not marry him unless I am the only queen. I will not share his bed with any other wives."

"But Olympias, Macedonian kings have many wives. They are parts of alliances."

"I don't care," she said, stamping her foot. "Then tell Philip I will marry him only if I remain his chief wife. My children with him will be his heirs, and not any from other wives. That is my answer."

The king presented her conditions to Philip, who was so taken with Olympias that he accepted. "Tell her that I will accept her as my queen and mother to my heirs." This was a princess whose will and ambition matched his own. He did not promise, however, not to take other wives.

Philip could not get Olympias out of his mind and returned to Pella and announced the marriage and alliance with Epirus. Philip's subjects were overjoyed and looked forward with happy anticipation to the first wedding of their king.

Olympias was equally attracted to Philip and looked forward to sharing a bed with the man who was making Macedon a powerful kingdom. The wedding was a royal celebration in the city that Philip was building into a Greek capital. Three days of festivities culminated with the royal couple appearing on a balcony outside their wedding chamber, waving and smiling at the happy crowd. Macedonian generals and nobles stood next to those from Epirus, and all raised their voices in congratulation. People filled the courtyard and beyond, dancing and singing praises to the royal pair. All prayed for a son and heir as a speedy issue.

Afterward Olympias told Philip that she had a dream during their wedding night. "I dreamed that a lightning bolt struck me as I slept and all was aflame around me. I felt the lightning strike within me. It was Zeus impregnating me."

Philip laughed. "It was not a god; it was me. My lightning bolt entered you. See? It's ready again." He reached for her.

She kissed him and made love, but didn't forget the dream. She would remember and retell it.

* * *

Olympias and Philip shared a consuming love, for both were passionate with excitable tempers and intelligent energy. Philip enjoyed drinking and partying with the men, and, of course, hunting and fighting. Olympias became active in the Dionysian rites that the women of Macedon and Thrace were addicted to. The cult, known for its excessive rituals, gave her wild Molossian temperament free rein. She developed a reputation for communing with the gods and possibly even sorcery. Snakes in particular fascinated her, and she avidly took to dancing with them and even kept them in the palace.

One night, Philip came to her bed after carousing with his fellows, pulled back the covers, and saw a snake coiled around Olympias' naked waist. It was green with black spots that looked like eyes over its glistening body. It raised its head toward Philip, candlelight refecting in the slitted eyes, and flicked out its wet tongue, as if tasting Philip's scent. He recoiled in shock, almost dropping the sheet, a stifled scream caught in his throat.

"Hush," Olympias said. "It is the God Apollo. Don't disturb him." She stroked its head, and the snake extended its quivering tongue. Philip was shocked into silence. Disgusted, he left the chamber and slept with his men.

This scene, and others similar to it, repeated itself over the years. Even though they shared passions of love, energy, and ambition, the fires gradually cooled. Philip would wander to other beds and his other wives, while Olympias' jealousy raged hot. Tired of competing with divine lovers, Philip turned his attention more and more to other women.

* * *

Aristotle and Phidias had heard the tales of Olympias' jealousy of Philip's other wives and sexual meanderings. They were told that she was a woman of intelligence and strong will who possessed a fiery temper and were warned not to be taken in by her intrigues.

"The queen has asked for us to pay her a visit," Aristotle told Phidias. "She wants to meet Alexander's new tutors."

Phidias sat down in a chair, facing his mentor and friend. "I suppose, as his mother, she has an interest in who his tutors are."

"It's not that simple," Aristotle confided. "She is angry that the king replaced the other tutors she had obtained. She means to control Alexander and resents that Philip has taken him from her. She uses Alexander as leverage against the king. It's the old-fashioned power struggle with the son as pawn."

"I see," said Phidias stroking his beard thoughtfully. "Perhaps we should refuse to see her."

"We can't do that; she's the queen. But we must be circumspect. Don't say anything to deserve her anger. Remember, you are here only to be a tutor for her son. And I was the one who was invited by the king and brought you as my assistant."

"I'll be careful what I say," agreed Phidias.

* * *

Olympias was anxious to meet the new tutors from Athens. She knew that Philip's dismissal of the other ones she had provided for Alexander was part of his plan to undermine her influence with her son. Well, maybe she could use these new men.

She first met with Aristotle, who had proved to be invulnerable to her. He told her that he had Philip's confidence and had total control of Alexander's education. Perhaps this man Phidias would be more pliable, she thought.

She asked him to come to her chambers. "Sit down, Master Phidias." She motioned a slave girl to pour the wine. "Would you like some fruit?" She waved to a bowl at the table next to them.

"No thank you, your Majesty."

"And how do you like Pella so far?" she asked, smiling. "The weather is pleasant in the summer but can be quite cold in winter." She spoke of generalities to disarm him before asking, "And what is your opinion of young Alexander?"

Phidias was wary of the queen's jealousy and competition with the king over their son, and his answer was guarded. "He is an intelligent young man, eager to learn. He has much physical energy as well, much more than other boys of his age. He will make a fine king."

"Of course he will," she said with pride. "As a mother, I am concerned with his education. I'm sure you can appreciate that. I want to be informed of his progress. You will report directly to me weekly."

Phidias bowed his head. "With all respect, your Majesty, I cannot do that."

A dark shadow furrowed Olympias' brow, and the pleasantness left her voice. "I command you," she said, her voice rising to impress her point. "I am the queen."

"Yes, you are, but I am under the authority of Aristotle and the king. If they wish for me to report to you, I will, but I cannot agree to do so on my own. I hope you understand."

"I understand, Master Phidias. I thought we could be friends, but I see it is not to be. I trust you will be more skillful in teaching than you are in ingratiating a queen. I am sure we will have other meetings in the time you are here. For now, you are excused."

"Thank you, your Majesty." Phidias bowed and left, realizing that he may have made an enemy of the queen.

CHAPTER 16

Alexander, not yet fourteen, was a precocious boy physically and mentally when Aristotle and Phidias arrived in Pella. He was an adolescent anxious to grow up and enjoy the freedom of adulthood. His new tutors would have their hands full, like trying to cap a roaring volcano.

Aristotle would take Alexander as his sole charge, while Phidias had the responsibility of tutoring his half-brothers and the sons of nobles, although he also taught Alexander history and geography. Both tutors soon became aware of the passionate temper Alexander came by naturally from both parents. At first Aristotle had less success with Alexander than Alexander had with Bucephalus.

The thrill of taming that royal steed had only whetted his appetite. He sought out wild horses that were brought to Pella and dared other youths to tame them with him. One day, Alexander went with four other boys, all fourteen or fifteen years of age, to the corral, having heard that some new horses were brought in from Thrace. They climbed up on the fence and looked at the animals running around the enclosure. "Let's each pick one," Alexander said, excited. "Whoever can tame his horse first will get a new bow."

"What new bow?" asked a boy.

"A guard in my father's palace has it from a battle. He said I could have it when I turned fifteen. I'll bet I can talk him out of it now. Let's see who can tame a horse. I pick that white one with a black streak on its nose."

All the other boys picked out horses, and the rough sport was on. In the course of the contest, one youth was bitten, another was kicked and suffered broken ribs, and another was thrown and broke an arm. Alexander suffered no injuries and was the first to control his horse and ride it around the corral.

In spite of their injuries, all the boys laughed and poked fun at one another. "Let's celebrate our victories," Alexander said. "We can have a party tonight. The wine steward will give me the wine, and we can meet outside the gymnasium."

They all knew they could sneak out of their houses after dinner, and Alexander was already known for his wild parties. He was beginning to have a taste for wine, like his father.

And indeed, the party got rowdy. Wine can bring out aggression in some people, especially boys who like to bully. One of the youths, who was big for his age, pushed another who had bumped against him. "Watch where you're going, horse's ass."

The other boy pushed back. "Who are you calling a horse's ass? Your face looks like one, you son of a whore."

The larger boy grabbed the smaller one by the tunic and swung him into a group of boys Alexander was standing with. Alexander picked up the fallen boy, who was a friend of his, and spoke to him. "Cleitus, he may be larger and stronger than you, but he's clumsy, already stumbling from too much wine. You can beat him. Remember what we were taught about fighting."

Cleitus straightened up and threw off his tunic. "Yeah, I remember." He ran at the other youth, who also had shed his tunic, and ran headfirst into his gut, winding him. While the boy was bent over getting back his breath, Cleitus hit him under the chin with his fist, then punched him in the nose. The other youths cheered and yelled. Cleitus reached back and, with all his strength behind it, delivered a roundhouse punch to the big boy's jaw. The boy fell over unconscious.

"Victory to Cleitus!" Alexander yelled. "Let's all celebrate," he said as he passed around another jug of wine. "Let's all go hunting tomorrow," he said to no one in particular.

"But Alexander," one youth replied, "we might not feel so well after tonight."

"Horseshit!" Alexander shot back. "If you're going to be a soldier, you'll have to learn how to drink hard and fight hard the next day. Anyone who has the courage will join me after the sun rises. Bring your horse and spear, for we will hunt boar."

They all knew that was a dangerous sport, for hunters could be killed by the sharp tusks of an enraged boar. They also knew that, if they wanted to remain friends with this high-tempered youth who would probably become king, they would join him.

* * *

Aristotle realized he had to get the attention of this lad, who would rather hunt and tame wild horses than read Greek literature and philosophy. He knew he would have to make learning down to earth if it was to be interesting, so he mixed his thoughts about ethics and the purpose of a good life with practical matters. He showed how mathematics and scientific laws governed objects, compared dissected animals with men wounded in battle. He consistently taught Alexander how to live like a civilized man by maintaining the virtues of courage, justice, knowledge, and moderation. With time and patience, he calmed the tempestuous energy of youth and turned some of it to an appreciation of wisdom.

One morning after Aristotle had been in Pella a year or so and had succeeded in getting Alexander's attention to more serious matters of learning, Philip came to pay him a visit. Aristotle and Alexander were discussing some of Plato's thoughts on government. Philip listened and nodded with approval as his son asked probing questions of the philosopher.

Aristotle looked at Philip, obviously wondering why he would come to their discussion. "What can I do for you, Sire?"

"I don't mean to intrude in your lessons, but I was so impressed by my son's reasoning," Philip said. "He agrees with me, that even though a ruler should be educated and wise, government should not be in the hands of philosophers. You know as well as I, that they would always argue with one another and nothing would get done."

All three laughed.

"The reason I came was to talk to you and Alexander. My son is becoming a man. He lives with his brothers and noble youth. You and Phidias have been doing well in taming their wild nature and making them civilized Greeks."

"Thank you, Sire," Aristotle said. "Alexander is a bright boy. He knows the Greek books and can quote from Homer. He also has a keen interest in the study of plants and animals."

"Master Aristotle makes those things so interesting, Father," Alexander said. "He knows so much."

"Yes, my son, which is why I brought him to teach you. Alexander, you will soon put on the robe of manhood, which has its responsibilities as well as its privileges. You must work harder at controlling your temper and your impulsive actions.

"Someday, if the gods agree, you will be king. If you are to sit on my throne, you must learn how to be a king. Your tutors can teach you how to read and how to think, and those are important, but they can't teach you how to rule men and lead them into battle. That is my duty. Learn from me, not how to drink wine and bed women, any man can do that, but how to be a general and a king. Will you learn from me as your tutor?"

"Yes, Father, I want to be like you, strong and brave and a leader of men in battle. I want to be king."

"Good, then come with me tomorrow. I'm leading a party to hunt for lions. Bring your bow and spear and Bucephalus, and be prepared to leave from the courtyard at dawn."

"Yes, Father." Alexander replied, the light of excitement dancing in his eyes.

"Good, I will see you then," Philip said and turned and left.

After his father left, it was hard for Alexander to think of anything except lions, so Aristotle said he could spend the rest of the day in the exercise yard.

* * *

Aristotle spent four long years preparing Alexander's mind and character for kinghood. He had succeeded in constructing the veneer of civilization over the wild nature this lad had inherited from both parents.

Aristotle had Alexander read Homer's famous epic, *The Iliad*, and they discussed it at length. "Before Achilles could decide whether to go to Troy and fight, and possibly to be killed, he asked the advice of his mother, a goddess," Aristotle said. "She told him that he could decide to stay at home and marry and raise a family and live a long and peaceful life, but no one would remember him. Or he could go to war and do courageous deeds and be covered with glory, even an early death. Then he would be immortal. "What do you think Achilles decided?" Aristotle asked the teenager.

"Why of course he went to Troy and he was killed, but we remember all his glorious deeds."

"That's right. A man should do what his destiny calls him to do. He should examine his life and live it according to what his true virtue calls for."

At the end of a year of studying and memorizing passages of the *The Iliad*, Aristotle gave Alexander his copy. "I have written notes in this book and give it to you as your own," he said.

"Oh, Master Aristotle, I will treasure it." Alexander hugged it to his chest. I will always keep it by my bed."

And he did, until the day he died.

By the time Alexander was eighteen, he showed love and admiration for his teacher, more so than for his own father. Later he was heard to say, "I have received life from one, but the other has taught me the art of living. Aristotle gave me the ancient adage, 'Life is the gift of nature, but beautiful living is the gift of wisdom '."

Toward the end of those years, his father had made an effort to have Alexander spend as much time with him as possible, allowing him to observe the art of ruling, political maneuverings, and military strategy.

Alexander absorbed the lessons he learned at his father's side with intense interest and showed his ambition to lead by asking to fight in skirmishes. He avidly listened to messengers who came from other cities, especially Greek ones, sometimes questioning them about their native lands. Alexander admired his father and sought to emulate him, but not out of love. His mother's son, he was fiercely loyal to her. She had molded him and formed his ambition, for she shared it with him

* * *

Philip liked stalwart, hearty men who would risk their lives in battle and carouse with him all night. His sexual appetite, moreover, could not be satisfied with only one woman, and he tasted other fare. After a rowdy drinking party, at which some of the dancing girls were passed around, Philip staggered back to his rooms as the sky was beginning to lighten. He threw off his robe and fell heavily to Olympias' side, pulling her to his chest and smothering her with rough kisses.

Olympias pushed him away. "You reek of old wine and young women. Let go of me. Go to your sweaty men and sluts."

"Oh, come on, my love. We were just having fun. You're my wife; this is our bed. Give your king the love he desires."

"I don't have to give you anything. I'm the queen. It's all right with me for you to have sex with whores and dancing girls, but I don't have to tolerate your philandering with other nobles' wives and daughters. Now get out of my bed. I want to go back to sleep."

"Your bed? It's mine too."

"Not anymore. You can sleep in the adjoining room. I'll tell you when you can come into my bed."

Philip grumbled, angrily grabbed his robe, and stomped into the next room. He collapsed onto the bed and was loudly snoring within minutes.

Philip's sexual escapades and other marriages caused Olympias' jealousy to rise to a crescendo. Her tirades were heard throughout the palace as she shrieked and smashed pottery. Attendants and guards fled in terror from her violent outbursts. Philip lost his patience with her jealousies and violence and banished her from his palace to a separate house.

He began spending more time with his favorite son, teaching him skills and tactics. Alexander excelled in sports and military training and was quick of intellect. Philip allowed him to sit in on the negotiations with other leaders to listen to the messages brought him. He was training him to be king, but Alexander remained faithful to his mother.

One day Alexander, sweaty from his exercise with arms, went to visit his mother in her house. He stomped into her sitting room and threw down his helmet. Falling exhausted onto a couch, he shouted, "I hate him!"

Olympias looked up from her loom. "Whom do you hate, my son?"

"My father."

"What has he done now, Alexander?"

"He upbraided me for giving the wrong order in a maneuver with the cavalry. He embarrassed me in front of the men."

"Maybe he thought it was to teach you a lesson, to discipline you to follow his orders."

"Perhaps, but I have had enough of his ordering me. I am almost eighteen. I'm a man who could lead men, and I will lead armies and conquer cities like him. I'll show him."

"Calm down, Alexander," Olympias soothed her son. "It will do you no good to openly oppose your father now. He is too powerful. The generals and entire army love him. He has led them from one victory to another and rewards them with gold and women. Bide your time and be patient. His power will come to you."

"But I'm ready now."

"You have much to learn, my son. Philip may seem hard and unfeeling, but he is a brilliant military leader. Learn everything you can from him, so that you may also be successful."

"But how am I to learn, if I hate him?"

"Hide your hate; bury your resentment; show loyalty, obedience, and a son's love for his father. You must do these things and be patient."

"But, Mother…"

"Trust me. The gods and I will help you to become great. You will surpass Philip in conquests and glory."

"But Mother, I've never commanded an army; how can I conquer Asia?"

"Believe me Alexander, it is your destiny. You will become king, and I will help you. Do as I say, and you will succeed."

"Yes, Mother."

Alexander showed the natural talent of a leader early, for he had inherited his strong will from both sides. Most of his half-brothers and other youths accepted his leadership, although some were jealous. He built a coterie of loyal companions who trusted his leadership. Before Alexander was to accompany his father to the battle of Chaeronea, Olympias sent for him.

Alexander came at Olympias' bidding, attired in his new armor. She admired it.

"Isn't it beautiful?" he asked, beaming. "Father has given me command of The Companions. We are preparing to march to Greece and face the Athenians and their allies. They have chosen war."

"Yes, I know," Olympias said. As a mother, she had mixed feelings about her only son going to his first war. "I'm proud of you. I know you will be courageous and lead your men well. You have the blood of Achilles within you, for, as I told you, I am his descendent. But be careful; don't take unnecessary risks."

"I'll protect myself, Mother." He reached over and kissed her on the cheek.

"There is something else I want to tell you before you leave." She reached up and caressed his cheek.

Alexander sat down, his curiosity aroused. "And what is that?"

"I have not told you this, but Philip is not really your father."

Alexander was shocked. "What? Am I not legitimate and heir to the throne?"

"You are not only heir, but the son of divine Zeus. On the night that you were conceived, Zeus struck me as a lightning bolt, catching me afire. He sired you. You have within you divine blood. As the son of the great god Zeus, you will have his protection. You will be the king of our nation and lead a great army in conquest of Asia. The priestess of Dionysus told me that the Oracle at Delphi prophesied it."

Alexander was overcome with emotion. Was he truly the son of a god? Other noble Greeks in literature were the sons or daughters of gods, even Achilles himself. Whether or not he accepted Olympias' tale of his birth, a part of him wanted to believe it.

Olympias saw the shock on Alexander's face. "As the son of Zeus, and descendent of Achilles, you are destined to do great things."

"But how can I," protested Alexander, "if my fath…if Philip conquers all of Greece and Asia and accumulates all the honor? I don't want to inherit a kingdom and sit on a throne and be bored. I don't want a peaceful rule. I want to lead armies, and conquer cities, and gain glory and honor."

"And you will, my son; you will become a great king."

Olympias would help him to fulfill that ambition.

IV Allies and Enemies

CHAPTER 17

Old Isocrates was the respected founder of the most successful school of rhetoric in Athens, which predated Plato's Academy by eight years. Political influence in the public affairs of the city depended on a man's ability to speak well before the Assembly and the courts. The art of speech and argument was the goal of public men, and Isocrates' school had trained many of Athens' leaders. He taught his students how to use language effectively to win their arguments and sway their listeners.

No great orator or statesman himself, Isocrates influenced public opinion through his talent of writing and distributing pamphlets. He addressed his long speeches in the form of essays, which he sent to the Assembly and later to Philip and the Pan-Hellenic Games. His reputation as a sound thinker with high ethics and the teacher of many of the political leaders of his day gained him a respectful audience.

Before the Second Sacred War, in which Macedon established its power in Greece, Isocrates rose in the Assembly and read part of a pamphlet that he had circulated in Athens, praising the city for its leadership in learning and culture. "So far has our city distanced the rest of mankind in thought and speech, that her pupils have become the teachers of all the world. But all around our culture are barbarians. It saddens me that the barbarians are becoming stronger, and Persia is lord over all the Ionian Greeks, while our Greek states consume themselves in incessant wars.

"For as many as there are evils that are common to the nature of man, we have invented even more than those by engendering wars and factions among ourselves. Greeks do not weep over the calamities of other Greeks, and view with complacency the many terrible sufferings that result from our state of war. They are so far from pity that they even rejoice more in each other's sorrows than in their own blessings.

"If Greeks must fight, why not fight the real enemy? Why not drive the Persians back to their homeland? I predict that a relatively small army of disciplined and determined Greeks can defeat the Persian hordes. Our soldiers have proven their prowess and courage so valiantly that even the Persians hire them as mercenaries. Why should Greeks fight for the Persians when they can fight for Greece? It is a war that will be blessed by the gods, a war that at last will give unity to Greece and a choice between Greek unity or triumphant barbarism."

A thunderous applause interrupted him, and old heads nodded knowingly to each other. They had seen too much of Greeks fighting one another.

Isocrates raised his hands for quiet. "I also want to stress another point. We are proud of our Greek culture and heritage. We have seen it spread with our commerce and settlements to the far reaches of the inland sea. Other peoples, who were not Greek, have adopted Greek language, arts, learning, and ways of doing things. Greek identity therefore is no longer merely the race of Greeks. Non-Greeks who have taken on Greek institutions can also become Greeks. Thus, the people of Asia outside the Ionian cities, of Sicily, and Italy, and even further west, may be called Greeks. Our ideals of the city-state can then be exported further to the east beyond Asia." Applause again congratulated his speech, for Greeks saw this again as an excuse to export their Greek influence by war as well as by trade. No one yet could name a potential leader for a possible invasion of Asia to face the Persians. Some in the audience fervently hoped for one. Others reported the speech to the Great King of Persia, who was always wary of Greek designs on his territory.

* * *

Athens had been urged by Philocrates, an elder statesman and member of the peace party, and Aeschines to conclude a treaty, recognizing Philip's conquests in the north. This had allowed Philip to easily defeat the Phocians and their allies in the Second Sacred War without the threat of Athens intervening.

Philip sat at a table littered with maps and letters from cities throughout Greece. His view from this room in his palace overlooked the city his architects were creating—a Greek city to rival Thebes or Corinth. He noted that the ionic columns of the Temple of Apollo, God of learning and the arts, were ready to receive its roof.

He turned to Antipater, his friend and advisor, "I am satisfied. I have secured the alliance of many Greek cities, and I have peace with Athens. Sparta and Thebes aren't threats."

Antipater nodded, "Athens should be satisfied also. The treaty preserves her grain supply from the Black Sea." Athens had been worried that Macedon's conquests in the northern Aegean could block those grain shipments she relied on.

The king looked down at a map. "We can withdraw our forces from Greece and prepare for our next step."

"I don't think we're ready to invade Asia," said Antipater.

"You're right, my friend. I have designs on expanding our kingdom north beyond Thrace. Then we can plan for Asia."

Antipater got up and walked to the window. "You don't have a navy. You must have one if you're to free the Ionian Greeks and supply your army." He turned to face Philip, awaiting an answer.

Philip replied, "That's why the treaty with Athens is so important. Athens has the navy I need. I'll persuade her to join me and the rest of the Greek cities in a war with Persia. I'll send emissaries to all the city-states, urging them to help me free the Greeks of Ionia from Persian rule. They need a leader to unify them. Surely they'll see the wisdom in following me."

Philip had no sympathy for hardheaded Greeks like Demosthenes, who insisted on their independence. He saw these cities as led by corrupt politicians or greedy merchants and bankers.

Antipater reflected Philip's thoughts. "Not all the Greeks oppose your leadership. The smaller cities welcome your protection against Athens, Thebes, and Sparta."

"I know," said Philip, "but there are voices in Athens, especially that of Demosthenes, that oppose me and the war with Persia. He probably receives Persian gold for his support."

"We have friends in Athens, also, Sire. We can rely on them to oppose Demosthenes."

Philip nodded. "See that they receive any aid that's necessary."

Antipater said with a smile, "I'll see to it." He bowed slightly and left.

* * *

In Athens Demosthenes continued his "philippics" against Philip. He denounced him as the tyrant of the north, bent on crushing all Greece under his heel. A talented orator, he urged the people against any accommodation with Macedon. He and his ally, Hyperiedes, led the party of war against Philip's ambitions.

Aeschines and Phocion, the leaders of the party urging peace with Philip, met in Phocion's spacious villa outside the gates of Athens. "Not all of Athens agrees with Demosthenes," Aeschines was saying. "Many will listen to your sound advice, for they hold you in high esteem."

Well-known for his integrity, Phocion had studied philosophy in Plato's Academy and was a capable orator. Although he had served in many wars, he was an advocate of peace.

Phocion replied, "It's obvious to me, and to any man who is reasonable, that Athens does not have the military strength to fight a war with Philip. We no longer have our empire or allies that we can draw men and money from."

"We have our navy still," Aeschines said.

"Yes, but it is not as large or ably led as in the past. Besides, what can it do against Philip's war machine? No, we must make peace with him."

"Who else supports us?" Aeschines asked.

"Philocrates, of course, who brokered the peace and alliance between Athens and Macedon."

"Demosthenes has branded him a traitor because of that peace. He has been quiet of late."

"Then there is also good old Isocrates, who continues to plead for Greek unity against the Persians. Perhaps Athens will listen to his seasoned voice," Aeschines said.

"The old man's logic is drowned by the torrent from the mouth of Demosthenes," Phocion said with a tone of sadness. He rose and paced across the room to look out onto his courtyard as if in thought. He turned and said, "The merchants and bankers don't want war, of course; it would ruin their trade. The wealthier classes realize that we don't have tribute from an empire to support a war. It would have to be paid for with increased taxes. The Assembly might even vote to confiscate some of their property."

"What of the Assembly, Phocion? They must vote for war or peace. I'm afraid that if the masses vote for war, we will be very unpopular, and even our lives may be at risk."

"You know what I think of the Assembly, my friend," Phocion replied. "They are a bunch of mindless animals, easily led by the most persuasive speaker, and Demosthenes is capable of doing it. The last time I addressed the Assembly, I was warmly applauded. I turned and asked a friend of mine whether I had inadvertently said something wrong."

Aeschines laughed. He had risen from poverty to a comfortable living by his own hard work. He had been a teacher and an actor and thus had learned to become a fluent speaker and noted orator. He could speak extemporaneously without the prepared text most orators used. He had served in many wars with Phocion and was committed to him in advocating peace with Philip. Even though the Macedonian king paid him, it merely increased his enthusiasm.

"Yes, I realize that we walk a precarious line," mused Phocion. "We must continue to urge peace among the upper classes and influential men. You can use some of Philip's money to help me."

"I must be circumspect in doing that," Aeschines said. "But in public, I'll speak against Demosthenes in the Assembly."

* * *

Demosthenes called a meeting with some of his war party to plan their strategy. "Phocion is talking with many of the wealthy men and leaders in Athens."

"He's trying to frighten them," said Hyperiedes. "He tells them Athens doesn't have a strong army. He warns them that they will be taxed heavily and may even have their property confiscated to hire mercenaries."

"He's partly right," admitted Demosthenes. "We will have to raise taxes to support a war, but we can also enlist our own citizens. I have a plan to do that. But we must blunt Phocion's campaign. We must not come under Philip's power."

Another man spoke up, "Phocion has such prestige. The people, rich and poor alike, honor him. You can't attack him directly."

"No," agreed Demosthenes, "but I can attack his friend Aeschines. I'll bring another indictment against him on the charge of receiving Macedonian gold."

"Of course," said Hyperiedes, "that will shut him up. He'll appear to be supporting peace with Philip only because he's paid to do so."

The trial was held, and most of the citizens of Athens came to witness again the duel between the two greatest orators of the day. Demosthenes eloquently laid out his arguments that Aeschines should be convicted of receiving bribes from a foreign power—a crime that deserved banishment. He sat down after his speech, convinced of his victory.

Aeschines rose in his defense, denying that his support of peace with Philip was bought and insisting that it was for a sincere concern for the safety of Athens. He then turned to face Demosthenes. "What hypocrisy," he shouted. "He accuses me of being in the pay of Philip of Macedon, and he receives gold from the Great King of Persia. It is no secret. He claims to support Athenian independence, but at what price? It is a far greater crime to support war with Greeks and their allies because of bribes from Persia. The Great King rules over our brothers in Ionia. Demosthenes would accept his money and bow down as well. I say you should acquit me of these ridiculous charges and bring the same charges against Demosthenes."

Aeschines arguments convinced the jurors, and they acquitted him. Demosthenes fumed as he left the proceedings with Hyperiedes. "This is not a defeat," he vowed, "merely a temporary setback. I will continue to attack Philip and Aeschines and his peace party in the Assembly. They will listen to me. We will have our war with Philip yet."

* * *

Isocrates, now ninety years old, addressed an open letter to Philip , praising him, yet advising him: "I foresee that you, Philip King of Macedon, will unite all the Greeks under your leadership. The Greek states need a strong leader who will prevent them from the fratricidal wars to which they are prone. I beg you not to use the power that you will obtain as a tyrant, for we Greeks have had our fill of those. Rather, you must use your political and military influence to unify all the Greek states in a war of liberation for our Greek brothers of Ionia from their Persian masters. We hail you as the unifier of the Greeks. Lead us to victory over the Persians."

Hyperiedes finished reading the letter Demosthenes had given him and threw it to the floor "What an old fool!" he said, stomping on the letter in disgust. "This sounds like a slave asking his master to beat him."

"He asks Philip not to be a tyrant," Demosthenes said, laughing. "Oh, please be a good boy. Don't sell us all into slavery."

Hyperiedes continued to fume. "That old fool is calling for nothing less than for all Greeks to surrender themselves to the Macedonian despot. I will resist that to my death."

"I agree, my friend," Demosthenes replied. "Philip will continue to gobble up parts of Greece, and the small city-states will support him until he is king over all of it. I will denounce the letter before the Assembly."

Demosthenes friends spread the word that he was going to make an important speech before the Assembly at its next meeting. The seats were full and people stood around to hear the fiery orator who was bound to entertain his audience.

Demosthenes read Isocrates letter to Philip, then proceeded to tear it apart. He called Isocrates a cringing dog, licking the feet of Philip and picking up the scraps left by him. "Does he think Philip will be kind to us, just because we are his slaves? The Macedonian tyrant will lead us by the nose and force us to fight a war against the mighty Persian Empire, just for his own glory."

He castigated Isocrates for encouraging the King of Macedon and branded him a traitor to Athens. "The old man has lost his mind, if not his loyalty to our city. He must be silenced or banished from us."

Demosthenes continued to work up his fiery rhetoric until the crowd cheered in martial hysteria. They booed Isocrates and chanted against Philip. Demosthenes' philippics were coming to fruition.

He drew short of charging Isocrates with treason, but the old teacher was humiliated, his pen silenced for the next few years.

Philip's strategy was working. His diplomacy had gained him leadership of the Thessalonian League and, with it, the finest cavalry in Greece. Year after year his influence advanced down into Greece. The obvious growth of Philip's power added weight to Demosthenes' campaign, who chided the Athenians and the Assembly for doing nothing to hinder Philip's advance into the heart of Greece. He called them cowards and again appealed to their patriotism. Shamed by Demosthenes, the Assembly voted to raise a citizen army and pay them with the theoric fund. Taxes were raised. Athens was preparing for war.

Furious, Philip threatened to choke Athens' grain supply. Demosthenes knew Philip would respond in this way. It played into his hands, and he screamed at the Assembly that he had warned them of this power-hungry monster. He urged the Assembly to vote for war against Philip. He said that he would help Athens collect allies and that Thebes would surely join them. His long campaign had at last borne fruit. The Assembly declared war.

* * *

Athens soon raised its citizen army and enthusiastically marched north to join with Thebes to fight Philip. The combined force consisted of ten thousand infantry and six hundred cavalry from Athens, twelve thousand infantry and eight hundred cavalry from Thebes, and the Sacred Band of three hundred devoted fighters. Along with other allies and mercenaries, the total added up to thirty-six thousand infantry and two thousand cavalry. Epaminondas had helped form the Sacred Band, which consisted of Greek lovers, who pledged to defend each other and the band to the death in battle. The veteran Macedonian army of thirty thousand infantry and two thousand cavalry proceeded south to face the allied force near the town of Chaeronea, not far from Thebes.

Philip arrayed his formidable phalanx and awaited the battle with his usual emotion. He loved battle: it was the element he thrived on. His heart beat louder, his head cleared, his eyes focused on the field, and his mind developed his strategy. He was also proud of his oldest son, Alexander, who was fighting his first battle. He had enough confidence in him that he gave him command of the elite cavalry, The Companions, on the left flank, assisted by senior generals and the Thessalian cavalry.

A remarkable youth of eighteen, who'd undergone extensive military training by his father, Alexander was ready. He had learned the strategies of phalanx and cavalry, of siege warfare, and of supply. His heart beat in anticipation, for even though it was his first major battle, he wasn't afraid. His father's son, he felt at home on a horse, leading men, a spear in his hand.

Alexander rode Bucephalus—strong, proud, and as excited for the coming battle as his youthful rider. Alexander's honey-colored curls bounced and caught the sunlight as he galloped along the lines of his men urging them on to victory. He wanted all the men to recognize him before he put on his helmet. His enthusiasm was contagious, and his men cheered him as he passed.

"We will route the Greek cavalry on our end," he encouraged them. "After we have chased them from the field, we will attack the Thebans on the left and engage the Sacred Band. Follow me, my Companions, and we will celebrate a great victory today."

The cavalry yelled, "Victory!" and made ready for the charge.

Philip commanded the right flank, opposite the Athenians. His plan was to draw the Athenians and the Thebans apart and then attack as a wedge between them. The allies had never fought together and were unfamiliar with the Macedonian tactics. A general who was ignorant of military tactics commanded the Thebans on the left. The Athenian general on the right, by contrast, was rash.

The king gave the signal for the battle to begin. The Macedonians gave a great roar and beat their shields, advancing slowly. The Athenians advanced as well and grappled with the wall of spears.

Philip's orders were for the phalanx in the center to draw the Athenian infantry to them and hold them. He led his cavalry against the Athenians, who beat them back. For many hours, the battle was doubtful. Thinking that victory was in sight, the Athenian commander urged his cavalry to pursue Philip's flank on the right. Philip ordered his phalanx to turn on them and thus retrieved his loss. The long spears of the Macedonians could not be breached by the Athenian infantry or horses and bore down everything before them.

Meanwhile, Alexander urged his cavalry to repeated charges against the Thebans on the left. Horses thundered over ground already dampened by blood, and yells filled the air as spears and swords clashed with shields. The horses' whinnies mingled with the cries of dying men, who fell beneath the crashing hooves.

As the Athenians on the right advanced to a perceived advantage, the Thebans on the left were gradually pushed back. They were anchored on the left flank by the Sacred Band, the strong arm of brave Epaminondas. Alexander saw the space that was opening between the Thebans and Athenians and yelled at his companions to charge into it. The disciplined cavalry galloped through the breach, and Alexander wheeled it around to the left around the Theban infantry. He turned to his men following him and pointed at the Theban Sacred Band. "Attack them in the rear!" he yelled above the din of battle.

Philip, meanwhile, was able to break the ranks of the Athenian infantry and pursue its cavalry from the field. He ordered his phalanx to advance in the opening between the Athenians and Thebans. The Thebans took to flight after they saw Alexander turn their flank. The Sacred Band stood their ground, and was killed to the last man.

The victory was complete. Dead and dying men littered the blood-soaked field. The Athenians and Thebans each lost at least one thousand men killed and suffered about seven thousand wounded. The panicked survivors were harassed by Philip's men as they fled to their cities. It was a disaster for the Greek allies. Alexander also showed his ability to use his cavalry and his quick perception on the battlefield to take advantage of the enemy's weakness. This was to be a great weapon for him in future battles.

Demosthenes had encouraged his fellow Athenians and their Theban allies that they fought for freedom against a man who would be a tyrant over them. He fought bravely but was no soldier. Seeing that his fellow Athenians were no match for Philip's phalanx, he began to falter. When he saw the line give way, he threw down his shield and armor and fled.

Hyperiedes found two horses and helped Demosthenes onto one. As they rode away from the slaughter, he turned to Demosthenes. "Better to live and resist Philip than to die on this field."

"Perhaps you're right," Demosthenes said, lowering his head in shame, "but how will the Athenians see me? As a coward running away from the battle."

"You led the good fight against the tyrant and lost," Hyperiedes said. "There is no lack of virtue in that. Your strength lies in your ability as orator and political leader, not as a general. Live and continue to fight Philip."

They rode on to Athens, considering their limited options.

After the battle, Alexander was hailed as a hero. Some of the Companions carried him on their shoulders into camp. The Macedonians cheered him as they bore him to his father's quarters.

Philip received him, hugging him in his huge arms, his face beaming with pride. "I am proud of you, my son. You have proved today to be my true heir. You will lead Macedon to new victories."

"Thank you, Sire, but you must leave some for me." Alexander smiled and embraced his father.

The men cheered, "Hail to Alexander! Hail to the future King of Macedon!"

Philip acknowledged the soldiers and told them with spirit to celebrate their triumph. He bade Alexander to follow him inside his tent. "Now the work of peace begins, Alexander. It is more difficult and less exciting than the thrill of battle, but it is important to solidify the gains of victory. You will watch what we do. I will need you to lead a delegation to Athens."

"Will we ask for the heads of Demosthenes and his friends? Will we garrison the city? What will you do with Thebes?"

"All in good time, my son. However, I see you are already thinking about the political options. Let's celebrate our victory tonight. I can already taste the wine." Philip laughed.

Alexander laughed as well. Then he slapped his father's back and left to change clothes and wash the blood from his body.

* * *

When news of Philip's victory reached Athens, Isocrates realized that his dream of Greek unity had finally come true. "But at what a price?" he lamented to a friend. "I wanted Athens to unite peacefully under Philip in his march against Persia. Instead, Greek blood covers the field of a forced alliance. My beloved Athens lies prostrate and humiliated. The joy of unity and peace, and the disappointment and sorrow of defeat mingle in my breast."

His friends tried to comfort him. "You have seen the unification of Greece, Isocrates. Now, we can invade Asia and free our brothers of Ionia."

"My old eyes are tired," Isocrates said. "They may never see our victory over Persia. Leave me alone now with my feelings of triumph and sorrow."

Yes, he thought sadly, his wish for Greek unity had come true, but at the price of defeat on the bloody battlefield. Philip's leadership would be resented instead of welcomed. Greeks would go to Persia and fight against him. He resigned himself to the reality that he had done what he could.

"I have lived long enough," he confessed to a friend. "Let me die in peace."

Isocrates starved himself and died five days after the battle that had unified Greece. He was ninety-eight.

* * *

Philip's diplomatic triumphs after Chaeronea matched his victory on the battlefield. First, he humbled Thebes. After selling the Theban prisoners into slavery, he disarmed what remained of her army. The Sacred Band had been destroyed and was not allowed to be re-formed. He put to death some of the Theban leaders. "I will appoint a governing council that is favorable to us," he said to his generals. "I will also place a garrison in their fortified acropolis, the Cadmeia. That should keep the Thebans quiet."

Another general spoke up. "What shall we do with Athens?"

"I have already decided that." Philip turned to Alexander. "You will go with Antipater to Athens. Return the Athenian prisoners, and give them back their arms."

"You are being very generous, Sire," said Antipater, "but you've always had a soft spot in your heart for Athens."

"I'm being practical, my friend," said the king. "I want to show them that I am not the monster that Demosthenes has painted me. Their power to wage war is broken, and I need their navy when I invade Asia."

"What of Demosthenes?" Antipater asked. "Should we demand that he be handed over to us?"

"He will be forced into exile, and his mouth has been shut for now. His fellow citizens have seen the folly of his leadership and his cowardice in fleeing the battlefield. Tell the Athenian prisoners that they may also take their slain with them back to Athens for honorable burial. In return, Athens must acknowledge me as leader of all Greek forces against the Persian foe."

"That is very civilized of you, Sire," Alexander said. "Antipater and I will do as you say."

Athens was relieved at Philip's leniency, for they had expected much harsher terms for leading the fight against him. The Assembly was so overjoyed that they welcomed Alexander and Antipater and consented to Philip's terms. Not only that, but they covered Philip with compliments, referring to him as the new Agamemnon, the conqueror of Troy.

* * *

Not long afterward, Philip convened an assembly of all the Greek states in Corinth. All came except Sparta. As usual the Spartans responded to the invitation by demanding that they be the leader of any federation or alliance. Philip ignored the Spartans, who by then had lost what military and political power they once had.

"Greeks, my brothers of the south," Philip addressed the gathered delegates. "We have gained Greek unity. Yes, it was bought with blood, but may that blood be the mortar that seals the peace. I ask only that you elect me as your commander of a united force, which I will use to defeat the Persians and free our Ionian brethren.

"I ask that each city-state among you pledge armed men and money, according to your population, to my army. I also require that you pledge not to fight me or each other. Remember, we all must fight the common foe.

"For my part, I grant that each Greek city may govern itself. They will have their individual freedom as long as their governing bodies are sympathetic to me. I will withdraw my forces to Macedon, trusting that you all will keep the peace among you."

Representatives discussed Philip's proposals and realized that they may have lost a measure of individual freedom, but had exchanged it for unity and a stable peace. Besides, if they acquiesced to Philip's call for arms, it was a small price to pay to keep him away from their walls. They also knew that they were defenseless if he should return from Macedon with his army.

One of the Athenian delegates rose to speak. "The purpose of our league is to avenge the Persian insults. Xerxes burned the temples on our acropolis and insulted the gods. They cry out for revenge. This is our opportunity to do that by uniting behind a man who will lead Greece once more against the Persian menace."

The assembly cheered and voted to name Philip commander-in-chief of all Greek forces for life. The Corinthian League, as it was called, was a brilliant piece of diplomacy for Philip. He had unified Greece, and they had accepted him as leader—and he had done this without having to garrison troops throughout Greece. He also was wise not to proclaim himself king over them, for he knew about Greek sensibilities on that matter. He had learned how to use diplomacy rather than conquest to gain his ends.

CHAPTER 18

The celebrations after the battle and diplomatic victories of Chaeronea making Philip master of Greece, continued over several weeks. Now seeing his way clear to an invasion of Asia, he sent his generals, Parmenio and Attalus to foment rebellion among the Ionian Greeks. Every Macedonian soldier and officer knew they were preparing for war with Persia. But for a while, they would exercise during the days and have drinking parties at night.

After Attalus returned from across the Hellespont, he met with Philip and reported on the progress in Asia. Slaves poured wine for the two men.

Philip was pleased and raised his cup to Attalus. "You and Parmenion have done well. I will send an advanced guard across to Asia next year. Before I join them with the main army, I must first rest my wounds from Chaeronea. My leg still pains me." He put down his cup and rubbed his leg, which was propped up on a stool.

"The army is ready, Sire. You get your strength back to lead it. I have an idea for a celebration. What about a wedding?"

"Whose, Attalus? Yours?" He laughed.

"No, I was thinking that you could strengthen your ties with the Macedonian aristocrats. What about an alliance between your house and mine?" Attalus was a member of an old, established family. "My sister's daughter, Cleopatra, is a beautiful girl."

Cleopatra was a popular Macedonian name, the same as that of Philip's sister.

"I have noticed your niece. How old is she?"

"She is eighteen, Sire, the right age to produce children."

"I can always use more children to carry on my conquests. Cleopatra will be my seventh wife, a lucky number."

"What about Olympias? She will be even more jealous if you marry a woman of Macedon instead of a foreign one."

Philip slammed down his empty cup. "What of her?" He raised his angry voice. "I am sick and tired of her tirades and little intrigues. I know she tries to turn people in court against me. She even makes Alexander resent me. I will not have her undermine my son's loyalty to me." He pounded his fist against the chair.

"They say she is a sorceress and talks with snakes," Attalus submitted.

"Not only that," added Philip, "but she consorts with gods and spirits. She said that a snake in her bed was Apollo." A thought occurred to him. "I know. I will accuse her of infidelity. That will be grounds for me to get rid of her."

"Why don't you send her to her brother, the king of Epirus?"

Philip nodded. "An excellent idea. I will banish her, so I won't have to put up with her acid tongue and jealous conspiracies."

"Then we will have a wedding?" asked Attalus.

"Let us have a wedding, my friend."

Attalus poured another cup of wine for the two of them to toast the coming wedding.

Over the course of the next few months, the wedding preparations were made. The ceremony was to be in the spring, and Olympias was to leave for Epirus in the summer after the spring rains. Alexander's mother had told him about her banishment. Although aware of his mother's violent and jealous nature, he loved her and was angry at his father's treatment of her.

"Your father will marry this Macedonian," Olympia said, angry and bitter, as she and Alexander talked in the sitting room of her house outside the palace. "This will not be like his other wives, who are alliances with foreign powers. This will be of his own court, the niece of his general. You will have to be on your guard to protect your inheritance."

"What do you mean?" Alexander exploded. "I am his eldest and heir. I am a proven leader in battle."

"True," said Olympias, "but Attalus is shrewd. He will use the marriage of his niece to increase his own influence with Philip. He may even convince him that a son of a true Macedonian should inherit the throne."

"He dare not!" Alexander spit out.

"He is not incapable of it. Just be on your guard, my son."

She continued to stoke the fires of anxiety and jealousy within Alexander.

A few days later at the wedding feast following the ceremony, celebration and heavy drinking and eating filled the huge hall. Alexander sat with his friends, quietly brooding. He raised his cup to the toasts for the wedding couple but did not share a drink. He thought about what his mother had told him and realized she would no longer be in Pella to help him. He would have to defend his position himself, but he knew he had good friends that he could rely on.

He looked at his father, who had drunk many toasts, and how he pawed at his new bride. He swallowed the last of his wine and slammed the cup to the table in disgust.

At that point, Attalus arose. "I wish to propose a toast to the king and his new bride. May the gods bless this marriage and send us a legitimate Macedonian son."

Alexander saw Attalus glance in his direction and understood the thinly disguised remark. Anger rose like a fire lit by his clenched fist, to his heart, pounding in his chest, and finally to the crimson flush of his face.

He stood with his empty goblet and threw it at Attalus. "Am I, then, a bastard?" he screamed.

Attalus raised his hand to deflect the cup aimed at his head. Philip yelled at his son, "You dare throw your cup at the uncle of my new bride! You insult him, and me, your father, at his own wedding!"

He rose and reached for a spear from a guard. He tried to come at Alexander, but too many cups of wine and his wounded leg caused him to stumble and fall.

Guests nearby gasped and reached to help the fallen king.

Alexander laughed and pointed at the prone figure. "Here, Macedonians, is the man who would lead you across to Asia, and he cannot cross from one couch to another."

Turmoil broke out as Philip bellowed, trying to stand between two men. Alexander's friends came to his side. Having seen what drinking and violent tempers could do, they quickly hustled Alexander from the hall.

The next day Alexander learned that he was also banished, along with most of his closest friends. He made plans to accompany his mother to Epirus. Over the next few weeks, Alexander heard that Attalus had been promoted and loaded with honors. He saw that his fear was turning into reality—that Attalus would promote a son of his niece to replace him as heir.

* * *

News of the squabbles of the Macedonian court spread through Greece. Some were happy with anything that vexed Philip, while others, who looked forward to his invasion of Asia, were concerned.

The representative of Corinth approached Philip. "We of the Corinthian League salute you, Philip, King of Macedon and captain general of the Greek alliance."

"Thank you. My generals are preparing for the invasion, and one is already in Asia. I have been preoccupied with personal matters here in Pella, or I would be with him."

"It is about those personal matters that I would speak with you. We of the Corinthian League are concerned that your energy is distracted. You have worked hard at bringing peace to Greece, yet you have brought war to your own family. A man who is to lead thousands in great conquests must first have peace in his own house."

"You are right, my thoughtful friend." Philip stroked his beard. "My personal problems have been a distraction. I am especially upset that Alexander dislikes me and is with his mother. She poisons his mind against me." He rubbed his troubled brow.

"Perhaps you should try reconciliation with her."

"How?"

"Does she not have a brother, younger than the one who is king of Epirus?"

"Yes, she does."

"And isn't your younger sister unmarried?"

"I am beginning to see what you're aiming at…a marriage between my sister and Olympias' brother?"

"Yes, Philip, that will accomplish several things. It will conciliate Olympias with another alliance to her family and will make Alexander more comfortable in his mind by sealing his legitimate right as heir. And bringing peace to your family will allow you to concentrate on preparing for war with Persia."

"That is sound advice. Now I see why your city appointed you as delegate to the Corinthian League."

Philip thanked the ambassador for his good counsel, and it was not long afterward that Philip proposed the marriage to the king of Epirus. He said that a marriage of the king's brother to his own sister would give a double bond to their alliance. The king of Epirus could hardly decline the offer of the most powerful man in the Greek world.

After the betrothal was announced, Philip sent word to Alexander and his friends that they were forgiven and allowed to return home. To prove his goodwill, Philip also told Olympias that she would be welcome back in Pella with her family. He would personally escort her back to the palace.

* * *

Alexander and his friends rode into Pella as if returning from a triumphant campaign. The army had come to love the charismatic hero of Chaeronea. The Companions, whom Alexander had commanded during that battle, surrounded him as he rode his magnificent Bucephalus. They cheered, threw garlands at him, and beat their spears on their shields. Philip, together with Alexander's friends who had not been banished, welcomed him at the palace.

Philip also welcomed Olympias and her family. The elaborate festivities, planned well in advance, celebrated the reunion of the royal family. Many dinners were given, and any excuse to carouse was anxiously used, especially among the hard-drinking men of the Macedonian army.

One of the parties was for the king's bodyguard. Attalus paid for the food and made sure there was plenty of fine wine to go around. He attended the party to see that the men had a good time, for he wanted to gain the favor of these men who were close to the king. By then his niece had a son by Philip, and he had hopes that perhaps he would be made heir to the throne, catapulting Attalus' star to the highest heaven.

After the food and entertainment was finished, the crowd passed around more wine, and the party became loud as men talked of battles and women won. The revelers staggered around, laughing, spilling wine, embracing and slapping each other on the back. Attalus joined them, seeing that his party was a success.

Spilled wine made the stone floor slippery. More than once a man lost his balance, spilling more wine. This, of course, exacerbated the riotous atmosphere of the party. One of the older guards fell on his face, throwing a full cup of wine onto the youngest member in the hall. The men around laughed at the beardless youth of only twenty with fair skin and long hair, by the name of Pausanias.

One of the guards nearby said to his neighbor, "Let's have some fun." He then grabbed Pausanias by his wine-soaked tunic. "Here, Pausanias, let's help you with your soiled clothes."

At the signal, several men jerked Pausanias' clothes off.

"My, what a handsome body," one said. Laughter exploded.

"I'll bet you're a virgin, aren't you?" another said.

More loud laughter. The youth blushed.

"Let's show him what it's like!"

Two heavily muscled men held Pausanias face down as, one after another, several of the guards, laughing and making nasty comments, mounted him. The young man knew that struggling would be useless and clenched his teeth, sweated, and groaned with agony as the men had their fun. He could hear laughter fill the hall and recognized Attalus as he stood by and enjoyed the fun at his expense. Finally, they let him up. He didn't allow them to see the tears in his eyes, but wiped the saliva and blood from his lip that he had bitten and reached to pick up his tunic.

The men were still laughing and poking one another. Another besotted guard spoke up. "Wait a minute, Pausanias. I'll bet the stable boys would like to have some fun also!"

With that, they jerked Pausanias' tunic away from him and hustled him to the stables, where the hands had their way with him.

In Macedon the king was available to listen to anyone who had a grievance, particularly if he was a member of the army. He was the chief dispenser of justice. Two days after his traumatic experience, Pausanias asked to speak with the king. He told him of the shameful behavior of his fellow guards and what they did to him at the party. He was abused and humiliated. "Not only that, Sire, but your general, Attalus, stood by and did nothing to stop it. In fact, he seemed to enjoy watching the men take advantage of me." He was shaking with anger.

"What would you have me do, Pausanias?" the king asked.

The youth's face was livid. He stomped his foot and his voice shook. "I want redress for the insult. I want Attalus to apologize to me in public and for the main perpetrators to be punished."

Philip showed some sympathy for the abused young man. "That was indeed a bad thing they did to you. The men had too much to drink. However, I consider it a playful escapade. No harm was done, other than to your feelings. You will get over it. Consider it only as rough men's sport and put it behind you."

"But Sire, I insist that you punish them. Not only were my feelings but my honor was also damaged," Pausanias said, beating his angry fist against his chest.

Philip held up his hand for Pausanias to calm down. "I will not punish them. Attalus is the uncle of my wife. The others are members of my bodyguard." He paused as if considering and folded his hands in front of his body. "But I'll tell you what I'll do. I will give you a promotion and increase your pay." He stood and raised his right hand, as if indicating that the discussion was over. "Now that is all. Just forget this unpleasantness and return to your duties."

Pausanias left, feeling betrayed at having received no justice from the commander he looked up to. Resentment and anger smoldered within his breast. Every day that he went to the bodyguard review, he saw smirks and knowing looks from his fellows. The embarrassment ate at his soul, which cried for revenge.

He went to Olympias. He knew that he would get sympathy from her, for she had no love for Attalus and his niece. He told her of the affair and of Philip's reluctance to redress his wrongs.

"That was a shameful thing that Attalus allowed to happen to you," Olympias said. She saw before her another possible ally to use against Attalus and his niece.

"I can't face my fellow guards without imagining what they think of me! They laugh behind my back. Even the stable boys smirk and tell jokes. I want to kill them all."

"You can't do that, of course."

"Then I would like to kill Attalus!" Pausanias said.

"You can't do that either, because he is protected by Philip."

"I am angry at the king that he did not give me justice and punish my assailants! I can't live with this dishonor. What can I do?" His anger made him tremble.

"You must show that you are a man equal to them. Show your courage in battle." She paused, picked up an apple from a bowl at her elbow, and gazed at it, as if contemplating, realizing.she could use this young man's anger and resentment. She looked up at Pausanias, who was waiting for her to continue. "There may be an opportunity for you to achieve your revenge."

"What is that?" he asked her with hope in his eyes.

"Act as if you have forgiven this affair and that all is well with you. Be courteous to your fellow guards, Attalus, and particularly the king. The wedding will be in a few days. Philip will be at his ease, celebrating the marriage of his sister to my brother. He has made peace with Alexander and doesn't pay any attention to me."

She rose and walked to a window overlooking the palace courtyard. "As a member of the king's bodyguard, you will have an opportunity to get close to the king." She turned to face Pausanias. The light from the window filtered through her hair, giving the appearance of flames emanating from her face. "Hide a dagger in your cloak—and use it." She smiled, realizing that this fool would be her fist of revenge and make Alexander king.

Pausanias squinted at this apparition before him. Was she really a sorceress? "But what of Attalus?"

"Alexander and I will take care of him and his niece after Philip is removed."

"Will Alexander be part of this?"

"Alexander has no love for his father and is anxious to be king. I will not tell him of our plot, even though I'm sure you will have his sympathy. He will no doubt reward you afterward with a new command. Then you can laugh at the fellows who dishonored you."

Pausanias smiled at the thought. Revenge would leave a sweet taste in his mouth. "My old teacher told me something. He said to me, 'Do you know how you can become the most famous man in the world? Kill the most famous man in the world.'"

"Yes, Pausanias," Olympias agreed. "Your name will be famous. You will be remembered as the man who killed Philip of Macedon. No one must know of this conversation, for I will deny it. Now go and do your duty for your honor—and for Alexander and me."

* * *

The wedding festivities were to begin the next week, and the royal guests made their way to Aegae, where the arrangements were prepared. Aegae, the ancient capital of Macedon before it was moved to Pella, had a large amphitheater used for important festivals, and was to be the setting for the wedding ceremony. The festivities would last for three days.

On the first day, the bride and groom would meet and pledge their troth, the families of both acknowledging the betrothal. Ceremonies and sacrifices would follow in the temple, and all would drink to the couple.

The second day would see the formal marriage ceremony in the large amphitheater, with all the ambassadors and representatives in attendance. Feasting in the old palace and drinking into the night would follow. The married couple would be accompanied, with much merrymaking to their bedchamber, and the party would return to the banquet hall for more celebration.

On the third day, after noon, the wedding couple would emerge from their room and acknowledge the congratulations of their guests and general people outside the palace. Such were the plans for this marriage between two royal houses.

On the day of the actual ceremony, Philip prepared to enter the theater, crowded with his generals, nobles of both kingdoms, and representatives of many cities. He wore a new purple robe embroidered with gold thread. A cleverly crafted, heavy gold chain hung from his neck, and a new crown set with a large red jewel adorned his brow. He stroked his beard and inhaled the expensive oils that anointed it. Before he started down the covered passageway to the orchestra, he turned and looked around him.

He said to his bodyguard, "Do not walk ahead of me or surround me as I enter the amphitheater. I don't want everyone to think I am afraid to go to my sister's wedding without a guard." He smiled, and the officer of the guard nodded to his men, who parted away from the king.

Philip walked down the covered walkway and noticed Pausanias. He remembered the guard who had been abused by his fellows and nodded to him. Pausanias bowed his head to the king. As Philip passed close to him, Pausanias pulled a knife from under his cloak and thrust it deeply under the king's ribs. He pushed it up to the hilt with all his anger behind it, hoping to reach his heart.

Gasping and stumbling, Philip fell to his knees coughing blood. As Pausanias withdrew the dagger, a spout of red followed the knife and began to flow down the stone walkway. The king's crown fell to the feet of Alexander, who picked it up and knelt by his father, lifting his head and holding him in his arms.

Alexander could hardly believe what was happening. He bellowed like an animal, tears filling his eyes. He screamed, "The king is murdered!" Blood covered his hands and cloak as he tried to staunch the crimson flood coming from Philip. He looked around for other conspirators who would assassinate him also, but none threatened him.

Pausanias was immediately disarmed and grabbed by nearby guards. His defense was useless, as his bloody knife lay at his feet. Alexander saw Attalus make his way to the king and look at his mortal wound. He glanced at Alexander with a warning look and walked over to Pausanias. He slapped the young man hard. "You have killed our king, who would have led us to conquer Asia!"

Pausanias spit in his face. "I care not about Asia. I killed him because he would not redress the wrongs that you allowed. I will have my trial and shout to the world how you let your men ravage me!"

Attalus picked up the fallen knife and calmly wiped it on Pausanias' cloak. "You have had your trial, and you are found guilty of the murder of King Philip of Macedon. A sentence of death is passed."

He reached up and grabbed Pausanias' hair, jerked back his head, and slit his throat. Pausanias choked and crumpled, blood pouring from the gaping wound.

Alexander watched Attalus execute Pausanias and then looked down at the dying figure in his arms. His father's eyes were fluttering, the light of life fading. He could see that his lips were trying to form his last words. "Alexander, my son…" Then he gave a last sigh, and his eyes became fixed.

"The king is dead," Alexander croaked. He could barely register the fact. This man, who had Greece under his fist and would conquer Asia, was gone. What would happen now? Who would take his place?

CHAPTER 19

Philip was only forty-seven and at the height of his power when Pausanias cut him down. The bravest of the brave, even his enemy, Demosthenes, grudgingly admired him. A true leader of men, he commanded from the thick of battle, leaving a part of himself on every battlefield. He had lost an eye, broken a shoulder, and partially paralyzed an arm and leg to fulfill his goals of strengthening Macedon, unifying Greece, and preparing to invade Asia.

He left Alexander an impressive inheritance. In addition to the best trained and equipped army in the world, Alexander inherited lands directly governed or allied to Macedon from the Adriatic to the Bosporus, and from the tip of Greece to the Danube. Under Philip, Greece was unified and politically stable. He had done what Greeks had never been able to do for themselves.

Even so, many Greeks, especially in the larger cities of Thebes and Athens, found Philip's controls hard to bear. Political stability for them was not worth the price of the loss of liberty to conduct their own affairs. Alexander had also inherited this rebellious attitude of the Greek states. But first he had to secure his position as heir to the throne, which was not totally assured. The throne of Macedon was not hereditary, the kings being elevated by common consent of the army and its leaders.

Alexander put on mourning garments and followed the carriage that carried his father's body back to the capital. Philip's generals accompanied him, as did the representatives of allied cities. The news had preceded them to Pella, and the citizens lined the streets, weeping, wailing, and tearing at their clothes. Army officers and soldiers followed the king's cortège to the palace, where the body was laid on a stone altar.

The generals took Alexander out onto the balcony of the palace, overlooking the large plaza and the assembled Macedonian troops. The soldiers and citizens in the open area and streets leading to it watched in hushed anticipation. The chief generals flanked Alexander. On his right, Antipater raised Alexander's arm and shouted, "Hail Alexander, King of Macedon!"

He knew Alexander was Philip's chosen heir, and he had proven his leadership and courage in battle. The army loved this handsome young warrior with a magnetic personality. The people all yelled, "Hail Alexander, King of Macedon!" as the troops beat their spears on their shields.

He was only twenty years of age, and the ambassadors who had gathered for the wedding were skeptical that this inexperienced boy could hold together Philip's kingdom, much less the allies and the Greeks.

Alexander was no young fool, however. His father had been carefully preparing him for years. He had observed closely how power worked, both in the palace and in the world outside of Macedon. He was precocious in mind as well as body. His father had left him in charge at Pella once when he was only sixteen. His judgment of men and their loyalties was keen, and he had an uncanny ability to manage events in crises.

In his veins flowed the blood of two very different individuals. Alexander had his father's talent for organization, military strategy, and leadership. He had also inherited his weakness for drunken excess. From his mother, Alexander received his sense of divine destiny, his belief that he was a descendent of the gods. She had also given him his darker nature, which could lead to bloodthirsty slaughter and torture. He would exceed both.

Olympias moved quickly to gain Alexander's ear. "You must kill anyone who has any claim to the kingdom," she said. She sat in the large chair she had used when she was mistress of the royal palace and wore a long robe of red and blue wool with threads of silver. Her snake belt of woven gold encircled her waist, and she fingered a bronze replica of a snake in her lap.

Alexander paced in front of her. "I know what I must do, Mother."

"Attalus, his niece Cleopatra, and her son by Philip must die," she demanded.

"I have already given the order. They will be taken care of."

"What about your half-brothers? Surely all the sons of Philip's other wives have to be eliminated."

"I don't want to appear as a Persian tyrant, who kills all his brothers when he attains the throne," Alexander said. He faced his mother and spread out his hands. "After all, some of my half-brothers are close friends, who are loyal to me, and will serve me well. I will find out if any of them plan anything against me."

"How will you know whom to trust and whom to arrest?"

"I have my informers."

Alexander listened to his mother and knew what he had to do. He left her and began his plans. He was threatened from all sides, from within and without. Conspirators at home were anxious to carve up the kingdom. Rebellions in the north and in Illyria broke out. Demosthenes had returned to Athens and was again making trouble among the Greeks. Some of Alexander's generals advised him to let the Corinthian League and the Greeks go their way and to concentrate on securing Macedon.

Alexander met with Antipater, for his father's closest adviser was now his. Alexander stood before the raised platform and chair the king sat upon, when addressing important gatherings in this large room. Paved with colored marble, the hall was lined with stone benches, above which were carved and painted scenes of Philip's victories.

"I will not give in to rebels in the north or in Greece," he was explaining to Antipater. "If I let them have their way, I will appear weak. If they succeed, then what is to stop others of our allies from breaking away? Our neighbors will invade us."

"That is sound reasoning, Alexander. But you must act soon, before our enemies can gather strength."

"What do you suggest, my old friend?"

"First, you must be sure of the loyalty of the generals. They command the army. Without it, you have no power whatsoever."

"That is very true." Alexander stood, silently considering his strategy. "The Companions and rank and file of the phalanxes and cavalry love me. I am convinced of that. I must assure myself of the generals." He faced Antipater with his legs wide, hands on his hips. As if issuing a command, he said, "Bring all the chief officers to this room at noon tomorrow. Tell them we must prepare our plans."

"Yes, Sire." Antipater bowed his head slightly and left.

Alexander faced the situation with the decisive energy that set the pattern for the rest of his life—not to wait for events to play out, but to face them with decision and action. He knew that he had to appear as a king and act like one. Before the meeting with his officers, he put on his carefully polished best armor. He entered the room after everyone had assembled and strode purposefully to the raised platform. He sat on the throne until the room fell silent, then rose and addressed the men.

"I am Philip's son and true heir. I have demonstrated that his blood flows in my veins by my command and victory at Chaeronea. He built

Macedon into its greatest power. Now his alliances and victories are threatened by revolt and conspiracies, planning to finish the work of Pausanias. They wish to kill me and divide the kingdom, to return to the old days in which tribe and noble and general all fought one another for petty power.

"As Philip's successor, I will not allow that to happen. I will protect the legacy he left me and carry on his plan to invade Asia. Though the name has changed, the king remains."

The generals looked at one another, gauging support for the young king. Most wore their armor, some only a short undergarment or tunic. These were hard men, veterans of many wars, and were accustomed to the discipline of Philip's army. This was an untried youth on the king's dais. He had proven himself in one major battle, but he was king in name only. He still had to prove himself in their eyes.

Alexander continued his speech, stirring up their patriotism and their loyalty both to Macedon and to King Philip's legacy. The generals all agreed with their young leader, nodding and from time to time saying yes or beating their chests in salute.

"With your help," Alexander continued, "I will destroy any conspirators; I will crush the northern rebels; I will bring the Greek allies back under our protection; then, as ordained by the gods, we will invade Asia and fight our true enemy—Persia." He raised his voice to a shout. "Are you with me?"

They all yelled, "Yes!"

"Do I have your undying loyalty unto death?"

They all yelled again, "Yes!"

"We are with you, Alexander," one said.

"We will follow you as we followed your father," said another.

They all began to affirm their loyalty, and Alexander held up his hands for quiet, as well as to acknowledge their affirmations. He knew now that he had them behind him. "Thank you all. I know you will serve me, as you did my father. Now we must make plans." He turned to the officer in charge of the king's security. "Aretas," he said, "round up any persons suspected of conspiring or aiding conspirators against us. Torture them if you must to uncover all the traitors.

"My generals, mobilize the army and prepare it to march south into Greece. We must show them our strength and that we mean to enforce the League of Corinth and all of its stipulations."

He turned to another officer. "Lead a scouting party north and find out what the northern tribes are doing. Take with you Thracians and Illyrians, who know how to infiltrate and spy."

Alexander again addressed the entire group. "Now let us all get busy, and we will retain the power Philip left us."

His contagious energy filled his generals, not only with the desire to do his bidding but with the will to conquer all opposition. They knew now that they had a leader they could follow, and set about their duties with enthusiasm and determination.

Within a few days, suspected conspirators filled the cells. Alexander condemned a few of them to death. "All possible opposition must be removed at home before I can safely venture to face our enemies abroad. I want to make an example of them. I want them to be beaten in public and beheaded."

His orders were obeyed. Some of his half-brothers, as well as Attalus, Cleopatra, and her son, were murdered in private.

* * *

In Athens, on hearing of the assassination of Philip, Demosthenes rejoiced and put on festival garb. He had the major streets and meeting areas festooned with banners and flowers. People walked through the streets shouting and celebrating the news. Many of the leaders of the party opposing Philip copied Demosthenes and put on their more colorful clothes, placing vines and wreathes around their heads.

Demosthenes called for the Assembly to meet and mounted the speaker's platform with a garland of flowers on his head. He acknowledged the cheering throng that spilled out of the seating area and raised his hands for silence. With a smile as big as the Parthenon, he said, "I rejoice that the despot, King Philip of Macedon, who would enslave all of Greece, is dead."

All the people rose in hysterical shouts and applause. Those who had supported Philip were not present. They feared that the young Alexander would not be as forceful a leader as his father, and their hope for Greek unity was lost.

Demosthenes continued, "An assassin's dagger has freed all of Greece again. We Greeks love our freedom and chafe under the yoke of tyranny, especially when it is disguised. No one shall tell us what to do, even if it means Greek unity. For the price of unity is too high, if it means slavery.

"The northern tribes in Thrace and Illyria are already in revolt. Many Greek cities have renounced their allegiance, and Ambraciotes has expelled its Macedonian garrison. Athens and Thebes must lead the way in demolishing the League of Corinth.

"The great King of Kings, Artaxerxes of Persia, has boasted that it was he who instigated the killing of Philip. No doubt his gold is still finding its way into the pockets of certain people in Macedon, who would be opposed to invasion of Persia. Artaxerxes says that he has nothing to fear from the stripling who has taken Philip's place. I say that we should not fear this boy either. We must take this opportunity to revolt against the fist of Macedon."

Shouts of approval filled the air. "Death to Alexander!" yelled some.

Others shouted, "Down with Macedon!"

Still others screamed, "War!"

Demosthenes raised his hands for silence. "As a symbol of that rebellion, I place before the Assembly a proposition that it vote a crown of honor for Pausanias. He gave his life so that ours may be free. He was not an assassin but a patriot, who delivered us from the bloody hands of a tyrant."

The Assembly roared with approval and unanimously voted the honor to Pausanias' memory.

Not long afterward, the rest of Greece declared itself absolved from Macedonian rule, since Philip was dead. The revolt of all Greece was imminent.

* * *

News of the events in Athens and the rest of Greece came quickly to Pella, as Philip had placed his ears throughout those cities. Alexander knew what he must do. He must show decisive will and overwhelming force in pacifying Greece before he could fight the rebels in the north. The generals had prepared the army, and it was ready to march. Within days the surprised city of Thebes found it at its borders, and the Greeks realized they were not dealing with a weak heir of Philip. The alarming news of the Macedonian advance spread throughout Greece, and Alexander soon received delegates from the Greek cities.

"Most of the Greek states have renewed their allegiances, Alexander," a senior general reported. "They have reconfirmed on you all the rights and honors they had given to your father."

"What of the League of Corinth?" Alexander asked.

"A meeting of all the Greek states, except Sparta, of course, has proclaimed you captain general of all the Greeks and has promised to contribute men and supplies for an Asiatic campaign."

Within a few days, Alexander heard from Athens. "Athens sends you its profuse apology," said the meek ambassador.

"What of that thorn Demosthenes and the Assembly he leads by the nose?" Alexander asked with squinted eyes.

"Demosthenes has been silenced. Those who oppose him have convinced Athens that she alone cannot resist your power. The Assembly bowed to that reality. In fact, they voted to give you two crowns of victory and conferred upon you divine honors. I present you with those laurels." The ambassador laid the two wreaths at Alexander's feet.

Alexander saw how fickle the Athenian Assembly was. He was also aware that marching armies and cold steel create the true reality. "Tell the Assembly that I accept their honors. I am flattered to receive them. As a mark of my good intentions, I will send notice to all the Greek states that are members of the League, that all dictatorships are to be abolished. Each city shall be free to live according to its own laws. I merely ask, like King Philip, that they do not war against me or each other." Alexander had taken a page out of Philip's book and coated the cold steel with honey. He knew how sensitive the Greeks were about their precious independence, and he needed their support.

"Thank you, Sire." The Athenian representative was relieved by Alexander's generosity and left to report it to his city.

Now assured of his security in Greece, Alexander returned to Pella to put the capital in order and prepared to quell rebellion in the north.

CHAPTER 20

Only a day after Alexander had returned to his capital, Olympias came to see him. "The news preceded you that the Greeks have reconfirmed Philip's powers on you. Congratulations, my son." She kissed him on the cheeks.

"Thank you, Mother. Even the Athenian Assembly voted me divine honors."

"As well they should, since you are the son of Zeus."

"All dangers are not resolved, however," Alexander admitted. "I must put down the revolts in the north."

"You must also crush any thoughts of rebellion here at home," Olympias insisted "There are still grumblings about your succession. I think you must arrest and execute all your half-brothers, and anyone else who has given aid or comfort to the conspirators."

"The army loves me," he assured her. "They respect my courage and leadership. They will follow me."

"Yes, Alexander, but you will be taking the army with you to conquer Asia. No opposition must be left behind. Even your generals cannot be fully trusted if you show weakness."

"I will have any conspirators executed," he insisted.

"Not just executed. They should be made examples. You must torture them without mercy. Flay them alive, and then have them burned."

"Mother, I will have them whipped and then beheaded. That is punishment and example enough. I will not show Molossian barbarism by skinning them and burning them. I must show that I am a Macedonian."

"You are not just a Macedonian, Alexander. You are the son of Zeus. You have a destiny. You will conquer the world. Nothing can stop you, because your father, Zeus, will aid you."

"Yes, Mother." He held up his hand to stop her. "I believe it. I will fulfill my destiny. First, I will destroy my enemies at home and those abroad. I will put Antipater in charge of Pella, while I lead the army north. He will arrest any conspirators."

"But Alexander, I demand…"

Alexander put up his hands in front of his face. "That's enough," he silenced her. "I will take care of matters. Now leave me so I can make plans for my campaign."

* * *

While Alexander campaigned, Olympias continued her grasping for power and influence. She demanded of Antipater that he be more aggressive against possible conspirators. "Put them all in prison and torture them," she commanded him.

"I cannot imprison all of Pella," he complained.

"Then do so for anyone who might oppose Alexander—all of his half-brothers, all their followers and relatives, even their tutors."

"But Olympias, even their tutors?"

"I suspect that Athenian, Phidias, who tutored Alexander's brothers and sons of the aristocrats. He is known to teach about democracy, and rights, and such nonsense. I believe he is a spy and has encouraged their conspiracy."

"What evidence do you have for such accusation?" Antipater put forth.

"Evidence? I need none other than my suspicion. Arrest and torture him; he will confess."

Antipater saw that further argument would be useless against this willful, vengeful woman. He bowed and left to fill the prisons with suspects.

Antipater had Phidias thrown into a prison under the walls of the palace, along with other suspected conspirators. Moisture seeped through the mold-covered walls in the dark cell. Occassionally a rat scurried under the straw that was the only bedding for prisoners. Frightened and depressed, Phidias shivered against the damp chill, hugging his torn and dirty robe closer. From time to time men would be dragged from the cell, followed by sounds of blows and screams echoing back through the halls. Afterward, the bloody and beaten form would be thrown into the cell, the partly conscious victim moaning in agony.

Phidias was horrified. He had not witnessed the effects of torture firsthand before, and he imagined that he might be the next victim of the torturer. He sat despondent with his head bowed between his knees, pondering his fate—most likely a painful one.

Some of Phidias' former students also shared his cell and were shocked to see him there. They knew him as an intelligent, calm teacher with no political ambitions.

"Master Phidias," said Crastas, one of Alexander's half-brothers. "My brothers and I know why we are imprisoned, but we also know that you had nothing to do with any conspiracy. Aretas and his men have orders to arrest anyone under the least suspicion. Certainly you had nothing to do with any conspiracy. Have you probably been arrested because you were our teacher?"

"That is possibly so, Crastas, but what can I do?" Phidias asked. "I am helpless and will probably share your fate. Sometimes there is no justice, and the innocent suffer along with the guilty."

"But surely Alexander doesn't know you're here. He loves and respects Master Aristotle, and you are his friend. He holds in highest regard the philosophers of Athens, as did his father. Surely he will listen to you. You must proclaim your innocence in this matter."

Phidias thought a moment. "You may be right, Crastas. I must be allowed to speak with Alexander, and convince him of my innocence. I'm sure he'll listen to reason. But he is in the north. How will I get word to him before the torturer works his will upon me? I am not a strong Macedonian like you and will likely admit to anything under torture."

Phidias sank back against the cold, damp wall in hopeless dread.

* * *

Alexander marched his army from Pella to suppress the northern barbarian tribes. In a series of swift marches, decisive strategy, and bloody battles, he subdued the closest of them. Then turning to Thrace, he put down the revolt there and accepted its allegiance. Not pausing in his swift campaign, he moved north through the Balkans, fought his way to the Danube, crossed it in a surprise move, and destroyed all resistance. The northern tribes were awed into submission and never gave him trouble again.

While his army was engaged that far north, the Illyrians to Macedon's west seized the diversion and invaded that country. In a brilliant and decisive action, Alexander's force marched two hundred miles and surprised the invaders in their rear. Soundly defeating them, he drove the survivors back to their mountain homes, left his army there to recover, and sped back to Pella to make sure the situation there was under control. These campaigns and battles proved Alexander's strategic genius and solidified his support among his officers and men.

Meanwhile Phidias had despaired of getting any word to Alexander. He sat in a filthy cell eating spoiled food, his clothes almost rags. His turn had come with the beatings. His eyes were blackened and blood matted his hair and beard, but he had denied that he was a spy or knew of any conspiracy. A rat ran across his feet, but he was too distracted to kick at it. There must be someone who can help me get to Alexander, he thought. It suddenly occurred to him. Of course, his friend Aristotle. So obvious. Why hadn't he thought of him before? He rose, shuffled to the door, and called out to the guard.

The guard slowly walked over and spat at Phidias. "What do you want, Athenian dog?"

"Let me speak with your captain."

"Why should I? You will all die in a few days, and good riddance."

"Please. I must speak with him. Here is a gold coin for your trouble."

The guard snatched the coin from his hand and said, "I will ask the captain if he wants to see you. I promise nothing."

The captain came about an hour later. "I got your message, philosopher. What is it you want of me?"

"Captain, I implore you. I am innocent of any wrongdoing. I have nothing to do with Macedonian politics. You may not believe me, but there is one who will. Would you please send a message to Aristotle to come and see me? I have a little money on me. It is all yours if you will do as I ask. Please."

Phidias handed a small coin purse to the officer.

The captain took the money and said, "I don't know if I should help a spy and conspirator. Athens has been treacherous in opposing Macedon. However, because Kings Philip and Alexander respect Athenian philosophers, I will take your message to Aristotle myself."

"Thank you, Captain. You will not be sorry."

"We shall see," he said as he turned, leaving Phidias in the dark, foul-smelling dungeon.

Aristotle came within the hour after receiving Phidias' message. "I heard that you had been imprisoned and will be executed for aiding the brothers of Alexander. I was shocked and tried to see you but was not allowed. Is it true?"

"No ! I had nothing to do with any conspiracy. In fact, I warned against it."

"To whom? Can you prove it?"

"One of Alexander's half-brothers, Melias, approached me. He asked that I enlist you and that we both give our support to him and his half-brothers. They said that they should inherit something of Philip's kingdom."

"What did you say?"

"I told him that they should all profess their loyalty to Alexander," Phidias explained.

"Will he corroborate your statement?"

"I don't know. I haven't seen or talked with him. He must be in another cell…or already dead."

Aristotle took Phidias' right hand between his and said, "If Melias is here, I will find and speak with him. Don't despair, my friend. We will set this matter right, and you will be freed."

"Please hurry, before I die of the beatings or am beheaded," Phidias pleaded.

"I will," Aristotle assured him. He went to the door and yelled for the guard. He asked to be taken to the captain.

"Do you have Melias, one of the king's brothers?" Aristotle asked the captain.

"Yes. Melias is here," said the captain. "He is in a cell with some of the main plotters."

"I would like to speak with him."

"I don't know if I can allow that."

"You know who I am. I am Aristotle, whom King Philip brought to teach the young Alexander, now your king. Do I have to tell him that you refused to allow me to speak with a prisoner?"

"All right, Master Aristotle. Follow me," said the captain.

Aristotle found Melias with black eyes and split lips, his tunic torn and bloody. "Are you all right?" Aristotle asked.

"I have been better. My consolation is that the suffering will soon be over. Why have you come to see me, Master Aristotle?"

"I don't know if you are aware that your teacher, Master Phidias, is also imprisoned."

"Not Master Phidias! What has he done?"

"Nothing. His only crime seems to be that he taught you and your brothers. He told me that you approached him to draft me to aid you."

"That is true, but he refused. In fact, he told us to profess loyalty to Alexander."

"That's what he said. Would you be willing to tell Alexander that?"

"Certainly, but why would Alexander listen to me? I am to be executed along with everyone else."

"That is precisely why he may listen. You have nothing to gain from him. You may, however, gain the freedom for your innocent teacher. If I can get Alexander's permission for you to speak with him, will you support Phidias and recount what he said to you?"

"I will, gladly."

"Good. I will speak with the king."

Before he left the prison, Aristotle told Phidias that he had found Melias and that he would support his innocence. "I will get word to Alexander somehow, my friend. Don't give up hope."

* * *

Alexander returned to Pella and received reports from Antipater and Aretas of the situation in the capital and of the conspirators who filled the prisons. He went over the list and said that he would speak with some before pardoning them or condemning them to death. He was surprised at one name. "Phidias? Is this Master Phidias, the friend of Aristotle?"

"Yes, Sire," Antipater was apologetic. "Your mother insisted that I arrest him."

"What has he done? Has he confessed anything?"

"No, Sire," Aretas said. "He maintains that he is innocent."

"As a matter of fact, Alexander," Antipater added, "Aristotle has asked to speak with you as soon as you returned. I didn't think it was important."

"It may be important," Alexander said thoughtfully. "It may be about his friend in prison. Bring him to me."

Aristotle told Alexander of Phidias' plight and of what Melias and Phidias had told him. Alexander knew that his half-brother Melias had plans of obtaining part of the kingdom. For Aristotle's sake, he would listen to what Phidias and Melias had to say.

"I will have them brought here. I want you to be present also," Alexander told his teacher.

Phidias and Melias were allowed to wash off the dirt and blood, and were given clean clothes before being presented to Alexander. Phidias was brought in first.

"I have respect for you, Master Phidias," Alexander said. "I know of your reputation as an intelligent, kind teacher, and have also learned much history from you. I am told that you have been imprisoned as a spy and advisor to those who would conspire to assassinate me. Is that true?"

"No, Sire, I am innocent. I am no spy and am part of no conspiracy."

"You were tutor to my brothers and sons of nobles for three years. Did you not teach them of the governments of other Greek states and foreign countries?"

"I did."

"Did you not tell them of Athens democracy and how power is shared with the people?"

"I did."

"Those are dangerous ideas for Macedon, Master Phidias. We are not as civilized as you Athenians. We need a strong leader with discipline to guide the army and rule our allies."

"I am aware of that, Sire."

Alexander continued, "Then isn't it plausible that suspicion should be placed on you as an Athenian spy and instigator of rebellion against me?"

"It's plausible," Phidias stammered, "but I…"

"However," Alexander interrupted, "because you are Master Aristotle's friend, I will listen to what you have to say for yourself."

Phidias stood erect and stated his case with conviction. "I am no spy, Sire. I am but a teacher with no political interests other than what is historical. I did not influence your brothers, the sons of nobles, or any army officers to oppose you. In fact, I implored them to reaffirm their loyalty to you. Apparently they did not heed my advice. Ask Melias if this is not true."

"But you knew of the plot and did not report it."

"I knew of no plot. But even if I did, and had given my oath, I could not break it, even for a king."

"I appreciate your integrity, Phidias. Now I know you would keep an oath to me as well."

Alexander turned to a guard, "Now bring Melias in."

Phidias stole a glance at Aristotle, who had been standing to the side. Aristotle nodded his assurance to his friend.

Melias was brought in. A deep cut above his right eye had not healed, and a large bruise colored his left cheek. He did not bow, but stood with courage and pride before his half-brother, now king.

"As for you, Brother," Alexander addressed Melias, "I am disappointed that you would oppose me when I could use your leadership in Asia. I don't know if I should trust anything you have to say."

"I will speak the truth on my honor as a Macedonian officer," Melias stated. "I am not ashamed of my wish to share your power. After all, I am King Philip's son also."

"True, but I'm afraid that you and some of your half-brothers would continue to plague me and my country if I spared you, and might also be manipulated by foreign enemies, including Persia. You know what your fate must be. But that is not why I had you brought here. Master Aristotle asked that I listen to what you have to say concerning Master Phidias."

"My brother," Melias began, "I know that you will order my execution, and I accept my fate. I will not beg or cry for mercy." He straightened his back and winced at the strain on his torn muscles. "I opposed you because I feared you would exile or kill most of us anyway. We know well how your mother despises the other wives and sons of Philip and how you are influenced by her cruel plans. We all believed she would have you murder us."

Alexander held up his hand to silence Melias. "Enough of my mother. I didn't bring you here to listen to you speak ill of her. What of Phidias?"

Melias bowed his head in obedience. "As for Master Phidias, he is innocent." He recounted how he had approached his teacher to enlist Aristotle to help them. "He refused. In fact, he pleaded with me to bend the knee of loyalty to you. I rejected that advice and must pay the price. I do not apologize for it. I wish no harm to come to Master Phidias because of my action."

Alexander replied, "I accept your statement as a Macedonian officer. I am convinced that Master Phidias is innocent. You have asked for no mercy, and I respect that. Therefore, I will shorten your stay in prison and have you and the other conspirators executed in the morning, without further torture." He turned to Phidias and nodded. "Master Phidias, you are free."

Outside the chamber, Phidias fell into Aristotle's arms and wept. "Thank you, my friend," he said. "I feared I was going to be executed. I did not fear death itself, but only the pain of the beatings."

Aristotle held Phidias at arm's length and said with tears in his own eyes, "We should all face death as if it is inevitable and order our lives as if each day could be our last. It is not the immediate happiness of today that a man should be satisfied with. His happiness should be in the realization that he has done something to make his life meaningful. We are all in this world to improve it and ourselves.

"Our death is not the end of our influence, only of our earthly existence. The people we touch, the students we teach, will carry on and influence the generation after that. The books we write will survive long after us, and, because of them, we will live on as well. Therefore, be thankful that you have had to face death. Learn from that experience. It will help you give meaning to your life."

"Thank you, Aristotle. You are very wise. I thank whatever gods there may be for sending you into my life. I will try to do as you have advised."

They went to Aristotle's chambers, where Phidias enjoyed the first good meal and wine he had had in several weeks. Then after a warm bath, he fell into an exhausted sleep.

CHAPTER 21

Rumors reached Athens that Alexander had been killed while campaigning in Illyria. Demosthenes was at first incredulous. "This news is too good to be true," he told a friend. "He has not been king yet a whole year."

"Why not?" his colleague replied. "He had to put down conspiracies in Macedon and then marched off to fight rebels along the Danube and in Illyria. He has been beset by troubles."

"Who brought this rumor? Let me speak with him," Demosthenes demanded.

A man from an allied state, who had lost an eye fighting for Alexander, was brought to Demosthenes. He walked with the aid of a crutch, a dirty rag covering his right eye. "What is your name?" Demosthenes asked.

The man told him.

"I hear that you saw Alexander of Macedon slain. Tell me of it."

He spoke slowly as if the pain he had received in battle came back to him in the retelling. "It was at the battle of Pelium in Illyria. We were outnumbered by the enemy, who also occupied the surrounding hills. Alexander devised a clever ruse and surprised the barbarians who retreated. He led a charge with his Companions cavalry. I saw him in the thickest of the battle. A sling stone hit him in the head, and he fell from his horse. Before he could regain it, he was clubbed from behind. I saw him fall, blood streaming from his head. He didn't get up. The wound appeared fatal."

"Then we can assume he's dead. Praise the gods. Get this man some food and clean clothes." Demosthenes was jubilant. He turned to his friends. "Make sure the exiles from Thebes know of this, and spread the word through Athens."

There were several Thebans living in Athens, who had left their city after the battle of Chaeronea and Philip had placed the Macedonian garrison there. Eager to use any opportunity for Thebes to throw off the yoke of Macedon, they met with Demosthenes.

"Will Athens support Thebes if she expells the Macedonian garrison?" their leader asked.

Demosthenes sat with other Athenians who opposed Macedon. "I can assure you that Athens will support you. I will also send letters to other Greek states. Now that Alexander is dead, none of them owe allegiance to Macedon. Persia will also give aid."

"What if the Macedonians come back to attack Thebes? They are still led by Philip's generals. Will Athens send men?"

Demosthenes comforted the Thebans. "I believe I can persuade the Assembly to send an army to help if necessary. I will send a letter with you supporting the Thebans in their rebellion and assuring them of Athens' aid."

"That is all we need. I and the other exiles will leave tomorrow for Thebes."

A group of about twenty exiles approached the gates of Thebes after dark. They had sent word ahead to some friends, who met them.

The next day the leaders of the revolt spread the news throughout the city. Armed citizens besieged the garrison, killing two Macedonian officials in the process. One of the leaders of the Thebans yelled in triumph, "Send a message to Athens of our action, and request the aid Demosthenes has promised,"

"Persia has also offered money," said another Theban. "But I don't think that what is left of Alexander's army can be here anytime within a month. They're still in Illyria."

"We shouldn't waste time my friend. The Macedonians will return and try to relieve their garrison. We must prepare for them."

Thebes sent messages to other Greek cities for support and prepared her defenses by building a rampart and stockade along the south side of the city between two rivers, just outside the hill of the Cadmeia.

When news reached Alexander about Thebes, he was furious. One of his generals explained, "The rumor that your injuries in Illyria were fatal spurred Thebes and Athens to rebel again. They have asked for Persian support."

Alexander had returned from Pella to Illyria, where the army was recuperating and refitting. He paced in his tent, fuming at the Thebans' act of treachery, not recognizing it as an act of passion for their freedom.

"How dare they act this way! It is ingratitude and perfidy. I was so generous during their last revolt, after my father died. My officials and garrison were there to help them. We have even taken Theban youths to train in our army."

"It seems," stated Antipater, "that the Greeks have forgotten the lesson of Chaeronea, and the Thebans their loss of the Sacred Band."

"They may think that Macedon has lost its king again," said Alexander, "but I will assure them that I am alive. I will lead the army to Thebes." He pounded his fist on the table.

"Sire," another general spoke up, "the army is still recuperating from our hard-fought battles. We have lost several hundred men and must replace our arms and supplies. Perhaps we can be ready in a month."

"We don't have a month!" Alexander exploded. "The longer we wait, the stronger the Greeks will get. They will use Persian gold to obtain mercenaries. No, we must invade now. We must surprise them, for they will least expect us."

"But Alexander," Antipater said, "Thebes is a three-hundred-mile march. The army is exhausted."

"And have I not endured the same battles and wounds that they have?" Alexander demanded. "I would not ask of my men any more than I myself would endure. We cannot allow the Greeks to succeed in defying Macedon. I see my standing in Greece in grave danger, unless this revolt is nipped in the bud. If they're successful, we cannot proceed with plans to invade Asia.

"It is Persia that is paying the Greeks to oppose us. We must cut off this arm of the Great King before we can face the main body of his army. Therefore, my generals, it is my order that you rearm and supply your men. We will march to Thebes in five days."

The army was ready in record time. After thirteen days of arduous marching, they reached Thebes. The Thebans were completely surprised to see the Macedonian army encamped outside their walls and at first refused to give battle. They could see, however, that many of their jealous neighbors in Boeotia were aiding the Macedonians and ravaging the countryside. Their Athenian allies urged them to give battle rather than starve, knowing that if they did not stop Alexander here, he would march on Athens. Athens sent a contingent to reinforce them.

The Thebans sallied out of their walls to face Alexander, whose mighty phalanx and irresistible cavalry made short work of the Thebans and Athenians. The dead and moaning wounded littered the battlefield. The Macedonians quickly dispatched the dying and wounded, and disarmed and rounded up the prisoners.

That evening, Alexander held a council including his generals and Thebes' ancient enemies of Plataea, Phocis, Thespiae, and Orchomenos.

Alexander addressed the meeting. "The Thebans and their Athenian allies have been utterly defeated. The city is defenseless. This is the third time we have had to meet these cities in battle. I am weary of these stiff-necked Greeks who do not appreciate peace and security under Macedonian protection.

"Once more we have defeated them, but will they rise and rebel again? It seems they must be given a lesson that is not soon forgotten. Thebes must be punished and a message sent to the rest of Greece. I will not make the decision alone, but ask the opinions of all who fought. What should we do with Thebes?"

One of Alexander's generals gave his opinion. "Even though Thebes has rebelled against us and needs to be taught a lesson, she is a city with a great past. Your father, King Philip, lived with great Epaminondas while he was in Thebes. It is my vote that we should take all the men of fighting age and put them in garrisons along the frontiers. The younger women and children can be sold into slavery. A reinforced Macedonian garrison should be placed in the refortified Cadmeia. Otherwise, the city should be spared. We can use it later as a stronghold in Boeotia."

The representative from Phocis said, "We have no love for Thebes nor honor the memory of Epaminondas, for he ruled us with an iron hand. I vote that Thebes should be burned."

The representative from Plataea replied, "Thebes drafted our youth for its army and kidnapped our women. She has been our ancestral enemy, and I vote that all its men should be killed."

The representative from Thespiae agreed. "Thebes should be destroyed. All its inhabitants either killed or sold as slaves."

The representative of Orchomenos and other enemies of Thebes added their voices of approval.

Alexander wanted to show the rest of Greece an example of the fate that would befall any who would rebel against his power. This would give the other rebels a lesson, and he could blame it on Thebes' enemy neighbors. His own troops would not have Theban blood on their hands, despite being the instrument of her defeat. In addition, his depleted treasury would gain from the sale of the enslaved population.

"I will sign the order," he said.

A yell of bloodlust filled the air.

"I will turn the city over to the Macedonian allies, but with the following provisions. You are to spare the house of Pindar the poet and all of the temples. The lives of all priests and priestesses and of all Thebans, who can prove that they opposed the revolt must also be spared."

Burning and butchery marked the next day. Even relatives killed one another, as Greeks mercilessly murdered each other. They plundered and torched houses and raped women. Even the old, women, and children who fled into temples for sanctuary were not safe, as children were torn from their mothers and mutilated. Every corner of the city was piled high with corpses. It would go down in history as one of the worst atrocities Greeks visited upon fellow Greeks.

The Macedonians and their allies slaughtered more than six thousand Theban men, women, and children in the streets, including all the prisoners. The rest, more than thirty thousand, they sold into slavery. They burned the city to the ground, except for the house of Pindar and the temples. They tore the walls down, and parceled out the surrounding lands to the neighboring cities that had joined in the slaughter. Thebes was never to rise again. The ancient city with a colorful history was wiped from the map of Greece.

This was a novel event in Greek history. No previous disaster had instilled such horror and dread. It was an act of deliberate terror, sponsored by Alexander and conducted by his proxies.

The destruction of Thebes was but a first taste of the vengeance that Alexander's wrath could take. He later said that he looked back with shame on this violent revenge, and atoned in part by showing leniency for Athens, even though she was the instigator of the revolt.

"Sire," said one of Alexander's generals, "surely Athens must also share the blame with Thebes. If you do not desire to burn the city or enslave its citizens, then we should at least arrest and kill Demosthenes and the other anti-Macedonian leaders. She should also be forced to pay a large indemnity."

"I hear what you say, Melliotos." Alexander had absorbed from his father a respect for Athens. Aristotle had also made a place in Alexander's heart for Athens as mother of philosophy and science. "No, I will not punish Athens even though she violated her pledges made to me only last year. Demosthenes and his party now have no teeth with which to harm us. We will take her army and navy with us to fight Persia. She and the other Greek allies will have no men at home with which to rebel. I will send a commission to Athens to see that this is done. Now get the army ready to return to Macedon."

Before he left the ruins of Thebes, Alexander exacted a renewed allegiance of all the Greek states. They all agreed—except, again, Sparta. Satisfied, Alexander returned to Macedon to prepare for his invasion of Asia.

* * *

News of the slaughter and destruction of Thebes reached Pella before Alexander did.

Horrified, Phidias spoke of his concern to Aristotle. "I thought we had educated Alexander. I thought we had given him civilized virtues. Instead, he has shown that he is still a Macedonian barbarian."

Aristotle shook his head. "It saddens me also to see that the bloody violence he inherited from his mother and father is but under a veneer of Greek culture. I tried my best during the past four years. I still have my hopes for him."

"But Aristotle, if he invades Asia, will he repeat this barbarism? Will his bloodlust overwhelm what you have taught him?"

"I have instilled in him lessons in how to be a good king, an enlightened ruler. I will have more conversation with him after he returns. Perhaps we can have a continuing influence on him after he attacks Persia."

"I hope so, my friend," said Phidias. "For Alexander's sake and for the sake of his enemies, I hope so."

Plans were made for the most daring and romantic undertaking of any European king up to that time. Persia was a huge empire with many millions of inhabitants. Very wealthy, it had a well-trained, effective army made up of contingents of several ethnic groups who fought with their own skills and armament. It was reported that the Persians could muster a million men for its army and cavalry. Only thirty thousand infantry and five thousand cavalry made up Alexander's invading force. However, they were hardened veterans, trained to a honed edge.

Alexander called a meeting of his senior generals. "We are preparing for a continuation of the war between Europe and Asia. Our ancestors invaded and sacked Troy. The Persians in their turn invaded Greece twice and even burned Athens. Now it is our turn to take up where Agamemnon, Achilles, and Odysseus left off. We will not only retrace their steps to Troy but will continue to conquer all of Asia.

"I had hoped to fight Persia as the champion of all Greece. I realize, however, that half of Greece prays that I will be killed. How can I count on the Greek allies to aid me, when many fight as mercenaries for the Persians? In fact, those Greeks will give us more trouble than the Persians themselves.

"Antipater ," Alexander addressed one of his older generals.

"Yes, Sire."

"You will remain behind in command of twelve thousand to guard Macedon and keep watch over Greece. You have been one of my father's most trusted generals and have proven your loyalty to me. I will take the forces of the Greek allies to serve as a rearguard and garrison the cities we have taken. I do not trust them in the front of battle. They are not as trained and effective as our Macedonian phalanx. Besides, they may not want to fight their brother mercenaries when faced with them."

"Sire," said Antipater, "I am flattered that you would leave me in command of Macedon in your absence, but I would rather be fighting at your side against the hated Persians."

"I know you would, loyal Antipater. It is because I can trust you that I leave you in charge. Now let us prepare to cross the Hellespont."

Alexander sent an invitation to Aristotle and Phidias to have a quiet dinner with him. They both greeted Alexander enthusiastically, kissing him and thanking him again for sparing Phidias' life.

"It was fortunate that you brought Phidias' plight to my attention, Master Aristotle," Alexander said. "I never want to be the cause for any harm to come to a teacher or philosopher, especially one from Athens. Come let us enjoy some simple food and good wine. As you are well aware, I am preparing to cross into Asia and embark upon an arduous campaign. It may be several years before I can enjoy a dinner with my teacher and his friend and discuss philosophy."

"Alexander," said Aristotle, "your campaigns in Asia should not be solely of a military interest. They can be a source of unlimited benefit to science. Take scholars with you who have knowledge of animals, plants, and geography. I would also ask you to send back to me whatever they can collect of interest. I want to add to my collections. It would increase our knowledge immensely to have specimens of plants, animals, and rocks from all of your journeys."

"I will certainly do as you ask," Alexander agreed. "But why don't you accompany me? You have knowledge of many things. You can also advise me about philosophical issues during my exploits."

Aristotle replied, "I am truly tempted by the opportunity to visit new lands and observe customs, plants, animals, and man-made wonders at first hand. However, I feel I must return to Athens. Xenocrates became the head of Plato's Academy. He is a good master, but he follows Plato's philosophy, with which I have many disagreements.

"I would like to start my own school. It could be a place for my collection of specimens, of books, and for my research. I would like to continue to teach and write. Now that the Macedonian party is in power in Athens, I will feel safe there."

"I understand your wish to return to the city you love, and I applaud your decision to establish your own school. How will you pay for it? Do you have land or buildings?"

"I have nothing. Your father supported me when I was your teacher, but I have no funds of my own."

"Then I will be your benefactor," Alexander said. "I will help you build your school. I give you my promise that I will send the first part of any booty I capture."

"Thank you, Alexander. I hope I have instilled within you a love for science. You always were a little impatient with philosophy, but perhaps you can take philosophers with you." Aristotle had considered how Alexander might continue to get philosophical advice even though he would not be with him.

"Whom do you suggest?"

"I suggest you take Gorgas, Pharacrates, and Callisthenes. Callisthenes is my nephew. He can act as your official historian and keep accurate record of all of your exploits. Gorgas has knowledge of animals and plants. Pharacrates is expert in minerals, geography, and the weather. And, oh yes, you should ask Phidias here to accompany you."

Alexander began, "I had never thought…"

"But Aristotle," interrupted Phidias, "don't you want me to go back to Athens with you?"

"I think it would be a great experience for you, my friend," Aristotle replied. "This is an opportunity of a lifetime to accompany my student, who, by the will of the gods, will conquer Asia and Egypt. You can be my eyes and ears also."

"Will you accompany me then, Phidias?" Alexander asked. "I could use a philosopher who has been trained like Aristotle. You can advise me about the customs and history of the Persians and other peoples we may meet. After dealing with hard soldiers all day, I would welcome the opportunity to talk with a person with a calm mind of things other than death and destruction."

Phidias abhorred war. He had fought in battle, been wounded, and seen his closest friend killed. He realized what Aristotle was doing. Aristotle couldn't be there himself, but perhaps he could send someone to temper Alexander's hot Macedonian blood with a cool Athenian head. Phidias looked at his friend and gave a bare nod. Bowing his head slightly to Alexander, he replied, "I would be honored to go with you and be your philosophical advisor. I can help collect material for Aristotle and even make notes for a history of barbarian peoples, if I decide to write one."

"Good, then it is settled," said Alexander. "Let's have a toast to a successful campaign."

"To the progress of scientific knowledge," said Aristotle.

"To the spread of Greek ideas," said Phidias.

"To the conquest of Persia," said Alexander.

V. THE ADVENTURE BEGINS

CHAPTER 22

Alexander trusted Antipater, whom he had left with an army to keep an eye on Macedon and Greece. He distrusted the Greeks, who may not have learned the strong lesson of Thebes. Demosthenes remained active in Athens, although the Athenians were not likely to revolt again soon. The northern tribes had also been chastened. However, who could guarantee that a rebel leader or exiled Macedonian might not cause trouble?

Alexander was filled with the excitement of his adventure. His father's dream of invading Asia and freeing the Ionian Greeks had inspired him since he could remember, and Aristotle had fertilized his imagination with the legendary exploits of the great Achilles. He fancied himself as the spiritual reincarnation of the hero of Troy in leading Greeks to battle in Asia. He had put much of the *Iliad* to memory and quoted passages as he approached the reputed site of Troy.

He ordered most of the army to cross the Hellespont, but Alexander chose to lead a smaller party to the place where Agamemnon supposedly had landed. Alexander was the first to set foot on the shore where the Greeks landed to attack Troy. He threw down his shield and helmet, knelt, and kissed the ground. "Hail, Achilles; hail, Odysseus; hail, Agamemnon. I have come to avenge the Persian invasion upon our sacred soil. I pledge to uphold your honor by reliving your deeds, following your courage, and using your cunning to defeat our foe."

He rose, and the army cheered.

"Let us march to Troy!" he yelled.

They retraced the path to legendary Troy and approached the site of Achilles' tomb. He knelt there, feeling a spirit of ecstasy wash over him, as if the soul of Achilles himself had risen and filled him with its valor. Cold sweat broke out over Alexander's brow, and, after a few moments, he stood up, pale on shaky legs.

He turned to his officers who had gathered around him. "Let us rest tonight, and tomorrow I will honor Achilles."

The next day, Alexander and his men gathered for a ceremony at the tomb. He stepped forward and poured sacred oil on it as he prayed to the gods. "I give honor to Achilles and to all the Greeks who fought against Troy and all Asians. Help us, all ye gods of Olympus, in our fight against the enemy, bless our arms, and bolster our courage."

He then crowned the tomb with garlands. Turning to an officer, he handed him his helmet. Other officers helped him remove the rest of his armor and clothes. He stood naked before the tomb of Achilles, and, after bowing in acknowledgement, ran around it. After doing so, he faced the tomb and exclaimed, "Happy Achilles to have had in life so faithful a friend, and after his death so famous a poet to celebrate him."

He made a sacred pledge. "I vow to you mighty and heroic Achilles and to all the gods, that I will continue the struggle between Greece and Asia, which was begun at Troy. I pledge my honor, my fortune, and my blood to carry through this contest to a successful end."

His officers and soldiers cheered and also made pledges.

Soon afterward, the main force joined Alexander and marched south. He knew that the vast Persian Empire was composed of diverse peoples, cultures, and languages, with no deep loyalty or affection for the Persian rulers. He counted on this and hoped that, not only would these peoples not resist an invading army, but may even join it in throwing off their oppressors.

The first Persian contingent met him at the river Granicus. The Persian forces arranged themselves on the opposite side of the river, forcing the Greeks to come across the river to engage them. This was not a large army and was to be mainly an engagement of the cavalry of both sides.

Alexander pointed out the Persians' deployments to his generals. "Look how they have protected themselves behind the river banks. This shows that they choose to fight defensively, a cowardly move."

"Alexander," explained Parmenion, "these have been evasive tactics of the Asian armies for hundreds of years. The Greek historians have written of them."

"I have contempt for such faint-heartedness," Alexander snarled. "That impels me even more to find the Persians' strongest point and to attack it. Prepare your men. I will lead the attack in the center."

Unlike the traditional Greek generals who fought on foot and were indistinguishable alongside their hoplite soldiers, Alexander dressed in ostentatious armor and helmet. He led his men with infectious courage and plunged into the melee, relishing the thrill of battle.

The generals were too familiar with the young king's apparently inexhaustible energy, especially when it came to the prospect of facing an enemy in battle. The planning of war and battles energized Alexander. His personality fed on it, as if he drank the blood that was spilled on the battlefield. War became an uncontrollable passion, the sound and sight of battle an intoxication. He seemed to forget sometimes that he was the commanding general and threw himself into the thickest of the fray. Time and again, his soldiers saved him and pleaded with him to go to the rear for fear that they would lose him.

Alexander led his cavalry across the river and attacked the Persians behind their embankment, attempting to push them to the open ground. The Persians resisted, barring their crossing and hurling them back into the river.

"Come on my companions. We can break this cowardly enemy," he yelled.

His men responded with shouts and renewed attacks until they forced the Persians from the embankment to the ground behind.

Alexander screamed encouragement again as he plunged forward into the enemy, thrusting and hacking. He likened himself to a modern Achilles, who measured his worth by the number of enemy he personally speared, unhorsed, or slashed.

Alexander was hotly engaged with a Persian cavalryman on his left side, unaware that another enemy was maneuvering from behind his right. Cleitus saw the threat. "Alexander!" he cried, but the clash of swords and spears against shields mingled with the sounds of dying men and horses prevented Alexander from hearing the warning. Cleitus screamed and sped his horse as he saw the enemy horseman move closer to Alexander with his sword raised.

Cleitus reached the enemy before he could strike, and with a slash severed the raised arm of the Persian. Only then as he heard the cries and sound of the stroke did Alexander realize that his life had been threatened, and that it had been saved by the action of Cleitus. He touched Cleitus' shield with his sword and said, "Thank you, my brother."

Alexander's gamble of attacking the Persian strength proved exactly correct. The Persian main force broke and fled, discarding their arms. The unexpected catastrophe rooted in their places the Greek mercenary infantry, who were in the second line. They stood their ground and fought like the disciplined soldiers they were.

Alexander turned his cavalry flank to attack the mercenaries. He exhorted his men, "Have no mercy for those Greeks, who fight for the enemy. We must teach them that they must not fight against fellow Greeks and Macedonians!"

With that, his men surrounded and massacred the mercenaries. Perhaps fifteen to eighteen thousand Greeks were killed, more than had fallen to the Persians in their two invasions of Greece.

Alexander led his men in riding down and slaughtering the retreating Persians, as many as twenty thousand perishing under their swords and spears. The Macedonians destroyed the Persian army outright.

This was a new type of warfare that Alexander had inherited from his father. War meant not merely the defeat of the enemy and signing of a treaty but the complete annihilation of opposing forces and humiliation of those who would dare to field further opposition.

He spared two thousand of the mercenaries and sent them back home in chains as a warning to other Greeks who would oppose him. To impress upon the Greeks at home of his first victory, he sent three hundred suits of Persian armor to Athens with the message, "Alexander, the son of Philip, and the Greeks, except the Spartans, have won this spoil from the barbarians of Asia." This one statement expressed not only his contempt for the Persians but his greater contempt for the Spartans and his conviction that all Greeks were united in furthering the Greek cause in Asia.

The wanton slaughter of fellow Greeks appalled Phidias. He watched the next day as officers gave orders and the men stripped bodies, heaped them into piles, and burned them. He saw Alexander astride the magnificent black Bucephalus in his clean, resplendent armor, overseeing the collection of booty from the Persians. Always clean-shaven, he introduced the custom of shaving into the world he conquered. Phidias had heard him say that the beard offered the enemy a handy thing to grasp.

Alexander saw Phidias watching the handling of the corpses and walked over to him. "Master Phidias, I would like you to come to my tent tonight for a quiet dinner and conversation."

"I would be delighted, Sire."

"Good. Then also invite Gorgas, Pharacrates, and Callisthenes. I would like to see what the scientists and historians have to say about the campaign so far."

That evening Alexander and his philosophers discussed things until the late hours. Alexander had been a good student but was consumed by responsibilities too early to develop a mature mind. As with many men occupied by action and ambition, he was sorry he could not also be a deep thinker. He had a passion for learning that would always be with him and delighted in reading when he had time, but Alexander's world was one of action—not contemplation. He attempted to intersperse learning and learned discussion between marches and battles. It was a joy to him, after a day of marching or fighting, to sit up with scholars for half the night.

Alexander welcomed the philosophers into his tent. It was large, as befitted the King, but not luxurious. The men sat at a table and were served fruits and vegetables from the countryside and a light stew. The wine was watered down.

Alexander did not gorge himself with heavy meals like some of his generals, even after a hard march or battle. He was not averse to drinking heavily, although Aristotle and others had warned him to drink moderately. This night was to be one of serious discussion, so he remained sober.

"What do you think of the Persians so far?" Alexander asked. He had told these philosophers to refer to him by his name while they were in private. He respected them and wanted to relate as a fellow scholar.

"They are very clever people with an advanced civilization," said Gorgas. "I have talked with their mathematicians and astronomers. They are excellent builders and have a vast network of roads that connect all parts of the empire."

"It is a vast empire," said Pharacrates, "composed of diverse peoples who dwell in cities, mountains, valleys, and deserts. It is not like Greece that is broken up into small kingdoms by many mountains."

"You are my official historian, aren't you Callisthenes?" Alexander asked. "Your uncle Aristotle instructed you to keep a record. Have my generals given you an accounting of the number of enemy dead, and how much armor, horses, and treasure we have captured?"

"Indeed they have, and I am writing a good account of your campaign so far. I have observed how you attacked the enemy with such courage, unafraid of possible injury to yourself. I was told how Cleitus saved your life at the Granicus. Don't you fear that you might be injured or killed, and therefore our army will fail?"

"I live a charmed life," Alexander smiled and waved his arm. "Know you not that I am the son of Zeus? He will watch over and protect me from the enemy's arrows and swords. I also believe my courage is an example to all our soldiers. It encourages them."

"But what if you are unhorsed or lose contact with your generals?" asked Callisthenes.

"My generals know what to do, for we discuss our strategy before the battle. But as any battle progresses, it may take an unpredictable course. The generals who serve me also served my father, and they know how our phalanxes fight and how to conduct a battle. They can make their own decisions in the midst of it without me."

"I see," said Callisthenes.

Phidias spoke up. "I would like to say something about the Persians, Alexander."

"What is that, Phidias?"

"Unlike the Greeks, the Persians have a very strong and centralized command at the top and very little initiative or leadership ability below that. Their general, or the King if he is present at the battle, stays in the rear and sends orders to his officers. If our general is killed or disabled, another takes his place. With the Persians, if the leadership is destroyed, the whole army is leaderless and capitulates."

"Thank you, Phidias. I guess I knew that intuitively. That's why I like to attack their strongest point, because that is where the leaders put themselves."

"The Persians are very clever people and very rich," Phidias said. "It is that cleverness and wealth that may be their undoing. They are smug in their vast empire and huge cities. They haven't had an invading army in three hundred years. They believe their polyglot peoples are firmly under control of the Great King and his *satraps*, or governors. It is my opinion that the empire is rotten at its core and is open for a strong invader, such as you. I think if Darius is killed or captured, the entire empire will fall into your hand like a ripe plum."

"I hope you are right," said Alexander. "That is what I'm counting on. Let's not be over confident, however. The engagement at the Granicus was just a taste of much larger battles to come. We must remember that the enemy outnumbers us by a vast figure. My destiny is to conquer Asia, and, with the help of Zeus and the other gods, I will."

The next day, Alexander gave Phidias a letter. "Here is a letter I have written to Aristotle. Please enclose it with your letters and specimens that we have collected."

"I will do that, Alexander."

"I enjoyed our discussion last night, Phidias. I learned a lot about our enemy. It is extremely important to understand your enemy. Don't you agree?"

"It is. However, it is more important to know yourself and your own forces. Know what your weaknesses are, so that you can correct them and the enemy cannot take advantage of them."

Alexander frowned. "Do I have weaknesses, Phidias?"

"Every mortal has weaknesses. That is why we may become ill, injured, or die. Men are also susceptible to greed, gluttony, excessive drink, or cruelty. The wise Socrates said to know thyself, that the unexamined life is not worth living. Look deeply into your psyche, Alexander, and find your weaknesses. Do not succumb to them, or you may be your own worst enemy."

"Thank you for your insight, friend. Aristotle was right when he advised me to bring you with me. Thank him for me, won't you?"

"I certainly will," Phidias agreed. "I will also tell him about our discussion last night."

"Now I must go and confer with my generals and prepare to meet Darius' main army."

Phidias read Alexander's letter, which stated, "For my part I had rather surpass others in the knowledge of what is excellent, than in the extent of my power and dominion."

Noble words, thought Phidias. *Aristotle has given him good values. He is an idealistic youth with good intentions, high ideals, and lofty dreams. He truly yearns for knowledge and appreciates fine thought and discourse.*

Having a kingdom and all its responsibility thrust upon him at the age of twenty, Alexander's formal education ended. Yes, he can converse brilliantly, but only if the subjects are politics or war. He might be able to think in universal terms, but he is still a slave of superstition. He listens to soothsayers and astrologers and performs magical ceremonies to various gods.

I am afraid that Aristotle's careful grooming may be only a coating over his inherited barbarian ways. He likes to partake in strong drink, sometimes to have a good time with his fellow soldiers but sometimes to dull the fires in his soul. I hope he will discover and control this weakness before it controls him.

CHAPTER 23

While marching through Asia Minor, Alexander became ill at Tarsus. "It must be some of that damned Asian food," said Alexander between abdominal cramps. "I don't see how the barbarians can keep down all that spicy food."

One of his advisers spoke to him sympathetically, "Sire, you cannot get off your couch except to move your bowels. You cannot eat or drink without vomiting. Let me call your physician, Philip."

"Yes, he may be able to help me. I have been two days without relief."

Philip came and diagnosed the problem as intestinal cramps due to tainted food. "I must go and prepare a purgative for you. I will return shortly, Sire."

"Thank you, Philip, but come back as soon as you can."

Cleitus entered the tent and announced that he had an urgent letter from Parmenion.

"What does the letter say, Cleitus?" Alexander asked. "I am too weak to read it."

"It says that you should not trust your physician, Philip. Darius has bribed him to poison you. Darius has many spies and Greeks in his pay."

"Thank you for that information. Philip will be returning momentarily with a medication for my illness."

Alexander considered his options. Should he arrest him? Torture him? Execute him? Should he distrust and suspect all his men as possible agents of Darius? Would any of them put their trust in him as their leader if he distrusted them? He would have to use this as an opportunity to impress his leadership.

At that moment, Philip returned. "I have prepared a purgative for you to drink. It will ease the cramps and allow you to keep a simple broth on your stomach."

Alexander took the cup. "Thank you, Philip. Here, read this letter from Parmenion while I drink it."

Philip took the letter and started reading as Alexander raised the cup to his lips. He blanched as he read, and Alexander watched him as he started drinking.

Alexander finished the draught and put down the cup. "The elixir was quite bitter. I hope it works," he said.

"I think you will feel much better tomorrow, Sire. I can say that Darius attempted to bribe me, but I returned his gold. Thank you for putting your trust in me. I will continue to serve you loyally. Your trust will not be wasted. Now you must rest."

The next day Alexander rose, dressed in his armor, and emerged from his tent, refreshed and ready to give new orders. The prescribed potion had produced its promise, and Alexander acknowledged its accomplishment. He rewarded Philip with more captured Persian gold than Darius had ever promised him.

Alexander allowed his army to rest, heal their wounds, and resupply themselves before resuming his march down the coast of Asia Minor, where numerous Ionian Greek cities were located.

"I believe the Ionian Greeks will welcome us as liberators from the Persians," said Alexander. "We need to purchase food and supplies from them. I'm sure they will open their gates to us."

Craterus, one of his senior generals, replied, "I am not so sure they will, Alexander. The Greek mercenaries we fight are mostly from those cities. They are glad to get Persian gold, whether it is to fight Macedonians or fellow Greeks. What if they close their gates to us? Will you besiege them?"

"I cannot waste time and manpower fighting other Greeks, even Ionians. I am not as pessimistic as you. I will offer them democratic self-government under our protection. We will free our fellow Greeks from the Persian yoke."

Alexander's prediction proved precise. The Greek cities opened their gates without resistance, welcoming him as a liberator. They not only supplied his army with food and material but helped to fill his ranks. "We would rather fight alongside you against the Persians than against fellow Greeks," one of the leaders from Miletus said. The wealthy merchants and bankers were generous with loans and supplies, and Alexander's refurbished army resumed its march south.

* * *

About a year after the battle at the Granicus, Alexander met the main army of the Persians under Darius himself at Issus. An army of mixed contingents from all parts of the vast empire numbering about 160,000 met Alexander's army of one-third the size.

Darius had brought his army to the Syrian coast behind Alexander's line of advance, thus forcing Alexander to turn and regain his line of communications. In their eagerness, the Persians took their stand in a geographical bottleneck, a mile-wide coastal area between the hills and the sea. They again formed their battle line behind a stream. But because of the cramped space, Darius could not take advantage of his numerical superiority. The rear half of the army could only watch the action of the front ranks.

Alexander's observers brought reports of the disposition of the enemy. He addressed his two chief generals. "How are the Persians arrayed, and where are their strengths?"

"Alexander," said Craterus, "the enemy vastly outnumbers us. Fortunately we are in a narrow space, and they cannot come around our flanks. Nevertheless I think we must keep our flanks strong to prevent such a movement."

"I agree. What fortifications has the enemy made?"

Ptolemy spoke up, "Darius himself leads this army. He has risked his presence as a moral show of strength. The Persians have built up palisades in the center, where he has stationed himself and his generals. This indicates to me that he is a man of no spirit."

"That is what I have heard," agreed Alexander. "These Eastern armies rely too much on their king or leader. If the leader is killed or put to flight, the whole army disintegrates. Therefore, we must strike directly at Darius. Let us rest today and attack at early light."

Alexander opened the battle by ordering his phalanx in the center to cross the stream rapidly, so as to give the enemy bowmen little time to unloose their arrows. The center was thrown well forward toward the center-left of the Persians, where Darius was stationed.

At this moment, the unexpected happened. The Macedonian phalanx crossing the stream lost its cohesiveness. The Greek mercenaries on the opposite side pressed forward to take advantage of the confusion. This movement by the Greeks in the Persian center opened a gap between the center and its left. Alexander turned his quick perception of this flaw into decisive action. He wheeled his cavalry's right wing inward, charging into the flank of the Persian center and widening the gap with its left. Darius and his nobles were immediately endangered. Perceiving the peril they quickly fled, with the rank and file soon following their example. Only the Greek mercenaries stood their ground, dying stoically as they were assailed from all sides.

The Persian disaster was complete, with estimates of more than one hundred thousand slain, while Macedonian losses were only four hundred and fifty. Any orderly retreat was impossible in Eastern armies except among the most disciplined, and the Greeks mercenaries did not retreat. Thus the pursuit and the slaughter of broken ranks turned into a one-sided massacre lasting for hours over many miles.

Darius fled, leaving the camp and its treasures, his wife, and even his mother. There was even a sumptuous feast laid out for his victory celebration. Alexander came across and gazed at the delectable food and rare wines set out with gold and silver plates and jeweled goblets. He forbade his men to touch it. "First we will tend to our wounded. Then we can dine on Darius' food," he said to them.

An officer brought the wife and mother of Darius to Alexander. He arose and greeted them courteously. "Explain to them that I will do them no harm," he said to a translator. "You are welcomed to dine with me. You may keep your slaves and handmaidens, and I will send you with an escort of your soldiers back to Darius."

Darius' mother came up and kissed his hand. Through the translator, she said, "Thank you for all your courtesies. You are a brave leader. I wish that you were my son."

Alexander smiled, acknowledging the compliment and the backhanded slap at the cowardice of her own son. Like his father, Alexander knew that generosity and justice can temper the cruelties and demands of war.

Although Alexander had obtained an overwhelming victory, he knew that as long as Darius was still alive, he could form another army from his vast empire. Instead of pursuing Darius, however, Alexander marched down the coast of Syria into Egypt. It was to be almost two years before the two great armies would meet again.

Continuing his march down the coast, Alexander found his way impeded by the ancient fortified city of Tyre. The old city still stood on the coast, but a new city had been built on an island half a mile from the mainland. It had a north and south harbor and was completely surrounded by stout walls. Alexander could see that the siege and capture of this important city would be a major undertaking. He could not leave it at his rear because its navy would interrupt his supply line from Greece. He would have to construct a mole or bridge to the island from the mainland.

This would have to be a Herculean task, but Alexander was undaunted, especially as he claimed to be a descendent of Hercules. The defenders fought with desperate courage. Each time the Tyrians developed a new defense, Alexander and his strategists had to devise a remedy. The besieged put up a fierce resistance but were reduced to awaiting the final breach as the Macedonians brought the seven-month-long siege to an end.

In his rage at the stubborn defense of Tyre, Alexander allowed his men to massacre eight thousand Tyrians in the streets. They crucified two thousand men as a lesson of the futility of resisting him. They sold the remaining twenty to thirty thousand women and children as slaves. Tyre, like Thebes, had ceased to exist as a city.

After the battle of Issus, Darius sent a messenger with an offer to Alexander. The offer of peace with an alliance was extended to him as King of Macedon and Lord of Greece. However, Alexander, feeling that Darius was making the offer from a position of weakness following a defeat, scorned it. He told Darius' messenger, "I reject your master's offer. Tell him that if he wants to deal with me, he must send the offer to me as Lord of Asia."

During the long siege of Tyre, Darius again sent an offer, this time with better terms. Alexander and his generals received the representative who brought gifts and bowed to Alexander as Lord of Asia. Alexander accepted the gifts and compliment. "What does your master offer me this time?"

"The great Darius, King of Kings, extends to you the offer of ten thousand talents, the hand of his daughter in marriage to seal an alliance, and the overall lordship of the lands west of the Euphrates. You will rule them, but they will still be part of the great Persian Empire. Our two powers will support one another militarily and will prosper economically."

"I will consider the Great King's offer" Alexander said. "As my guest, you will be taken to your lodging and provided with food and servants for your needs. I will meet with my advisers and let you know what I decide. You may go."

Alexander turned to Parmenion. "What do you think of Darius' offer?"

"I think you should accept it. Ten thousand talents and Darius' daughter are gifts for a prince. You are indeed lord of all Ionia, which was the object of our invasion. We have freed our fellow Greeks from the Persians and gained our revenge for Persia's invasion of Greece. Let's take his offer of all of Asia this side of the Euphrates. We will have territory and wealth enough."

"Enough for what? For you? For me? For our men? I have a bigger vision. We have seen how we can beat the Persians in open battle, and its cities have fallen into our hands. However, I wish to press down the coast and even invade Egypt. I believe we can take it, and then I will defeat Darius and conquer all of Persia."

"That is a wonderful dream, Alexander, but not easily done. This is a vast country."

"I say it can be done," Alexander insisted. "We have the trained army and siege equipment to do it. I say we go to Jerusalem, Gaza, and then to Egypt. Who will follow me?"

All the generals nodded, and Parmenion added his assent. "I will help you with all of my skill and strength to conquer Persia, but first we must get to Egypt."

As Alexander proceeded south, news of his successful siege of Tyre and the slaughter of its defenders preceded him. Jerusalem surrendered peacefully and was treated well. The walled city of Gaza, however, refused to surrender. Gaza was the last fortified barrier to Alexander's march to Egypt. The city, situated in a plain surrounded by mighty walls, was not assailable by rams or bores, the common siege engines of Alexander. A courageous and skillful Persian general named Batis commanded it.

"I will not allow this stubborn Persian to block my advance. We'll construct a mound to put our siege equipment on. Conscript men from the surrounding area." This tremendous labor produced a huge earthen hill 250 feet in height and 1200 feet in diameter. Alexander then placed his war engines on its top, and they took Gaza two months later. The Gazans fought courageously until every man was killed and every woman raped. Alexander's men beat the heroic Batis to death, bored his ankles, and put brass rings through them. Then Alexander dragged him, like Achilles did Hector, around the city walls.

Intoxicated with his victory over the Persian cities, Alexander succumbed more often to intoxicating drink. It seemed that the more violent the raging fires of slaughter and mayhem, the more drink it took to quench them and bring calm to the nerves of this conqueror of armies and cities.

CHAPTER 24

Alexander, at the head of his triumphant army, marched through the Sinai into Egypt. Phidias enlightened him on his way to the Egyptian capital. "Egypt is a very ancient country. Its pyramids and tombs were built centuries before Achilles attacked Troy. They worship many gods. Some may be the same as ours, but by a different name. Their chief god, Ammon, is probably the same as Zeus."

"Yes, that is what my mother told me. She said that I am his son."

"I don't know about that, Alexander, but you are indeed mortal. Your injuries in battles and your sickness in Tarsus are evidence of that. Nevertheless, the priests of these ancient gods command tremendous wealth and power. They have accumulated it over centuries from the gifts of many pharaohs. As a matter of fact, it is understood that the pharaoh, even though he was considered a living god, had to have the support and blessings of the priesthood. Woe to the pharaoh who opposed them. On the other hand, if he had their support, the priests could get the people to do anything for the pharaoh."

"Thank you for your lesson, Phidias," Alexander replied. "I will respect and listen to their priests."

Arriving in the ancient Memphis, Alexander was hailed as a divinely sent liberator. After several days of feasting and celebrating there, a priest of Ammon asked to speak with Alexander. He arrived with an interpreter, who was a Greek trader.

"What is it that you want, Holy One?" asked Alexander.

"All honor to you, conqueror of Egypt. You have won great victories, Asia and Egypt lay at your feet, and the great Persian Empire is within your grasp."

"These facts I already know. What new things do you have to tell me?"

"You have the face, body, and character of a god," said the priest. "Certainly you have divine blood within your veins."

"My mother told me that my true father was Zeus. Wise men of Greece say that Zeus and Ammon are one. Do you agree?"

"Ammon is truly our chief god, and I am aware that Zeus is the Greeks'. Whether or not you are his son, I do not know. But there is a way to learn the truth."

"And what is that, Holy One?"

"In the Western Desert, many miles from Memphis, is an oasis named Siwa. This place is sacred to Ammon, and his spirit resides there, as does his oracle. One with the proper consecration of his spirit may approach the oracle and ask of him important questions. I believe that if you are properly prepared, you may ask the oracle about your true father."

"That is indeed something I would like to do with all the strength that is within me. I am eternally grateful for this information. Where is this oasis, and how do I prepare myself for the oracle?"

"Come tomorrow to the Temple of Ammon in Memphis. Bring nothing except the simple robe of a supplicant. Be prepared to spend three days with us. We will do no harm but welcome your divine presence. Tell your generals where you will be, but they are not to disturb you."

"What will I be doing for three days?"

"That, I cannot tell you. The rites and ceremonies are ancient and not to be revealed to anyone who has not participated in them. You will be consecrated and prepared to approach the oracle with your inquiries."

"Thank you, Holy One. I will come to your temple in the morning."

After the priest left, Cleitus advised Alexander, "You should not go. They will murder you and throw your body to the crocodiles."

"Cleitus, they claim that I am divine, so they will not harm me. I'll ask the oracle of Ammon if I am the son of Zeus. They will help me."

Alexander went to the temple and submitted himself to the priests. They gave him a ritual bath and anointed him with sacred oils. He sat for hours in front of strange gods, human bodies with animal heads, while the priests chanted and burnt incense. On the last day, they dressed him in a snow-white linen garment, placed an Egyptian headpiece on his head, and hung an amulet of lapis and gold around his neck. Finally, the chief priest laid his hands on his head and prayed a long prayer, ending with the only word that Alexander understood, "Ammon."

Two days later, Alexander was ready to visit the oracle at Siwa. With a company of soldiers and supplies, he crossed the desert. The Macedonian and Greek soldiers were unfamiliar with the endless soft shifting sands and ceaseless sun of the Western Desert. Many times, one would point to the distant horizon and exclaim that there was a lake of water. The Egyptian guides explained that this was only the appearance of water. The God Ra, who controlled the sun, used it to trick the stranger into believing there was relief from his burning rays.

At last they reached the Oasis of Siwa, an island of water, date palms, and grass for the animals in the midst of a vast sea of sand. There in the center, on a small hill overlooking the water, stood a jewel of a temple. Steps led up to an open plaza in front of the white limestone structure, which was supported by thirty-foot columns shaped like lotuses. On the plaza in front stood a twenty-five-foot statue of the God Ammon. He stood in the traditional way, with his right foot slightly in front, his right hand extended palm up, and his left hand at his side. Dressed in the ancient Egyptian skirt, his torso was bare and on his head sat the double crown of upper and lower Egypt. His left hand held an ankh, a cross with a loop on top, while in his open palm he held a symbol of the sun, a disc with radiating rays. The Egyptians explained to Alexander that Ammon, the ruler of the world, held the symbols of the God Aton, the ankh, and the God Ra, the sun. They said the oasis showed that he brings life and comfort from the searing sun and sand of the desert.

The Egyptians took Alexander to a small house, where they dressed him in traditional Egyptian attire. They gave him oil, fruit, and wine and guided him to the temple to present them as sacrifices to the god. After this ceremony, they took him into the temple and on into a smaller room that opened from the back of the main hall. This room had a low, dark blue ceiling dotted with gold stars. A small, still pool of water in the center reflected the only light in the room, which came from the numerous candles around the walls. Incense rose from a bronze brazier in a corner. In the center of the back wall stood a raised platform with a large, ornate chair. On this sat a hooded figure in a long, flowing white robe. His hands were folded within his sleeves, and his face was completely in shadow. Nothing of his face or body could be seen.

Alexander was told to stand by the circular pool facing the seated aparition on the other side. The faceless figure spoke in a rasping voice that was hard to discern yet reverberated around the small room. The translator behind Alexander said, "The oracle asks why you have come to this holy place."

"I have come to seek answers from the God Ammon," stated Alexander.

"Why do you deem yourself worthy of approaching mighty Ammon?"

"I have won battles and captured cities from the Persians and have freed Egypt itself from their empire. I believe I have earned the right to speak with Ammon's oracle."

"Who told you that you have the right?"

"The priests of Ammon told me that I have within me a divine light. My mother has said that I am a son of Zeus. Greek and Egyptian wise men believe that Zeus and Ammon are one. Therefore, I have the right to address Ammon and ask if he is my father."

"Well spoken. A good answer you have made. State your question, and I will address it to the God Ammon."

"Oh, Ammon, mighty God and ruler of the world, am I, Alexander of Macedon, your son?"

The oracle rose, walked over to the smoking pot, and threw something into it. There was a flash and a puff of acrid smoke that rose, surrounded the hooded figure, and then filled the room. After chanting, the oracle stood like a stone statue facing the censer. Finally he turned, walked slowly to the dais, mounted it, and sat again in his chair.

He spoke slowly in the same rasping, hollow voice. The translator listened to all of it and then told Alexander what the oracle had said. "The oracle said divine blood flows in your veins. Your face shines with the light of the gods. Ammon has told him that indeed you are of his seed. He, Zeus-Ammon, will guide and protect you. You will fulfill your destiny."

"Did he say what my destiny is? Will I conquer all of Persia?"

The oracle was silent.

The translator spoke to Alexander. "He will not say. We cannot ask further questions. That is all the oracle will answer. He will speak no more. We are to go."

Alexander left with mixed emotions. He was elated that Ammon, through the oracle, had confirmed his divine paternity. He felt the power of the god within him. On the other hand, the oracle would not say what his destiny actually was. Alexander was convinced that it was to conquer whoever opposed him, and he would fulfill it.

While returning to the Nile Delta, Alexander conceived the idea of building a new city in Egypt. It would be Greek in style and culture and bear his name, Alexandria. It would be the new capital of Egypt.

Back in Memphis, he asked for his chief architect and engineer, Dinocrates, to meet with him. He told him of his plan to build a city in Egypt and call it Alexandria. "Search for a good site, for it will be a Greek city, grand in style, impressive as the new capital of Egypt. It must be worthy of its name, Alexandria, the name of a god and conqueror. It will represent a new era for this ancient land, the Greek era."

Dinocrates agreed that he and his engineers would look for a suitable site.

A few days later, Dinocrates took Alexander to a site they had selected. Located to the west of a large tributary of the Nile, it had a protected harbor large enough for a fleet of the biggest warships and plenty of waterfront for warehouses and buildings. It was far enough from the Nile that it would not be flooded.

Alexander was ecstatic. "This is beautiful. It will be the site of a great city. Let me mark out the main avenues, for I can see it in my mind."

Dinocrates looked at one of his engineers and raised his eyebrows. "Of course, Sire. Where would you like to start?"

For the rest of the day, Alexander paced the land, telling his engineers to make notes and pound stakes into the ground. He marked out the walls of the city, the main avenues, and the sites for temples.

"And here is where I want a palace complex built. It should also have a place where philosophers can gather, teach, and do science."

The engineers made notes and drawings.

"Dinocrates, I will not remain in Egypt to see its construction. I must fight Darius. I will leave you here to oversee the building of Alexandria. Make me proud. Make it a city worthy of my accomplishments."

"I will, Sire," he said.

Not long after, Dinocrates presented Alexander with a model of the city that was being planned. Wide avenues lined by noble buildings with Doric and Ionian columns graced a large harbor with a guarded entrance to the Mediterranean. Piers and wharves for a hundred ships lined the northern side, while stately buildings of the palace complex and government, a theater, gymnasia, palaestra, and temples occupied raised ground that would be constructed by a thousand workmen. The Egyptians were accustomed to monumental building, and Alexander, with his architect, Dinocrates, planned to build a city that would be a contrast to the huge, overpowering style of the ancient Egyptians. Alexandria would be a jewel of classic Greek architecture and art. Dressed in white marble, its glory would shine across the eastern Mediterranean and symbolize the new era of Helenization of the East.

Satisfied that Dinocrates would build him a city he would be proud of, Alexander turned his attention to his generals to make sure they were preparing for the campaign against Darius. The priests of Ammon sent word that they would like to meet with Alexander. "Hail, Alexander, Son of Ammon, the living god," said the Chief Priest as he and his assistants prostrated themselves before Alexander.

"Arise, Holy Ones. What do you wish of me?"

"We wish nothing of you, Sire. On the other hand, we wish to give something to you."

"What is it that you can give?" Alexander asked, smiling. "I already own all of Egypt."

"We wish to confer upon you the title that goes with that ownership. We wish to crown you Pharaoh, King of Egypt. You will join a long line of living gods who have ruled Egypt for centuries beyond number."

"I thank you for your compliment," said Alexander. "Can we do this in the next few days, for I am busy, as you can see?"

"Oh god-who-walks, the ceremonies that befit the deity must be performed in the great temple complex of Karnak. We must prepare the royal barge and make the coronation garments and vessels. We have not had a pharaoh since the Persians conquered us and placed their satrap here to govern."

Alexander acquiesced to the planning of a grand coronation. He was impressed by the wealth and the ancient monuments of Egypt and the opportunity to be crowned in a royal ceremony. The priests told him it would take two weeks to prepare the royal barge and make his vestments. The barge would sail up the Nile to the great Karnak, which would take three days. Then the ceremonies themselves would last four days, with a great feast afterward lasting two more days. The barge would then return leisurely back to Memphis, allowing the people along the Nile to cheer and give obeisance to the new Pharaoh.

Alexander was awed by the great power and enormity of the temple complex of Karnak. The priests told him that for centuries stretching back over two thousand years, more than fifty pharaohs had contributed to its temples and monuments. For four days, the Egyptian priests led him through ceremony, after ritual, after sacrifice. Finally, in a ceremony lasting two hours, the Chief Priest put in Alexander's hands the flail and crook—the symbols of the pharaoh's sovereignty, and he placed on his head the double crown of upper and lower Egypt.

Then he spoke the words in Egyptian and Greek, "Hail Pharaoh, son of Ammon, the living God, may you reign and live forever." He then prostrated himself in front of Alexander until his forehead touched the ground.

All the other priests and ministers repeated the words and gesture. The Greeks and Macedonians said, "Hail Alexander, Pharaoh of Egypt," but they did not prostrate themselves. This Egyptian and Persian way of obeisance was foreign to Greeks, who were not comfortable with it. To them this prostrating and groveling was a mark of barbarian weakness. They would later find out otherwise.

CHAPTER 25

Back in Memphis Alexander was again feted with dignitaries and officers. One day after a night of sumptuous feasting, Parmenion, his second in command, and his generals, Craterus and Ptolemy, asked to visit with him. Alexander, lounging on silk cushions and dressed in an Egyptian linen gown, welcomed them. His chief generals, without their breastplates, wore only the short Greek tunics.

"Hail, Alexander," said Parmenion.

"Hail, Alexander, Pharaoh of Egypt," said Ptolemy, bowing slightly.

"Hail, Alexander, conqueror of Asia and Egypt," said Craterus, also declining his head.

"Thank you, my friends. Please have a seat and help yourselves to wine. What is on your minds?"

"Know that we come to you as friends and fellow soldiers who share your hardships and love for your troops," said Craterus. "We speak not only for ourselves but for your officers and men. We think that this life of luxury, of feasting and drinking, is making us soft. They long to see you in your Greek clothes and armor riding Bucephalus and giving commands. These Egyptian priests and ministers are corrupting you."

"We enjoy Egypt," said Ptolemy. "It is an ancient civilization with much to teach us of architecture, engineering, and medicine. We may return here, but we have other work that is unfinished. We must defeat Darius, before he can gather more forces and attack Egypt."

"What say you, Parmenion?" Alexander asked. "You are my chief general, yet you have not said a word."

"Alexander, I have served your father and you. We have won many battles together. What Craterus and Ptolemy say is true. You cannot allow yourself to be seduced by Egyptian luxury and the fawning of priests. They mean only to use you. Their flattery is but empty words. You are a Macedonian soldier. The officers and men respect that. Do not lose that respect. Show them you are still the same Alexander, who will lead them to victory over Darius."

Alexander nodded slowly. "You are right as usual, Parmenion. You have always given me solid counsel. As to this Egyptian dress, you are also correct. These fine clothes are not those of a Macedonian King." He stood, tore off the linen garment, and stood naked before them. "Hand me my Greek tunic from that chest. I will not wear Egyptian clothes any longer. Tomorrow we will discuss the campaign that we will begin in the spring. Have the troops ready for inspection at noon. Afterward, we and the senior staff will gather here for lunch and planning."

At noon the next day, Alexander rode his magnificent black steed, followed by his chief generals. He wore a new silver and bronze breastplate and a silver helmet shaped like a lion's head. Beneath the armor he wore a white pleated skirt. Gleaming brass greaves covered his shins and silver sandals his feet. Bucephalus paced slowly down the ranks of disciplined soldiers with gleaming armor and spears.

Alexander nodded in recognition to some as they looked up and smiled at him. He was proud of these warriors. He would share their food and water, their hardships, and even their wounds—and they knew it. He led by example, daring them to follow him into the thickest of the battle. They loved him, as they knew he loved them, and they would follow him across the River Styx to Hades if he asked them to.

He addressed his troops from his horse. "Fellow Macedonians, fellow Greeks, fellow comrades, we have enjoyed the fruits of victory and congratulated ourselves with feasting and revelry. But now it is time to resume what we have come this far to do. The Persian King, our enemy, is still in his capital preparing to defeat us. We must cast off the softness of Egypt and harden ourselves for the conflicts to come.

"As you can see, I will no longer wear the Egyptian clothes but those of the hoplite, like you. I will eat your food and drink your wine, and I will train my body hard like yours. Today my generals and I will make plans for the campaign. You will also prepare by training and exercise. Obey your officers without question, and prepare for battle?"

"Yes!" the assemblage yelled.

"Will you make your bodies hard and your weapons sharp?"

"Yes!" they yelled again.

"Will you follow me to meet Darius?"

"Yes!"

"Will we destroy the hated Persians?"

Again they screamed, "Yes!"

"Then make yourselves ready." He turned his steed and rode away as all the army roared and beat their spears on their shields.

As the days grew longer and warmed their bodies from the night's chill, the soldiers' blood burned for battle. They knew it would not be long before they were ordered to march from this rich, green land into the desert called Sinai and beyond. The week before the Greeks were to break camp, Phidias called for Callisthenes, Gorgas, and Pharacrates to meet with him.

"It has been a while since we have met," said Phidias. "I am preparing a collection of letters to send to Aristotle. The ship will sail to Athens next week. What do you have for him, Gorgas?"

"I have collected many specimens of plants and animals from the Nile, all the way to the first cataract. I have many rolls of fresh papyrus for him to write his books."

"What about you, Pharacrates?"

"I have collected many papyruses, herbs, and medicines from Egyptian physicians, also chemicals used to preserve the dead. Aristotle can utilize these for his animal specimens."

"That is very good; the Egyptians are experts in preserving the dead. What do you have for Aristotle, Callisthenes?"

"I am keeping a detailed account of everything, which I will produce into a book when I return to Greece. As for my uncle Aristotle, I have written a report about Alexander's activity in Egypt. I told him mostly about Alexander's experiences at the Temple of Ammon, at Siwa, and at Karnak. I included some of my impressions for him."

Phidias gave them all some advice. "I want to admonish you to remind Alexander of his scientific and philosophic principles and of his promises to Aristotle. The exigencies of war monopolize his time. Try to engage him in philosophic discussions when he is not occupied with military matters, and attempt to keep him from bouts of drunkenness. He often becomes unreasonable and violent under the influence of too much wine."

"We will do the best we can, Phidias," said Gorgas. "Alexander listens more to you that to us, since you are Aristotle's friend and fellow teacher."

"He is hardheaded at times, especially when he drinks," agreed Pharacrates.

"Especially now that he is a god-king, Alexander thinks he can do no wrong. It is hard to criticize his behavior or even give him advice when his mind is set against it," complained Callisthenes.

"Do your best, gentlemen, as true philosophers and historians. That is all I can ask," said Phidias. "Now we all have work to do. May the god of nature, who watches over the world, watch over you also."

They all said their thanks and farewells and embraced Phidias. Callisthenes was the last, and as he put his arms around him, Phidias whispered for him to stay.

After the others left, Phidias said, "What are the personal impressions about Alexander you spoke of? I have an idea of what they may be."

"Alexander is taking too seriously this talk of his divinity. The Egyptians praise him as son of Ammon-Zeus and Pharaoh, a living god."

Phidias replied, "Don't the Greek poets talk of the Olympian gods having offspring with humans? Do we not speak of great men such as Socrates being the son of god? Why not Alexander?"

"Phidias, you know as well as I do that the term, 'son of god', is meant in a symbolic and allegorical sense. I do not believe literally in the Greek myths and the sexual activities of the Olympians. Their personalities and acts are to be interpreted allegorically to teach a lesson, not to be taken literally. I know that you and Aristotle believe the same."

"What you say is true, but the common people do not believe as you and I. They may want to believe in Alexander's divinity."

"His soldiers do not!" Callisthenes was emphatic. "I have heard the officers and men make fun of this divinity of Alexander. They revere him as their king and general, but they know he is no god. I fear Alexander is losing touch with reality and believes that he is divine. That would lose him the fealty of his men."

"That may be so, but you must not speak of it. Do not instill doubt or disloyalty among the men. That is dangerous. You might even be arrested for treason. Keep your opinions to yourself. You may write of them to Aristotle, but make sure no one else sees them. Do you understand?"

"Yes, I do. I will watch my tongue and my back, and I will continue to chronicle Alexander's exploits like a good historian."

The next day, Phidias sought out Alexander. "May I speak with you, Alexander? Are you busy now?"

"We are preparing to leave Egypt and march on Persia next week, but most of the major work has been done. My generals are taking care of the smaller details. I can always make time for my philosopher friend. What can I do for you?"

"Your successes in battles and sieges have been impressive, but the Persians have a huge empire with many men and resources that still oppose you. You must keep your perspective and not let your head be turned by luxury, flattery, and talk of divinity."

"Your advice has always helped me to put things into perspective, and I think I have developed a new one," Alexander replied. "Since being crowned Pharaoh, I have been overcome by a sense of world unity. If the gods of all nations are really the same, then why can't all people be united under one king, one culture, one language? I have united Greece with Macedon and then with Ionia, then with Asia west of the Euphrates, then with Egypt. I intend to unite this with all of Persia. We will have one nation, one monarch, one people. Isn't that a worthy dream?"

"It is a dream to be cherished and certainly to work toward," Phidias replied. "I believe you can attain it if you follow your heart and keep your head. I have warned you about drinking in moderation, and I have watched in approval as you limited your cups of wine or mixed more water in them as you feasted with your officers. That has helped you keep your violent temper under control."

"Yes, it has, my friend, but I still have those demons that haunt my dreams. I have nightmares of swimming in rivers of blood, surrounded by dismembered heads, arms, and legs."

"Those are the dreams of a military man. War is indeed a hideous nightmare. On those nights, awaken, put on a cloak, and go for a walk. Do not drink any wine but some warm milk, if you can get some. The night terrors will pass."

"Thank you, Master Phidias. I will try that."

"I have more serious advice for you, Alexander. I have watched how you enjoyed the ceremonies of the Egyptian priests, especially as they addressed you as living god. Perhaps you enjoyed it too much. The Egyptians have always addressed their pharaohs as such, and you see that they have all been very mortal. All men die. We are not gods, and you are not a god. If you persist in placing yourself on such a high pedestal above your men, who fight and die for you, you will alienate them. They will lose the adoration they have for you as a valiant warrior if you force them to adore you as a god-king."

"But they do adore me, Phidias. They love me. I see it in their eyes, I hear it in their cheers, and I feel it in my heart."

"True, but it is because they know you share their hardships and dangers. You lead them without fear into the thickest of the battle. They admire you more than adore you."

Alexander was silent a moment. "I see the difference."

"Most important, I would leave you with this advice. Do not let your own power, ability, and even courage blind you. Do not succumb to hubris, to overweening pride. Trust not solely in your own power but heed also the counsel of your generals and advisers. Remember the poet said, 'Those whom the gods would destroy they first make proud.' Do not be destroyed by your own pride, Alexander."

"Thank you for such good advice, my philosopher friend. I will take it to heart. Now I must prepare to meet and destroy Darius and conquer Persia."

"Go with the gods, Alexander," Phidias replied. "Please remember what I have said. Good fortune to you." Then he turned and left, wondering if his earnest words would be taken to heart and remembered by this impetuous young man.

CHAPTER 26

Spring in Egypt brought new life to the banks of the Nile. Papyrus plants raised their umbrellas and lotuses put out their showy blooms, while flocks of birds glided overhead to resting grounds or waded in the shallows for their lunch. The Macedonians, anxious to follow Alexander into Persia before the heat of summer and the Nile flood, were also feeling spring's rush of new energy.

Alexander met with his commanders and outlined his campaign. "We will march divided and fight united," he said. "It will be easier to manage our forces in two parts, yet be close enough to combine, if we observe the enemy."

His generals agreed to this plan.

"Parmenion", Alexander continued, "you will take half the army across the Euphrates at Thapsacus. I will gather the Greek mercenaries from the coast and follow you."

"Sire," one of the generals spoke up. "You think it wise to spread our forces so much? Darius will surely take advantage of our temporary division and attack and destroy us piecemeal. He has enough men for four armies, each bigger than our combined force."

"I do not share your pessimism, Cleander. I believe the Persians will retreat before us. It is to their advantage to do so. Why should they give battle when they saw what we did at Issus? No, they will not attack us. But to assuage your timidity, I will allow you to wait for the mercenaries and lead them to me. That is all, gentlemen. Let us prepare to invade Persia."

Parmenion and then Alexander crossed the Euphrates, pushed northeast, and crossed the Tigris in September. Four days later, his scouts told Alexander that the enemy was encamped on the plain of Gaugamela near Arbela. Alexander was delighted. "I thought the coward, Darius, would continue to retreat as his advanced guard has done the past two months. Now we will test his courage and that of his army. This battle will decide the fate of Asia."

However, as Alexander topped a small rise and viewed the vast multitude spread out on the plain before him, he was dismayed. There, over a hundred thousand men, thirty thousand horses, chariots, and even elephants spread out before him. Twenty-four nationalities with their colorful uniforms and varied weapons were encamped: Persians, Armenians, Parthians, Cappadocians, Carians, Bactrians, Indians, and of course Greek mercenaries still fought in the pay of the Great King.

Alexander turned to a captain. "I could never imagine such an army. What if we are surrounded and overwhelmed by their sheer numbers? All our victories will be canceled by one defeat."

"Be of good cheer, Sire," his veteran captain said. "Do not fear the great number of the enemy, for they will not be able to stand the very smell of goat that clings to us."

Alexander laughed heartily. "You're right; they will hold their noses, turn, and run. Let us camp for the night and engage them tomorrow."

Just after sundown, while there was still enough light to see, Alexander and his generals, Parmenion, Craterus, Philotas, and Cleander reconnoitered the battleground.

"Look," said Philotas, son of Parmenion and commander of The Companions, "the ground has been completely leveled.".

"It appears like a parade ground," exclaimed Craterus. "Even the stones have been removed and the field stamped."

"It is to prepare it for the chariots," said Alexander. "Darius wants to leave nothing to chance."

The men decided on the deployment of their forces. Parmenion would command the left. "Philotas and I will lead The Companions cavalry on the right," said Alexander. Craterus agreed to command the forward phalanx in the center.

"I want a second line of phalanx behind Craterus, and the Thracians behind them as further support." Alexander drew lines in the dirt to illustrate his strategy.

"We should guard against our flanks from being turned by this superior Persian force," said Parmenion

"I agree," said Alexander. "We can use Cleander's veteran mercenaries."

Cleander spoke up, "I will place them on the flanks and angle backward."

"Excellent," said Alexander. He had the largest army he had ever commanded. The recruited Greek mercenaries and reinforced cavalry units brought his total to forty thousand infantry and seven thousand cavalry. He was still outnumbered by at least 4 to 1, some say more, but Alexander was satisfied with his observations and deployments. "Let us return to camp and make sacrifices for a great victory," he told his generals.

In the twenty months since the battle of Issus, the Persians had made an effort to build a reputable fighting force. The famous archers and ten thousand "Immortals" who had been the backbone of the heavy infantry that had forged an empire no longer existed. Other than the Royal Guard, the infantry mostly consisted of untrained levies and tribesmen. The best part of the army was the cavalry, including the Cappadocians, who had link armor, a thrusting spear, and a longer sword. Darius had brought back the chariot with scythed wheels, which had not been used for a long while. Two hundred of these chariots were drawn up in front of the infantry. In addition, Darius had fifteen war elephants that he placed in front. Horses disliked confronting elephants, and they could be very effective against Alexander's cavalry. His cavalry Darius placed on his flanks, as did Alexander. Having made his dispositions and eaten a light supper, Alexander went early to bed and slept well into the morning, rested and ready to give battle. Darius, on the other hand, made his men stand at their arms all night, a foolish move that only tired them before the battle even began.

While Alexander was forming up his forces before the battle, An officer of the Companions rode up to him. "Look Alexander our Companions are opposite Darius' scythed chariots. If we charge around them it will leave a gap in our lines."

"I can see that," agreed Alexander. "Order the Companions to move to the right and bring our phalanx opposite the chariots."

He sent an order urgent to Craterus who commanded the infantry, now opposite the chariots. "As the chariots charge, have the front ranks throw their javelins at them, then allow them to pass through. The second rank of infantry will take care of them."

Darius observed that the Greeks might shift too far to the right off of his carefully leveled ground, so he immediately launched his heavy cavalry under Bessus against Alexander's extreme right. Men and horses clashed in a desperate fight. Instead of committing all his cavalry at once, Alexander sent in fresh units where they were needed, thus skillfully holding back the Persians.

Darius saw an opportunity and gave the order to launch the chariots at the Macedonian center. As the chariots charged, volleys of Macedonian javelins threw the chariots into confusion. The drivers and horses had not had effective training and the horses panicked, often running into other chariots, spilling men and vehicles over the battlefield. The chariots that survived the chaos and reached the front line of the phalanx passed through the parted ranks and were annihilated by the second line.

Darius shook his fist in frustration at the failure of his chariot attack. One of his officers reported that Alexander had thrown in his last cavalry reserve on the right, Darius yelled, "Order the entire Persian cavalry to move forward and envelop the Macedonian and Greeks on both flanks. Surround and destroy them!"

Alexander at first observed the mass of enemy cavalry aiming at his wings with dismay, but quickly recovered. "Prepare the Companions to take their attack," he said to Philotas. As the enemy cavalry maneuvered, Alexander noticed that instead of the Persians coming directly at the Companions, they veered far to the right in order to envelop the right wing.

Alexander saw the move and smiled to himself. "The Persians have made a mistake," Alexander gloated. "This will create a break in their line." It was part of Alexander's military genius to see an opening in the heat of battle and instantly take advantage of it.

He gave the order. "Wheel the Companions and part of the phalanx to the left and wedge through the gap in the Persian lines. Philip's training and discipline allowed the Macedonians to instantly execute the maneuver. Alexander yelled at the top of his voice, "Follow me my Companions!" as he galloped through the weakened opening and straight toward Darius himself.

A fierce hand-to-hand struggle ensued, with Darius' guard putting up a vigorous fight. The dense Macedonian phalanx followed the cavalry, and it's long bristling lances cleared all resistance before its advance.

With alarm an officer at Darius' side pointed at Alexander, whose unmistakable helmet and armor charged on his black stallion directly at him. Darius panicked at the threat, lost his courage, and reining his horse around fled from the field. His guards valiantly stood their ground and died almost to a man.

The Macedonians had not won the battle yet, however. When the phalanx advanced and turned, the Persian cavalry broke through the gap, cutting the phalanx in two. Then the enemy made another blunder. Instead of turning to go behind the center of the phalanx and destroy the hard-pressed Greek left, the Persian cavalry rode straight on to loot the baggage.

Parmenion on the left sent a desperate message to Alexander for help on his flank. The note reached Alexander as he was completing his successful charge on the right. He noted with disgust and regret that Darius had run away. "Philotas," he yelled, "the phalanx can take care of Darius' guard. Your father needs our aid. Follow me with the Companions." They crossed the battlefield and encountered the Persian guard and Parthian and Indian cavalry.

Some of the fiercest cavalry fighting continued on both flanks, horses and riders crying and falling under the thundering hooves. Word spread among the Persian troops that Darius had fled and they began to lose heart.

Alexander's charge relieved some of the pressure on Parmenion, and the Greeks and Macedonians on the left made another charge, collapsing the Persian right. Meanwhile, Bessus made an orderly retreat with the left flank of the Persians.

Alexander watched the enemy retreating with relief and realized he had won the battle. "Pursue them!" He ordered his men. "Kill as many as you can, for we don't want to have to face them again." The Macedonians and Greeks chased the Persians for thirty-five miles, as far as Arbela, pausing only for a short rest at midnight. The slaughter was unimaginable.

A combination of awe and affection for Alexander filled his men. They were awed at how the gods protected him from the utmost danger, and favored him with outstanding victories against overwhelming odds. They held him in affection because he shared their hardships, even their food and shelter. He held them as brothers in arms and knew their names. The Battle of Gaugamela wrote in stone the truth of Alexander's military genius and his victory over the Persian Empire. He was the master of Asia. Darius fled into the hills of Media, but Alexander did not pursue him, turning instead to the great cities of Babylon, Susa, and Persepolis.

Callisthenes wrote to Aristotle of Alexander's taking of Babylon, the winter capital of the Persian Kings: "On approaching Babylon, a deputation of officials from the city came to greet Alexander. They prostrated themselves before him and hailed him as their conqueror and master. They said that he would be welcomed into their city and asked that he spare it from slaughter, looting, and destruction. By sparing the city, Alexander showed restraint and foresight and taught a lesson to other cities of his mercy, if they surrendered to him."

Babylon surrendered much wealth to Alexander. He distributed some to his soldiers, which satisfied them since it prevented them from looting. The chief priest invited Alexander to the main temple so they could honor him. "Alexander climbed the steps of the Temple of Ishtar in his gleaming armor, carrying flowers and a vial of oil," wrote Callisthenes. "The priests said prayers, burnt incense, and blessed Alexander. They said that the Babylonian gods have also claimed Alexander to be a living god. Then Alexander placed the flowers at the foot of the statue of the goddess, poured the oil on her feet, and bowed down while the priests and the people beamed and nodded with approval. He then turned and spoke directly to the people. Through a translator he told them that he would restore all the city's sacred shrines that the Persians had removed.

"I must admit, Aristotle, that even though we Greeks do not approve of bowing down and giving obeisance to foreign gods, Alexander charmed the Babylonians. They love him as if he is a god himself. The Babylonian priests have convinced Alexander that they have strong influence with their ancient gods and that indeed Alexander is one of them. These declarations of the Egyptians, and now the Babylonians, that Alexander is divine, trouble not only me but the soldiers. The Asians are familiar with this type of god-king, but we Greeks are not."

Callisthenes continued his description of Alexander's habits in another letter to Aristotle: "As you know, Alexander has always had a wild and restless spirit, always seeking new adventures and delighting in courting danger, even injury or death. He cannot stand resting and is always thinking of new things to do—innovations, military tactics, worlds to conquer.

"He made fun of his generals recently because they had so many servants they had nothing to do. I quote what he told them: 'I wonder that you with your experience do not know that those who work sleep more soundly than those for whom other people work. Have you yet, to learn that the greatest need after our victories is to avoid the vices and weaknesses of those whom we have conquered?'

"He begrudges time needed for sleep and is sparing in his eating. In drinking, he enjoys lingering with his friends and occasionally with us scholars over a goblet of wine. Occasionally, however, after he has ordered unforgivable slaughter, he will drink longer and deeper. I am fearful, uncle, that during these bouts of drinking, when his coating of social conscience is washed away, a ferocious barbarism will emerge and consume him."

By the end of that year, Alexander reached Susa, the summer capital of the Persian Kings, which welcomed him. Callisthenes again wrote to his uncle: "Alexander protected the city from pillage but satisfied his troops with some of the fifty thousand talents he found in Darius' treasure houses. He sent some of it back to Platea in Greece, which had bravely resisted the Persian invasion a hundred and fifty years ago. He also returned to the Greek cities on the Asian coast the donations he had elicited from them early in his campaign. He is indeed showing himself to be a magnanimous conqueror. Perhaps he has learned something from you and Phidias in how to show his humanity. He had me compose a letter to be circulated among the Greeks of the entire world announcing that they are now completely free of Persian rule."

Alexander did not tarry long in Susa but was anxious to capture Darius' ceremonial capital at Persepolis. In midwinter he crossed the mountains and seized the capital so unexpectedly that the Persians did not have time to hide the royal treasury. The treasure he collected was so vast that it took twenty thousand mules and five thousand camels to remove it.

As Alexander and his men approached Persepolis, they came upon a hundred Greeks, who had been captured by the Persians. One of his captains brought the unfortunate men to Alexander, who was horrified by the sight. "Oh, ye gods!" he exclaimed and broke down into tears at the sight of the mutilated captives. Some had their arms, legs, or ears cut off, while others had their eyes gouged out.

Alexander reflected the fury his soldiers felt at this outrage. "The Persians will pay dearly for this," he vowed. He turned to his captain. "See that these unfortunates are given lands in Persia and slaves to work for them."

Possibly because of this mutilation of fellow Greeks, Alexander this time allowed his men to loot the city, ravage the women, and slaughter the men. Alexander tried to wash away the two days of bloody savagery with heavy drinking. As if on a whim, he decided to perform one more act of revenge. "Burn the Palace of Darius," he ordered a general.

"But Sire, it is such a magnificent edifice. Surely you could occupy it yourself."

"I said burn it!" he screamed through a drunken haze. "I order you to do it to avenge the Persian invasion of Greece and the burning of Athens."

Phidias was appalled. "What a shameful waste. We could have learned so much of the culture and history of Persia in that palace." He shook his head and wondered about Alexander's judgment, especially when he'd had too much wine.

Alexander indeed had a complex personality, with fits of slaughter and destruction moderated by lofty ideals of universal brotherhood. Throughout his life, his demons would continue to haunt him.

VI DANGERS AND ORDEALS

CHAPTER 27

Alexander's generals congratulated him on his conquest and subjugation of Persia. "Surely your goal of conquering the world's largest and richest empire is fulfilled," said Parmenion. "When can I tell the men they may return to Macedon and Greece?"

"But Sire," said Cleitus, "Darius is still alive and may yet raise another army. Although he is a coward, he has able generals like Bessus and Mazaeus."

"Cleitus is right," said Alexander. "All in Babylon, Susa, Persepolis, and the other cities we have captured consider me as rightful King of Persia by conquest. However, as long as Darius lives, my rights to that throne may be questioned. We must pursue and capture him and force him to abdicate, and then I will marry his daughter to cement the legitimacy of my reign. Parmenion, tell the men to rest and enjoy the spoils of war for now. In the summer we will march north in pursuit of Darius."

As summer swelled the warehouses with grain, Alexander's army provisioned itself and once again marched, this time to capture Darius and destroy any pockets of resistance. Alexander had almost caught up with his quarry when he received a message.

"Sire," Cleitus announced, "we have received a message from Bessus, the chief Persian general. He said that he and the other generals were disgusted with the cowardice and mismanagement of the Great King in this war. Their long resentment flared into rebellion, and they killed Darius. They ask for peace with you. It is my opinion that he would ask some reward from you for removing this threat to your throne. He might seek to be appointed a satrap of one of the provinces."

"We shall see about that," said Alexander. "It was my hope that I would capture Darius and force him to make obeisance to me and acknowledge me as the King of Persia. Now I have been denied that fulfillment of my dream by a cowardly act."

"But you are now the undisputed Great King. We will have the official ceremony when we return to Susa."

"But it is still a disappointment."

The next day, Alexander came upon Darius' body and sent it with due honors back to Persepolis for proper burial in the royal resting place of the Persian Kings. A new flame of revenge grew in Alexander as he pondered the lost opportunity and the humiliation of his vanquished foe.

"We will pursue Bessus and destroy the last of his army, even following him into the far territories if necessary. I will avenge the murder of Darius."

His advisers were disappointed that they could not rest from campaigning after seven years, but they could not dissuade Alexander and followed him as if he were Apollo himself.

Unsatisfied by his conquest of Persia and the death of Darius, Alexander decided to subjugate the tribes on the eastern borders of Persia. This had not even been accomplished by the great Cyrus, but Alexander could not satiate his lust for battle and conquest.

Callisthenes followed Alexander to record his exploits, while Phidias remained in Babylon. Callisthenes sent back reports to Aristotle through Phidias. "His campaign into Sogdiana, Ariana, and Bactria was bloody. He now controls the lands that had belonged to Darius. However, he achieved little," wrote Callisthenes, "except winning some victories, finding some gold, and leaving enemies everywhere. Near Bokhara he found Bessus, and Alexander made himself the avenger of the Great King. He had Bessus whipped almost to death, cut off his nose and ears, and then sent him to Ecbatana. He was executed by having his arms and legs tied to two trees that had been drawn together by ropes. When the ropes were cut, the trees pulled him to pieces. Aristotle, I am afraid that as Alexander is removed further in distance and time from Greece, he is acting less and less like a Greek and more and more like a barbarian king."

Phidias read Callisthenes' letters with a mixture of emotions. He was satisfied that Alexander had exhibited mercy and forbearance when he captured Babylon and Susa. He'd shown generosity with the spread of some of Darius' treasure among his soldiers and Greek cities, and pity and a generous spirit were his when he saw the mutilated Greek captives.

However, these were thrown away by wanton slaughter and the burning of the Palace in Persepolis. *History may never forgive him for that*, Phidias thought. *What had Alexander to gain except the shedding of more blood and self-aggrandizement by invading the tribal areas the Persians had never completely subjugated?* Phidias thought the barbarian blood of Olympias boiled in

Alexander's veins and wondered which part of Alexander would finally win out.

Phidias also was concerned about Callisthenes' obvious criticism of Alexander. Would that color his objectiveness as a chronicler of historical events? It would be a shame if his prejudices tainted his historical record.

What bothered Phidias the most was that if Callisthenes' criticism of Alexander became overt, Alexander would punish him or send him home. Alexander had brought Callisthenes as historian as a favor to Aristotle. It would be an insult to Aristotle if he were sent back to Greece.

* * *

After completing his conquest of the Persian Empire, Alexander decided to turn south and enter India. He had to cross the daunting Himalayas, and his generals advised against it.

"Alexander, the men are reluctant to go beyond Persia across those mountains into a strange land. They are tired and want to go home, at least back to Babylon," argued Ptolemy.

"Reluctant? Were they reluctant to follow me in the conquest of Persia and pursuit of Darius? Were they reluctant to bask in the glory of our victories? Were they reluctant to share the riches I have collected for them? Was I reluctant to share all the dangers and hardships they suffered? No.

"Part of that country on the other side of the Indus River was ruled two centuries ago by the first Darius. I know my history, my friend. I am determined to recapture it for my own empire. Tell the men I will share all the wealth we capture, and I will personally lead them into any battle."

"Alexander, I'm sure they will follow you, even though they may wish to return to Susa or Babylon. They need only hear your order, and they will obey. They honor you because of your example as our leader."

"Good, then we will cross the Hindu Kush. Tell the men that it is my order."

Alexander, with about twenty-seven thousand men, followed the Kabul River down to the Indus and crossed overland to the Hydaspes River. There, near a place called Jhelum, Alexander fought one of his most difficult battles. The enemy under King Porus had a well-trained army several times the size of Alexander's. He also had war elephants, which rendered Alexander's cavalry useless. The enemy stood arrayed on the far side of the river. Alexander showed his military genius by feinting a series of attacks and then attacking from an unexpected quarter, defeating Porus and his army

"We fought their elephants with our phalanxes and long spears. They could not break our ranks," reported Craterus. "More than twenty thousand of the enemy lay dead on the battlefield."

"I am overjoyed with our victory," replied Alexander, "but also saddened at a great loss. One of the casualties of this battle was my beloved Bucephalus." He was heartbroken and cried over the death of his magnificent steed his father had given to him. "He carried me over thousands of miles and through countless campaigns. I will leave a city built to his honor and memory at the site of this struggle. We will call it Bucephala."

After resting and refitting his army, Alexander told a meeting of his generals, "We will advance deeper into India."

"But Alexander," Craterus complained, "the men are tired of marching and fighting. What reason do we have to go further east?"

"Must I instruct you in your geography, General? Greek scholars have told me that a great ocean encircles the world. We must only reach the eastern shore, and then we can sail back to Babylon."

The army reluctantly followed its commander, but at the Hyphasis River, a deputation of his captains approached his tent.

A senior captain Alexander knew and admired for his bravery and leadership spoke. "Sire, the men are grumbling. They say they could see the reason for the campaigns in Persia, but now we have conquered it. They are reluctant to march further away into the unknown. They have heard of vast deserts, fierce warriors, and armies of elephants in the lands ahead."

"What, are they afraid of elephants? Darius and Porus had these, and we defeated them. Are they afraid of unknown lands and difficult terrain? We have campaigned in many strange countries and crossed mountains, deserts, and rivers. Are they now shivering women, cowards who would not follow their King?"

"No, Sire, they are not cowards. They are tired. We have been gone from Macedon for over eight years of hard campaigns and battles. They yearn for home, where they may spend the fruits of conquest with their families."

"Order the men to prepare to march tomorrow."

"They will not march, Sire. With respect to you as their commander and king, they will not go further."

Callisthenes wrote to Phidias: "Alexander waited three days on the banks of the Hyphasis River for them to change their minds. When they would not, he agreed to return home. He had his men erect twelve altars to the Olympian gods in gratitude for his many victories."

Alexander decided to divide his army on the return march. "A part of the force will take a northerly route back. I will lead the rest of the army back through the southern regions. We have yet to explore that part of Persia," Alexander said.

"But, Alexander," Ptolemy objected, "doesn't the large Baluchistan desert lie in our path? It will be a dangerous march."

"Have you not been accustomed to dangerous marches, Ptolemy? We will have experienced guides who know the desert and where the watering holes may be found. I want to see that part of my empire on our way back to Persepolis. Tell the men to prepare to march and that we will fight on our way, if we must."

On the way down the Indus Valley, Alexander and his men fought their way through hostile tribes. During the attack on one city, Alexander led the advance upon the walls and was severely wounded. After the victory was complete, his men carried their seriously stricken leader to his tent.

Hardened veterans with tears in their eyes passed his wounded form and kissed his garments, overcome with emotion by his courage and sacrifice. So serious were his wounds that Alexander spent three months convalescing before resuming the march to the Indian Ocean, where he sent part of his forces back by ships. Callisthenes went with them.

With his remaining men, Alexander turned northwest, where his route lay through the scorching desert of Baluchistan. The heat was so intense they had to march by night.

"We have not seen water for several days," Alexander said to a captain. "Send the guides to me."

The captain returned with one of the guides, who said through an interpreter that they had missed a landmark but were sure to find it the next day.

"Tell him that if they do not find our way out of this desert soon, we will all die, but he will be the first because I will personally flay him alive," Alexander threatened.

The guide did not flinch. He replied through the interpreter that he was not afraid to die but that if Alexander killed him, he would never find his way out of the desert.

Alexander told him to go and do the job he was supposed to do. For the next two hundred miles, the guides did not find the way. Food supplies ran out, and the baggage animals had to be sacrificed and the baggage abandoned. Water became extremely scarce. A little was found and sent to Alexander.

Alexander took the cup of precious water. "I cannot accept this cup when my men cry with thirst. I will suffer with them. They are my comrades, who give their lives for me." With that, he poured the water into the sand.

The heat killed thousands on this march, and thirst killed more. When Alexander finally reached Susa, he had lost ten thousand men and was himself half mad.

CHAPTER 28

During his recovery in the comfort of Susa, Alexander came to the realization that he would have to channel his energy from conquest to the consolidation and control of his vast empire.

Persian satraps or governors of the provinces, leaders of cities, and wealthy merchants came to Alexander, pleading for his control. They were concerned not only for their safety but for the security and prosperity of Persia.

As more and more territory fell under his control, Alexander realized that in order to hold his new empire, he had to govern it effectively, and to do that, he had to somehow merge it with the Greek world.

Aristotle had told Alexander to treat all Greeks as free men, but to consider all barbarians, that is non-Greeks, as slaves. During the nine years he had been in Persia, however, Alexander was surprised to find a high degree of refined taste and good manners among the Persian aristocrats. He admired the way in which the Persian Empire was organized and governed and wondered if his hardy Macedonians could step into the shoes of the Persian governors.

"In order to give a sense of continuity and permanence to my reign, I must abandon my role as a Macedonian King," he confided to some of his closest advisers. He had increased the number of Persian ministers who advised him.

"I must conceive of myself as a Greco-Persian Emperor. The Empire must be a mingling of Greeks and Persians who will be on equal footing. We will no longer be conqueror and conquered subjects but a marriage of cultures and blood."

His Persian subjects were pleased. They had charmed their master with their civilized manners and courtly ways.

"I will also follow the expedient example of my predecessors and tolerate local religious and social customs. Each province or ethnic group will be able to maintain its own identity, but Greek ideas and culture will be infused throughout my Empire. In order to do that, I will create new Greek cities over the land and encourage Greeks to settle in them."

He encouraged colonizers to come from Greece, where they scratched a living from impoverished soil, and he founded no fewer than sixteen cities that bore his name.

Alexander had been too involved with his conquests and political problems to have had much energy for the opposite sex. He had not seemed to care much for the company of women. Like his father, he enjoyed the camaraderie of men, fighting, carousing, drinking, and conversing. His closest and dearest companion, some thought even his lover, was Hephaestion. Alexander fought side by side with him, often sharing his tent and meals. It may have been that Alexander in his mid-twenties just enjoyed physical activities and the companionship of other men.

Alexander, who seemed to have an endless supply of energy, belittled his officers who succumbed to luxury. He confided to Hephaestion, "Sleep and sexual activity make me realize that I am mortal. After all, the weariness that leads to sleep and the pleasure derived from the sex act belong to the unthinking weakness of human nature. They remind me that I am a man who has human frailties and feelings. If I am to be a god, I must overcome those shortcomings."

Nevertheless, while campaigning in Sogdiana and Bactria, Alexander was smitten by a princess named Roxana. Whether he was captivated by her beauty and seductiveness or because of political expediency, he married her. Many of the soldiers had already taken native women and, following Alexander's example, married them. These numbered into the thousands over the years.

Three years later, in Susa, Alexander considered more ways in which he could consolidate his empire. At a dinner with his top officers and advisors, Cleitus rose to toast him. "Let's all raise our cups and honor the new Great King, Alexander. He, with the help of his generals and the courage of his men, has put an end forever to the threat of Persia. May his reign be long and prosperous."

All present yelled their approval and drank to Alexander.

Acknowledging the compliments, Alexander stood and toasted his officers in return. "It is three years since I have mounted the throne of Darius. All of the old Persian Empire, including Egypt, the Ionian Greeks, Macedon, and Greece, acknowledge me as their King. It is now one realm and should be one culture, although comprised of many nationalities and tolerating many religious traditions.

"I have instituted several policies in order to consolidate my new empire. We have merged the Persian cavalry into our own, and tomorrow I will send out the order to have thirty thousand young Persian men trained in Macedonian military tactics. Persian administrators work at maintaining the provinces. To further the melding of our peoples, I have opened lands in Mesopotamia and Persia to colonists from Greece. This will not only relieve the pressure of feeding excess population but diffuse some of the class warfare in our home country. Landless Greeks can now settle across Asia and bring with them the Greek language and culture.

"In the next few days, I will announce to the entire world that I am to marry Statira, Darius' daughter, and Parysatis, daughter of Artaxerxes, the predecessor of Darius. Although these are political unions, they also symbolize the union of our two peoples. I want my top eighty officers to marry eighty Persians of the nobility. All of you present will gain wives who will also bring you wealth and lands. As wedding presents, I will give the officers twenty thousand talents. We will have a great public ceremony and celebrate all the marriages in the great Court of the Palace in Susa. The priests of all religions will make sacrifices to all the gods and bless our nuptials.

"The centuries-long quarrel between Europe and Asia will end in a great wedding feast. Unity and peace will rule the world. Let us drink to our weddings, and to our Empire."

During the talk, the officers smiled and winked at each other when Alexander talked of uniting the two nations of Greece and Persia. Having been away from home a long while, they appreciated the beauty of the Persian women and welcomed the prospect of marrying noble girls. They rose, drank, and yelled approval of Alexander's marriage plans.

A few weeks after Alexander's new wives moved into the palace with all of their retinue, Alexander also increased the number of his Persian attendants and began wearing Asian clothes. His servants used many of the Persian modes of service such as bathing, dressing, and serving food and wine to Alexander. All of them made obeisance by prostrating before him, and it was not long before Alexander asked his fellow Macedonians and Greeks to do likewise.

Callisthenes wrote to Aristotle: "Alexander first put on barbarian dress perhaps to gain the affection and approval of the Persians in his effort to bring Greek civilization to them. Nothing gains more impression upon men than conformity to their customs. Let it be noted that he did not affect the ostentatious show of the most opulent of Persian dress. He moderated his taste by adopting a middle way between the Persian and Macedonian modes, being not so pompous as the one, yet more flaunting than the other.

"The officers and soldiers see the change in Alexander, not only of dress and manners but in his personality. They mourn the loss of their leader to Asia and miss the affection and time he once showered on them. They are being softened by oriental luxury and grumble at any of his orders to train or garrison. They have forgotten his generosity and speak of desertion and going home. For his part, Alexander seems to lap up the flattery the Persians spread on him, like a dog with honey. He resents the soldiers' lack of appreciation and prefers more and more the society of the Persian nobility.

"When Alexander asked his soldiers to follow the Persian custom of prostrating themselves before him, his captains were affronted by this. They thought this implied worship, and they did not think Alexander was a god. They told him it was not their custom as Greeks and refused to prostrate themselves.

"I am afraid, uncle, that there will be open rebellion and even threat of violence against Alexander. There are many, including generals, who scoff at his ideas and resent his forcing the Persian ways upon them."

Alexander was aware of the resentment of his Macedonians, who saw him favoring Persians and even copying their dress and manners. He called together his Persian and Macedonian officers.

"You must realize now that we have made the world smaller by the unity of our countries. You must regard the whole world as your home and all good men as brothers. The idea of universal brotherhood must be left to philosophers, but for us it is a reality. It is politically expedient that we hold together our multilingual empire. Therefore, I urge my Persian captains to feel as though they are the equals of the Macedonians, and I urge the Macedonians to accept this equality."

The assemblage applauded and thanked him, the Persians more enthusiastically than the Macedonians. Alexander's actions and words may have mollified the conquered Persians, but the victorious Macedonians resented it.

Phidias had also noted the resentment generated by Alexander's policies, but wrote to Aristotle about a new problem: "Alexander has sent an announcement to all the Greek states except Macedon that he wishes to be publicly acknowledged from this time as the son of Zeus-Ammon. He omitted Macedon because he thought this might be taken as an insult to the memory of his father, Philip, and arouse resentment. I have heard that most of the Greek states complied, even the Spartans, replying that Alexander can consider himself to be a god if he wants to. After all, we Greeks are familiar in our history with heroes being semidivine or divine.

"I believe there is a purely political side of Alexander in wanting to be considered divine. Many of the members of the Hellenic League like Macedonian overlordship. It keeps the power of large cities like Athens and Sparta in check. On the other hand, Alexander is obviously aware of Greek sensitivity to being ruled by a king.

"Thus, as a god, he stands outside the cities. They can maintain their own form of government and a sense of individuality. As the supreme commander of the league, he knows that he cannot order but can only persuade. This may be one of Alexander's more brilliant moves. It allows the Greek city-states to remain as political entities. And even though many Macedonians mock his divinity, his closest associates admit that it is politically expedient.

"The Egyptians have always considered their pharaohs to be gods. The priests at Siwa and Babylon, who were believed to have special knowledge in this respect, all assured Alexander of his divine status. It is quite unlikely that Alexander really considers himself to be a god, for he has come very close to death from sickness or wounds. Yet since his self-deification, he has become more arrogant. He sits on a golden throne surrounded by sycophants, wears sacred vestments, and has incense and candles burned around him. Sometimes he even wears the horns of Ammon on his head. If anyone disagrees with him, he becomes very irritable and berates them.

"For my part, I do not believe he thinks he is divine, for he continues to give sacrifices to the gods. This would be unheard of if he were divine himself. I think he is promoting his deification to easier rule a superstitious and heterogeneous population. No doubt he feels that the common people of our two worlds will more likely give him reverence if his divinity is accepted by the upper classes.

"We Greeks, of course, don't accept Alexander deifying himself. That is unheard of. If men sometimes are so honored, it is because it is bestowed upon them by the gods or by other men. Alexander's puffed-up ideas of god- emperor are becoming obnoxious to his men."

As Alexander's ideas and plans for unifying Greeks and Persians filtered through the Macedonian ranks, they made little headway.

"We are not political philosophers," complained a soldier to his fellows. "I leave the idea of brotherhood with barbarians to them. I am a Macedonian soldier."

"I agree," said another. "After all, we conquered these people. They should be our slaves and we their masters."

"Yeah," added someone else, "he should govern this barbarian country like he did Macedon and Thrace."

"And I resent his treatment of the Persians as our equals," said the first soldier. "He has placed some Persians over us as commanders and has even made some governors."

They had no sympathy for Alexander's dream to unite the empire and govern it responsibly with fairness to all its peoples.

One of the older Macedonian veterans, who had only been listening, added his thoughts. "I feel that our King and Commander has put himself on a pedestal. He is too much taken with his titles and power. He has abandoned the comradeship that has always been part of the Macedonian army. His father drank and ate with us and made himself always available if we had a problem. Alexander wants us to grovel like his Persian lackeys."

Alexander increasingly felt this resentment and heard the grumblings of his officers and men. More and more he feared conspiracy, revolt, and assassination.

CHAPTER 29

Marching east of Susa, Alexander stopped with his men in the town of the Zarangians, and the local king invited him to take over his rude castle as his headquarters. The army was encamped outside the town. That evening he was having a bath to wash off the dusty march before dinner when one of his squires burst in.

Surprised to come in on Alexander naked in his bath, the squire was embarrassed and speechless. "What is it, Metron?" Alexander shook him aware. "What is so important?"

"Sire, there's a man outside who says that he has heard of a plot to kill you."

"What? Where is he?"

"He is under guard in a locked room."

"What's his name?"

"Cebalinos."

"What is it that he said?" Alexander asked as a Persian slave boy dried him off and dressed him.

In bits and pieces, Alexander drew out of the squire what he knew. Apparently Cebalinos was told by his brother, Nicomachus, that Dymnos of Chalesta had approached him to join a conspiracy to kill the King. "Dymnos told Nicomachus that he would kill him if he didn't join, so he pretended to agree but told his brother. That's why Cebalinos came to tell you."

Alexander called for the captain of the guard and told him to arrest Dymnos, then he went with a guard and the squire to the room where Cebalinos was guarded. When Alexander entered the room, the terrified prisoner knelt and started babbling, "Oh, Sire, thank goodness I got word to you before it was too late!" He told him how Dymnos had felt slighted by the King and had collected others who resented Alexander.

"What others?"

Cebalinos told him the others his brother had named.

"How long did your brother know this before he told you?"

"As soon as he could find me, he told me to tell you."

"Are you saying this happened today as we were making camp?"

"No, Sire, it was two days ago. That's why I came now, to report directly to you."

"Two days!" Alexander exploded. "You knew this for two days and didn't report it because you are in on it, aren't you?" Alexander glared at him through slitted eyes.

"No, Sire," Cebalinos insisted with a croak. "I went as soon as I heard to your tent and reported it. The officer said you were busy, but that he would tell you as soon as you were free. Again the next day I reported to him, and he gave me the same answer. Then, when my brother saw that Dymnos and the others were still free, he said that I must report to you in person myself."

"Your brother was right. What officer was it you gave the report to?" Alexander looked at him with expectation.

"General Philotas, my King."

Alexander repeated his name, at first in disbelief, but then with a look of understanding washing across his face. Philotas was the son of Parmenion, Alexander's second in command. He was the Commander of the Companions, the most prestigious cavalry unit, which Alexander himself had commanded under his father. Even though he had been friends with Alexander since childhood, he had made no secret of resenting Alexander's claim of being a son of Zeus and of his taking credit for all the army's victories.

Alexander told Cebalinos that he and his brother would not be harmed and for him to bring Nicomachus to his headquarters for questioning. Back in his room, Alexander ate a light supper and called for his senior officers.

Hephaestion, Ptolemy, Perdiccas, and Craterus appeared, and Alexander ordered that all roads out of the area be closed and guarded. Then he told them of the plot. They heard Nicomachus tell his story, and then Alexander sent for Dymnos.

Guards brought Dymnos in on a stretcher, blood pouring from his chest and trickling from his mouth.

"Who did this?" Alexander yelled.

The head guard was white-faced but finding his voice said, "He did it himself, Sire, apparently as he saw we were coming to arrest him."

Alexander bent over the soldier he knew and saw him choking at the blood filling his throat. "What have I done to wrong you, Dymnos? Tell me."

The dying man's eyes focused with apparent anger and coughed out, "Barbarian," then they became fixed and he breathed no more.

That night around midnight, all the conspirators were arrested—Philotas last. He was brought before Alexander and the generals, still not completely sober from a drunken sleep.

Alexander confronted him with what Cebalinos had told him. "Why didn't you tell me when you first heard of this?"

Philotas tossed it off with a little chuckle. "I thought nothing of it. Alexander, do you want to hear of every grumble and drunken threat from anyone who feels a slight?" Alexander could hear the scorn in his voice, as if talking down to a boy.

Alexander calmly looked him directly in the eyes and said, "Dymnos has killed himself. He will not stand trial, but you and his other conspirators will. Guards, take him away."

The news quickly spread around the camp the next day. Trial by the army was to be in the afternoon. It was amazing to the Persians that the King could put no Macedonian to death without their vote. Their Great King would have immediately had the conspirators roasted to death.

The conspirators all confessed and implicated each other. Brought before the assembled troops one by one, they were shouted as guilty and taken away.

Finally, Philotas was brought before the company. The brothers gave their testimony, and many of the soldiers recalled Philotas' pride and insolence against the King on many occasions. Whether he was a member of the conspiracy or merely failed to report it with hopes it might succeed was never proved. They voted him guilty of treason and sentenced him to death.

The executions would be the next day. Stakes were placed into the hard ground and the prisoners tied to them. The lesser soldiers were stoned while the general faced a squad with javelins.

After the executions, Alexander ordered the death of Parmenion. He was campaigning in Ecbatana. As second only under Alexander, he had his own army that he could pay out of treasure he had captured. Philotas had been his only living son, two others having died during their campaigns in Persia.

"Did Philotas implicate his father?" asked one of Alexander's generals after hearing of the order to kill him. "If he did, it was under the most vigorous torture."

"It doesn't matter," Alexander dismissed the question. "He must die because he may seek revenge for his son's death. Other officers and generals may join him in casting me aside. I can't trust anyone. Do as I say and send messengers with orders to kill Parmenion for treason."

The messengers went to Ecbatana. Parmenion had heard of neither the plot nor execution of his son. One of the messengers went to Parmenion with a letter from Alexander. It was a routine appearing message complimenting Parmenion on his campaign and requesting a report. The other messenger went directly to his senior officers and gave them Alexander's order. They read it and, without question, put on their armor and swords and marched to Parmenion's tent.

The old general sat at his desk looking at maps when they entered unannounced. "What can I do for you, gentlemen?" He looked up and saw that they were armed.

"We have received a message from Alexander."

They walked toward him.

Parmenion rose. "And what is it?"

His second in command displayed the letter. "He has ordered your death."

They drew their swords.

"But why?"

Those were the only words Philip and Alexander's most loyal general could utter before he was cut down.

From that moment in which Alexander ordered the murder of his most able and oldest general to the end, the relationship between Alexander and the men in his army became increasingly fractured. The officers and men became ever more discontent, as Alexander became ever more suspicious and isolated.

Alexander at first exalted at the uncovering of the plot to kill him and the deaths of the conspirators. He drank congratulations to himself and to his fate, which he believed was protected by the gods. The bouts of drinking became more frequent and longer as the realization seeped to the surface that it was his most loyal and ablest officers who were conspiring against him. Fearing that he could trust no one, he isolated himself in his Royal Palace, surrounded by barbarians. Heavy droughts of wine could not bring back his sense of comradeship with his Macedonians.

Alexander replaced Philotas with Cleitus and Hephaestion, giving both command of The Companions. They were his closest friends, yet he gave them joint command, expecting that neither would act against him without the other knowing and warning him. Cleitus had been Alexander's closest advisor ever since he had saved Alexander's life at the Granicus.

Two years after the deaths of Philotas and Parmenion, Alexander was campaigning with his men in Sogdiana. After the successful campaign, he planned a victory banquet in Samarkand. The food was sumptuous, as befitting the Great King and his officers. Wine ran freely, and all drank deeply, congratulating themselves on their recent victories.

One officer after another rose and toasted the leadership and bravery of Alexander and the fortitude of the men. Some of the officers were comparing Alexander's military genius with that of his father. Some defended Philip's generals, whereas others thought Alexander outfought them.

One of the officers, who had recently been promoted, rose to speak. "I was a young officer in King Philip's army and fought at Chaeronea with him and Alexander. Alexander's action during that engagement won the battle for us. I saw that his decision in the battle of Gaugamela turned near defeat into overwhelming victory. I think Alexander's military genius far outshines that of his father. I toast our King."

The officers drank from their cups. As they were refilled, Cleitus rose to speak. Wine had loosened his tongue with candor, as it had weakened his self- restraint. "I take exception to your demeaning the memory of King Philip in praising Alexander. It is true that Alexander is brave, but he is not the military and political man his father was. Remember, King Philip made Macedon and our army strong. He unified Greece and made possible our invasion of Persia. I think King Philip's achievements were much more meaningful than Alexander's."

Alexander choked on his wine and spit it out when he heard those words. Before Cleitus could propose a toast to Philip, Alexander, equally intoxicated, stood in anger at the affront. "Why you ungrateful…" He raised his hand to strike Cleitus.

Ptolemy, seated on the other side of Cleitus, saw what Alexander was going to do and grabbed Cleitus, pulling him away.

Alexander lost his balance and fell back into his seat. "You call yourself my friend!" he yelled. "You're no friend!"

Cleitus shot back, "More of a friend then your Persians who kiss your feet!"

They both screamed insults and obscenities while Ptolemy pushed Cleitus out of the hall.

The assembled men went back to eating and drinking, having put aside the argument between the two men as merely drunken behavior. Alexander pulled deeply at another cup to quell the jealousy and anger that filled his gullet.

Ptolemy was escorting Cleitus down the hallway when his charge broke away. He had more to say, the wine still ruling his judgment. He stumbled back into the room to continue his tirade and reeled drunkenly to the center of the men. Alexander watched him through a wine-soaked haze.

"You did not win our victories. Your officers and men did!" Cleitus screamed. "You acted like a thoughtless youth running into danger. I saved your life at Granicus, as others saved it in other battles. You may be brave, but it is we who won your battles!"

Alexander's mind clouded with rage as he turned and grasped the spear from one of the guards behind him. Before anyone could stop him, he hurled it with all his strength at the figure in front him, yelling, "You're a traitor!"

The spear ran straight and true, penetrating Cleitus' chest and extending out of his back. He grasped the shaft protruding from his midchest, a look of shock and pain on his face. He coughed as blood filled his mouth and spilled down his chin. Then his eyes glazed, turning up into his brows, as he stumbled and fell on his side.

Everyone in the room was struck dumb with shock at the horrible scene that ended with the murder of one of Alexander's closest friends. Hephaestion, next to Alexander, said in a barely audible voice, "You killed Cleitus."

The rage in Alexander reinforced the alcoholic haze that shrouded his mind. He was not fully conscious of what he had actually done, as Hephaestion and Ptolemy put their arms under his and led him out of the hall. Staring between the men who held him up, he ranted incoherently about traitors and ungrateful officers, still unaware that he had just murdered his closest adviser and second best friend.

It was almost noon the next day when Alexander stirred and awoke in a red fog. His head pounded and his stomach rebelled at the abuse of too much wine. He sat on the side of his bed, his head in his hands. He saw that he was still in his clothes and did not remember coming to bed. Fits and flashes of the memory of drunken revelry of the night before began to seep through the hazy curtain. He vaguely remembered arguing, yelling, scuffling. He called to the guard.

"Yes, Great King?" asked the youthful Persian guard, bowing deeply.

"What did I do last night?"

"What do you mean, Great King?"

"Was there an argument? A fight? Was I violent? What happened?"

"You killed Cleitus, Great King. You threw a spear through his chest."

"Noooo!" Alexander screamed, squeezing his temples and tearing at his hair. "NO! NO! NO! NO!" He beat his chest, ripping at his clothes. "Noooo!" He staggered from his bed, grabbing anything he could reach and flinging it at the walls.

The frightened young guard slowly backed out the door and quickly shut it behind him.

Completely devastated, Alexander groaned and cried with remorse. "What have I done? He was my loyal friend. He saved my life." He tore his clothes off and cut his hair. "I don't deserve friends; I only murder them!" he ranted. He refused visitors and even food for three days.

Hephaestion and other concerned officers listened at the door to his hysteria. When Alexander seemed that he would kill himself, they barged into the room. "Alexander," Hephaestion pleaded with him, "you must listen to reason. You are the King. We need your leadership. If you killed yourself, you would throw your new empire into chaos!"

Alexander at last listened to reason, cleaned and dressed himself, and asked for food. Calming down, he refused wine and returned reluctantly to assuming his duties. He plodded through official acts and meetings with ministers but was obviously depressed.

His Persian officials sought to reassure him. "Great King, since you are a living god, your actions cannot be wrong. Cleitus must have deserved the righteous punishment you gave him. After all, he insulted your divine being." Alexander listened and nodded his head, not convinced by the Persians' arguments.

Anaxarchus, a Greek philosopher from Abdera, tried philosophic reasoning. "Alexander," he said with calm logic, "it would not be just for you to take your life, for you as Great King are justice personified. Thus, logically, your action against Cleitus could not have been unjust."

Phidias also tried to talk reason to the tormented king. "Remember the promises you made to yourself to bring peace and brotherhood to your empire. You also promised me to be moderate in your drinking. Do you see where intemperance leads? You lose your judgment. Emotions take control and anger rules. Thoughtless acts are the result, for which you are sorry afterward. But they cannot be undone. The only thing is to learn from your errors and misdeeds and go forward with new resolve. Now shake off your inertia and fulfill your duties as King and Commander. It is your destiny."

Such reasoning failed to mollify Alexander's conscience or restrain him from trying to drown it in wine. Nor did this vacuous logic prevent others from openly criticizing or secretly conspiring against Alexander.

With Alexander's increasing descent into isolation and drunken paranoia, Callisthenes became more openly critical. He refused to prostrate himself to Alexander and sent letters to Aristotle detailing Alexander's excesses and the murders of Philotas, Parmenion, and Cleitus. He was not overly critical of Alexander personally, however, because he knew Aristotle was having to defend his actions in Athens.

Not long after the episode with Cleitus, Alexander's spies uncovered another conspiracy against him. This time it included one of Alexander's pages, Hermolaus, whom he had unjustly punished for a minor offense. Under torture the youth implicated Callisthenes, among others.

Alexander summoned Callisthenes and questioned him. "It is difficult for me to comprehend the possibility that you, my official historian, the chronicler of my campaigns and victories, would conspire to kill me."

"I did not say that I would kill you and deny that I am part of any conspiracy that would," replied Callisthenes.

"You cannot deny that you do not condone my actions. You do not prostrate yourself before me as I have ordered and are openly critical of those who do. You even criticize my Persian robes of royalty."

"Yes, I have spoken openly of your Oriental ways, Alexander. You're not a god and cannot make yourself one. You can suffer pain and death as well as I and any other mortal. Your fellow Macedonians and Greeks feel degraded when forced to grovel like barbarians before you."

"Callisthenes, you do not understand the implications of my actions. You cannot see the larger worldview because of your narrow Greek vision. I can imagine a world empire, a union of peoples as my father unified all of Greece. In order for that to come to fruition, I have to gain the loyalty of all my subject peoples under me as their leader. I must be a living and visible symbol of political and religious unity. You and the Greeks and

Macedonians do not consider me a god, but you must give lip service to it. You all must give me the same obeisance as the rest of the peoples I have mastered.

"I am Alexander, the King of Kings, the conqueror of Asia, and ruler of the Greeks."

"You are a product of your time, Alexander. You had a father who was a military and political genius and inherited talented generals and a well-trained army from him. You were fortunate to face a corrupt and cowardly Darius in battle. The gods favored you, and his well-administered, wealthy Empire fell into your lap. You will rule and die and pass into history. Alexander and his exploits will only be known to posterity because of Callisthenes. It is I who will make you immortal."

"Silence! I will not listen to any more of your boasting. Take him to prison."

Alexander had the plotters tortured and hanged. "Let Callisthenes stay in prison," he commanded, unable to bring himself to order the execution of his beloved Aristotle's nephew.

Callisthenes stagnated in prison, and Alexander put him out of his mind. Nevertheless, his jailers mistreated the philosopher and fed him spoiled food. He finally succumbed to a combination of poor treatment and disease and died while imprisoned. Alexander showed no remorse.

Phidias was at a loss to comprehend the death of Callisthenes at Alexander's hands. He saw that paranoia, fed by alcoholic bouts, ruled Alexander's judgment more and more. He had murdered his best general and his son, his closest adviser, many of his officers and retainers, and now his philosopher-historian. Who would be next? How would it end?

He wrote to Aristotle of Callisthenes' death and of his own impressions of what was becoming of Alexander.

Aristotle read the news with dismay. "He is lost," he said to a fellow philosopher and teacher. "I can no longer defend him or his actions."

CHAPTER 30

In the army, discontent verged on open mutiny. In order to mollify his troops, Alexander announced to his generals, "Tell the troops that I will send back to Macedon the oldest veterans. I will pay them each a bonus of one talent. This is in addition to their regular pay, which will continue until they reach home. They should be very grateful for this generosity, for it will allow them to purchase farms and retire in comfort."

After receiving this apparently good news, the generals were surprised to hear from their officers that there was still grumbling among the troops. The leaders of the complaining troops sent word that they wanted to meet with Alexander. Six veteran soldiers addressed the King.

"Sire, we are tired of Persia. We are tired of fighting. We don't want to die here, even in the midst of all this luxury. We miss our homes. You've discharged the oldest veterans. Now, we wish for you to dismiss all of us. After all, since you are a god, you no longer have need of our services to realize your purposes."

The last was a veiled insult, and Alexander lost his patience and his temper. "Guards, arrest these men! You will all be charged with sedition and spreading mutiny among my troops and will be executed in the traditional manner, stoning by your own comrades. Take them away."

After the execution, while the troops were still assembled, Alexander addressed them. "My comrades-in-arms, do not think that I don't appreciate all the sacrifices you have made for me. Yes, we have lost thousands of our comrades in battles and to disease, thirst, and starvation. Many more have lost arms, legs, or eyes. You who stand here bear scars of fighting. I dare any of you to show more scars than I have. My body shows the signs of every battle and the marks of every weapon of war.

"You have helped me destroy Darius and win his empire. You have gone with me into the farthest provinces, into India, and across great deserts. But I have rewarded you for all your effort and sacrifice. You now live as conquerors in luxury. You have shared the wealth of Persia. You have married its beautiful women. Now you want to leave all of this and return to the poor mountains, hills, and plains of Macedon and Greece. You should be ashamed for your ungratefulness. However, I grant your wish. I now offer you all permission to go home. Yes, all of you. You are discharged. Go back and report that you deserted your King and left him to the protection of conquered foreigners."

He immediately turned his back to them and disappeared into his palace, where he secluded himself and refused to see anyone. It was a calculated gamble. Either his soldiers would take his permission to leave and go home, or they would be embarrassed and ashamed of their whining and ingratitude. Alexander knew his men and predicted what they would do.

Alexander's speech had slapped his men in their faces. They spoke to one another, ashamed of their rebellion.

"We feel guilty for our ingratitude," one of the men told his officer.

"As you should," he replied. "The King has been very generous to you, and you have thrown it back into his face."

Shame for their action grew through the troops until, after three days in which no one had seen Alexander, they decided to march to the palace. Assembled below his window, a leader of the men pleaded, "Alexander, our King and Commander, please come out and hear us."

They waited, but he did not appear. "We are sorry for our complaining and ungratefulness!" they shouted.

He still did not appear. One of the junior officers spoke, "Sire, please forgive us and accept us back into your army."

Another officer pleaded, "We will not leave until you forgive us."

Finally, Alexander appeared on the steps of the Palace, dressed in his shining armor. They yelled their fidelity and affection with tears in their eyes, as he held open his arms as if to embrace them.

The Macedonian army's tradition was like a fraternity, and here was its leader. Alexander motioned for quiet and shouted, "I forgive you! I love you, as I know that you love me!" His eyes were moist.

The men broke into tears with exclamations of joy and appreciation and surged forward to their commander, pleading with him to allow them to kiss him. He relented, and they kissed his hands, his clothing, his armor, his feet, and his hair.

Showing his love and forgiveness, Alexander was reconciled with his men, who left with warm feelings for their king and leader and marched back to their camp, singing songs of thanksgiving.

Alexander was moved by this show of affection and loyalty. His spirit lifted and he began to dream of further conquests. He ordered his generals to meet with him and to bring in maps.

When they were settled, Alexander said to them, "The men have shown their loyalty and love for me. I don't want them to get soft with all this luxury and forget that they are Macedonian soldiers." He looked around at his senior officers. "I want to plan future campaigns with you. Let me see those maps."

The generals exchanged looks. They raised eyebrows with questions behind them of what Alexander was going to propose.

"Look here," he said, pointing to Arabia. "This is an area south of Mesopotamia. It is hidden behind its wall of desert." He pointed to another area adjacent to his empire. "And here, around the great Caspian Sea, are areas we have yet to explore."

The generals nodded that what Alexander said was true and let him prattle on.

"We can also go west of Greece. There are still fresh troops in Macedon, which we can join with Greeks in Sicily and southern Italy. We can conquer all of Europe to the Gates of Hercules."

His generals allowed Alexander to dream and plan further campaigns that they knew he could not and would not attempt. They congratulated Alexander on his health and told him that they would consider his plans and return with suggestions.

After they left, the generals discussed the meeting. "I am glad he is feeling well enough to plan new conquests," said one, "but his body will not let him do this."

"He looks much older and weaker," said another. "His once magnificent body has suffered from injuries and disease."

Craterus agreed, "His campaigns, battles, and near death through the desert have taken a terrible toll on him."

Ptolemy spoke up, "His spirit has also been wounded by the conspiracies of his officers and the mutinies of his men. He has sought to numb his mind with heavy drink."

Lysimachus summarized their thoughts. "In spite of his bravado and unrealistic dreams of further conquests, there lies in Alexander a corrupted body and spirit."

They went to their homes agreeing not to encourage Alexander's plans for future campaigns.

Not long afterward, Alexander received devastating news from Ecbatana. While with part of the army there, Hephaestion, Alexander's dearest companion, had died of disease. Alexander was heartbroken, crying and tearing his clothes.

As the body of Hephaestion was being brought to Susa, Alexander prepared an elaborate funeral. He read a report about his friend's illness. It stated that he had a fever and that his Greek physician was treating him.

"Yes, Sire," one of Hephaestion's officers said, "but the physician left his side to attend the public games. While he was gone, his patient became worse and died."

Alexander exploded in rage. "Arrest that ignorant physician for the murder of my companion! Have him whipped to death. With each lash, maybe he'll be sorry for leaving his patient to die."

When Hephaestion's body arrived in Susa, Alexander had it put in a place of honor in his palace. He lay prostrate across it for hours, tears staining the expensive robes he had it dressed in. He cut off his hair in mourning and refused any food for three days.

When told that his orders for a gigantic funeral pyre and memorial celebration for his friend would cost ten thousand talents, Alexander shouted, "I don't care! How much is a dearest friendship worth? Ten thousand talents? A million? It is priceless."

After the funeral, he sent word to Ecbatana. "In the campaign, have the next tribe that opposes you completely slaughtered as a sacrifice to Hephaestion's spirit."

Phidias again felt dismayed over Alexander's excesses. Nothing he could say or do any longer would dissuade the troubled young man. He knew that Alexander was haunted by his thoughts of Achilles, whom he had long identified with. The hero of Troy did not long survive the death of his own dear friend and lover Patroclus.

All men have monsters that lurk within them, eating at their entrails, waiting to emerge and destroy them and all that they love. They try, and most succeed, at keeping the monsters submerged, but drink, or drugs, or emotional loss, or violence will unchain them. Alexander, too, had his monsters—inherited tendencies to violence, jealousy, and insatiable ambition. His angst was that he wanted so badly to fulfill his dreams of the unity of peoples and nations, yet they were thwarted by the selfish interests of others and his own weaknesses of drunkenness and violence.

Phidias was conscious of the conflicts in Alexander's spirit. Alexander struggled to discover the self within, to be noble, magnanimous, farsighted, and philosophical in the largest sense, to live up to the ideals Aristotle had tried to instill in him. However, the dark side of his nature arose from time to time to overshadow the good, the altruistic, and the noble. He could not forever campaign and fight battles to keep the bad tendencies at bay. Violence and bloodshed of battle only seemed to dehumanize him and feed the evil side. The inactivity and boredom of peace allowed the nightmares of death and destruction to haunt him. He tried more drink to drown the black memories in a sea of wine, but they continued to float up and consume him.

After the death of Hephaestion, Alexander and his court moved to Babylon. Day after day and night after night, he abandoned himself more and more to heavy drinking. During one night of revelry with his officers, he proposed a drinking match. "To whomever can drink the most wine, I will give a talent in gold."

The men all yelled in excitement and competed for the prize. One of the younger lieutenants downed twelve quarts of wine. Amid shouts of congratulations and approval, Alexander bestowed the prize on the drunken officer. He staggered off but never enjoyed his prize, for he died three days later.

Shortly afterward, at another of the seemingly endless schedule of banquets, Alexander quaffed a large bowl of six quarts of wine. He passed out afterward but attended another dinner the next night and drank heavily again. Alexander slept most of the next day and awoke complaining of a raging headache.

One of his Persian attendants brought in some hot soup. "The weather has turned cold, Great King. Your guards did not cover you or light a fire when they brought you to bed last night."

Alexander coughed. "I'll be all right. I'll just go back to sleep."

"Let me call the physician. He is Persian and will help you feel better."

"Perhaps he can give me something," Alexander agreed. "My muscles ache and my head throbs."

The physician examined Alexander. "Your exhaustion and drinking have weakened your constitution, Great King. You have a fever. I will prepare a draught for you, but you must remain in bed."

The fever raged for ten days while Alexander grew weaker and weaker, and finally could not speak. His officers became alarmed. One by one his captains filed past his bed, touching his garments or kissing his hand. Tears filled their eyes as they looked at the spent body wracked with fever.

Alexander was unable to do anything more than lift a hand or blink in a sign of recognition. On the eleventh day, he died, not yet thirty-three years old.

Phidias had watched Alexander's sad decent into alcoholic debauchery, illness, and death and commented to his philosopher friends. "In a frenzy of drunken excess, the darkening storm clouds of unthinking barbarism finally overwhelmed his noble intentions and clear reasoning, and he killed his friends and himself. What a tragedy. What a waste. A talented and heroic life thrown away at its zenith. Such potential lost, flung away by a senseless act, which was again a flaw in his character."

"I must admit," Gorgas replied, "Alexander was the bravest of soldiers, but not the brightest of generals. He supplied the inspiration for the courage and ferocity of his soldiers. His perseverance and reckless energy, regardless of the impossibilities, led to unprecedented victories. But it was most likely his generals' organization and tactics that supplied the strategy for his victories."

Phidias added, "He had great leadership abilities, reinforced by his brilliant imagination, the fire of his oratory skill, and the sincerity with which he shared the hardships of his men."

"Whatever his weaknesses of character," Pharacrates replied, "history will remember him as a conquering genius. It may have been just as well that he died at a young age, while still at his peak. More years would surely have brought more sorrow and disappointment. He could never have fulfilled all his dreams. They were more than he could accomplish, even if he were a god."

"So true," lamented Phidias, "but perhaps a mellowing age would have taught him to love governing more than he loved war."

Gorgas said, "Alexander could not resist the inexorable force of Nemesis, the spirit sent by the gods to punish prideful mortals."

Phidias added his opinion as a historian. "We who write and study his history feel a natural sympathy for this tortured hero. We know that, despite his cruelties and superstition, he was, at base, a generous and affectionate youth. He was undeniably a brave and able leader who fought against his own heritage of bloodthirsty barbarism. Through all the savage battles, bloody sieges, and executions, he kept in front of him the dream of bringing the light of civilization that came from Athens to a larger world."

Later in his chambers, Phidias wrote down in his notes. "When Alexander left Macedon to invade Asia, he would never see Europe again. He would live only eleven more years, but in that time, he would conquer the largest empire up until his day. He would meld the civilizations of Greece and Persia together and create a new culture. He would found a dozen cities and give them his name. He would leave a brilliant legacy of heroism and military genius.

"Alexander endeared himself to his men and officers by his openness, generosity, and kindliness, risking their lives but feeling their wounds as if they were his own. His reputation for fairness and mercy helped him in his campaigns, enemy forces and cities allowing themselves to be taken without fear of slaughter. On the other hand, the blood of the Molossian tigress flowed within him and arose in paroxysms of cruelty. The occasional spasms of sadism and barbarism made bitter his final fate.

"Many historians, emphasizing his superhuman victories and conquests, may tend to overlook the darker side of his personality. Other historians will chronicle the bloodletting, wanton slaughter, torture, and murder he ordered. I knew both sides of his brilliant yet tormented character.

"He could lead tens of thousands of men in battle, conquer vast lands, and rule millions, but he could not control his own temper. Unable to recognize his own faults and limitations, he would allow his judgments to be influenced by flattery and praise. He became convinced of his own invincibility and that he was indeed divine. In his own mind, he could do no wrong and thus was prone to violent and impulsive acts. He lived in a maelstrom of action, victories, and glory and so loved war that his mind never knew a time of peace.

"Nevertheless, we remain amazed by the exploits of this young conqueror, who was never defeated in a hundred battles; who unified the eastern Mediterranean world all the way to India; who spread Greek civilization, language, and ideas; and who will probably remain one of the most brilliant and enigmatic personalities of history."

CHAPTER 31

Before Alexander set out to invade Asia, he ensured himself of a stable and complacent Greece by leaving behind governments that were favorable to him. The populations of those cities remained hostile to him, however, even if he was a conqueror of Persia. In particular, Athens, because of its long tradition of freedom and the history of its own empire, resented the brilliant world conqueror as a despot.

Demosthenes enflamed the populace with his fiery eloquence as he spoke from the areopagus. "…And where is your Empire now, oh Athens, your navy that ruled the Aegean, and your treasure that overflowed from your temples? Have you forgotten the glory brought by Pericles? You and Sparta threw back the Persians in defeat. Now you are asked to bow down to Alexander, the god-king who has taken the place of the Persian despot.

"How long must we suffer under the heel of the Macedonian overlords? They say that they have left Athens to govern itself, but that is a hollow and meaningless concession. What do we govern? We have no army, no navy, and no empire. We cannot make alliances or treaties. And, we must pay taxes to maintain the Macedonian army that oppresses us.

"Show these Macedonians that we resent their oppression! We do not share in their adoration of Alexander. Tell them to go back to Pella and let us govern ourselves, so that we may once again enjoy the wealth and power that once was Athens."

The people yelled their approval. A band of youths roamed the streets afterward, beating up Macedonians they happened across. They spied a small detachment of soldiers coming from the harbor and began to pelt them with stones. The soldiers quickly drew their swords and chased the youth, catching one unfortunate fellow and splitting his scalp open with the flat of a sword.

Aristotle had left Pella the same year as Philip's victory at Chaeronea. After a four-year period of traveling, he returned to Athens. He naturally associated himself with the Macedonian party in his approval and support of Alexander, not only because Alexander had been his student, but because he was conquering and unifying Asia under Greek rule. He much preferred unification and pacification of Greece over Athenian patriotism, realizing that philosophy would flourish in Athens when the petty squabbling and rebellion ended.

Aided by funds from Alexander, Aristotle opened a school of rhetoric and philosophy on his return to Athens when he was fifty-three years of age. He chose as the site of his new school a group of buildings comprising the most elegant of Athens' gymnasiums. It was dedicated to Apollo Lyceus, the God of shepherds, and shade trees, gardens, and covered walkways graced it. Even in the hostile environment of Athens, pupils flocked to the teacher of the King of Kings.

The school was soon called the Lyceum, from the fields dedicated to Lyceus. In the mornings Aristotle taught advanced subjects to his regular students and in the afternoons gave lectures to a popular adult audience on rhetoric, poetry, ethics, and politics.

The Lyceum was no mere copy of Plato's Academy, which Xenocrates now headed. Even so, a sharp rivalry developed among the three main schools in Athens; the Lyceum, whose students were mainly middle class; the Academy, whose members were from the aristocracy; and the school of Isocrates, whose students were chiefly colonial Greeks. Although the Academy was devoted mainly to mathematics, speculative philosophy, and politics, the Lyceum concentrated on biology and other natural sciences while Isocrates' school emphasized rhetoric. Thus, the specialized fields of the three schools eased the rivalry among them with time.

Alexander's hunters, games keepers, gardeners, and fishermen sent material to Aristotle from all parts of the new Empire. He also used the money Alexander gave him to hire a thousand men scattered over the expanded Greek world to collect flora and fauna of every land. This plethora of specimens enabled him to construct the first great zoological and botanical gardens the world had ever seen. Aristotle and his successors used this wealth of material for biological research. It was in the science of biology that his energy and genius really shone.

Aristotle instructed his students to gather and coordinate knowledge in every field they were capable of. They studied the customs of foreign peoples, the governments of Greek cities, the habits and internal organs of animals, the types and distribution of plants, and the history of science and philosophy. Aristotle's interests were so varied and universal that his works, which probably numbered in the thousands, comprised a library of their own, grouped into works on logic, science, aesthetics, and philosophy, which included ethics, politics, and metaphysics. Aristotle was the first after Euripides to compile a library, and in fact developed the principles of library classification.

To Aristotle's reputation as the most brilliant of Plato's students and the tutor of the conqueror of the Persian Empire was added his unequaled respect as Athens' genius scientist and philosopher. His repute was recognized throughout the Greek world. But just as prophets are reviled in their own cities, so sometimes are philosophers, especially in Athens. Love and admiration for Aristotle was not shared among the common people and those who supported Athenian patriotism.

Two men were discussing politics as they approached an open area in front of the Temple to Apollo in the heart of Athens. "It is a bitter taste in my mouth that we must grovel under the shadow of Macedonian rule. Alexander wants us to accept him as a god. That's ridiculous! I'll never consider him divine. He's the son of a barbarian king."

"Now that Aristotle has returned to Athens, he adds his support for his former pupil," said the other. "He has a considerable reputation over the Greek world, but there is no love for him among many in Athens, because he defends Alexander."

"What is that statue they're erecting on the pedestal in front of the Temple?" interrupted the first.

"I noticed them building a pedestal, and now they're unveiling a statue. You think it's Apollo? No, the head is fairly bald, and it has a beard."

"It's Aristotle!" exclaimed someone else in the crowd. "That traitor!"

Some in the crowd started to shout at the workmen and threaten them. They quickly finished their work, picked up their tools, and left the shouting, angry crowd.

"Demosthenes is right," the first man said. "How much longer do we have to tolerate the Macedonians? We don't have Alexander himself to vent our anger at, but we have a statue that he erected. Aristotle can be our target." He picked up a stone and threw it at the statue. It missed and bounced off the steps of the Temple. "Please excuse me, Apollo, for tossing a stone onto the steps of your Temple," he murmured. He turned to his companion. "Let's go before the god gets angry. We will have our revenge on Aristotle some other day."

* * *

On a brisk spring morning, as the laurel and oak trees burst with new growth, Aristotle was discussing the basic political nature of men as he and his students strolled leisurely around the botanical gardens. Every now and then Aristotle would point out a particularly interesting plant and describe its source and characteristics.

"You have taught us, Master, how men should behave, that they should seek happiness and that they should be educated. But what is the best form of government that a state should have for the happiness and well-being of its citizens?" "That is a good question, Eucliedes. I have thought much about that subject and will put it down in a book. This afternoon, as a matter of fact, I will address a group of interested men on my thoughts concerning government. You're all invited to come and listen."

Aristotle was conservative by nature. As a typical scholar and man of science, he prized order, peace, and security. He had personally witnessed the conflicts and disasters that had come from Athenian democracy. He said that in general, the habit of lightly changing laws is an evil that may not be immediately recognized but may reveal itself later under other circumstances.

The announcement had been spread through the city that Aristotle was going to speak his thoughts on government. Many men of all political persuasions came to hear what the man of philosophy and science would say, for even if a citizen disagreed with his politics, they admired Aristotle for his mind.

The audience exceeded Aristotle's expectations, and the session had to be moved to the largest of the buildings. Even so, the excess of citizens and students spilled outside under the pillars and down the steps.

"I am flattered that you have come to hear what I have to say about politics and the state," he said. "The science of politics is about society's happiness, for the function of the state and its government is to organize a society for the greatest happiness of the greatest number of its people. Man is by nature a social and therefore a political animal. A person is not born into a void but into a society already organized.

"What are these societies, and what are their types of government? Which ones are best? I and my students have collected the constitutions of one hundred and fifty-eight Greek cities and have studied them. I have divided them into three types: monarchy, aristocracy, and timocracy, that is, government by power, by birth, and by excellence. Any of these may be good at any given time and place, though one may be preferable over others."

An older man in the front row asked, "Isn't democracy the best government? Athens was at the height of its power when the Assembly held power under Pericles."

"That is partly true, Paeonias. But Athens also was defeated and lost its empire twice under the Assembly. Let me compare the three systems of government. First, there is monarchy in which a single ruler has all the power. This can be the best form of government if the monarch is good, able, and wise. It can also be the worst tyranny if he is selfish, stupid, or power-hungry. In practice, this is usually the worst government, since great power and great virtue are seldom held in common.

"An aristocracy in which governing power is held in hereditary families can be beneficial but will, in time, deteriorate. Noble character may be high in one or two individuals of a family and then degenerate in later generations into foolishness, selfishness, or insanity. The trouble with hereditary power is that there is no economic base. As the new rich gain more and more wealth, political power goes to the highest bidder. This makes wealth more important than ability, and the whole state becomes avaricious. The government then becomes an oligarchy, ruled by the wealthy few.

"Democracy—that is, government by the common citizen—may be just as dangerous as oligarchy. It is usually the result of rebellion against a plutocracy or oligarchy. This temporary victory of the poor over the rich in the struggle for power often leads to chaos and strife for the state. Democracy is at its best dominated by peasant farmers and at its worst by a landless urban rabble. When a democracy is dominated by the lower classes, the rich are taxed to provide money for the poor, who continually want more, because they do not produce any wealth of their own. Continually giving more money to them is like pouring water into a sieve."

"Yet, Aristotle, a wise conservative will not let people starve. That is inhumane. It is not virtuous," said another in the audience.

"That is very true, Empedecas. The true patriot in a democracy should see that the people are not too poor but all have sufficient wealth. This is also advantageous to the rich, who then would not fear violence or confiscation.

"However, and this is the most important point, government requires special ability and knowledge. I would not want to have judges who were not knowledgeable of the law. How can a laborer, tradesmen, or hired servant be able to acquire excellence, training, or good judgment? All men are created unequal, gentlemen, whatever anyone says to the contrary. They may be equal under the laws, however. Equality is just, but only between equals. The upper or lower classes will rebel if an inequality is enforced or is extreme. Democracy, on the whole, is inferior to aristocracy."

"You only say that, Aristotle, because you are of the aristocratic class!" yelled one from the rear. "Are you saying these things because you don't think people are capable of governing themselves? Don't you trust the people?"

"I say it because I distrust the uninformed masses. Democracy is based on the false notion that those who are equal in respect to the law feel they are equal in all respects, that because they are equally free, they are absolutely equal. The result of this is that their numbers can be manipulated by orators and demagogues. Because the people are so easily misled and fickle in their opinions, the ballot should be limited. The citizens who are allowed to vote should be intelligent and at least be able to read our language."

"If, as you say, all these forms of government have their weaknesses, what form do you think is best?"

"What we need is a combination of the best parts of aristocracy and democracy," Aristotle replied. "We can achieve this with a constitutional government. The best practical constitution is a rule by the middle class."

"Why the middle class, Aristotle? Is it because you distrust the rich as much as you despise the poor?" This came from a wealthy landowner who supported the Patriotic Party.

"My friends, it is not only because the middle class is that moderation between the poles of rich and poor, it is because it possesses some property and is likely to follow a middle course. It avoids extremes and resists radical change. The middle class is more likely than either the rich or the poor to be guided by reason and what is best for the state. Middle class rule will give stability and a rational control. It is the golden mean between a democracy and an aristocracy.

"In all the state governments we have examined, those that were the most stable and prosperous were the ones in which the middle class outnumbered the rich and poor. Whenever the middle class was small, either the rich or the poor over-powered them and gained control. Whenever the rich or the poor gain power, neither will establish a free state.

"Those qualified to rule should be male, own property, and have at least a modest education. The state then will be sufficiently democratic if the path to office is open to all, and sufficiently aristocratic, if the offices are restricted to those who are fully qualified, have traveled the road of experience, and are prepared."

Aristocus, a friend of Demosthenes, rose and shouted, "Those are very sound arguments and pretty phrases, Aristotle, but you do not support in practice what you preach in theory. You support the Macedonian Party in our city, which is an oligarchy imposed upon us by a foreign king. Our Assembly is helpless, and the people have no voice. You are a hypocrite."

"It is true that I favor a party that has brought peace and prosperity to Athens. I favor no oligarchy, but I yearn for stability. I gladly relinquish some personal freedom to gain security, and so should you. It is the whimsical opinions of the unwashed masses that can be swayed by the likes of Demosthenes that I most fear."

"You should fear the revenge of the people more if your Macedonian Party ever loses control," Aristocus replied.

Many men rose and started to speak and yell, raising their fists at Aristotle.

Aristotle spoke above the din, "My lecture is concluded. You are free to discuss among you or with me afterward any questions you might have." He turned to some of his friends nearby. "Please stay close to me and see that some of those who hate my politics are not tempted to advance their argument by thrusting a knife between my ribs."

When Aristotle heard that Callisthenes had died after Alexander imprisoned him, he lost confidence in Alexander and stopped supporting him. However, the Athenians still considered him a proponent of Macedonian rule. When news of Alexander's death reached Athens, Aristotle's safety was threatened.

CHAPTER 32

The magnetism of Alexander's personality had kept his far-flung empire together, but after his death, it began to fall apart almost immediately, as the generals and successors jostled each other for power and territory. The Empire in theory was held together in Babylon by Perdiccas, as holder of the treasury, and Craterus, as commander of the army. Antipater, who was left as the commander in Macedon and Greece, continued to rule it. Lysimachus ruled Thrace, Antigonus Asia Minor, and Ptolemy held Egypt. The conquests in India went back to local rulers.

Alexander's successors had been Macedonian leaders and generals who ruled by personal power and the sword. They dismissed democracy as an ignorant corrupt way to govern and continued to strive with one another for position over several years.

The Greeks of the mother country were aware of the increase in trade and opportunities for immigration for the poorer classes, that were made possible by Alexander's conquests. However, most chafed under Macedonian rule and rejoiced that the successors of Alexander were occupied with fighting each other.

During Alexander's victories and conquest of the Persian Empire, Demosthenes' fortunes had not fared well. In the year before Alexander's death, an accusation of accepting a large bribe was brought against him.

"What, another accusation?" Demosthenes exploded. "My enemies have done this before, and I have beaten them."

"This time it may not be so easy," said his friend Hyperiedes. "I have the indictment here. The Macedonian authorities insist that you be imprisoned until your trial."

"They're afraid I'll flee Athens."

"They know you will continue to cause trouble for them."

"And they're right! Athens and Greece must be free from the Macedonians."

"But you have to be realistic, my friend," Hyperiedes said. "The Macedonian Party in Athens has all the power. They will probably have you convicted."

"You're probably right," Demosthenes admitted. "Then they'll have me executed. Even if the jury doesn't convict me, they'll have me assassinated. I must find a way to escape."

"I'll ask our friends to try to get you out of prison. Don't despair."

Demosthenes was imprisoned, but Aristocus and other members of the Patriotic Party bribed the guards, who released him. They met him at the prison gate. "Thank you so much, my friends," the orator and political leader said, relieved. "You have saved my life."

"You aren't safe yet," one of the party said. "Here is some food and money. You must flee tonight and find a safe place to hide."

When his enemies found that Demosthenes had fled, they were glad to be free of his acid tongue, even if they were cheated of his execution. Their relief was short-lived, for within months, news of Alexander's death reached Greece. In Greek city after city, revolts arose against the Macedonians. In Athens the Patriotic Party led the way. "Out with the hated Macedonians!" they chanted.

"The Thebans, who escaped the destruction of their city, have besieged the Macedonian garrison on the Cadmeia," said one of the leaders of the Athenians. "We must force out the Macedonian Party."

The Athenians feasted and wore garlands in celebration of Alexander's death. They lined the streets and shouted insults at the fleeing Macedonians and their supporters. Many spat at them or threw rotten vegetables. "You are fortunate we don't kill you!" one man shouted as he threw an egg.

A member of the Macedonian Party ducked the egg, but some fruit hit him. "These Athenians are singing victory songs. You would think they had vanquished Alexander themselves!"

His fellow replied, "It won't be long before their victory songs will change to dirges of defeat. Antipater will return to Greece with his army."

Demosthenes had been in exile nine months when Aristocus called the leaders of the Patriotic Party together. "We have control of Athens now, but old Antipater will come and try to reestablish Macedonian power. I propose that we call Demosthenes back to Athens. We need his leadership, and he can help us gather allies."

* * *

Aristotle's life had become very complicated after the death of his nephew, Callisthenes. He angrily reproved his former pupil for Callisthenes' death. Alexander flippantly replied to Aristotle's protest that it was within his power as a god-king to put even philosophers to death. This certainly made more complex Aristotle's defense of Macedonian rule to the Athenians. It was not because he favored Macedon but because he felt that peace and Greek unification would be a fertile ground for culture and science to flourish.

The patriotic fervor following Alexander's death swept away all supporters of Greek unity under Macedon in favor of Greek solidarity in rebellion. Aristotle was caught up in the Athenian backlash. After the Macedonian Party fled the city, he was defenseless.

The chief priest of one of the temples of Athens brought charges of impiety against him. "I charge him with teaching that prayers and sacrifices to the gods are useless. He said they were of no avail in either bringing fortune or preventing misfortune. This blasphemy undermines all Greek religion and is against all our tradition and practice. It is the teaching of an atheist. I can support this accusation by citing passages from his own books. They will be the witnesses against him."

The judges brought an indictment of impiety against Aristotle and scheduled him for trial. Aristotle knew that he was unpopular in Athens because of his support of Alexander and the Macedonian Party. The supporters of Plato's Academy and the school of Isocrates were also jealous of him as a rival and critic. He knew that any jury that would listen to his case would be much less sympathetic toward him than the one that had condemned Socrates to death, on the same charge of impiety.

Aristotle met with his friend and fellow teacher, Theophrastus, at the Lyceum. "My friend, I am afraid that I must leave Athens soon, before the mob kills me."

"You're probably right to think that. The people and the Assembly are definitely against you. Now that Alexander is dead and the Macedonians have fled, you have no defenders. It is reported that Demosthenes, your old nemesis, will soon return from exile to enflame the city more in revolt against Macedon."

"Demosthenes' presence will make even more certain the prospect that a jury will condemn me to death. I will not give Athens a second chance to sin against philosophy. I will never forgive her for murdering

Socrates. He chose death rather than to escape into exile, to show that he would obey the law that condemned him to death.

"I have no need to make a moral point, for I have already done so by publishing my works. The convicted person in Athens always has the option of exile. There is no cowardice in this. I do not believe there is dishonor in preferring exile over death. What will my death gain for philosophy? It will only dishonor Athens again. I will not let them do it, so I will leave in two days."

"Where will you go?"

"I will go to the home of my mother's family in Chalcis. I want you to take over and lead the Lyceum. You are its finest scholar and will be a fitting successor to me. Please protect my library and maintain the collection of plants and animals. Surely this city will not destroy them. Defend our school against the jealous Academy and school of Isocrates. I wish you well."

"Thank you, Aristotle, for your confidence in me," Theophrastus replied. "I can never truly take your place. You are a giant in whose shadow we mere mortals but grope around."

"You flatter me, my friend. I am flesh and blood like you. I have used the talents I have been given and my intelligence to enrich my life, and I hope, the lives of others.. I have always tried to teach as many as would listen, that the pleasure of contemplation for truth is a continuous joy that does not come and go. This search for truth and the contemplation of it characterizes the highest life of all. We must, as best we can, strain every nerve to live in accordance with the best that is within us. Always remember that, Theophrastus, and you will do well. Good fortune to you. Now I must ask you to go so that I may quickly decide what to take with me to my exile and what to leave behind."

Aristotle fled during the night and traveled to Chalcis. The trial against him was held in his absence. The priests presented their accusations of impiety and read from his books, and leaders of the Patriotic Party accused him of treason for supporting Alexander and the Macedonians. A verdict of guilty was returned and a sentence of death imposed. "If he ever returns to Athens, we will make him drink hemlock like Socrates," said a priest.

The crowd ran from the trial cursing Aristotle for cheating them of his death. They streamed to the forum where his statue stood. Screaming in anger, they tore it down and smashed it to pieces.

A friend and former student of Aristotle went to Chalcis to tell him not to return to Athens, for he would be executed. He found him in bed ill. "What is the matter, my friend?" he asked as he sat on the side of his bed. Aristotle's room was small and made smaller by the crates of books and specimens that lay about. His face was pale and his skin dry and hot with fever. He had lost weight, and the hollows of his temples exposed a weak pulse.

"I have not felt well since I arrived here. Perhaps the stress of flight and spoiled food along the way caused this abdominal illness. I can eat only the simplest of broths."

"What can I do for you, Aristotle?" his friend asked with painful sympathy in his eyes.

"There is nothing you can do to help me. I have brought some herbs with me that my father used to use for abdominal troubles. I have been using them and will try some others." He pointed a weak finger at an opened crate. "I want you to return to Athens after you have rested and tell Theophrastus that I hope he keeps the Lyceum thriving in my absence. I believe now it will not be hampered by my political unpopularity. I do not think I will see Athens again. I will miss her."

"I will also miss you, Master." He clasped Aristotle's thin hand and kissed it as tears traced a course to his lips. As he left, he looked at the phials and flasks in the crate, some labeled with the names of poisons he was familiar with. He looked back at the tired, frail figure in the bed as he left the room. The intellectual giant looked all too mortal in the colorless clothes that covered his gaunt frame.

News reached Athens a few months after Aristotle's departure that he had died. He was sixty-three. Some rejoiced but most were aware that they had lost one of Athens' most brilliant lights. Whether he died of his illness or by his own hand we will never know, although there was speculation on both sides.

Aristotle, like Plato, believed that human intelligence was not only divine but immortal, linking humans to the gods and giving them the ability to grasp the truth. If true, then the magnitude of Aristotle's intelligence and his numerous gifts to human understanding certainly gained him immortality.

On hearing that Aristotle had died, Phidias shed tears and tore his clothes. "He was my friend and teacher," he cried. "Different from Plato, he was more a scientist. They both are with the immortals in that divine and eternal realm, where truth is universal. I will miss him, but now he belongs to the ages."

It was not long after his death that revenge and defeat were visited upon Athens.

* * *

Demosthenes returned to an Athens that was complacent in its new freedom but unprepared to meet a vengeful enemy. "We must rearm ourselves," he said. "The Macedonians will surely come back in force."

"We can't face them alone," Hyperiedes complained.

"I'll take a delegation to Sparta and other cities to raise allies," said Demosthenes. "They will certainly join us in a war of liberation."

He succeeded in convincing Sparta and some others in forming an army. They marched north, filled with the ardor of Greek liberation. Too many times a military force that is filled with patriotic valor believes that the righteousness of its cause will be defense enough. The hard lesson that patriotic pride was no match for the Macedonian phalanx had been forgotten and had to be relearned. Antipater's forces completely destroyed the Greek armies.

"Those stupid Greeks will never learn that they can't resist our phalanx," said Antipater as he surveyed the Greek slain scattered over the battlefield. "I have lost all patience with rebellious Athenians. I will teach them a lesson this time that they will not forget."

One of his generals advised him, "Remember that Philip and Alexander had much admiration for Athens and her culture. They spared her of harsh punishment or even a garrison."

Antipater replied with disdain, "Look at what it gained us. They only listened to that hornet, Demosthenes, and rebelled again and again. They must be dealt with harshly this time. They must pay all the costs of the war. Athens must give up all its democratic government, including the Assembly and the courts. There will be a governing council and governor appointed by us. We'll leave a garrison to enforce our will." Antipater issued an order that all citizens who possessed less than two thousand drachmas in property were to be deported to Asia as colonists.

"What of Demosthenes and the other agitators?" asked one of the generals. "Demosthenes, Hyperiedes, and Aristocus must be surrendered to us for trial," he said.

Knowing that if handed over to the victors, they would be summarily executed, the three anti-Macedonian leaders fled in different directions.

Demosthenes went to a nearby town, where he claimed sanctuary in a temple. The priests supplied him with food and water. It didn't take long for the people who sought Macedonian favor to tell them of his whereabouts. A detachment of soldiers was sent, and Demosthenes soon found himself surrounded.

The Macedonian captain called to him, "Demosthenes, you cannot escape! We can't violate the temple and come in to arrest you. However, we will not allow food or water to enter the temple and you will eventually die of starvation. Why not save yourself that ignominious death and come out to face your trial as a rebel like a courageous man?"

Demosthenes called out from the temple, "I will surrender to you after dawn tomorrow. I will use this night to sacrifice to the gods."

The captain agreed. As the sun began to peak from the horizon, he called for Demosthenes to come out and surrender himself.

After drinking a phial of poison he had brought with him, Demosthenes appeared at the top of the steps of the temple and began to speak, the words coming slowly and with difficulty. "I have been a true citizen of Athens and fought hard for her freedom against tyranny and oppression." He paused and leaned against a pillar. Raising his head, he stammered with all his remaining strength, "Long live Athenian liberty." With that, he lost his support and fell down the steps, dying at the feet of the captain. He was sixty-three.

Thus it was that he died within months of Aristotle at the same age. So within one year, Greece lost its greatest ruler, its greatest philosopher, and its greatest orator.

VII REWARD

CHAPTER 33

When Alexander was ill and obviously sinking to his death, his generals and friends gathered around the bed of their revered king, who had led them through so many conquering battles and asked, "Alexander to whom do you leave your empire?"

Alexander opened his feverish eyes and slowly gazed around at the eager, ambitious faces he knew well. He raised his right hand with difficulty from his side, as if to point to someone, and said, "To the strongest." With that his hand collapsed and his eyes closed.

The powerful men looked at each other as if gauging one another. They tried to get Alexander to speak again, but he would not and died soon afterward. His body had not yet gone through the elaborate funeral ceremonies, before his generals and administrators began jockeying for power.

Perdiccas was the administrator in Babylon and also controlled the treasury. He could probably have assumed the throne, but a vote of the Macedonian Army confirmed Philip Arrihaeus, Alexander's feebleminded half-brother, and the yet-to-be-born son of Alexander by Roxana as co-heirs. Perdiccas was given the title of regent and, with the veteran army commanded by Craterus, maintained his power.

Antipater was confirmed in his role as regent in Macedon, while Lysimachus was assigned Thrace, and Ptolemy was given Egypt. Antigonus was confirmed as satrap of Asia Minor. Some of these governors supported a unified empire under the heirs of Alexander, while others sought to divide it and retain their own part as independent rulers.

After these appointments were confirmed, Phidias approached Ptolemy, "May I speak with you, General?"

Ptolemy replied, "Master Phidias, you have known me since you taught me about the history of government. Please call me by my name. What can I do for you?"

"I know Alexander didn't name an heir. For now the Empire is administered by Perdiccas, and regions have been divided among powerful generals. It is knowledge that you will have Egypt."

"Yes, Alexander actually assigned me as satrap before he died."

"But you were wise in desiring it. Egypt is not only wealthy and already well-administered, but easily defended also."

"You are very discerning, Phidias. Those were my reasonings exactly."

"When will you leave Babylon for Egypt?"

"As soon as possible. My men are collecting supplies and what treasure Perdiccas will allow us."

"I wish to go with you," said Phidias.

"Why is that? I thought you would be glad to go back to your home, like the other philosophers."

"I foresee troubled times ahead. Athens will undoubtedly start another revolt, now that Alexander is dead. Antipater will have his hands full there. The other satraps, including you, will not be content under Perdiccas. There will be war among you."

"Why do you say that, my friend?" Ptolemy asked. "Perdiccas is regent for Alexander's baby, and Antipater is co-regent for his half-brother. They both will continue the reign of the Argead House."

"That is true for now, but there are men who do not want to see the Empire ruled by a half-wit and an infant. The satraps will want to control their own spheres as independent rulers. I repeat that there will be civil war among you. For those reasons, I fear for my life here in Asia as well as in Athens."

"Don't repeat any of those thoughts about conflict and division of the Empire. Perdiccas and Craterus would not like it."

"Then will you take me with you to Egypt?" Phidias asked. "There is another reason for me to accompany you."

"And what is that?"

"I want to start a museum and library that Alexander wanted built in Alexandria."

"That is a noble reason, and I will support that enterprise. We will have to see what Dinocrates has built since we left him. So the answer is yes; I will take you with me."

"Thank you, Ptolemy. I have quite a collection of artifacts, plants and animals, and books. I was going to take them with me back to Athens, but I fear now for their safety. They will be a nucleus around which to build the museum and library."

"It is decided then," Ptolemy said. "Prepare to leave for Egypt within a fortnight."

More of a shrewd political maneuverer than a strategic general, Ptolemy was as realistic and clear in his thinking as he was open and generous with the people who served him. He improved his hand by claiming the body of Alexander. "I will have him entombed in a sarcophagus of gold and placed in the temple at Memphis, where he was first proclaimed god and Pharaoh." He also took Alexander's mistress and housed her in his palace. He later married and sired two sons by her.

* * *

Soon after arriving in Memphis, Ptolemy had a meeting with his ministers. He outlined broad plans for the development and administration of Egypt. He was fortunate in having a vast Egyptian bureaucracy already in place. All he had to do was appoint competent Greeks and Macedonians over them.

After visiting Alexander he met with Dinocrates and Phidias. "I am very impressed with what you have done in the nine years since we left Egypt," he said to Dinocrates.

"Thank you, Sire. Alexander wanted the city laid out as a rectangle with the central avenue fifty paces wide, running east and west. Another of the same width crosses it, running north and south. The main thoroughfares are lighted at night, and kept cool during the day by miles of covered colonnades. The western half will be occupied mostly by Egyptians, while the northeastern part will be for foreign merchants. The southeast quarter will contan the royal palace, public buildings, and temples."

"What about the museum and library?" Phidias asked.

"It will be housed in this temple," Dinocrates said, indicated it on his plan.

"That's not big enough," Phidias complained. "Alexander said he wanted several buildings in the palace complex dedicated to science and philosophy."

Dinocrates slammed his fist on the table. "What did he want, a school like Aristotle's? We have soldiers, traders, and administrators. You are the only philosopher. Where are your students?"

"The school with teachers will come later. What Alexander wanted was a museion dedicated to the muses—a place where science, the arts, literary activity, and philosophy may flourish."

Ptolemy spoke up, "I also want a place for learning. It will be no mere collection of artifacts and books but an institution where scholars can gather, do research, and teach."

"But, Sire, how much space will that require?" asked Dinocrates.

"As much as necessary." Ptolemy rose, stepped to the window, and looked out as if picturing the prospect. "I want to build the largest collection of books in the Greek world. I want to gather scholars from all lands and house them at public expense. It will be a grand project. Phidias here will help you lay out the space and buildings."

Phidias was excited by the enthusiasm of Ptolemy and quickly added, "I will write to scholars in Sicily, Rhodes, and Pergamum to join me."

Ptolemy's eyes filled with the vision in his mind as he scanned the grand monuments of ancient Memphis. "I want you to collect every book, or a copy of it, in the Greek world." He turned to Phidias. "I will help you develop this museion into the gem in Alexandria's crown. It will outshine all other places of learning in the world."

Phidias' eyes widened. He had not conceived of such an ambitious plan. "I will try my best," he said. "The museion, or House of the Muses, will be formally dedicated as a temple to them. The titular head should be a priest of the goddesses. I suggest you request one from the prestigious temples in Greece or Ionia."

"I will have someone look into that," agreed Ptolemy. "Now, I will have my hands full running Egypt and defending it from invaders. I trust that you will handle the museion." He turned to Dinocrates. "I will make sure there are funds for the buildings Phidias will require. Alexandria will be my capital one day. I want it to be a magnificent Greek city to outsparkle these huge but ancient and colorless Egyptian edifices."

Phidias and Dinocrates left, both extremely satisfied that they had the support of the Pharaoh of Egypt to build the most impressive city and institution of learning in the Greek world.

* * *

Unfortunately they were both frustrated in their plans, because Ptolemy was engaged in the serpentine alliances and wars among the successors of Alexander. Within a year, Perdiccas actually invaded Egypt, attempting to overthrow and kill Ptolemy. Fortunately for Ptolemy, Perdiccas was killed in the process.

As Phidias foresaw, Athens and other Greek cities revolted. Antipater called to Craterus for aid and, with the help of his ten thousand Macedonian veterans, crushed the rebels.

A complicated shuffle of alliances and civil war among the generals ensued over the next several years, and Ptolemy's preoccupation with these conflicts and political intrigues prevented him from giving much attention to Phidias and Dinocrates. When the dust of the first civil war settled, Perdiccas and Craterus were dead and Seleucus was appointed as satrap of Babylon.

News of the revolts in Greece against Macedon following Alexander's death spread to Alexandria. Phidias was fearful for Aristotle's safety. *Aristotle had many enemies in Athens*, he thought. *Many resent his support of Alexander. What will happen to him? Will they arrest and put him on trial? Will he flee from Athens? What will happen to the Lyceum if he does? Politics is the cause of so much chaos and wasted energy. Will Athens ever have peace so philosophy can flourish again?*

Not long after, Phidias received news of Aristotle's death. He was devastated. With tears in his eyes, he spoke to a group of his colleagues. Ptolemy had sent his condolences. "He was more than my friend, my mentor, and my teacher," Phidias mourned. "He was my brother in spirit; we shared our souls. No one, not even the great Plato or even Socrates, had the breadth of knowledge he possessed. He did research, talked, and wrote books on every subject. He looked at the world through eyes that have had the cover of ignorance, superstition, and unfounded religion removed from them. His head was not in the clouds in some ethereal realm. He looked keenly to our earthly existence and what made it work.

"I will miss him; you all will miss him; the world will miss him."

They burned incense, poured wine libations, and spoke prayers for their departed master of philosophers.

* * *

While the other generals who had inherited parts of Alexander's empire continued to conspire and fight to conquer one another, Ptolemy concentrated on promoting Egyptian agriculture, commerce, and industry. He built a great fleet to project Egypt and its commerce. He helped Rhodes and some other Greeks of the Aegean maintain their independence of Macedon.

Antigonus, who ruled Asia Minor, was planning to extend his power. Ptolemy allied himself with Lysimachus and Seleucus, and later with Cassander, Antipater's son and successor, to resist Antigonus.

After Ptolemy's survival from the first war of the successors, Phidias was anxious to show him what progress he had made. He showed Ptolemy the plans for the museum. "It will be a magnificent and lasting monument to you and to Alexandria. The House of the Muses will be dedicated to and promoting all the arts and sciences. I have been collecting specimens and historical artifacts from all over Alexander's empire. Many scholars will come and help me collect books and conduct research. Dinocrates has left areas near the Palace for the museion.

"You have done a fine job of starting this project that Alexander wanted," said Ptolemy." I am occupied with matters over my expanded territories, but I trust that you will handle the museum. I will make sure you have funds dedicated for your work."

Phidias thanked Ptolemy and returned to the temple he was using to house the books he was collecting. He had written to Aristotle about his project when he left Babylon and had received from him instructions on how to organize a library.

The books and artifacts were indeed growing. Phidias had written to scholars around the civilized world. Many had indicated their interest, and some had said that they would come after Ptolemy moved his capital to Alexandria.

But Phidias was worried. Even though Ptolemy seemed to have secured his power in Egypt, the other successors of Alexander continued to scheme and shift alliances. Any year could see one overthrow Ptolemy and ruin everything Phidias was building with such energy and dedication.

CHAPTER 34

Ptolemy at first ruled Egypt from the ancient capital in Memphis. He had obtained a magnificently run country, rich in food and natural resources. Most importantly, the ruler was the proprietor, and his vast army of priests and supervisors administered it. He inherited the sacred tradition that all the land and its production belonged to the Pharaoh as god-king. The peasant was not a slave, but could not leave his land without government permission. Ptolemy and his successors enlarged the system by appropriating great tracts of land from the Egyptian nobles and priests.

A great bureaucracy grew that completely managed Egypt as a huge state farm, telling the farmers what soil to use and what plants to grow. The state also controlled industry, owning the gold and copper mines and having a monopoly on oil from plants and subsidies for salt, incense, papyrus, and textiles. Minor industries were left in private hands, but the state licensed and supervised them, bought most of their production at fixed prices, and taxed the profits for the state treasury.

For the most part, slaves manned the factories, their low cost enabling Ptolemy to undersell their products in foreign trade. The government completely controlled commerce, all caravan routes and waterways being owned by the state.

Ptolemy I's successor introduced the camel, that wonderful ship of the desert sands, into Egypt. The Ptolemys built the largest commercial fleet in the Mediterranean, while the double harbor of Alexandria and its huge warehouses were the envy of other cities and the magnet for world trade. Alexandria also became the main port for reshipment of goods coming from the Middle East and India.

This great expansion of industry and commerce was augmented by innovative banking methods. Deposits, transfers, and withdrawals could be made on paper instead of performed physically. Banking was, of course, a government monopoly, and the central bank in Alexandria had branches in all the important cities and towns.

This Ptolemaic system was the most efficiently organized government in the world at that time. The centralization of the economy and forced labor for the government allowed the construction of great public projects such as building, road construction, flood control, and irrigation.

The Jewish population of Alexandria grew to probably twenty percent of the total. There had been Jewish settlements for at least three hundred years prior to this time, and many Jewish traders followed the Persian conquest of Egypt. Alexander had urged Jews to go to Alexandria and gave them political and economic rights equal to Greeks.

After Ptolemy took Jerusalem, he carried many captives back to Egypt, who were later freed, and invited prosperous Jews to establish businesses and spacious homes in Alexandria. A large number lived in the Jewish quarter in the northeastern quadrant, but it was not restricted like a ghetto. Jews were free to live in any quarter, except the one exclusively for officials and their households. They built temples that served as schools and meeting places as well as for religious services. The Greek-speaking Jews called them *synagogai*—places of assembly

Phidias' museum was gradually growing, for scholars came from all over the Greek world to come and do research with promises of support and funds from Ptolemy. Phidias continued to argue with Dinocrates for more space and traveled to Memphis repeatedly to request more funds.

"I promise you that your museum and library will have ample buildings. But first Dinocrates must complete my palace, for I will move the capital to Alexandria," said Ptolemy.

"When?" asked Phidias impatiently.

"Soon. Don't push me, philosopher. I have my hands full."

"Pardon me, Sire, but your supervisors run Egypt smoothly, as they have done for centuries. There are no threats to you from the other successors of Alexander."

"Yes, things are quiet at the moment. I can promise you this, that I will move to Alexandria before the Nile floods."

"That will be within three months?"

"Yes, Dinocrates tells me the palace interior will be finished, or at least habitable, by then."

"Good, then I would like for him to build more accommodations for the housing and feeding of the scholars. We now have over twenty."

"That many? That's impressive. You've been doing a good job, Phidias."

"The museum with the library will grow even more and make you and your son, who will succeed you, proud of it. It will be a sparkling jewel in the crown of Egypt."

* * *

In Macedon, Antipater, whom Alexander had left to rule Macedon and Greece, died four years after Alexander. As anticipated by the prescient Ptolemy, Athens revolted, putting to death old Phocion, who had ruled Athens at peace under Macedon.

"He was a puppet of Antipater," said the leader of the revolt. "Macedon is without a strong leader now. The other generals of Alexander are still fighting among themselves and will continue to do so. Now is the time for Athens to regain its freedom and reassert its power."

"But don't you think Cassander, Antipater's son, will attack?" asked another. "Macedon will not easily give up its power over us."

"I say let them come!" yelled another. "We can raise an army of citizens who are tired of the Macedonian yoke. I will be glad to raise, train, and lead a contingent myself. I suggest that you address the Assembly," he said, pointing to the leader. "They will listen to you and vote for an army. Death to all who support Macedon. Long live free Athens!"

All of those present raised their arms and voices in approval. Soon afterward the Assembly took a vote, and Athens prepared to defend herself and her freedom.

In Pella, Cassander quickly established his ascendancy to his father's throne as king. Veterans of Alexander's wars, anxious for battle and booty, flocked to Cassander's call to put down the rebellion in Athens. Athens had prospered during the peace, its warehouses full of goods and its merchant's pockets full of gold and silver.

History had shown that the basic principle of democracy was freedom that led to chaos and that the basic principle of monarchy was power that led to tyranny, revolution, and war. So it had been in Greece and continued through the revolt. Athens elected its generals, who quarreled among themselves over the best strategy.

"We cannot beat Cassander's phalanxes in the field, and we cannot match his cavalry. We should increase our fortifications and lay in food and water for a siege. He will soon tire and return to Pella," said one of the generals.

"That is folly," said another. "The Macedonians have mastered siege warfare as Alexander demonstrated in Asia. Our walls will be breached by their machines, and our city will be open to slaughter and pillage."

"I have an alternate plan," spoke up a third. "I propose that we send out our cavalry to run around Cassander's army and destroy his siege engines while our soldiers prepare to defend the walls."

"That is a sound plan," said the fourth general.

They all agreed.

Unfortunately, plans that look good in theory are not always successful. Cassander heard of the strategy from his spies and prepared his counter moves. His cavalry awaited the Athenians in ambush and scattered or captured them. When his army encamped before the walls of Athens, and his siege machines were drawn up, the Athenians realized the folly of their strategy.

They sent envoys to Cassander, begging for peace and sparing of the city. Cassander accepted the city's surrender and demanded that its leaders meet with him the next day in the Temple of Athena on the Acropolis.

"I should destroy Athens for its repeated rebellions as Alexander did Thebes," he told them. The Athenian leaders were dismayed, burying their heads in their hands, crying, and beating their chests. "However, I will be merciful, realizing that a prosperous and stable Athens will bring stability to Greece. Not only that, but I will enlarge the franchise to citizens who have one thousand drachmas of wealth. You can retain your Assembly."

A collective sigh of relief and thanks to the gods murmured through the Athenians.

"However," Cassander stressed as he raised his right hand, "all of its actions must have the approval of me and my regent in Athens. I hereby appoint Demetrius of Phalerum to be my representative here in Athens. He will have absolute power. Obey him and you will have peace, prosperity, and relative freedom. If you revolt again, I will burn the city. Now go to your homes, and thank the gods for my mercy."

A philosopher and scholar, Demetrius of Phalerum was not a politician or military man and did not have aspirations of power. By skillful persuasion and diplomacy, he kept the factions of Athens at peace with one another and supervised ten years of peace and prosperity in Athens. Of course, he was backed by the Macedonian power and threat to interfere if there was unrest or revolt.

* * *

Phidias' museum and library complex were growing beyond his dreams. Ptolemy had agents from Sicily to India collecting specimens and texts. No one could bring a book into Alexandria without surrendering it to be copied, which included scrolls in Persian, Phoenician, and Hebrew.

The institution was more like a research university that grew to more than thirty scholars who lived and worked in the temple complex. They ate in a common hall and were supported by the state. There were experts in mathematics, biologic and physical sciences, literature, history, and, of course, philosophy. As in any collection of intellectuals, there was bound to be jealousy and resentment.

"I am sick and tired of the bickering between scholars. They act more like children sometimes than intelligent men," Phidias complained to one of his assistants. "It reminds me of my old friend, Aristotle, who argued with Plato. Each thought his world view was correct. Philosophers will always argue about what they perceive to be right." Phidias shook his head.

"There is something more serious than that, Master Phidias." His assistant looked around to see if anyone was close by who might be listening.

"What is it?"

"I have heard that one of the mathematicians wants to replace you as head of the museum and library."

"What? Who?"

"Dyonatas of Syracuse. He says you're old and can't run the institution as it should be."

"How dare he! I built this place. It is my child."

"That is true, Master, but he has the support of other scholars."

"They're jealous. I still have the support of Ptolemy."

"I have heard that they may speak with the King himself."

"We'll see about that," Phidias said, slamming his fist on the table.

After that conversation, Phidias began to realize he was indeed tired from all his work and missed Athens. He sent a message that he wanted to see Ptolemy.

* * *

"I want to go back to Athens," Phidias said to Ptolemy. They stood on a high terrace of the palace looking at the sparkling water in the distant harbor with its plethora of multicolored sails and flags.

"Why?" asked Ptolemy.

Phidias told him of the bickering among the scholars, but more importantly about a movement among some to replace him as head of the institution. "They say I am getting too old."

"That's ridiculous. You're doing a great job. There will always be jealousy among intellectuals. They are very high strung, despite their logical and philosophic reasoning. I will always support you, my old teacher. You have my complete confidence."

"Thank you, Ptolemy, but I do feel my age and want to return to my home, my mother Athens. I want to teach at the Lyceum that Aristotle founded."

"Athens is not what you left when you followed Alexander, my friend. It is a conquered city ruled by Macedon."

"At least it's at peace under Demetrius of Phalerum," insisted Phidias. "Theophrastus at the Lyceum may need me. I feel that I must return."

"You cannot go," commanded Ptolemy. "I want you to remain here. You're a good advisor to me in the areas of philosophy and history, and you're doing wonderful work with collecting artifacts and books."

"Someone else can take over that job. I can teach a replacement…"

"I order you to stay in Alexandria," Ptolemy interrupted. "You do not have my permission to leave."

"But…"

"I said no!" Ptolemy yelled. "Your place is here in Alexandria to serve me. Now go and continue your duty. You are dismissed."

Phidias left, feeling in his soul that there was something he must finish, some destiny he must fulfill, that he could not do while still in Alexandria. He must return to Athens to discover that destiny and complete it before he was too old. He reluctantly returned to the collections he had accumulated. He dusted off the scrolls containing his notes of his journeys from Pella to Persia and to Egypt.

Something he must do.

He continued to work with the library and museum, awaiting an opportune time to approach Ptolemy again.

CHAPTER 35

Ten years after the death of Alexander, Ptolemy moved his capital to Alexandria. In those years he had strengthened its defenses, deepened its harbors, and built up his navy. The city prospered and teamed with people from every land: administrators, priests, soldiers, and, of course, scholars.

Alexandria's main avenue, called the Canopic Way, gathered speechless wonder from newcomers. Ninety feet in width, it could accommodate eight chariots abreast and was unmatched in scale in the ancient world. It was lined with carved granite columns in vivid colors, decorated with rich facades, and covered with canopies against the hot sun, hence its name, and lit at night. From east to west the city measured nearly four miles and was already becoming a beautiful metropolis of parks, baths, theaters, gymnasiums, courts, and temples, shrines, and synagogues. The side streets were nearly twenty feet wide and well drained. From the central crossroads of the two main avenues, a forest of colonnades extended along the ten-minute walk to the Palace and Temple complex, a wonder in its own right.

Ptolemy was justifiably proud of his capital and what he had built his kingdom into, but he was also aware of how fragile it could be. He had to balance nimbly among the shifting political realities of the Greek world in order to keep a powerful, hostile coalition from forming.

Antigonus ruled Asia Minor, which was the geographical connection between Greece and the rest of the empire of Alexander. Together with his son Demetrius, who styled himself as the new Alexander, they were planning to conquer and unite all the Empire under themselves. Demetrius was called Poliocretes, meaning "destroyer of cities," because he built huge, clever siege machines to conquer cities. Ptolemy saw the threat and had to counter it.

* * *

The dark blue of the Mediterranean was a deep contrast for the multicolored sails of the galleys in the harbor of Alexandria. Ships from Ionia,

Rhodes, Cyprus, Athens, and even Sicily and Carthage plied the commercial routes that came through Alexandria.

Phidias sat at a table in the portico of the Temple of the Muses, built on an elevation with a view down the wide avenue toward the harbor. He gazed at the busy harbor, allowing his thoughts to roam from the cataloging he was doing. The sea was not as iridescent as he remembered the Aegean. The harbor was much grander than the one at Piraeus, but he missed his homeland and especially Athens.

How long had it been since he had seen Athens? Almost forty years, he reckoned as he realized he was approaching seventy years of age. His legs hurt when he climbed the steps of the temple or museum, and his eyes had trouble reading the many manuscripts he had collected.

His attention shifted from the distant harbor to the slaves working in the museum. They were carrying in and arranging specimens of stuffed animals, insects and butterflies in containers, and reptiles and amphibians in jars. In another area, slaves carefully shelved scroll after scroll under the supervision of a Greek scholar, including books on every subject from anatomy, astronomy, biology, mathematics, history, biographies, and philosophy. The museum had collected so many books that Phidias was going to ask Ptolemy to build a large separate building for the library alone.

One of the young Greeks, who was supervising the cataloging of some books, approached Phidias. "Pardon me, Master Phidias, but could you help me catalog this treatise from Lachaetes of Syracuse? He has written on the teachings of Pythagoras. It contains mathematical theorems, of course, but also relates them in a mystical way to some of the new religions from the East. Should I place it in the section on mathematics or religion, or perhaps philosophy, next to those of Pythagoras and his followers?"

"Let me read the manuscript, and I will decide where to place it," Phidias replied. "Do you enjoy your work here at the museum, Cleanthes?"

"Oh yes, I am hungry for knowledge and devour what I can from the scholars here. I like to study the mathematics and science that the Babylonians and Persians developed. The collection of books is such a treasure of information. I hope to use that knowledge someday for great projects in Egypt."

"Books are my great love also," said Phidias. "I am caretaker of these books, and they are my children, since I have none of my own. I lavish my time and care on them. I read them, of course, add notes of my own, and have the slaves repair and copy them. They contain all the knowledge mankind has painstakingly found by trial and error and carefully collected and passed from generation to generation to us. We no longer have to memorize and recite histories as Homer had to do before there was writing. Knowledge doesn't have to be passed from father to son, some being lost, and some having to be rediscovered. Now each generation is free to add to the cumulative knowledge of the past."

"That is a wonderful message, Master Phidias. You ought to teach it."

"I was a student of the great teachers, Plato and Aristotle. I have their books. Their teachings will not be lost after those whom they taught are dead. They will live on, studied by future scholars. Thus it should be with all knowledge."

"Thank you. I will leave Lachaetes' book with you and get back to supervising the slaves."

Phidias opened a scroll but could not concentrate on the script. He had mentioned the revered names of Plato and Aristotle, stirring his recollections and bringing them into the vivid present. Alexandria might be developing into a center of culture and learning, but it would never overshadow the brilliant glory that was Athens. He loved his work here and had planted the seeds and nourished the beginnings of this museum. Ptolemy and the supervisors he had trained would continue the process.

He missed Athens—the lively arguments in the marketplace, the brilliant conversation in the symposia, even the political bickering. They were what made life interesting in Athens. He especially missed his friend Aristotle and the intellectual stimulation at the Academy. He longed to stroll the paths of Aristotle's Lyceum. He would write to Theophrastus and ask him if it was safe to return to his beloved Athens.

Phidias heard from Theophrastus of the peaceful atmosphere ruling Athens and again went to Ptolemy, demanding that he be allowed to return there. Once more Ptolemy demurred.

"I told you before that I will not allow you to leave Alexandria. You're doing a good job for the wonderful museum and library."

"But Ptolemy, the supervisors I have trained can take care of the facilities. The scholars that are here will draw others…"

"I said no!" Ptolemy slammed his fist on the maps he had been studying. "Antigonus is gathering an army and may invade Egypt. He is a very capable general, the best survivor of those who served Alexander. To tell you the truth, I am afraid of him. Now leave me from your pleadings to go back to Greece. "I will be occupied in trying to save Egypt and your precious museum. And now…go back to the good work you're doing."

Phidias left. He understood Ptolemy's anxiety over his political situation, but he felt even stronger in his desire to return to Athens. He would approach Ptolemy again when he thought the time appropriate.

* * *

During the revolt of Athens and other cities against Cassander, Olympias, Alexander's mother, led an army from her homeland of Epirus. While Cassander was busy in the south, she took Pella and visited wrath on many of her opponents.

"That witch!" Cassander exploded. "She caused my father unceasing trouble while he ruled Macedon for Alexander. Now she will give me more headaches."

"She has made it no secret that she wants to unite the Empire under Alexander's son," said one of his generals.

"And, of course, she will be his regent," said Cassander cynically. "She still considers herself Queen of Macedon. I will have to deal with her after I have finished with the Greeks."

After Cassander returned victorious to Macedon, he chased Olympias from Pella and had her executed.

The year after Ptolemy moved to Alexandria, Antigonus and his son, startied a war in an attempt to unite the entire empire under them.

"I will cross the Hellespont and attack Lysimachus in Thrace and Cassander in Macedon," Antigonus told his son. "I will cut off the source of supplies and mercenaries Ptolemy needs from Greece. Seleucus is in Babylon and is no threat for now."

"What about Ptolemy?" Demetrius asked.

"Take a contingent of about twenty thousand to Gaza. You can block him there if he comes out of Egypt."

Demetrius did that, but Ptolemy surprised him by bringing a large force across the Sinai, supplied by new ships. He overwhelmed Demetrius, who fled north.

Meanwhile, Antigonus was having trouble supplying his army due to a lack of naval power and soon withdrew back to Asia Minor.

Ptolemy followed up his victory by advancing up the coast and capturing Sidon, Tyre, and lower Syria.

The two sides called a truce and licked their wounds. All the allies except Seleucus signed what amounted to an armistice. Antigonus with his son planned to hunt down Seleucus. The war would resume four years later.

During the next year, when Antigonus and Demetrius failed to destroy Seleucus, Ptolemy took advantage and annexed the island of Cyprus, that rich source of copper from which it got its name.

That same year Cassander was also preparing to defend himself politically. "I can't allow anyone to use Alexander's son as a rallying point against me, like Olympias tried to do. He and his mother must die."

"But, Sire," one of his advisers replied, "won't that play into the hands of Antigonus? He had Alexander's sister murdered. He wants to unite the whole Empire under himself."

"That will take away his excuse that he is uniting it for young Alexander. He will thus show himself and his son to be naked agressors."

Alexander's half-brother had already been killed. Cassander executed Roxana and her son, Alexander, thus ending the Argead family line.

* * *

Phidias felt that the time was right for him to plead with Ptolemy once more. He waited until after the celebrations of his victory and the news that Cyprus was now a part of Egypt's growing territory.

Phidias asked for a meeting in the morning, before Ptolemy began his official business, and was ushered into Ptolemy's chambers. Ptolemy had finished his breakfast and was lounging in comfortable clothes on a veranda with a view of the harbor in the distance He would not see official visitors until after his bath and noontime meal. The sun was not yet hot, and a pleasant breeze caressed the open area. Ptolemy welcomed his old tutor and organizer of his museum.

"Sit down, my friend," he gestured to some fruit on the table. "Have some fruit. Have you had your breakfast? Perhaps some wine?" "No thank you, Ptolemy. I have not had the chance to congratulate you in person for your remarkable success against Antigonus." He raised a cup of fruit juice.

Ptolemy raised his own cup in acknowledgment. "And what important business brings you here?"

"There are no serious problems at the museum and library. In fact, they are growing steadily. More scholars are visiting us, and many have asked to stay. No, the institutions are doing so well that I feel I can approach you once more about my leaving Alexandria."

Ptolemy raised his brows and started to reply.

Phidias lifted his hand to continue. "I know you have been occupied with your own political security, but now you have it. I have carefully considered my arguments for you to allow me to return to Athens. I give you the following reasons why you should grant my wish: I am getting old, now seventy winters. My legs rebel at the thought of climbing all those steps to the library. My eyes cannot read the small script of the scrolls, and I must have younger men read them to me. I have trained others how to collect and organize the books that come from all corners of Alexander's empire, and my sources will continue to send them. The library is rapidly outgrowing its present facility. You will have to spend many talents constructing new buildings, and that will take years.

"There is peace for now among the successors of Alexander, and you have expanded your power. You are secure in your kingdom. Cassander rules Greece, and Athens is peaceful under Demetrius Phalerum."

Phidias paused and stood erect as if to emphasize his next statement. "The most important reason of all is that, even though you are King and Pharaoh of Egypt, I am not your slave. I am a free Greek and have the right to leave without your permission. I only seek it out of courtesy and friendship. If you do not grant it, I will leave with the summer winds in any case."

"You have made your arguments well, my friend," said Ptolemy. "It is true that I cannot force you to stay, but hoped that you would do so out of loyalty to me and the important work you are doing here. I grant you permission to return to your beloved Athens. I will make sure a proper vessel is provisioned for your journey. Not only that, but I want to reward you for your years of service to me. I will instruct my treasurer to give you five talents. You may take as many of your slaves with you as you may need. All I ask is that you remember me with charity when you teach or write your history."

"Thank you, Ptolemy. You have truly been a friend as well as a generous sponsor of my work for the museum. I will never forget your wisdom as a ruler and your friendship to philosophers."

Phidias took his leave and prepared for his journey home. He had not seen Athens for thirty-two years.

VIII THE ROAD BACK

CHAPTER 36

As the vessel rolled up its sail and the oarsmen carefully guided it into the harbor at Piraeus, Phidias' eyes filled with tears. He stood near the bow and noted how new shops and houses had sprung up along the shore near the port. His ship glided past many vessels, obviously not manned by Greeks. They seemed to be from every port in the Mediterranean, Aegean, and Black Seas. Colorful sails and pennants, exotic costumes, and foreign smells filled his senses.

He had brought with him some of his books, letters from Aristotle and others, and all his notes. He'd left behind all his slaves, whom he had freed, except for his old manservant, Pinocrates, who had followed him from Athens to Pella and throughout Asia to Egypt, and had been head of the household of over twenty slaves in Alexandria. Phidias had also brought Lydia, who refused to leave him, and would serve as cook and housekeeper.

Phidias had written to him that he was returning, and Theophrastus was overjoyed that his fellow student of Aristotle was coming. He had assured Phidias that a position was waiting for him at the Lyceum. Slaves took Phidias' belongings to a house that the head master had arranged for him.

As Phidias was led through the streets of Athens to his new home, he noticed the changes that the years of his absence had brought to the city. The people were dressed in costumes and colors of the rainbow, reflecting their varied origins from all over the expanded Greek world. Athens was not the monotonous undyed cotton or wool of its past years. There were purple cloaks from Tyre, scarlet caftans from Persia, and silk scarves and sashes from as far away as India in brilliant greens, yellows, and blues.

Many of the houses Phidias remembered had been torn down and replaced by larger homes of the new rich. The houses were also more colorful, as the newer style called for doors, shutters, window frames, and eaves to be painted in colors and patterns limited only by their owners' imaginations.

Finally, the servants of Theophrastus stopped in front of the gate to Phidias' new home. He noticed it too was freshly painted a forest green. Inside the gate, they crossed a small courtyard and entered the house proper. The house was small, by the standards Phidias was accustomed to in Egypt, but it would fulfill all his needs for the time being. He would use some of the money Ptolemy had given him to purchase larger accommodations when he found what suited him.

Over the next few days, Phidias visited the Lyceum and discussed teaching there. Some of the philosophers and scientists were either old acquaintances or men Phidias had heard of. They were anxious to meet this man who had followed Aristotle to Pella and then accompanied Alexander on his conquests. They asked him what were his experiences with King Philip, of Alexander, and of Ptolemy.

"You were with Aristotle when he was tutor to Alexander," said one. "What did he actually think of his student?"

Phidias sighed deeply and stared into the distance, as if reliving the years when he and Aristotle first saw Pella and the future conqueror of the Persian Empire. "Aristotle was excited about being the tutor of the son of a strong king and was encouraged to find Alexander an intelligent youth with a thirst for knowledge."

They enquired about Philip and Olympias, about Alexander's personality, and, of course, about Phidias' escapades in Asia.

"I can tell you," he said after an hour or so regaling them with tales of murder and mayhem, "that Aristotle became disappointed, that the bloodthirsty barbarism Alexander inherited from his mother and the wild drinking of his father began to overwhelm the civilized culture Aristotle had instilled in him. It tore at his heart." Phidias looked sadly around at the rapt faces. "After Alexander killed Aristotle's nephew, Callisthenes, Aristotle turned his back on him. I knew it must've pained him deeply, but I never saw or spoke with him again." He choked, unable to go on.

One of the other philosophers patted his back. "We miss him, also. He was such a brilliant man. It is a great loss to us."

Phidias nodded and thought to himself that it was a great loss for Athens, too. He could see that the brilliant minds of the Greek world were gravitating no longer to Athens but to Alexandria.

"Phidias," another philosopher interrupted his thoughts, "you have such detailed knowledge of these persons and events. Why don't you write them down in a book so that they can be shared and will not be lost?"

"Perhaps I will. I have my journals, but I have not put them in any readable order. It is such a daunting task. I have never written a book. I don't know if I can."

"You must," said someone, and they all murmured agreement.

Phidias fell silent, overcome with the thought that he should do something he felt unprepared to do. He shoved the thought aside temporarily and enthusiastically immersed himself in the intellectual atmosphere of the Lyceum.

* * *

A year or so passed and as Phidias made his way through the crowded streets one day, he noticed that ambling among the colorful people were dark men with rough, dirty clothes. Some walked in groups with menacing stares, obviously armed. Beggars with filthy rags over a sightless eye or a walking stick in place of a missing leg hugged the walls, holding out a hand or cup for passersby to drop a coin into.

Phidias knew these were not veterans of Alexander's army, who were all provided for by the dead conqueror. They were the victims of the violence between bands of hired thugs. Phidias had heard that Greece was riddled with petty lords who carved out pieces of the countryside and defended themselves against their neighbors with foreign or Greek mercenaries. As long as they pledged allegiance to Macedon, Cassander allowed these warlords to have their own sway. He shook his head in disgust as he watched a group of ruffians shove their way through the crowd, rudely pushing aside anyone too slow to move. Phidias backed to a wall watching the men go by, holding his breath at the stench that accompanied them.

"Good evening, Master Phidias," Lydia said as she opened the door to his house. She followed as he walked through the open courtyard with its small fountain. "Do you want to eat now? I made a stew with some fresh lamb I got in the market today."

"Not right now, Lydia. I'm a little winded after climbing that last hill to our house. Bring me a little wine to my room. I want to lie down for a while before eating."

Lydia brought him the wine, diluted about two-thirds with water. She had been Phidias' slave for almost twenty years. He had offered freedom to Lydia along with his other slaves in Egypt, but the old woman had said, "But Master, what will I do, and where will I go? You need me to care for you in your advancing age. Who would cook your meals and wash your clothes?"

Phidias agreed with her logic, and they grew inseparable as he relied on her and Pinocrates for all his bodily needs. He listened to her prattling and respected the down-to-earth wisdom she possessed. A daily visitor to the markets, she listened for the latest gossip. The slaves always knew what was going on in the homes of the rich and powerful.

Lydia chatted as she brought Phidias his supper. She placed the freshly baked bread on the table and said, "I had to pay two drachmas for a bushel of wheat to be ground into flour for this bread. A year ago it was only one drachma. I'm afraid you'll have to give me more money for the market, Master. Everyone is complaining. We see the rich merchants and landowners getting wealthier, while the poor have to scrape to get enough food to keep going. I think it's a shame. Demetrius better do something about it or there will be riots."

"You may be right," replied Phidias between swallows. "I noticed the public unrest since I came back. There always seems to be violence. Not only in Athens but throughout Greece, there are power-hungry men or else wealthy aristocrats or businessmen who have armed gangs. Athens always had a lively political atmosphere, but this is dangerous and degenerate."

"The people of the streets are afraid of these armed men," Lydia said as she tore some bread. "Supporters of one or another of these *plutonoi*, these new rich, often fight each other. I find that I have to go to the market very early before they roam the streets."

"They frighten me too, Lydia. They have no respect for older men and teachers such as me."

"Master Phidias, it is shameless that the younger generation flaunts the common morals by living openly with each other. I don't mean the homosexuals, who have always been accepted. I mean men and women who live together without the ceremonies of marriage. They often have babies, which they immediately abandon on the temple steps or expose in the hills. What is becoming of Athens?"

"I call it moral decay, Lydia. Athens is not like it was when I was younger. The old religion is no longer accepted by the educated and wealthy. Money is their god, and they are filled with the cynicism of Pyrrho, who is skeptical of everything. We are inundated with Oriental cults since Alexander's victory over the East has opened our doors to these foreign religions. But now I'm tired and will take the rest of my wine to bed. Thank you for the supper; it was delicious."

"Thank you, Master. Good night."

* * *

One day after he taught a class about the government and the economy of Egypt, Phidias walked over to where Theophrastus was talking with some youths. He listened as they asked him about some of the new plant and animal organization in his book. After the group broke up, Phidias approached and said, "Friend Theophrastus, may I have a word with you?"

"Phidias, my esteemed friend and colleague, I am always happy to talk with you. You know, we must continually learn from nature and from each other, or we might as well be dead."

Theophrastus became head of the Lyceum on the death of Aristotle and, as a naturalist and scientist, surpassed his teacher. He was an avid gardener and knew every aspect of plants and gardening, having recently written his ninth book on the medicinal properties of plants. Before he died, he would write over a hundred books on almost every subject from love to war.

"If you don't mind, Phidias, walk with me along the path through the Lyceum grounds. I want to show you some of the new plant specimens I have obtained from Egypt and Asia." He enthusiastically pointed out plants with exotic aromas, ostentatious blooms, or healing powers. When they reached a bench under an ancient oak, he indicated that they should sit down. "What is it you wanted to talk about?"

"Theophrastus, you knew Aristotle almost as long as I. However, I followed Alexander and stayed in Alexandria while you became a teacher here at the Lyceum after Aristotle built it. He told me you were a very popular lecturer, attracting as many as two thousand students. You were more scientist than philosopher, so it was natural that Aristotle picked you to succeed him."

"Thank you. Indeed, Aristotle liked me. I suppose he was impressed with the way I lectured. My birth name was Lysander, but Aristotle said I should be called Theophrastus, which means 'he spoke like a god'. Now no one recalls my original name."

Phidias changed the subject. "Xenocrates died recently. He was the head of Plato's Academy."

"Yes, for about twenty-five years. I knew him well. He was a true philosopher and wore the mantle of Plato with distinction."

"I heard that he led a very simple life and never married," said Phidias.

"Xenocrates refused all fees and became so poor that he was on the verge of being imprisoned for taxes, when Demetrius Phalerum paid them for him. I believe his only mistress was philosophy. Athens will miss him."

Phidias shook his head. "It seems that with the passing of Xenocrates, the essential philosophy Plato espoused is exhausted. Most of Plato's successors are mathematicians or moralists. It also pains me about the trend in Isocrates' School."

"Pyrrho, the cynic, teaches there," admitted Theophrastus. "He has quite a following. He is very persuasive in his arguments, although I disagree with him."

"I knew him in Asia," said Phidias. "He followed Alexander to India and studied there with the *gymnosophists,* the naked holy men. I'm afraid he came back with his nihilistic view of life. He teaches that certainty is unattainable, and since all theories are probably false, one might as well accept the conventions of his own place and time."

"That is so completely negative to me," said Theophrastus with exasperation.

"That is what he believes and practices. What bothers me is that kind of teaching is also undermining our traditional Greek values. He says that the same practice may be moral or immoral, depending on where and when we live, and that everything is opinion and nothing entirely true. How can a person live his life that way? This cynicism is replacing traditional values. Foreign cultures are diluting our Greek ways. What is happening to Athens? It troubles me greatly."

"I agree with you, my friend, but you cannot turn back time. Since Alexander's conquest, we have a new world, one that is not limited to Greece but looks outward. Yes, we have intermixed foreign cultures and religions, but I think we are richer for it. Athens is still the center of philosophy. Our Lyceum, Plato's Academy, and even Isocrates' school train philosophers, mathematicians, and scientists for the world."

"It has changed greatly since I left. I guess I have seen so much of strange lands and peoples that Athens appears to be another city than the one I knew."

Theophrastus patted his hand. "It's hard go back to a place you knew when you were young. You remembered good times and pleasant memories, and were disappointed when you see how dirty, crude, and selfish the people really are. The grass is not as green, the trees are not as tall and the houses are not as grand as you remembered them."

Phidias nodded as he sadly accepted the reality of his friend's reasoning.

"Look, Phidias, you know so much of the history of Greece and Macedon during those years of Philip and Demosthenes. You followed Alexander and knew him intimately. Why don't you write a history of those times? You're such a good teller of tales. The students tell me how they enjoy your stories of past glory and heroes."

"Not all was glory and heroes, Theophrastus. There was much ugly slaughter, drunken murders, sinister plots, and self-centered, power-hungry men. I do have a lot of memories and I have many notes I have collected over the almost seventy-five years of my life. I don't know if I can ever write them down in a book. Perhaps I should. You have written many books. Would you help me?"

"I will certainly help you in any way I can. It is getting late, however, so let's continue our discussion another time."

* * *

That night, after Lydia cleared the table of the dishes, Phidias asked that she bring him his scrolls and light the oil lamp. His thoughts began to churn as he passed his fingers caressingly over the papyrus rolls and the straps that bound them, each with dates, places, or names written on it.

He recalled his conversation with Theophrastus and realized how much the schools of Athens had lost in the passing of their founders. The reputation of Athens would fall with them. He decided he must do what he could to ensure their legacy and that of the great men he had known.

At times, it was difficult for him to put down the subtleties of ideas, the fire of controversy, the complexity of politics, and the agony or exhilaration of battle in his writings. Much more was in his memory than he had noted down, but he felt he must find the energy to rouse himself to the task of putting it to paper. Sometimes he thought he was writing in a lucid and informative manner, but, read now, it came out stale and uninteresting. How was he to transform dry facts, the utterances of dead men, the numbers of slain on battlefields, into living, feeling, breathing history, that people would read and want to continue to read long after his stylus had left the papyrus and the book was placed on a shelf? He realized that this was the mystical force that had urged him back to Athens. He had to fulfill a goal—one that gave meaning to his life.

He opened another scroll and started to read. Suddenly he choked and grabbed at the pain that was squeezing his chest over his heart. He yelled out, as his right hand swept the scrolls from the table and spilled the lamp onto the floor. Pinocrates rushed in and threw a cloth over the scattered oil, and Lydia brought a cold, wet cloth and placed it on his head. She and Pinocrates gently helped him to his bed.

Phidias felt as if he was dying as dark spots and colored flashes swirled through his vision. His mind was filled by a drumming that didn't allow him to think. He let them help him to his bed. Someone propped his back up on cushions, and he felt himself able to breathe better. His heart, which had been pounding against his chest wall, seemed to settle into a calmer rhythm. "The color is coming back to his face," said Pinocrates. "How is the pain, Master?"

"It is lessening. I think it is passing, old friend."

"I will sleep on a pallet on the floor by your door tonight."

"No," Lydia said. "The floor is too hard for your old bones. I will put cushions in this large chair and sleep in Master Phidias' room tonight. I will keep the lamp burning and will call you if I need you."

Pinocrates reluctantly left, while Lydia made herself as comfortable as she could.

Phidias lay in his bed, his breathing becoming normal, the sweat drying on his forehead. His thoughts rushed like flashes through his mind. Would he die that night in his sleep, the next day, or the next week? His remaining life was short, he admitted to himself. Would he be able to write down all his experiences and memories before it was too late? He was thinking about all the important people he had known—all dead now—as he drifted into a restless slumber: *Plato..., Aristotle...,, Philip..., Alexander..., Demosthe...*

CHAPTER 37

The next day, Phidias felt as if he had died and been reborn. Although he felt weak in his body, he was renewed in his spirit. He was determined now to become strong and to fulfill the destiny that was driving him. After a week of eating Lydia's soup and going through his notes scattered about his room, he became restless. He needed some fresh air to help stir his creativity, so he could actually start writing.

Ignoring the pleas of Pinocrates and Lydia, he dressed and went out. "I promise I will only walk to the market for some fruit and come back home."

As he walked slowly to the marketplace, Phidias' thoughts turned to feelings about his life. He had wanted to be a philosopher, a teacher, and a historian, ever since he had been a student with Aristotle, and these he had accomplished. However, when he examined his life more closely, as the great Socrates had admonished, he realized that he also had other feelings and needs that he had ignored. He had left the only love he had known and had tried to cover his broken heart with paper and ink, but the scars remained. He had survived hardships and near death to finally return to his beloved Athens, but he still had not fulfilled that goal that eluded him.

He was paying for some fruit when he noticed an older woman purchasing some vegetables at one of the stalls. The color and style of her dress caught his eye. Her body was bent, and gray hair still streaked with light brown peaked from behind the brightly colored scarf wrapped around her head and lower face.

He stepped up to the stall alongside the woman and started picking out some vegetables. Politely he turned to her and said, "I see by your dress that you are of the hetairai. Do you mind if I ask you a question?"

She lowered her eyes and said, "I was a hetaira, but no longer. What is your question?"

"Do you know of a hetaira by the name of Thais? Is she still alive? If so, is she still in Athens?"

"I know a woman named Thais who was a hetaira. She still lives in Athens. Who wants to know?" She examined the baldheaded old man with a white beard and sun-weathered face.

"Tell her that her old friend, Phidias, asks about her health. We were lovers when we were much younger." Phidias choked down the words that he still loved her.

The woman slowly lowered the scarf that covered her face and said, "I am Thais, Phidias."

They fell into each other's arms, tears of joy falling down their cheeks. The bands of years of repressed feelings suddenly were released as emotions of rediscovered love burst from their hearts. Completely overcome with happiness, like seeing a loved one thought to be dead, they clung to each other, unable to speak.

Unwilling to let Thais go, Phidias held her at arm's length. He was so overcome with the joy of finding this loved one, whom he thought he had forever lost, that his mouth could only mumble questions. "Are you well? Where are you living? What are you doing? You must tell me everything." He didn't dare ask the question of other lovers, perhaps even one she lived with.

"Yes, my health is good, although I feel my age." She seemed to know his unuttered question. "After you left, I never took another lover. My money ran low, and I moved into a small house with another retired hetaira. We live simple lives, just getting by."

They spoke in excited syllables, as if trying to catch up on a lifetime of memories, both filled with the joy of just being together again. Phidias at last noticed the sack of fruit at his side and remembered that he had told Lydia he would not be long. He didn't want them to worry, and yet...he couldn't bring himself to leave Thais. He felt that he might lose her again.

His mind filled with an unconscious urging,."Are you free for tonight?" he asked. "I would like you to come to my house for dinner. Lydia, my housekeeper, is a wonderful cook. We have much to catch up on. So much has happened to me that I would like to share with you."

"I would love to have dinner with you. I have no other plans. No one invites an old hetaira to dinners."

"Tell me where you live, and I will send my manservant for you at sundown. I am so excited to see you again."

They parted, and Phidias returned home with a bag full of fresh fruit and vegetables, hardly aware of his feet trodding the hard cobblestones, his head in the clouds drifting across the bright Athenian sky. His heart felt warm and young again, completely healed from his close call with death.

Phidias' path home carried him past the Temple of Aphrodite, Goddess of love. Although he did not believe in all the old Greek gods, he had a feeling that a divine force must have brought Thais back to him. He felt he must thank someone or something for his good fortune.

He entered the temple, his eyes becoming accustomed to the cool, dark interior lit by candles and smelling of incense. Dropping a coin into the poor box, he slowly knelt down, holding onto a pillar. "Thank you," he murmured. "Thank you for saving my life twice. I am indeed a new man. I promise never to let her go. I will protect her and keep her with your help. I will fulfill my destiny."

He rose with difficulty, unconcerned with his aching knees, renewed in heart and mind.

That evening Phidias welcomed Thais and ushered her into the small dining room. Lydia had set the table with fresh flowers and candles. He had told her that a lover from his youth was coming for dinner, but he didn't elaborate.

They talked of his years in Pella, Asia, and Egypt. "My life has not been as exciting as yours," she admitted. "After you left, Demosthenes aroused Athens periodically with revolts against Macedon, always with disastrous results. But my life has been without excitement."

"Surely you had friends. What did you do?"

"Oh yes, I had many friends, other hetairai. I have met many men, but none as lovers." She looked down, obviously filled with confused feelings.

Phidias broke the awkward silence and reached for the pitcher. "Would you like some more wine?"

She nodded, "Please."

They said no more of lovers past or present and spent the rest of the evening remembering pleasant times.

At last she said, "It's getting late, and I have no one to escort me home. The streets become dangerous at night."

"Pinocrates will escort you home. He carries a heavy staff and can take care of you. When can I see you again?" Phidias was so glad to have found his woman.

"I usually go to the food markets in the mornings. Now I must go." She rose, and they briefly hugged.

Phidias escorted her to the door and watched as Pinocrates' lantern outlined their figures until they disappeared around a corner.

After their dinner together, Phidias felt his love grow steadily for the woman he had left so many years before. He longed to be with her every day, and met her frequently in the markets, where he would buy fruits or vegetables for her to take home. She thanked him politely for his generosity.

They talked of their lives since they had parted and would take walks in temple porticos, the gardens of the Academy, or the Lyceum. He told her of his experiences in Asia and Egypt, of Philip and Alexander, and of Ptolemy.

"But enough of me and my life. What about you?" he asked.

"Since you left, my life has been simple. I have a few friends among the hetairai. We get together for dinner and discussions and attend the plays and festivals."

He noticed that she had worn only three or four dresses and the same cloak at all of their meetings. The cloak had frayed sleeves and stains around the hem. She said she had not taken other lovers, and he could see the signs that she had slipped into near poverty.

He brought her gifts daily—a fruit or vegetable basket with some silver or gold coins in the bottom, flowers, or sweets from Asia.

She thanked him politely and did not mention the money she found in the baskets. It was a matter of pride for her. She held his hand when he reached for it on their walks and modestly kissed him when they met or parted. She did not speak of love to him, although Phidias could sense it growing stronger within her.

Phidias moved into a house of his own that he had purchased. It was more spacious with a large, open courtyard, softened with flowers and a splashing fountain. "Will you come to my new house for dinner? Perhaps you can give me some pointers on decorating it."

"I would like to see your new house. Yes, I will come for dinner tomorrow night."

Phidias greeted Thais dressed in a new cloak and held her hand while he showed off his house, ending in the dining room, which was lit with scented oil lamps. His heart was bursting with emotion. He could not help but touch her hand, her shoulder, her dress, which he also noticed was new. They enjoyed the dinner Lydia had prepared and drank sparingly of the wine. Phidias' face was flushed with emotion as he reached into his belt. "I have a present for you," he said.

Thais looked up in surprise. "You do? You have already been so generous."

"I would give you the whole world, if it were mine to give," he said in a voice filled with emotion. He handed her a small, carved wooden box. "I hope you like it. It's something that Alexander himself gave me. He said it came from Darius' treasure."

Thais opened the box and took out a long strand of exquisitely matched pearls. They gleamed in the lamplight. "Oh, they are beautiful. I love them." She held Phidias' hands as he held the box and looked into his eyes. Her vision blurred with brimming tears as she took the pearls out of their box. "I will wear them for you." She placed them around her neck, then reached over and kissed him.

Phidias reached for her hand. "Please move into my house," he pleaded. "I will take care of you. I have plenty of the money left that Ptolemy gave me. I have it invested with the bankers."

She didn't answer but looked down, one hand in his and the other fingering the pearls.

Phidias continued. "I want to be with you all the time, not just meeting here and there. I cannot ever let you go again. Please say you will live with me."

Thais looked up and met his eyes, slowly shaking her head. "I don't think we are ready for that. I know you say that you love me, perhaps you do. I have strong feelings for you too, but…I don't know if you have changed." She remembered the younger man who was filled with erotic energy but lacked a deeper sense of emotional commitment. His true loves had been philosophy and history.

"What do you mean, I haven't changed?" He was animated. "Can't you see I'm older and wiser? I've experienced wars, murders, and cruelty beyond imagination. I've seen unbelievable wealth and dire poverty, fabulous cities, magnificent mountains, and wide rivers. I have seen how men can cynically plot and plan assassinations, even of close companions. Believe me, I have changed."

"I don't mean it that way. You must show me how you have changed," she said quietly.

He took her in his arms and kissed her deeply, passionately, pouring all the love of his heart into the embrace. Hoping that the passionate kiss showed her his true feelings, he held her in his arms and said, "I don't want you to move into my house because of my selfish desires or need to own you, although I do want you all to myself. I want to give myself to you also. I want to marry you. Will you marry me?"

"Phidias, we are in our seventies. Why do you want to marry? We have no children. We can simply remain friends and lovers if you wish."

"I…I love you…with all my heart. I lost you once; I can't bear to lose you again. I want to give you back the love we missed all those years. I want to live the rest of my life with you. I want to give you all that I have, including my heart."

"That's wonderful, but it's not enough. You said that to me forty years ago. What is different now?"

"What is different now is that I know myself better. Yes, I am older and have seen more and have had many adventures. I mean that I see now what is important. Books and philosophy are not what is important; it is people, and relationships, and feelings. My love for you and our relationship are what are important.

"I have come to this realization late in my life, and you have helped me. I realize that what is important to me is to share the rest of what life I have left with you. Without you, my life is not complete." He reached with trembling hands to hold hers. "Please, will you marry me?"

Thais saw that this old man was speaking from his emotionally filled heart, completely different from the person she had known, the one who had been interested in her only sexually, the love he expressed then born of a sensual need. Yes, now she could see that he had changed. She did not answer, but tears filled her eyes.

Phidias confessed a deeper yearning. "I need you to help me, Thais. I must fulfill a destiny that fate has given to me. I can't do it alone. We can do it together. Please say you will," his voice choked with pleading.

Thais realized Phidias had finally admitted that he could no longer rely on himself alone. He needed someone, someone to aid in his quest, someone he could trust. Perhaps he needed the magic that a woman could bring. He was willing to give up his proud independence and ask for a partner. Yes, she admitted to herself, he had changed. She looked into his pleading eyes as a tear ran down her cheek. "Yes, I will marry you. I will be glad to be your wife, your lover, your friend, and your partner."

"Oh, Thais, my love." He fell to his boney old knees at her side holding her hands, his tears bathing them as he covered them with kisses.

Phidias realized at last that real love is when a person truly, truly cares about another, not for what they represent as a means, but as an end in itself.

They were married in the same Temple of Aphrodite in which Phidias had made his promises. He invited all the faculty and students of the Lyceum and all of his and Thais' friends. He gave one thousand drachmas to the head priestess of the temple and asked her to officiate at his wedding, with all the proper ceremony and sacrifices.

The temple was filled with guests who were flanked by candles and bouquets of flowers. Incense wafted to the ceiling as the priestess asked the goddess to bless the marriage. The elderly couple, dressed in their finest clothes, held hands and spoke to each other from their hearts. Phidias choked several times as he spoke, and Thais could hardly finish her words. Tears of joy filled their eyes as they embraced and kissed. The priestess herself wiped away her tears as the assembly raised their voices with hopes of blessings and good fortune.

IX RESURRECTION

CHAPTER 38

Not long afterward, Phidias made his way one morning to the Lyceum. He walked slowly, leaning on his stick as he moved through the people already crowding the narrow streets. He wrapped his robe around him and threw it over his shoulder against the brisk breeze that blew from the ocean only a few miles away. Winter was coming, and it was cool in the mornings for his stiff old bones. Sounds of tradesmen opening their stalls, yells of food vendors, and the laughter of children running and playing joined with the shrill voices of women bargaining with the sellers of everything that fed the life of Athens. The bright clothes of the crowd mixed with the hues of cloth, jewelry, and foods of all sorts, creating a mélange of color. Phidias relished the smells of the market, the bustle of the people, and the energy of the tradesmen.

As he walked through a street lined by fruit and vegetable vendors, he spied some fresh apples laid out like giant rubies sparkling in the sun. Stopping to pick out one, he said to the vendor, "Good morning, Petros. How fresh are your apples?"

"I just got them early this morning from the port. They are as crisp as the morning air."

As Phidias picked one up, he was struck in the back and yelled at, "Turn around old man and give me your purse!"

Phidias slowly turned as the man stepped back. He had dark, swarthy skin and greasy black curls tied back with a dirty red cloth. His short yellow shirt was tied at the waist with a rope. He held a small knife and pointed it menacingly at Phidias' belly.

"Don't you know who this is, you ruffian?" Petros said. "He is a philosopher at the Lyceum."

"I don't care who he is. What use have I of philosophers? They don't make or sell anything. But he has money to buy apples, so I can take it to feed myself." His appearance and accent told Phidias the man was from Asia. He thought ruefully, how many of them were seen in Athens since Alexander had conquered Persia. "Quick, old man, your purse!"

"Here take this," said Phidias as he tossed the man his apple.

With the thief's attention distracted, Phidias arced up the bottom of his walking staff and struck him hard between his legs. The man groaned, dropped his knife, and grabbed his groin. Phidias then used his stick like a club and hit him across the ear. The robber screamed and fell to the ground, one hand on his groin and one on his bleeding ear.

"That will teach you to try and rob a citizen of Athens. Now go back to Asia where you belong!" Phidias offered a coin to Petros for the apple, which he refused. He then stepped around the still moaning thief and went on to the Lyceum. He had learned many tricks and how to fight from his travels with the Macedonian army.

He reflected on his way about the incident with the Asian ruffian and how it was a symptom of how Athens had changed. There seemed to be no respect for age or intellect. Only wealth and power were the currency of the Empire. Mercenary soldiers roamed over Greece, hiring themselves to the highest bidder for their private armies.

Returning from the Lyceum at the end of the day, Phidias entered his courtyard breathless. Pinocrates took his outer cloak and helped him to where Thais was embroidering a scarf. He sat down heavily in a chair. "What is wrong, Phidias? You look as though you have the weight of the world on your shoulders like Atlas."

"The decay in Athens is beginning to stink." He told her of his episode with the thief.

"That is terrible. Are you hurt?"

"No, I'm not hurt. I'm just disgusted. My soul aches."

"You should be more careful. You're not the young adventurer anymore. That thief could have stabbed you. He could have had a partner."

"I realize that now. I will be more careful. Athens is full of foreign riffraff these days. It does not have the feeling of spirit, of citizen loyalty anymore, The classes are only concerned about what they can get from the state. Something is missing, as if it is dead."

"Did the thief shake you up so much? Have you given up on Athens?"

"I haven't given up, but Athens is sick. Not only is there rot in the streets, but there is intellectual decay as well. Timotheus, the leading mathematician at the Academy, and two of our main scientists at the Lyceum, Simonides and Polydorus, are leaving for Alexandria. Some of their students are also going with them. We are losing some of our best talent. It saddens me to see this happen to Athens." He shook his head and wiped the perspiration from his bald pate.

"I have seen other sad signs," she admitted. "Athenians are limiting their families. Some have only one child while many have none. When a child comes, especially a female, it is often exposed and left to die in the hills or by the ocean. I am afraid the citizen population will fall, and we will be populated only by slaves." She changed the subject by pausing and looking squarely at him. "Phidias, look me in the eyes and answer me. Why did you come back to Athens?"

"I wanted to teach at the Lyceum."

"You are not needed at the Lyceum. The great philosophers are gone, and only Theophrastus holds the Lyceum together. Even, the students are going outside of Athens for learning and adventure. Why did you return to Athens?"

"I came back to find you."

"No you didn't. You found me accidentally. Now look into your heart. What do you see? What is there that told you that you must return? What is it that you came back to do?"

He looked up at her with extended, open hands as if pleading. "I love Athens, Thais, more than I love anything, more than I love you, more than I love myself. I was drawn back to her as to a lover, as a slave to a beloved master. I see that her soul is dying. Her sense of patriotic pride, her intellectual leadership, even the creative energy of her artists and writers has faded.

"It seems to me, that not only Athens, but all of Greece has passed a distance marker. The many wars of polis against polis weakened us, and now Macedon rules Greece. By conquering the Persian Empire, Alexander has spread Greek culture throughout the eastern world. It has enriched the other civilizations of the world, but it has opened Greece to their influence as well."

He finally began to realize what she was asking. "When I recovered from my close call with death and I found you, I made a sacred promise that I would fulfill my destiny, the destiny I would find in coming back to Athens. It was not clear to me before what that destiny was.

"My youth was spent in sports, in eating and drinking with my friends, in arguing in the streets about politics, and even in brawls. I was no deep thinker or leader of men. I was rather weak in virtues. My teachers at the Academy, especially Plato and Aristotle, helped prepare me for my experiences with Alexander, that truly made me a mature person. I have literally gained a world of experience." He raised his eyebrows as if a lamp suddenly flamed behind his eyes.

"You have forced me to open my eyes and realize what my real desire was in coming back to Athens. It is that I must write a history of all the events I've experienced, so that posterity can have a record of what transpired in Greece, and Macedon, and Persia, and Egypt. It is my task to document those momentous events and personalities that defined our times. It will be my gift to Athens and to the world."

"Yes, Phidias, that is why you have returned. I see it in your face and hear it in your voice. I know your heart, and you have found your destiny. Now document the exploits of Alexander and his golden age before it is forgotten."

"I know I must do it, but it is such a huge task. It spans my whole lifetime and half the known world. My notes are a hodgepodge, more like a diary. Some are merely fragments, thoughts, impressions, or a name of a person or place."

"I will help you. Tomorrow, instead of going to the Lyceum, bring out all your notes, and I will help you arrange them."

The next day after breakfast, Thais told Lydia and Pinocrates to clear all of the furniture out of one of the spare rooms. She told them to place a table with writing materials against the wall under the window. Then she told Phidias, "We will bring all the scrolls containing your notes, and lay them out in some order on the floor. You can open and refer to them as you write your history."

As Thais was helping Phidias arrange his notes, she said, "I have something I must tell you."

"What is that, my love?"

"Remember when I told you to go to Pella with Aristotle, because I didn't love you anymore? I said some pretty harsh words."

"They broke my heart. Yes, I still remember."

"Aristotle told me that you must accompany him to Pella for your own growth. You had to see more of the world than Athens, and indeed he was right."

"I saw almost the entire world. I saw many wonders and had many adventures, but I would have traded all of that for your love. You mean more to me than all of that."

"You say that now, but I knew that you must go. You had to go with Aristotle. He convinced me. You don't know how it broke my heart to say those things to you, but I did it for you, for your welfare," she said, putting her hands around his cheeks.

Phidias replied, "I could not believe in my heart then that you meant those words. I was crushed. My world was destroyed, but now I understand everything. It was for my benefit that you hurt yourself. It makes me love you even more for your sacrifice."

"Aristotle was your friend, and teacher, and mentor. Now he is gone. You must carry on and finish what he has trained you for. I will try to take his place. I will prod you along and keep you going. Now, let's get to work."

Although he knew this was what he came back to Athens to do, he was afraid that he might not be up to the task, but with Thais' encouragement he would begin.

* * *

"I can't read some of my notes," Phidias said exasperated one day soon afterward. "My eyesight is getting so bad."

"I will read them for you," Thais said.

"You can't. Some are just brief statements, abbreviations, barely legible even to young eyes. I can't finish."

"Don't keep making excuses. There must be a way. Perhaps one of your students from the Lyceum can help read them for you."

"No one can read them but me. But there might be a way. You mentioned the Lyceum. Maybe someone there can help me. Leontinas, a teacher of physics, has been making glass lenses that will focus the sun's rays to burn paper. He says he can also use them to study small insects. Perhaps I can use one to read my small script."

"If it is possible, that would be wonderful. We will pray to the gods that it will work."

He returned from the Lyceum the next day and, bursting through the gate, he began to shout for Thais, Pinocrates, and Lydia. "Hurry! Come see what I have."

They all came running and met him in the room in which he was working on his book.

He showed them a lens he had obtained from Leontinas. "Look how it makes the letters larger. I can read even the finest of writing merely by moving it farther from the paper. Look!"

They all took turns with the lens, marveling over it.

"Now, Phidias, you have no excuse," said Thais.

"Yes, Master, you can finish your book now," said Pinocrates.

. "The gods are looking after you, Master Phidias. You must not disappoint them," said Lydia.

"You are right, all of you. I have been told in so many different ways that I must finish this task. By everything I hold sacred, I will do it. Now everyone except Thais, leave me…and we will get to work."

CHAPTER 39

The days became weeks and the weeks became months as the two of them labored on the book. Phidias still went to the Lyceum occasionally, for he enjoyed talking with the students and his fellow teachers. As the winter winds grew colder, Pinocrates had to keep a fire in a small stove in the room. Phidias had to rest his cramped, arthritic hands occasionally, warming them by an oil lamp kept on his table.

After lunch each day, Thais made him lie down and rest in his room for an hour. Then they would resume work, take a break for dinner, and then work some more for a few hours before going to bed.

"I am tired," said Phidias one day.

"I know. You just walked up that hill from the Lyceum."

"I don't mean I am tired of walking, or just today. I mean, I am getting tired in general. I feel my years, almost seventy-five now. It is hard for me to get myself moving and keep up the energy to finish each day. I am getting old, Thais. I feel I don't have much longer in this world."

"Don't talk like that. You are almost through with your book. After we finish, we can take a trip to Alexandria. You said you wanted to show me the city and the library you started. You can even take a copy of your book and place it there."

"You're right. That would be something to look forward to after I finish. I have learned that life is a gift, and that a person must take it as it comes and make each day count. Let's get back to work," he said as he picked up his stylus.

A few days later, Demetrius Phalerum, the regent in Athens, came to visit Phidias. "I came to see how you are feeling. You haven't been to the Lyceum for some time, and I missed seeing you there."

"I am feeling well," Phidias replied, "perhaps a little tired. I have been working hard in finishing my book about my experiences."

"You must let me read it when you are finished."

"I will do better than that. I will have a copy made for you. I also will send a copy to Ptolemy in Alexandria. He encouraged me to start the library there."

"I would like to visit Alexandria someday, for I hear that Ptolemy has built a beautiful city," Demetrius said.

"It is not only beautiful, but it is becominge a center for scientific and academic study. But the library and museum are only beginning their growth. I told Ptolemy he needs to expand it and hire more scholars. Why don't you go and help him, Demetrius?"

"Cassander needs me in Athens to keep the peace. However, I will keep in mind what you have told me."

"Demetrius, you are no politician. You must use your talents as a philosopher ."

"Thank you for your compliment, Phidias. However, you are the true philosopher. I am sure that your book, when you are finished with it, will bring honor to you."

"I hope it will bring honor to Athens and to the people whose lives I have documented. I seek no honor for myself."

"That is the virtuous statement of a true scholar," Demetrius replied. "You will always be remembered through to your devotion to scholarship." Demetrius said good-bye and warmly embraced the old man.

* * *

A few months after Phidias' meeting with Demetrius, news came to Athens that Antigonus was at war with Lysimachus and Cassander. While Antigonus's army occupied the Macedonians in the north, his son, Demetrius Poliocretes, marched down into Greece proper.

Athens was in turmoil. The leaders of the Athenian resistance to Macedonian rule secretly met. "Demetrius Poliocretes will probably win his way to Athens," one of them said. "Some Greek cities support him, and many more will support Athens in throwing out the Macedonians."

"What should we do?" asked another. "Cassander's garrison rules the city under Demetrius Phalerum."

"We can gather what arms we can in secret and prepare to besiege the garrison if we must."

"There are still Athenians who support Macedon. They believe Demetrius Phalerum has brought peace and prosperity to our city."

"At what price?" another spat out. "We have no say in Athens' politics; the aristocrats have gotten wealthier; the poor have been forced to immigrate to Asia."

"We must support Demetrius Poliocretes in any way we can, and hopefully he will restore our freedom."

Macedonian soldiers from the garrison nervously patrolled the streets, looking for signs of revolt. Demetrius Phalerum paced in his villa. "I can't fight Demetrius Poliocretes. Cassander didn't leave me enough men; besides, I'm no general. Will Poliocretes kill me?" He asked, shaking.

"Probably not," his adviser said, "since you pose no military or political threat to him. But you should be prepared to leave Athens."

"I hope you're right. Start packing up my things, especially my books."

Not long afterward, a messenger arrived from Poliocretes, calling on the city to surrender peacefully. The Macedonian garrison would be spared, and there would be no reprisals against those who supported Cassander.

"He said that I must leave," Phalerum said. "I and all the governing council that Cassander appointed are expelled. Where will I go?"

"Perhaps to Egypt," said his adviser. "Ptolemy is an ally of Cassander, and you can sail with an Athenian merchant ship."

Demetrius remembered his conversation with Phidias and went to visit him the next day. He found the old man writing in his courtyard. Someone had brought a table and chair and placed them in the warm spring sunshine.

Phidias greeted his fellow philosopher and asked his servant to bring up a chair. Lydia brought out fruit and wine.

After pleasant greetings, Demetrius came to the point. "This is no social visit, my friend. As you know, Greece is being invaded, and Demetrius Poliocretes will be in Athens soon. The city is in political chaos. The democratic party is raising arms."

"What will you do?" Phidias showed concern. This reminded him of the time when his friend Aristotle's safety had been threatened by the same people.

"I must leave Athens. I was thinking of Alexandria."

"Excellent idea. I told you before that you should see the library and museum I started. You will love it. Many scholars are there, doing wonderful work."

"You think Ptolemy would welcome me?" Demetrius was hesitant, yet hopeful.

"Of course he would. He welcomes all philosophers. He loved Aristotle and was a generous supporter of my labors. Besides, he is still an ally of Cassander, is he not? I can't keep track of all their shifting alliances and wars."

"I tell you what," Phidias added. Reaching for a fresh papyrus, he dipped his stylus. "I will write a letter for you now that you can take to Ptolemy. Have some fruit and wine while I compose it."

He blew on the ink to dry it before rolling up the scroll. "You can continue to build the museum and library, for you have good skills in organization."

"Thank you, Phidias." Demetrius took the scroll handed to him. "I promise to give all my creative energy to the library and museum in Alexandria. Perhaps we can make it the best in the world."

"I trust that you may." Phidias rose and embraced Demetrius. "Have a safe trip, and may the gods protect you."

Demetrius left, knowing that he would never see Phidias, nor probably Athens, again.

* * *

Demetrius Poliocretes entered Athens, threw out the oligarchy supported by Cassander, and restored democracy, allowing the Assembly and courts to resume their authority. There was general rejoicing in the city.

"Athens has its freedom again," Thais said to Phidias. "There are celebrations all over."

Phidias smiled, "And they should. But Athens has no power of her own. She will be at the mercy of whatever faction of the warring Macedonian successors is most powerful. The party of democracy is in power now but will lose it again. That is the way with politics and those who would wield its power."

"You sound so cynical," Thais replied.

"I have lived a long time and have watched the changing fortunes of Greek politics. The times may change, but people will not. They will continue to make the same mistakes. It is the nature of man." He slowly shook his head and turned back to his writing.

X THE ELIXIR

CHAPTER 40

A few days afterward, Phidias looked up from his work and said to Thais, "We are almost done. I will probably finish this last part in the morning, and then I can rest."

"You deserve a rest. You have worked very hard these past few months. Perhaps we can sail to Crete or Cyprus, where it's warmer, and relax in the sun."

"No, my love, I don't want to leave Athens, for I believe my time on earth is short. By rest, I mean an eternal sleep."

Thais frowned. "Phidias, don't say those things. We have only found one another again, and I don't want you to leave me. You must not give up your spirit. You still have so much you can do. You can teach the students."

"I feel the years weighing down my weakened, tired old body. I'm just being realistic. It greatly hurts my aching heart when I realize the sorrow it will bring to you. However, death is the inevitable end of life, for all living things must eventually die. Only the gods, if they truly exist, are immortal. When it's my time, you must let me go. I am not afraid of dying. It's only the pain before death that people fear, and that is only fleeting. Death itself is like a dreamless sleep with no feeling at all.

"We had no control over the time and place of our birth, but we can decide what to do with the time and life that is given to us. It is our duty to make it count for something, to give meaning to our lives. A person must discover his destiny or the purpose in life, then, in fulfilling it, he will further the progress of humanity.

"I've lived a full life. Tomorrow is my birthday, and I'll be seventy-five. I've experienced much more than most men, and I have found my only true love, who I thought was lost. Most importantly, I have discovered my destiny—to write the book that I can pass on to the world. You helped me do that, and for that I love you more than I can say."

The next day, after noon, Phidias laid down his stylus and said, "It is finished. The book is done. He turned to Thais, who sat at another table in the room, his thoughts turning to his mortality.

"I know nothing of a life after this one," he said with his eyes focused on a distant vision. "Plato spoke of the eternal realm, where perfect forms dwell. Perhaps the perfect part of me, a soul, if there is one, will go to reside there. I favor Aristotle's opinion that the soul, or consciousness, cannot live without a living body. I believe that only the creations of my mind, my writings, will live after me. Therein lies my immortality." He read aloud the last words he had written:

"For my beloved Athens, even though her philosophers and scientists and writers may perish, and her houses and temples crumble into dust, her bonfire of genius will serve as a beacon down the centuries. Her outpouring of literature, art, and science will never die and will benefit human civilization forever."

Thais rose from her seat and came over to kiss him. "Those are wonderful words. Let's celebrate your book and your birthday tonight. I will have Lydia fix your favorite meal and serve our best wine. Why don't we dress in festival attire to commemorate the occasion?"

Phidias agreed, and a feeling of fulfillment went through him with a sense that he had accomplished his goal.

For dinner later, Lydia had covered the table with a fine Egyptian cotton cloth dyed a deep blue and placed a runner of scarlet silk down the center with decorative oil lamps placed along it. Their finest dishes and silverware graced the table. Thais poured some wine and water into two large silver goblets she had saved. The flickering light played across their faces and sparkled in moistened eyes as she raised her goblet. "Here's to you, my lover and my teacher. I love you so much. You have given us something that not many men have accomplished, something that will live forever."

"Thank you," Phidias said as they raised their cups and drank. "You called me your teacher, but you have taught me. By finding you and your love, I have grown; I have learned what life really means; I have become the person I was destined to be; and I have fulfilled my promise. I thank you."

They raised their cups again. Thais served him some of the roasted lamb cooked in olive oil and spices on a bed of scented rice. They ate heartily of the delicious fare, celebrating Phidias' great accomplishment. He told her to have copies made of the book and to send them to Ptolemy and Demetrius.

After dinner they went to bed, caressed one another, and fell asleep in each other's arms. Phidias' last thoughts before falling into an exhaustive sleep were how fortunate he was to have Thais. His destiny was fulfilled.

The next day Thais arose early and, letting Phidias sleep, went into the kitchen to help prepare some breakfast.

Phidias arose late and, stumbling into the kitchen, said, "I don't feel well. It is hard for me to breathe."

Thais told Lydia to fetch Pinocrates and to bring a cold wet cloth. They helped Phidias to his bed, propped him up on several pillows so he could breathe better, and placed the wet cloth on his head. Lydia brought him some broth, but he shook his head, refusing it. His breathing was labored, and a cold sweat beaded his forehead.

Tears welled in Thais' eyes as she leaned over and kissed his forehead. "I love you. I have always loved you."

"I always knew that, deep in my heart," he sighed, short of breath. "I always kept your memory with me. Go into the room with my books and look behind the bronze bust of Plato that I have in there on the top shelf."

A few moments later, she brought back a little terra-cotta figure of a woman. "Who is this, Phidias, a goddess you prayed to?" She ran her fingers lightly over the figure, noticing it was a little worn around the feet.

"It is a goddess. I kept it with me and talked to it daily. She comforted me. Turn it over and read her name on the bottom."

She turned over the little figure and whispered the name engraved there, *"Thais."* She choked and burst into tears, hugging the statuette to her breast. "Oh, Phidias, you always loved me." She handed it to him.

He nodded, "Yes, always." He took the precious figure, kissed it, and placed it gently beside him on the pillow.

"I love you so much," she said, as she hugged him and covered his face with kisses, her tears mingling with his.

"Let me sleep now," he said. "But stay with me." He slowly closed his eyes, a smile barely visible on his lips. His breathing became shallower with longer and longer pauses between breaths. It was not long that he stopped breathing altogether. Thais rose and hugged him again, her tears bathing his face. She lightly caressed his face for the last time.

Another of the great men of Athens has died, she thought. *He mourned the passing of Athens' glory and many people will mourn his death. We will sing his requiem.*

She found on his desk a poem he had written after finishing his manuscript. As she read it, drops of tears fell onto the page.

Paean to Athens

Sing to me, oh Muse, of Athens' golden story,
Mistress of the seas and victor over Persia's hordes.
Midwife of democracy,
Mother of philosophy and science,
World teacher.

Down from Olympus' heights did come
Athena to Attica's shore
And plant her foot on Acropolis mount
To found the city that bears her name
And became the ancient empire.

For a time, blessed by the gods,
Did she become rich
And extended her sway
With sword and spear, shield and ship,
'Til all Hellas followed her.

Yet hubris of power and wealth
Spoiled her morals and modest ways,
So the gods and allies forsook her,
And humbled by Sparta's arms,
All Greece conspired in mutual suicide.

Neither wealth nor conquest her immortality made,
But art and literature and philosophy
She has passed to the ages,
Taught us how to govern our cities,
How to live just and virtuous lives.

Her universities became the school of Hellas
Philosophers from Plato and Aristotle,
Lawgivers from Pericles,
Historians from Thucydides,

Many have enlightened our minds
Her art became an eternal name
For civilizations far and near.
While her poems and plays
Lifted our spirits with mirth
Or catharsis' choking tears.

As one decreed by fate,
Oedipus did say in his advanced years,
"Only to gods in heaven
Comes no old age, nor death of anything;
All else is turmoiled by our master Time."

So it is with Athens, that
Her glory days are gone.
All will pass into the dust of history.
Only the legacy that is created
For good lives on.

EPILOGUE

Our fictional hero, Phidias, died in 307 BCE at seventy-five years of age. Athens was at peace for a while, even though the successors of Alexander continued to war until 301 BCE. Antigonus was defeated and killed and the Empire was divided among Cassander, Lysimachus, Seleucus, and Ptolemy.

The same year, after Phidias' death, the new Assembly passed the famous law requiring the Assembly's approval in the selection of the leaders of all the philosophical schools. An indictment was brought against Theophrastus on the old charge of impiety—the same as that against Socrates and Aristotle. Theophrastus left Athens, but so many students followed him that businesses complained of the decrease in trade. Within the year, the law was abolished, the indictment was dropped, and Theophrastus returned to preside over the Lyceum until his death at eighty-five.

Demetrius Phalerum went to Alexandria and convinced Ptolemy to expand the museum and library. He suggested that Ptolemy would increase the illustriousness of his name and that of his capital by creating as part of the museum and library a university to rival those of Athens. He recommended plans for the erection of a group of buildings, not only to provide for a great collection of books but for scholars who would do all types of research.

Ptolemy I Soter and his son, Ptolemy II Philadelphus, created the new university buildings near the royal palaces. They consisted of a mess hall, a lecture hall, rooms for study and research, a garden and cloister, and the great library, which was to become the largest library of antiquity. It was said to contain over one million scrolls when it burned during the occupation of Julius Caesar. Untold numbers of manuscripts, works of science, philosophy, and literature were lost in one of the most tragic events of history.

Four groups of scholars, all Greeks, lived at the museum and library–astronomers, mathematicians, physicians, and literary writers. All received salaries from the royal treasury, and their function was to do research and conduct studies and experiments. In later decades, as students became numerous, its faculty began to give lectures, but the main function of the museum was always to be an institute for advanced studies, rather than a teaching university like those in Athens. It was the first establishment for literature and science set up by a state, and this was the contribution of the Ptolemies and Alexandria to the progress of civilization.

Demetrius suggested to Ptolemy Philadelphus about 250 BCE to invite some seventy Jewish scholars to come from Judea to Alexandria and translate the scriptures of their people. These seventy men translated the Hebrew Pentateuch, or Torah, into Greek. Later, the books of the prophets and other parts of the Hebrew Bible were also translated into Greek. This is known by its Latin name *Interpretatio Septuaginata*, the interpretation of the seventy, or simply the *Septuagint*. This was the Bible later used by Paul of Tarsus.

Ptolemy I wrote a history of Alexander. The original was destroyed but was quoted extensively by the historian, Arrian, whose works we still have.

Although Callisthenes was not alive to chronicle the events after Alexander's death, others did. They did not see Alexander's death as being the end of an age. Rather, they saw this as the start of new times in which Greek culture and science expanded into areas that Alexander had opened. Although Greek freedom had died, Greek civilization was alive and thriving. The vast Empire broke down barriers to communication, trade, and immigration. Greeks moved by the hundreds of thousands into Asia Minor, Palestine, Egypt, and across Asia, even to Bactria and India. Greek spirit, energy, and arts spread from southern France and Sicily all across Alexander's Empire. Greek letters and learning had never won such a vast conquest.

In the closing pages of the chapter, a new power was growing in the West—Rome. She engaged in a death struggle with Carthage, and some of the Greek and Macedonian cities unwisely supported Carthage. While campaigns against Hannibal occupied Rome, the Achaean League revolted against Roman authority. The Romans sent an army and a fleet, which overcame all Greek forces and captured Corinth, the capital of the League. Like Alexander's lesson against Thebes, the Romans decided to show the Greeks a lesson by destroying this rich city of trade. Corinth was burned to the ground, all its men slaughtered, and its women and children sold into slavery. Works of art by the shipload were sent back to Rome. Greece and Macedonia were made one province under a Roman governor, and Greek independence ended.

However, Greek civilization did not die; it only migrated to Rome and to Western Europe, as it did throughout the East to India. It lives on today in the great works of Plato and Aristotle, of Hippocrates and Archimedes, of Aeschylus, Sophocles, Euripides, and the great Homer. Her gifts of science, mathematics, astronomy, medicine, and of government of laws derived from the people have created the rich tapestry of human civilization. We must overlook its faults and weaknesses—the suicidal wars, inhuman slavery, subjugation of women, loose morals, class conflicts, and its tragic failure to unite and promote order and peace.

Even though the Greece and Athens of Pericles and Socrates are gone, their requiem is sung by the whole of humanity and will never be forgotten.

Made in the USA
San Bernardino, CA
26 June 2014